OAK KING HOLLY KING

SEBASTIAN NOTHWELL

Copyright © 2022 by Sebastian Nothwell

All rights reserved.

No part of this book may be reproduced in any form or by any electronic or mechanical means, including information storage and retrieval systems, without written permission from the author, except for the use of brief quotations in a book review.

Cover illustration by Jan of Thistle Arts Studio
Cover design by Kelley of Sleepy Fox Studio
Interior formatting by Diana TC of Triumph Covers

*Thank you to
Aden, Ari, Felix, Janet, Jess, Kyanite, Marcela, and Olivia
for their encouragement and support
in making this book possible.*

AUTUMN

CHAPTER ONE

The Court of the Silver Wheel
The Fae Realms
Autumnal Equinox

The crisp wind howled across the tourney field, scattering scarlet leaves. Their hue matched the blood trickling from the wounds of the fallen, who lay in a haphazard pattern as if the wind had scattered them as well. Some struggled upright and limped towards the boundary of the *mêlée*, where their squires and servants waited amidst the roaring crowd to staunch their wounds. Some crawled. Some could do little more than groan as they waited out the battle's end. A few would never rise again.

Two combatants remained on their feet, their sword hilts locked together in a contest of brute strength, their snarling faces inches apart.

Shrike, who had slain several of the corpses on the field, stared unblinking into the mercurial eyes of his opponent. These eyes belonged to a knight whom the court considered quite beautiful, and it was said those eyes altered their colour with his moods. To Shrike, they had appeared gleaming green when the battle commenced. Now they'd faded to an icy blue and paled with every passing second. The knight's lips had taken on a blue tinge as well, twisted in a lupine snarl to reveal doubled canines as sharp as his longsword. The blood-slicked blade crossed against Shrike's own to form a shining scarlet X between their close-pressed chests. The well-honed edges—Shrike's with more nicks and notches—scraped against the ringed mail beneath the knight's tabard and scored the leather armour over Shrike's tunic.

"Yield!" the knight hissed between clenched teeth.

Some scant moments before, an errant shield-bash had split Shrike's lip open. Shrike had cut down the shield's wielder, who now lay groaning into the dirt a stone's throw away. Still, Shrike's lip bled. He licked the blood from his chin now and darted his head forward between the crossed blades to crush the knight's mouth beneath his kiss.

The knight jerked his head back—or attempted to, at least, before Shrike bit his tongue.

And in that instant of shock and outrage, Shrike sank his dagger into the hollow beneath the knight's flailing left arm.

Blood poured forth. Each successive wave came weaker than the last, the blade having pierced the knight's heart. The hot torrent soaked through Shrike's tunic sleeve. The copper stench of fresh-spilt blood joined with the miasma of gore that hung over the tourney field.

Shrike stared into the knight's eyes as their ice-blue faded to silver-white. Then they rolled back, and the knight collapsed in Shrike's arms. His sword scraped against Shrike's cheek as it fell to the ground. Blood for blood, Shrike supposed, and dropped him.

The victory horn resounded over the tourney field. The rising cheer of the crowd swallowed up its echo.

Few of the fae scattered around him were dead. Fae did not perish so easily. Even a knife to the heart could heal with time. The mercurial-eyed knight, like most of his rank lying broken over the tourney field, had a squire, a page, and very likely a gentle lover to tend his wounds and mend his armour so he might fight another day. Shrike, as a mere knave, had none. He would not have been permitted to stride out on the tourney field at all if the queen had not called for a general *mêlée* in which fae of all rank could compete for her favour.

And as the pages and squires and gentle friends swarmed the battle-field to rescue the wounded, Shrike stumbled through alone, a single minnow swimming against their overwhelming current, towards his queen.

The Queen of the Court of the Silver Wheel sat at the northernmost end of the tourney field. Her servants had erected a temporary bower, coaxing a copse of hemlock trees to grow into a shelter for their queen. Their scaly trunks twisted together like a nest of snakes for a floor, and their flat needles of brightest green came together overhead to filter rays of the setting sun like stained glass. Stout lower branches forked into stools for handmaidens and courtiers. Thrust forth from the centre like the bow of a ship, a balcony emerged with two thrones. On the tallest and centre-most throne sat the queen herself, perched on the edge of her seat, her delicate white hands laid on the braid of branches that formed the balcony's rail. In the lower throne at her left hand, set back from the balcony's edge, sat the Holly King; her champion until Yule. A ring of knights, those whose service the queen deemed too important to permit their participation in the tournament, surrounded the base of the bower. Each wore her livery—a silver wheel on a cobalt blue field—and stood ready to defend her person and her honour.

At her nod, her knights withdrew to let him pass, and he climbed up into her bower.

The splendour without proved nothing compared to the splendour within. Paper lanterns filled with blue fireflies augmented the green sunshine. Handmaidens and courtiers garbed in feathers and silks twittered together like so many songbirds, yet all with at least one of their eyes on their queen, lest she should require their prompt service. Her servants, human and fae alike, had piled a feast on a raised dais in the centre of the bower. A whole roast boar formed the centrepiece, large enough for a half-dozen warriors to ride on. Its tusks now speared apples instead of flesh. A peacock, skinned for cooking and then meticulously re-dressed in its own brilliant plumage, spewed from the boar's propped-open mouth. Several swans had received the same treatment, flanking the boar with their spread wings. The boar's mortal blow, an enormous gash in its left side, gaped open to hold a fountain of wine, with bunches of grapes spilling from the lips of the wound. Amidst these showier pieces lay scattered piles of strawberries, apples, pears, citruses, bird tongues, whole roasted mice, and tiny knights and horses made of pastry and marzipan fighting all over the feast.

Shrike spurned it all.

The queen and her Holly King had turned their respective thrones—the living hemlock branches bending to their whims—to face into the bower where Shrike now stood.

The Holly King wore a crown of sharp green leaves that befit his title. The blood-red berries bejewelling it matched his crimson eyes, which burned into Shrike. As the Holly King turned this same gaze on everyone, however—and furthermore he wasn't by far the first fae to have turned such a gaze on Shrike in particular—Shrike paid it little heed. This day, halfway between Midsummer and Midwinter, marked the point at which the Holly King's power would begin to wane. As Shrike glanced over the Holly King now, he saw little proof of this; the Holly King's high cheeks had not hollowed, nor had his well-muscled limbs wasted away. His skin had a blueish tinge, but then again it always had, and the frost in his silvery hair glistened bright as ever.

Shrike had only ever glimpsed the queen from afar. Now, as he drew nearer to her than he had ever dared before, the radiance of her beauty proved no mere poetical affectation.

The autumnal winds blowing across the tourney field lost all their chill as he drew closer, the cold blood dripping from his wounds warmed, and the sunlight filtering down from gold to green through the hemlock needles brightened. Her hair shone the same strawberry gold shade as the sunset. It spilled forth from beneath her delicate diadem of heather and starlight and flowed down to pool at the trailing hem of her emerald-green gown which precisely matched the shade of her sparkling eyes. The rosebuds of her cheeks and lips provided all the colour in her otherwise milk-white flesh.

"Kneel, Butcher of Blackthorn," said the queen.

Shrike dropped to one knee and bowed his head. Pointed crimson leaves blew across the knotted branches beneath his boot-heels.

By this time the wounded and their attendants had withdrawn from the field. The remaining spectators, some thousand strong, regathered beneath the queen's bower. Shrike glimpsed them through the braided branches of the balcony rail, all staring upward to see what boon their queen would grant to the tournament's victor.

The queen's sword sang out as it left its sheath, the sweet ring of metal against metal. The slender blade, wielded with all the gentle precision of a moth's wing, came to its rest first on Shrike's left shoulder, then his right.

"And arise," the queen continued.

Shrike held his breath in anticipation of the title she would grant him. With it would come the loss of many freedoms, yes, but he'd tallied up the exchange long before he made the first move that brought him to this moment and considered the ensuing security worth the forfeit. If he laboured in her service and under her protection, he needn't suffer any knight-errant's raid. Furthermore, with a title from the queen, he could force all contenders to look him in the eye and acknowledge his skill and craft were worthy of his ambition. As to the form the title took, he cared not. More than likely he would be declared Knight of Blackthorn, as his minor freehold would become hers once she took him into her service. Or perhaps she would grant him a more creative sobriquet.

"King," said the queen, "of the Oak."

The taste of victory turned to ash on his tongue. His head shot up before he could even think of restraint. Shock parted his lips. Betrayal burned in his eyes.

The queen gazed down with an expression no less serene for the death sentence she had handed down on his head.

Behind her, just over her left shoulder, the Holly King's mouth twitched in something almost like a smile.

Shrike wasted a half-second staring at his predestined opponent, then snapped his eyes back to the queen. Still, she appeared unmoved.

"Arise," she repeated. "My Oak King."

Shrike staggered upright. All grace had flown from his limbs along with the queen's favour. His mind reeled. He'd won her tournament. Buckets of blood had spilled beneath his blade and flowed over his hands to prove his strength and fealty. He couldn't think what he'd done to displease her.

Perhaps, he thought as she smiled her inscrutable smile and cast a considering look over him from the crown of his head to the heels of his boots, he'd pleased her all too well.

The spectators surged forth with a joyous roar. The true feasting began, with servants carrying forth a half-dozen more wine-spewing boars from the bower into the crowd, and the throng tangling all limbs in a frenzied dance to celebrate the harvest.

Shrike withdrew from the queen's presence with a bow and slipped away in the ensuing chaos. A well-placed knee here and a sharp elbow there carved his path from the centre of the festival to the encroaching forest at its edge.

The illumination of the rising bonfires behind him didn't reach far into the trees, with their ancient trunks so broad and the undergrowth so thick between them. Shrike drew his sword and hacked his way deeper into the darkness. The dense greenery swallowed the noise of the revels, with only the rustling of new growth creeping up behind him as he went. It didn't grieve him to leave the celebration behind. He had no time to lick his wounds, much less join the throng.

He had a silver wheel to splinter.

Some minutes or hours after he began striking his own path through the woods, he reached a thicket ringed with pale mushrooms. He wiped his sword clean on the hem of his tunic, then sheathed it before collapsing at the base of an immense oak. Its roots grew as thick around as his own waist and formed a rudimentary throne. Fitting, he thought, as the queen had titled him after the same.

Yet he couldn't allow himself to wallow in bitterness. Nor could he yield to the siren song of sleep, with the sting of the cut on his cheek and the deep ache of the bruises beneath his armour. Instead, he plucked a silver strand from amidst his black locks, some thirteen inches long, and selected an acorn from the hundreds scattered across the ground. He tied the hair around the stem of the acorn's cap. Holding his left hand out before him, he dangled the acorn over it, a mere quarter-inch above his palm. He waited until it stopped swaying, stopped spinning, and then waited another moment for absolute stillness.

"I seek that which will allow me to prevail over the Holly King,"

Shrike intoned. "His current incarnation and in all his future forms. Where shall I find my quarry?"

The makeshift pendulum shivered on its thread, then began to swing, a hair's breadth at first, then further and further, rippling outward until its path traced a particular line etched in Shrike's palm.

Shrike frowned down at it. He clenched his hand into a fist, shook out the pendulum, and tried again.

It traced the same line with renewed vigour.

Shrike broke off the thread and popped the acorn into his mouth. It tasted almost as bitter as the queen's favour. Chewing it burst open the half-healed wounds in his cheek and lip. As the acorn crunched between his molars, he considered the directions it had given. He would not find his answer in the Court of the Silver Wheel, nor in any of the fae courts.

His quest, it seemed, must take him into the mortal realm.

Staple Inn
London, England
23 September, 1844

Fog swirled outside the thick glass panes latticed with leading. Its hue and viscosity looked almost identical to the grey sludge of milk and tea sitting in the chipped cup and mis-matched saucer beside Wren Lofthouse's inkwell. Every so often the dark speck of a sparrow would dart through the fog, coming perilously near to the window before veering off again. The dark specks of ink-spatter in Wren's tea never veered off.

Wren gazed down at these specks, and, unable to summon any feeling stronger than resignation, quaffed the whole remained in two gulps, ink and all, before returning to his ledger. On a day like any other spent clerking in Staple Inn, Wren might as well drink ink. It would make no difference. Indeed, it hardly seemed to alter the tea's flavour one jot. Which, Wren supposed, he could only blame on himself. After all, it'd been he who had brewed it in the copper kettle over the smouldering coals in the hearth.

Another sparrow swooped past the window. Wren glanced up at it, suppressed a jealous twinge, then looked across the law office to the desk opposite where sat the sole other occupant; Mr Ephraim Grigsby, Esquire. Mr Grigsby, a bachelor of some sixty years, had an unfortunate resemblance to an egg balanced on stilts. Still, he bore it up better than Wren bore any of his own burdens. Indeed, he seemed to thrive on the monotony of receiving rents, drawing up and executing wills, and rearranging columns of figures from one ledger to another. His weathered face remained in the same placid attitude as one might see on a gentleman fishing away the afternoon.

Wren, a bachelor of a mere thirty years, felt nothing like the same serenity with his situation and had resolved to take his razor to his throat if he ever drew near it. For the present moment, however, he dipped his pen nib into his inkwell with a sigh.

The muffled silence of the office shattered as the bell rang in the hall.

As if compelled by clockwork mechanism, Wren set aside his pen and rose from his desk to weave his way between bookshelves, cabinets, and stacks of ledgers towards the door at the opposing end of the chamber.

"Lofthouse," Mr Grigsby said without looking up from his desk.

Wren didn't slow his stride, much less stop to hear him.

Mr Grigsby continued on regardless. "I believe the penny post has arrived. If it wouldn't trouble you overmuch, would you be so kind as to go down and—oh, thank you," he said, glancing up at last to find Wren halfway through the open door, latch in hand.

A tight smile twitched at the corners of Wren's mouth—the old man deserved better, but it was the best Wren could manage on a Monday—as he slipped out of the office and pulled the door shut behind him.

Yet even as Wren stepped into the hall, he heard the thud of bootheels on floorboards, and as he peered over the railing down the steep and narrow staircase into the foyer below, he beheld a curious figure.

The figure stood tall enough that it had to duck under the doorframe to enter the foyer. Any other hint as to its shape remained hidden under an immense black cloak. The hood cast the face into deep shadow—assuming there existed a face at all beneath it. Wren began to doubt it as he watched the figure ascend the stair, looking as if it glided up the steps as smoothly as one might glide down the banister, and yet accompanied by the sound of heavy foot-falls beneath the cloak's sepulchral folds. The cloak's hem trailed behind the figure, flowing upwards like a waterfall in reverse, its dusty and tattered edges resembling black-and-grey feathers.

Wren, whose ceaseless prayers for escape from the tedium had never been answered before, stared in frank disbelief and quite forgot he was expected to do anything else until the figure had reached the upper landing and loomed over him like a gnarled oak.

Before Wren could address the astonishing shadow directly, a pair of hands gloved in black leather emerged from beneath the cloak and threw back its pointed hood to reveal an equally-pointed black hat with a long grey-and-black-striped feather adorning its black band.

The face beneath this hat proved no less bizarre. Wren beheld a black Venetian mask, its leather tooled in a feathered pattern, with a long, pointed nose like a beak. A ragged black scarf, so full of holes that it seemed halfway between fishing net and lace, swathed the stranger from throat to nose. Beneath the mask, two dark eyes smouldered like coals. The scent of wood-smoke—not just of a wood stove or a hearth, but that of a raging bonfire—hung in the hall.

The stranger could not be the queerest sight in all of London, but by Wren's estimation he was the queerest sight in Staple Inn. Certainly the queerest figure to ever grace the chambers of Mr Ephraim Grigsby, Esq., and clerk.

Still, on the off chance that the stranger was not in fact a wormwood-tonic induced hallucination, Wren felt he probably ought to say something.

"Your name, sir?" Wren asked, covering his confusion with his blandest professional tone.

The smouldering eyes beneath the mask flew wide.

Impatience drove out the last of Wren's wonder. "Your face, at least. You're quite in out of the fog, and you needn't fear its chill any longer."

The stranger's hunched shoulders relaxed, and the gloved hands came up again, this time to untie the mask, pull down the scarf, and sweep the hat from the head in a brisk bow.

Wren kept his own hair unfashionably long, with the tips of the longest strands brushing his collar, but he felt positively well-trimmed when compared against the unknown gentleman. Night-black locks shot through with starlight-silver spilled over the stranger's shoulders as he bent forward despite the leather cord tying them at the nape of his neck, just visible where the hood had fallen back.

As the stranger rose from his bow, Wren beheld his face at last. The stranger appeared not many years older than Wren himself. His dark eyes and high cheekbones would strike even the most discerning taste as handsome. His nose proved almost as long and pointed as the mask's beak, paired with the swarthy complexion and full lips worthy of an ancient Roman emperor or a modern gondolier. His sweeping black brows lent a stormy intrigue to his countenance. A raw red line with white pinched edges carved down his left cheek—a wound which had just begun to scar—proved his only flaw.

Wren realized not only was he staring at the stranger, but his own mouth had fallen open in the meantime. His teeth clicked together as he shut his jaw.

"Good morning, sir!"

Wren turned to find Mr Grigsby had wandered to the door and now looked over the stranger with an expression equal parts astonished and intrigued.

"Do forgive Lofthouse," Mr Grigsby continued. "I'm afraid I work him rather too hard, and he hasn't much patience left for conversation. But to the purpose—what may we do to assist you?"

The stranger looked almost as astonished to see Mr Grigsby. His black eyes swept from his bald pate to his knock-knees, then flicked over to Wren once more. With hesitation, the stranger asked, "Is this your master?"

"After a fashion," Wren admitted. It took him a half-second too long to do so, for to hear the stranger speak quite unsettled him. The stranger's voice rumbled forth from deep within his chest, low and looming, reverberating in Wren's ears.

The stranger returned his attention to Mr Grigsby. "Then forgive me, my lord, for it seems my purpose lies not with you, but with your squire."

Mr Grigsby appeared not in the least perturbed by this, which Wren put down to his being inured to sour dispositions and rude speech after suffering Wren's indifferent service for too many years. On the contrary —he laughed. "Squire! My, how fanciful! Very well, then, he is at your service. Only pray don't keep him over-long. Indispensable, he is, my good sir—indispensable!"

And, with the least-subtle wink Wren had ever seen, Mr Grigsby whisked himself away back into the office and shut the door behind him, leaving Wren alone in the hall with the stranger once more.

If nothing else, Wren supposed he could take Mr Grigsby's direct address of the stranger as proof that the stranger was not, in fact, a hallucination. Still, the possibility of a hoax remained. And while Wren might fail as a clerk in many respects, he'd be damned before he'd allow Mr Grigsby to become as much a laughing-stock as Mrs Tottenham.

The stranger furrowed his formidable brow at the closed office door, then looked down at Wren. "If you are not your master's squire, then you must be his page. Unless—is your master not a Knight Templar?"

"He most certainly is not," Wren replied, bristling. "He is a lawyer, sir."

"Then what are you?"

Wren did not often encounter anyone as blunt as himself. It almost tricked him into giving a true answer. Instead, he resigned himself to reply, "I am a clerk. I wish you would state your business at once, sir, as I have much to do and little time to spend standing about in corridors consulting with lunatics."

"If you have so little time as you say," the stranger countered, "perhaps we should meet elsewhere when you are more at liberty, for I've too much to explain at present."

How convenient, Wren thought. Aloud, and as much to appease his curiosity as to arrange a meeting, Wren asked, "When and where would you suggest?"

"Name your place and time. I am at your mercy."

Wren thought he'd prepared himself to expect anything from the stranger. Yet that final phrase gave him pause. In life he'd more often found matters quite the other way around.

The stranger, meanwhile, appeared unaware he'd said anything strange and awaited his answer with the patience of an oak.

"The Green Man," Wren blurted. "Tonight. Eight o' clock."

The stranger conceded with a nod. "As you wish."

He turned and descended the stair in the same queer fashion, reached the lower landing, and had his hand on the door-latch before Wren recovered his senses enough to reply.

"And whom shall I say is waiting for me, sir?" Wren called down, his frustration lending the question a bitter aftertaste.

The stranger paused at the bottom of the stair and glanced up to meet Wren's eyes again with that burning gaze.

"Butcher," he said.

Then he donned his mask, threw his hood over his hat, and stalked through the door.

The wind slammed it shut behind him.

CHAPTER TWO

Mortals might lie, Shrike considered as he stalked away from the Knights Templar's crumbling fortress, but scrying could not. The clerk held the key to his victory.

Still, Shrike's return to the mortal realm after several centuries' absence had not proved quite as smooth as he might have hoped. While the acorn guided him through the forest to the Grove of Gates, stepping into the portal felt like marching against a howling wind.

Forcing his way through, Shrike had found himself engulfed in an acrid fog.

He stumbled to his knees onto close-cropped grass. His flailing hand braced against a sapling to keep himself upright as he dry-heaved. Iron hung in the air itself. Its heavy ache seemed to fly at him from all directions. In past centuries this particular passage between the realms had led to the lands belonging to Westminster Abbey. What had happened to the mortal realm since then, he could not begin to imagine.

But he would find out.

Shrike hauled himself upright against the sapling. The rush of falling water mingled with more distant hoof-beats, voices, and metallic clanging in his ears. Glancing 'round, he found he stood in a copse of trees by a waterfall with a ring of small pale mushrooms surrounding him. Not a single tree-trunk spanned wider than his hand, and he felt certain the river had not existed on his last journey to the site.

Yet the acorn drew him away from the river, north and to the east.

Shrike staggered through the fog. His strides came surer with every step as he grew used to the fatiguing influence of the surrounding iron. Soon he stumbled on a well-trod foot-path amidst the close-cropped grass.

Glimpses of changing mortal costume had rippled through the fae realms in the intervening centuries. Certain courtly fae had habits of stealing whichever trends struck their fancy—or stealing the mortal tailors themselves—both of which meant fae attire often became a motley whirlwind of hundreds of years' worth of mortal innovation. While Shrike did not often venture out into fae society, he had caught a few hints of it amidst the wild hunt and had thought breeches, stockings, tricorn hats, and flimsy high-waisted gowns were the latest mortal fashions. Instead, when he encountered the footpath, he found mortals wearing trousers, shawls, and bell-shaped skirts with yards and yards of draping. These mortals appeared no less bemused by his own garb. While some wore capes, none wore cloaks, and nothing as well-crafted as Shrike's fur-lined hood or his tall leather boots.

Their sheer number proved likewise astonishing. Tens of thousands had walked London's streets when last Shrike wandered through the city. The population seemed to have multiplied a thousandfold since then. Everywhere he turned, he beheld mortals wandering to and fro. Most on foot. Some mounted on horseback. And still others rattling along in chariots.

One particular chariot almost ran him down as he strode towards his quest's object. The gelding pulled up short with a shriek and reared, its hooves striking the air inches from his face. The mortal at the reins shook his fist and called Shrike a blackguard. The passengers in voluminous skirts screamed almost as loud as the horse.

Shrike touched the brim of his hat and continued on. None of them would bring him his promised victory. That individual lay somewhere further beyond, towards the heart of the city.

The acorn guided him north-eastward. Shrike followed it in a straight line regardless of paths, plants, or people, which earned him many an odd look, but he cared not.

Until it brought him to iron.

Shrike halted some twelve feet from the fence. A thousand iron spears hung suspended from iron bars in a line that stretched from south to north and on through the fog beyond Shrike's field of vision.

While made of iron and standing as tall as his own shoulders, Shrike thought he could climb the fence if he had to—by throwing his cloak over it to shield him from the corrosive metal and taking a running leap, if nothing else. Still, it could not run on forever, and so he continued northward, maintaining a wary distance from the fence as he stalked its length.

Past an enormous bronze cast of a nude warrior with unsheathed sword and upraised shield, in the furthest north-east corner of the fence, he found a three-fold marble arch—the central passage flanked by smaller twins—and beyond it London teemed.

The central arch stood wide enough for two carriages to pass through alongside. Shrike held his breath and walked beneath it. The marble shielded him from the iron fence. A shudder ran through him all the same as he went.

Shrike followed his gut feeling down a formerly familiar path towards Temple Bar, where the Knights Templar had once reigned over their own court. The half-timbered inns appeared much the same, though their occupants had changed from knights to clerks. And one clerk in particular, Shrike knew, for when he had locked eyes with Lofthouse at last, he felt the warm rush of victory radiating from the acorn throughout his body.

And perhaps the warm rush of something else besides.

Shrike had no expectations of what might await him in the mortal realm. To find at the end of his quest a mortal man with the enormous, soft, dark eyes of a hunted hart in a shadowed glade—well, that was certainly a surprise, and not an unwelcome one. The eyes alone would have fascinated Shrike. In addition to this, a fine-boned face with nose, chin, and cheekbones honed to a keen edge, and a complexion as speckled as a sparrow's egg—even over the rosebud pink of the lips—all combined to captivate him. The sweep of chestnut hair low over his brow tempted Shrike to brush it out of his eyes and take that noble chin in hand. If he had but passed this delicate face in severe garb on the street, he would have halted his quest to learn more of the man. Fortunate, then, that the quest itself had forced their paths to cross.

Then those freckled rosebud lips had opened, and the question that emerged had set Shrike back on his heels.

"Your name, sir?"

The interruption of the clerk's master allowed Shrike to recover from the shock and realize that, like most mortals, the clerk did not actually demand to know his true name—just to know what he was called. Shrike could offer him that much on their first meeting. He would like to offer him much more anon.

At present, however, the clerk had set him on another quest.

The Green Man. A good omen, Shrike thought. An aspect of the Oak King and a symbol of summer's triumph over winter. He strode away from Staple Inn with renewed purpose. While the paths running through London had increased in population, the signs hanging above the doors of the edifices he passed had retained a great deal of their medieval origins. A scarlet lion over some thresholds, a white hart over many others, and, at length, the green-tinged head of a man with ivy spewing from his eyes, ears, and mouth.

Shrike entered. While the mortal behind the bar looked askance at his attire, he accepted his coin regardless. Shrike settled in to wait for the sharp-featured, sharp-tongued, fierce little bird wrapped in dark garb, and eagerly looked forward to the opportunity to prove himself worthy of his favour.

"Bless my soul!" cried Mr Grigsby the instant Wren returned to the office. "Is that your new muse?"

"What?" blurted Wren.

"Forgive me," Mr Grigsby added in a conspiratorial undertone. It seemed he supposed Wren objected to the volume of his words rather than their content. "I mean only to ask—is he to pose for your next piece? An engraving, perhaps, or dare I hope, a painting? I'm in eagerness to see it, whatever form it may take."

"No." Wren hadn't the heart to tell Mr Grigsby that he'd given up on his artistic aspirations long ago. Still, he could promise something. "If one of my works is to be exhibited, I shall tell you straight off."

Technically that wasn't a lie, for, as he had no intention of submitting any of his works to galleries, he need never tell Mr Grigsby anything.

It seemed to gratify the old gentleman, who gave him a warm smile and returned to his ledger humming a few tuneless yet cheerful bars.

Wren returned to his own work feeling far less sanguine. Butcher—if that was the bizarre stranger's real name, which Wren very much doubted—had set his brain afire. Bad enough if Wren had only glimpsed such a figure in a crowded street or a shadowed alley. To have spoken to him, however, and found his speech and manner as medieval as his garb…

All this aroused Wren's suspicions as well as his interest.

Checking to make sure Mr Grigsby wasn't watching him—which he never was, but Wren preferred not to leave matters to chance—he slipped his memorandum-book out of his desk and jotted down a description of the whole encounter in shorthand. Certain details, like smouldering black eyes and high cheekbones, may have taken precedence over others. No matter. Whether or not anything came of their crossing paths in reality, he would make something of it in pencil, ink, or paint.

Then, with the riddle of Butcher set down in black and white, Wren attempted to solve it.

There were few reasons Wren could think of why anyone, much less such a Gothic figure as Butcher, would accost him at his place of work. Money motivated most things, in Wren's experience. Yet as a clerk taking in not more than forty shillings a week, he had none—at least, not enough to make it worth anyone else's trouble. Nor did he have any debts which might provoke a moneylender to send out a large and imposing figure to intimidate Wren into paying.

Perhaps Mr Grigsby did have the right notion, in his own way.

Perhaps this Butcher was no hired brute, but a hired model. Or, more likely, a hired actor.

The more Wren reflected on this possibility, the more plausible it seemed. While he didn't have mortal enemies, there remained a certain coterie in the city who might consider him a sort of professional nemesis. Though they didn't want Wren dead—probably—they would delight to see him humiliated in his office. Furthermore, this certain coterie was the precise sort of people who would hire the queerest possible actor to do the job.

Except Butcher had proved a touch too queer. A great deal of craftsmanship had gone into his costume. Expensive craftsmanship at that, full of little details—all in black and with such fine tooling on the leather mask—that would not read well from the stage. Nothing in it matched any role performed in the city at present; medieval pageantry was not in current dramatic fashion. So it would have to be especially made, and that would cost a great deal more coin than Wren believed a certain coterie had at their disposal. Unless they had found themselves fortunate enough to make the acquaintance of an eccentric aristocrat who already had such a costume to hand mouldering away in some ancestral cedar chest.

Wren had one secret, of course. And while he'd never breathed a word of it to any living soul, save the other individual involved, one person had discovered it quite by accident, and there remained a few others out in the world who might have guessed it. And given this particular secret and those who knew of it, two of the three possibilities remained the same; blackmail, for those who suspected the secret had the habit of spending more money than they earned; or humiliation, as those who suspected the secret found obscure pranks particularly amusing, and would think it a grand lark to hire an actor to tease the secret out of Wren.

Out of the two, Wren thought the second—a humiliating prank—the most plausible. Because, if so, the suspected parties couldn't have chosen a more promising actor to carry out their plan. Whether they knew it or not, this Butcher, bizarre as he behaved, had precisely the sort of countenance, form, and figure that would most tempt Wren to reveal his secret.

All this meant that, after ten hours spent puzzling over the mysterious Butcher, Wren had no more idea of what to expect at the Green Man than when he'd begun.

When the clock over the mantle struck half-past seven, Mr Grigsby rose, stretched, and, as he did every evening, invited Wren to join him at the inn across the way for dinner. And like every evening before, Wren demurred. Mr Grigsby never took any offence at this. He had long ago supposed Wren preferred to dine with his artistic and literary peers, and for many years his supposition proved correct. Though the circumstances had changed, Wren saw no need to correct Mr Grigsby's assumptions. Regardless of the reason, the outcome remained the same. Mr Grigsby invited Wren to join him for dinner; Wren declined; Mr Grigsby bid him goodnight and departed for the evening; Wren stayed to finish what work he could before going to bed himself in the garret above the office and Mr Grigsby's own chambers.

Tonight, however, at quarter to eight, Wren donned his coat, locked up the office, and strode out into the night. A long, cold walk ensued over the cobblestones until he reached the hanging sign of a man's face overgrown with ivy. Wren braced himself before the green-painted door and, with a sigh, shoved his way into the bright bubbling chaos of scores of clerks making up for twelve hours of absolute boredom.

The noise of their excitement assaulted Wren's ears like a trumpet blast. A cluster nearest the fire had broken out in popular comic song which one of them had heard at a music hall; this young man stood on an ottoman to direct his fellows in following along his half-remembered lyrics. A still larger circle of clerks had gathered around this mess to laugh at the spectacle. The remainder not directly involved in the musical revue had all their own jests, gossip, and arguments to distract them, each raising his voice above the general noise to make himself heard, and thus each voice raising the general noise by exponential degrees. The resulting cacophony would've turned Wren right around and sent him out into the night again had he not determined himself to meet the enigmatic Butcher. So he nudged, pardoned, and surreptitiously elbowed his way through the throng, his black frock coat a dark speck of ink in the roiling tide of more fashionable orange, green, crimson, and pink waistcoats, neckties, and gloves of his fellow clerks.

It occurred to Wren, as he stepped away from the bar with a cup of coffee in either hand and searched the crowd in vain for anything like medieval garb, that convincing him to wait in a coffeehouse all night for a mysterious stranger who never arrived might, in and of itself, pass for a prank. A wise man, having recognized this, would no doubt cease his fruitless hunt and fight his way out of the Green Man the same way he'd come in.

Yet Wren also recalled the high cheekbones, hawkish nose, and haunting dark eyes of the imposing figure who'd appeared in his office as if summoned by Wren's wishful imaginings of something—or someone—to carry him away from the ceaseless drudgery of his own life.

Wren supposed he'd never been a wise man.

"Lofthouse."

Wren flinched and whipped his head 'round. The voice, its low growl cutting through the noisy cheer of the crowd, had spoken his surname directly into his hear. He looked over the heads of the assembled clerks, where he expected to see a particular long and brooding face rising above the throng but beheld no sign of the speaker.

"Down here," the voice growled again.

Wren glanced down and discovered a rough-hewn table tucked away in the back corner not more than two feet from his own left elbow. This position left it quite out of reach of the candles overhead and the merry flickering of the hearth-fire surrounded by armchairs full of clerks further off and cast the whole corner into shadow. Yet the shadow seemed deeper than it ought, as if it absorbed all light attempting to breach it. And in this fathomless shadow sat a hooded figure, no less imposing for his hunched posture.

"Butcher," Wren said, setting the coffee-cups on the table and pulling out a chair to join him.

As soon as Wren sat down, Butcher threw back his hood. He wore no mask this time. Wren supposed the proprietor of the Green Man wouldn't have allowed it. He appreciated Butcher's flair for the *dramatique* regardless.

Likewise, Wren appreciated how the clerks nearest to their table cast nervous looks at Butcher—further confirmation that neither Butcher himself nor his bizarre attire were figments of Wren's imagination. And for once, Wren was not the weirdest figure in the room. Though no doubt sharing a table with Butcher would mark him out for life. Still, Wren hadn't noticed any members of the Restive Quills amidst the crowd, and the noise of the clerks' revels would cover up his conversation with Butcher better than the curious muffled silence in the fog of Staple Inn.

Wren handed one of the coffee-cups off to Butcher, who accepted it with a solemn nod.

"A toast." Butcher raised his cup a hair's-breadth. "To the good health of your king."

"Queen," Wren corrected him.

Butcher's brows knit together. Then his expression cleared. "Of course. Elizabeth. Forgive me, I had forgotten."

Wren opened his mouth, thought better of it, and sipped his bracingly bitter coffee.

Butcher, meanwhile, quaffed the whole piping-hot cup as if it were water. "And now to our purpose."

Wren, who'd found it difficult to tear his eyes away from Butcher's throat as he swallowed, forced himself to meet that dark gaze once again. "And what is our purpose, exactly?"

"To defeat the Holly King, now and forevermore."

Wren blinked. "I beg your pardon?"

"The Queen of the Court of the Silver Wheel has chosen me as her Oak King," said Butcher, which did nothing to dispel Wren's confusion. "I must slay the Holly King on the Winter Solstice. The queen will appoint another Holly King in his place, who must slay me on the Summer Solstice, and so the Silver Wheel continues turning."

Wren stared at him. If he'd had any doubts as to who'd hired Butcher before, they vanished now. The medieval details and chivalrous themes of Butcher's speech were obvious allusions to his own interests—interests which only the Restive Quills knew of, and knew well at that, and had made no secret of their own impatience with Wren's treatment of such themes. He had to admire Butcher's talent, for he not only had his lines down by heart but spoke them as if he truly believed every word. What a wonder he must appear on the stage. Wren wished he might see him as Hotspur or Tybalt or Hamlet. Perhaps, after the Restive Quills had finished their laugh at his expense, Wren could wring his professional name from him and witness his work under the limelight.

Butcher leaned in, his dark eyes burning into Wren's like twin coals. "I do not intend to die on the Summer Solstice."

"Nor do I," Wren replied.

Butcher smiled as if Wren had said something both sensible and agreeable, rather than blurting out the first words which came to mind. Wren found he rather liked that smile. More the pity, then, that Butcher merely played a part. "I intend to slay the new-crowned Holly King and every one of his successors, for all the coming centuries."

"That's all well and good," said Wren. "But I don't see what any of it has to do with me."

Butcher furrowed his brow again. "Don't you?"

"No, I don't," Wren insisted. "Do explain."

Butcher looked at him a moment longer, then stared across the room into the fire and scratched the scar on his cheek in thought.

Wren watched him with a mixture of idle aesthetic appreciation and practical impatience—at least, until he recalled that not twelve hours hence, Butcher's scar had been a wound.

Yet even as he stared in wonder, Wren realized his mistake. The "wound" of that morning had been mere drippings of wax, which skilful fingers had arranged to look like broken skin. Actors on the stage often employed such tricks. Now, so much later in the day, the wax had fallen off—for the most part—and only the faint red streaks of irritated skin remained.

Butcher's rumbling voice broke through Wren's thoughts. "I don't know, either."

"What?" said Wren stupidly.

"I don't know what purpose you will serve in my quest. But,"

Butcher added, with a wry half-smile that made Wren's heart perform curious acrobatics, "I intend to find out."

"If you don't know how I fit into your 'quest,'" Wren said, forcing himself to pronounce the word with extreme scepticism, "what makes you believe I'm part of it at all?"

"Because the fates have said so," Butcher replied as though it were the most natural thing in the world.

"And pray tell, how do the fates speak to you?"

"Through ritual."

"What, scattering bird entrails across the cobblestones? Or do you inhale mystical vapours and babble prophecy in a stupor?"

"I made a pendulum of an acorn," said Butcher, "and ate it."

Wren stared at him.

Butcher did not elaborate. Nor did he seem in any way discomfited by Wren's continued scepticism.

As much as Wren enjoyed staring into so handsome a face, he didn't want the evening to come down to a mere staring contest. He cleared this throat. "Well, you've certainly learnt your book by rote, and your continued improvisation on it is commendable. But you really can't expect me to believe any of this. Not without some proof, at least."

Butcher served him a blank look. Then, catching Wren's eye to be sure he followed the motion, he raised both hands to either side of his head and tucked his hair behind his ears.

Prior to this moment, his raven locks had flowed down as straight and dark as ink poured from the bottle, shot through with strands of molten silver. The loose gather at the nape of his neck allowed for this remarkable hair to cover his ears. The shape of these Wren had taken for granted resembled his and those of other men.

Now, Wren's eyes widened as he beheld a pair of ears as pointed as arrowheads.

Even as he gawked, however, he had a rational explanation to hand. Startling and remarkable craftsmanship, yes—but mere waxwork, just like the wound-turned-scar, and no doubt if he reached out and touched them they would crumble beneath his fingertips.

Wren resisted the urge to do just that and instead replied, "You say your ritual brought you to me. Magic, I presume?"

"Aye," said Butcher.

"Why don't you show me some more of your magic, then. Go on." Wren gestured to the table between them. "Do a spell."

For the first time since they'd met, Butcher appeared almost offended. "I'm a sell-sword, not a witch."

"Yet you performed a spell to find me," Wren countered. "Do you deny it?"

"I deny nothing," said Butcher. "But the pendulum ritual—it's the simplest trick. Every hunter knows it."

"Thought you said you were a sell-sword."

"I am a knave, and thus of all trades." The wry half-smile returned to Butcher's lips. "Though I excel in the hunt."

Wren, who'd begun to feel rather hunted himself, swallowed hard.

"Right. Well," he said, rising from his chair, "until you have some magic to show me, I'm afraid your hunt is at an end."

Butcher watched him stand with a touch of alarm and a great deal more interest. "So be it. I know where to find you."

His eyes lingered on Wren's ink-stained fingertips, his blue-veined wrists protruding from his shirtsleeves, and the death's-head pin on the black neck-cloth tied beneath his throat.

Wren felt the colour rise in his cheeks. If Butcher had demanded to meet him in another sort of establishment, who could tell where their encounter might have led. Alas, in the Green Man, they could have nothing. And so Wren's secret remained safe, though it stuck in his craw.

"Give my regards to the Restive Quills," Wren said with more confidence than he felt and threw himself into the crowd without looking back.

CHAPTER THREE

For the next fortnight, as September passed into October, Wren expected Butcher to descend on Mr Grigsby's office at any moment.

If he were perfectly honest, Wren had to admit he felt more than a little bitter satisfaction in imagining the Restive Quills' reaction to his demand for proof. No doubt it would throw them into fits. He felt still more excitement in imagining what sort of street magic, mesmerism, or conjuring trick Butcher would use to prove his story. To say nothing of how, when Butcher returned to show off his so-called magic, Wren might have the opportunity to glean the man's real name at last.

As the days passed, however, and Butcher did not appear, Wren began to fear he'd set his challenge too high for the Restive Quills to meet.

Which was a shame, because no matter what his reasons for coming, Wren found he did want to see Butcher again. That imposing figure, those high cheekbones, those dark eyes—even his woodsmoke scent had begun to enter Wren's dreams.

Then, on a mid-October morning, the downstairs bell rang at last.

Wren leapt out of his chair before it occurred to him to conceal his excitement from his employer.

Mr Grigsby blinked at him. "Are we expecting something particular from the penny post?"

"Yes," Wren lied, glad Mr Grigsby had provided him with a convenient excuse for his behaviour. He went for the door without any further explanation.

But as he reached for the latch, the door swung inward of its own accord and brought an unexpected visitor along with it.

"Ah!" Mr Grigsby exclaimed in genuine delight, which Wren did not share. "Mr Knoll! What a marvellous surprise! Lofthouse, you ought to have told me—but no matter, you are here now, and must sit down and take tea with us."

"Thank you," said Mr Felix Knoll, a young gentleman of twenty years in a striking blue suit that matched his sapphire eyes. He swept his silk top hat from his lamb-like golden curls and handed it off to Wren without looking at him. "I'm quite famished."

Wren resisted the urge to cram the hat into Felix's mouth. Instead, he shut the door behind Felix and put the top hat in the coat closet beside his and Mr Grigsby's own *chapeaux* and umbrellas.

Mr Grigsby, meanwhile, rose from his own chair to offer it to Felix. "To what occasion do we owe this honour?"

"Oh, nothing particular," Felix answered with the exaggerated casual air that always bespoke his lies. He draped himself across Mr Grigsby's chair like a house cat in a sunbeam. "Found myself in the neighbourhood. Thought I'd drop in."

"Then we must give our thanks to Providence for allowing our paths to cross this day," Mr Grigsby concluded with an indulgent chuckle.

As a clerk, Wren feigned to take as little notice in Felix as Felix took in him. As an aspiring artist, however, he remained ever observant. And while he considered himself wise enough not to judge aloud, he knew in his heart he wasn't charitable enough to avoid forming judgments privately. He had formed his judgment of Felix four years ago, when the boy had first come under Mr Grigsby's legal guardianship, and nothing in Felix's behaviour since then had caused him to reconsider that judgment. On the contrary, his conviction only deepened with every minute spent either in Felix's presence or in going through the records of Felix's considerable inheritance.

Mr Grigsby, meanwhile, went to put the kettle on.

Mr Grigsby was not a clumsy man, precisely. He didn't often knock over ink-bottles or drop his teacup. Yet he moved as if he expected to become clumsy at any moment. A total lack of surety infused his limbs. He might raise his hand towards a ledger twice or thrice without actually touching it before he summoned the conviction to pull it down from the shelf. He did this with a grim determination suggesting that he fully anticipated the whole shelf would collapse at his fingertips, but have that ledger he must, and so he had resigned himself to his fate. When the shelf did not, in fact, crumble to splinters in front of him, he always seemed pleasantly surprised.

At present, Mr Grigsby employed a similar method when it came to fetching the box of tea down from the shelf where it sat between the years 1815 and 1816 in the endless line of annual rent records. He stood on the tips of his toes to grasp it like a schoolboy flailing at a box of forbidden treats put out of his reach.

The third time Mr Grigsby tried and failed to retrieve the tea, a snort of laughter rang out through the muffled atmosphere of Staple Inn.

Mr Grigsby paused and looked around in puzzlement. By then Felix had already whipped out his handkerchief and turned his laughter into a convincing cough.

"The fog is dreadfully thick today," Mr Grigsby observed. "But never fear! Lofthouse has stopped up all draughts, and a moment by the fire should put you to rights."

Felix nodded into his handkerchief, his eyes still sparkling with mirth.

Of all Felix's many faults, this was the one that most provoked Wren's wrath. Wren did not—indeed, could not—deny that Mr Grigsby's awkward habits held some humour now and again, but still he felt the least Felix might do would be to wait until he had departed before he indulged in laughter at the expense of his legal guardian and benefactor, who had behaved far better by half towards Felix than Wren felt he deserved.

Rather than give young Felix a blistering lecture on gratitude, however, Wren took the empty copper kettle out of the office and down to the water-pump in the courtyard.

By the time Wren returned, Mr Grigsby had succeeded in getting the tea-box down from the shelf and now clasped it before him with perfect contentment as he regaled Felix with his report on the past week's weather—fog, with intermittent rain, followed by more fog.

Felix did a better job at feigning interest than Wren, though Wren suspected this was only because Felix wanted to commit as many of Mr Grigsby's odd mannerisms to memory as possible, so he might impersonate Mr Grigsby to amuse his university friends at a later date. Even if Wren didn't already know the boy's character, he would've realised it in a moment from the way Felix kept biting back bursts of laughter and sniffling away his snickering beneath his handkerchief.

Wren entered the room without a word, shut the door behind himself with the softest click of the latch, and wove his way around the two gentlemen to hang the full kettle over the fire. Neither acknowledged his presence; Felix because he did not care and Mr Grigsby because he genuinely did not notice. At least, not until Wren approached him directly to take the tea-box.

"Ah, thank you, Lofthouse!" Mr Grigsby said, handing the tea over with a smile. "Now, Mr Knoll, we need do nothing more than twiddle our thumbs, for Lofthouse takes care of everything. I don't know what I'd do without him."

Prosper, most like, Wren thought but didn't say.

Felix cleared his throat. "Actually, I've just thought of something you may help me with in the meantime."

"Oh?" Surprise did not lessen Mr Grigsby's good humour by one jot. "Name it, my dear boy."

"I require an advance of funds from my father's trust," said Felix.

For a moment, the only sound that permeated the muffling fog of Staple Inn was the crackling of the fire beneath the copper kettle.

"Dear me," said Mr Grigsby. "I'm very sorry to bear bad news, but I'm afraid my hands are tied on the matter. The terms of your father's will are unmistakable. You are to have sufficient funds for your education, and—" Here Mr Grigsby named a sum that had dizzied Wren the first time he heard it and infuriated him every instance afterward. "—per semester to live on in a manner befitting your station. And, as it comes from the interest of your late father's trust, there is no margin left over from which to draw on. Quite impossible. I hope only the need is not great and the matter not dire?"

Felix waved off Mr Grigsby's genuine concern. "Oh no, nothing pressing. It's just I wanted to buy a particular necklace for Flora, as a Christmas present."

Wren thought Felix might at least have the decency to look abashed at his own lie, but falsehood altered the young man's fashionable features not a whit.

Mr Grigsby entertained no such suspicions. "How charming! I'm sure it would please Miss Fairfield very much."

Wren had never laid eyes on Miss Flora Fairfield in the flesh, but he had seen the miniature Felix kept of her. Indeed, the boy had shown it off to him like a prized racehorse when he'd first received it. From this, Wren knew Miss Flora had pale blue eyes, white-blonde hair, and an expression that fell somewhere between astonishment and boredom. Though, Wren supposed, the blame for the latter might fall on the artist rather than the subject.

In Wren's opinion, Felix and Miss Flora, with their matching fair hair and blue eyes, bore greater resemblance to a pair of twins rather than a pair of lovers. Indeed, as Mr Grigsby retained legal guardianship over both of them, one might call them siblings. But since no one asked for Wren's opinion on the match, he expressed it only to his manuscripts.

"Unfortunately," Mr Grigsby continued, "Miss Fairfield's appreciation does not alter the terms of your father's will. However, depending on the jeweller from which you acquire the necklace, it may be possible to pay some small amount at present and the remainder after the first of the year. Not that I suggest one ought to make it a habit to live on one's debts! But for this singular special instance, it might do."

Wren had long suspected Felix was no stranger to living on his debts but kept this to himself—save for a speaking glance at Felix.

Felix ignored Wren's accusatory gaze. "I'm afraid this particular jeweller will not make such a bargain with me. Is there absolutely nothing to be done?"

"Nothing whatsoever," Mr Grigsby said solemnly. "But fret not! Christmas is three months out, and I'm sure you can think up another equally suitable gift for dear Miss Fairfield before then. And the new year will allow you to withdraw the cost of the necklace from your father's trust—no doubt you have already resolved to tighten your belt to meet the demand—in plenty of time for her birthday, on which occasion I'm sure the necklace will meet with equal appreciation."

Mr Grigsby looked well pleased with the solution he'd drawn up for Felix's supposed predicament. Felix's own smile proved a pale imitation of such satisfaction. Wren saw through it as easily as one might see through a windowpane.

And no sooner had Wren thought this than something struck the actual windowpane behind Felix's head.

All three men whirled towards the sound, though only Wren dashed to the window itself.

A bird lay on the sill. It didn't move as Wren unlocked the window and threw it open. Wren supposed it had died in striking the glass.

"A sparrow, Lofthouse?" Mr Grigsby called to him from across the room.

"No, sir," said Wren. For indeed, it was no sparrow, but something with a fluffy grey coat and a little mask of black feathers over its eyes. "Some other sort of bird."

Just as Wren attempted to scoop its poor corpse onto a scrap of parchment, the black-masked eyes blinked open.

"Oh!" cried Wren as the bird hopped upright.

Despite its passerine shape, the queer little bird had a fierce gaze beneath its mask. It blinked at him several more times, shook itself all over, then hopped onto the parchment and from there onto the cuff of Wren's jacket.

Wren willed himself not to flinch, lest he startle the stunned creature.

Just as the bird seemed about to hop up his elbow and into the office, it blinked at something over his shoulder, then whirled away in a storm of feathers and disappeared into the fog.

"It's alive after all?" Mr Grigsby asked as Wren shut and locked the window. Without waiting for an answer, he continued, "Very good. Far preferable to the inverse outcome, I think we may all agree."

Felix belatedly returned Mr Grigsby's beaming smile. "Yes, well—thank you for the tea—I'm afraid I must be going."

"So soon?" asked Mr Grigsby.

Indeed, the kettle had not yet begun to whistle. Wren indulged in a raised eyebrow at Felix's expense.

"Yes," said Felix, pointedly avoiding Wren's gaze. "I've just remembered an appointment with another friend in town. Must dash. But thank you for your offer of tea and your advice. I shall use it in good health."

With this, he made a very pretty bow, which gave Wren enough time to fetch his hat from the cupboard. He handed it over to Felix, who did not trouble himself to thank him.

When the downstairs bell rang again the next day, Wren's heart leapt to think Butcher had come at last. He hastened to temper his enthusiasm; more likely it was Felix Knoll returned to make another attempt at his trust fund.

Mr Grigsby, absorbed in his newspaper, took no notice of Wren rising from his desk and crossing the office to answer the door.

Yet when Wren ventured into the foyer, he found not Felix Knoll, nor Butcher, but a gentleman with sandy hair, snub nose, and a receding chin propped up by the voluminous folds of his cravat.

Wren hurried to shut the door behind himself and hissed down the stair. "Humphreys? What are you doing here?"

Indeed, for a member of the Restive Quills to confront another in his place of work broke all the club's rules of secrecy. Though, since Wren had tendered his resignation, he supposed the tenets of membership no longer applied to him.

Humphreys bore a look that strongly implied he didn't care what rules he flouted in that moment. He mounted one foot on the stair and furiously stage-whispered, "What the Devil do you mean by sending over such a ridiculous creature to give us your regards?"

"What?" said Wren.

"When we asked him how he'd found us, he said the bones had shown him the path. The bones! Is that what you're calling yourself now?"

"What?" Wren repeated.

"Don't play coy. We all know it was you who set him on us and told him where he might find our gathering place."

"Humphreys," Wren said with complete honesty, "I haven't the faintest idea what you're on about."

Humphreys scoffed. "You know perfectly well! That actor you hired to play the part of your medieval Dick Turpin—Butcher, he said to call him."

Wren stared at him.

"Which, while it certainly cuts to the point of the matter, can hardly be considered a particularly clever pseudonym," Humphreys continued. "I'd thought your pride in your craft would demand something more. A pun, at the very least."

"I didn't hire him," Wren said stupidly. "You hired him."

"Me!?" Humphreys recoiled from the notion.

"The collective you," Wren elaborated, not bothering to disguise his impatience. The farce had gone on long enough. "The Restive Quills. You hired him to play a prank on me."

"We most certainly did not!" insisted Humphreys, sounding almost as indignant as Wren felt. "Of all the absurd—"

"It is exactly the sort of absurdity in which you all delight," Wren snapped. "Though I'd considered you better gentlemen than to try and convince me it was all my own idea."

"Whether or not Butcher was your idea remains to be seen," Humphreys sniffed, "but he certainly wasn't ours."

Wren knew he hadn't hired Butcher. However, he also knew that Humphreys couldn't spin a convincing falsehood any more than he could spin dross into gold—or ink into prose, for that matter. The man had no capacity for lying. Which meant Humphreys, at least, had nothing to do with Butcher.

This by no means cleared the remainder of the Restive Quills of such a charge. They all knew as well as Wren that Humphreys couldn't lie and might have wisely chosen to keep Humphreys in the dark as to their actual plans, lest he give the game away.

But it did give Wren pause.

"What exactly happened," Wren said slowly, "and when, and where?"

"At our last meeting," Humphreys answered. "In the coffeehouse at Cockspur Street. We were all sitting in our corner of the back room reading the minutes when this Gothic brute stormed in and demanded to know if he'd found the gathering place of the Restive Quills. Vincent informed him he had and asked how he knew where to find us, and he claimed that the bones had told him. Which was of course nonsense, and he proved it in the next moment by looming over us all and growling out: 'Lofthouse sends his regards.'"

Wren felt his dawning horror at war with a fervent wish to have seen the looks on all the Restive Quills' faces as Butcher passed on his message.

"So Vincent demanded his name," Humphreys continued, "and you'd have thought he'd asked for the man's own firstborn son, for how he smouldered at the question! But then he rumbled, 'Butcher,' and turned on his heel and stalked out. Well?" Humphreys concluded with evident irritation. "Does this account of your prank satisfy you? Or did your Butcher give you a better one?"

"Not my prank," said Wren, still digesting the tale. "And not my Butcher, either."

Humphreys scoffed. "As you like it. But know this—the Restive Quills will not forget this offence. All that follows, sir, you will have brought down on your own head!"

Wren, who knew full well that what followed would likely be little more than a satirical sketch in the margins of whatever literature the Quills produced in the coming year, resisted the urge to roll his eyes.

Humphreys took a pinch of snuff without offering any to him—not that Wren wanted it, but he knew from experience Humphreys delighted in the slight—and bid him an extraordinarily sarcastic good day as he whirled away from him. The three consecutive sneezes that resounded through the foyer after Wren had closed the door on him somewhat marred the impressive nature of his exit.

Mr Grigsby glanced up from his newspaper as Wren passed him on his way back to his own desk. "Glad tidings, I hope?"

The question jerked Wren out of bizarre musings, and it took him a moment to respond. "Interesting tidings."

Mr Grigsby seemed pleased by this and returned to his newspaper with no further questions, much to Wren's relief.

Wren found no relief from his own mind, which continued apace in its theorizing on the matter of Butcher.

Very little was accomplished in the way of clerking that afternoon and on into the evening. The next day brought no relief from the ever-twisting coils of the mystery. Wren spent the day scratching surreptitious notes on scraps of paper whenever Mr Grigsby wasn't watching—which was most of the time, to be perfectly honest. The sun rose and set somewhere beyond the fog over London. Mr Grigsby invited Wren to dinner. Wren declined. Mr Grigsby departed. Wren hunched over his desk and resumed his scribbling by candlelight.

The downstairs bell rang.

Wren's head shot up. His fevered brain flitted through the possibilities—another visit from the Restive Quills demanding an explanation? Perhaps Felix had come again to beg, borrow, or steal an advance on his inheritance, hoping to find the servant more willing than the master. If so, Wren would prove him very much mistaken.

More likely, Wren supposed as he rose and stretched the stiffness from his bones, it was Mr Grigsby, who had left his ring of keys behind and required Wren to let him in so he might retrieve them.

Wren opened the door.

There before him, in all his medieval majesty, stood Butcher.

CHAPTER FOUR

Butcher loomed in the doorway. As Wren blinked up at him in astonishment, so Butcher stared down at Wren with something like merriment and satisfaction twinkling in his dark eyes.

"What are you doing here?" Wren demanded.

"I've fulfilled the first object of your quest," Butcher replied in a rumbling voice that thrummed through Wren's own breastbone. "I've given your regards to the Restive Quills."

"So I heard," said Wren. "How did you find them?"

"The bones told me."

Just as Humphreys had said. How consistent of them. Almost as if they read it off the same script. Wren withheld a sardonic smile. "And, pray tell, what bones are these? How do they speak to you? May I see them for myself?"

Butcher's brow furrowed, yet his hand didn't hesitate as it dropped beneath his cloak and withdrew a fist-sized leather pouch to proffer to Wren.

Wren took it warily. The leather felt warm in his palm. He pulled open the tie at the neck and peered down into the pouch's depths.

Five knuckle-bones the size of dice gleamed white amidst the dark shadows.

"From a sheep," said Butcher. "I cast them on the stones, and they showed me where I might find my quarry."

Wren had to admire his use of theatrical property. He drew the pouch closed and handed it back. Butcher secreted it away in the folds of his cloak, revealing as he did so the silver rabbit-fur lining of the black wool garment.

"Where did you acquire your costume?" Wren asked.

For the first time in their short acquaintance, Butcher seemed reluctant to answer. Indeed, if Wren didn't know better, he'd say he looked almost abashed. Still, in the stirring bass voice with a hint of a burr, Butcher replied, "I made it."

Wren raised his brows. Butcher might take more pride in such an accomplishment—if it were truly his accomplishment and not the accomplishment of his theatre's dressmaker, which Wren thought the more likely outcome. "Did you indeed?"

Butcher cleared his throat and held out his left hand. Dark lines wore through his weathered palm like tree-rings, and his long fingers bore more than a few calluses. It looked more like a sailor or farmer's hand than the hand of a thespian or an aristocratic eccentric. "Tonight I join the Wild Hunt to slay the beast that has devoured the children of the Court of Moons. If you will venture out with me, I will show you that all I spake of rings true."

This, then, was the trick. No shell hidden beneath a cup or ha'penny pulled from behind an ear. Just a fairy tale to lure Wren out of the city. To what end, he couldn't fathom.

Yet even as his rational mind supposed that such an adventure could only end in mugging or murder, his Romantic soul stretched its withered wings and soared at the notion of leaving the suffocating fog of Staple Inn behind to venture out into the wilderness beneath the full moon.

Furthermore, if he did end up murdered, it meant he'd never have to copy out another account-book again. And if he must end in murder, Wren supposed he'd rather have a strapping specimen like Butcher slide the knife into his heart.

A morbid smile curled Wren's lips. "Very well. I accept your challenge."

So saying, he grasped Butcher's hand with his own. Warmth suffused his touch and flowed up his arm to the elbow. He'd quite forgotten what the touch of another person could feel like, much less a handsome stranger. Recognition tingled in his fingertips and kindled a voiceless longing in his heart.

All too soon, Butcher broke off their handclasp. Not unkindly, and with a look that suggested to Wren's fevered imagination that he wished for more as well, but he broke it nonetheless and turned to glide down the staircase with heavy tread.

Wren snatched his coat and hat from the cupboard and fumbled locking-up twice in his haste to follow him.

Though the almanac declared this the night of the full moon, none of its silvery light penetrated the fog that hung over London. The yellow flame of the gaslights lining the streets proved a poor replacement. Still, they sufficed for Wren to keep sight of Butcher as he took two quick steps for every one of Butcher's lengthy strides. Butcher led him north out of Staple Inn onto Holburn and turned westward. Holburn became Oxford Street. They passed fewer and fewer clerks returning home after a long day and more and more unfortunates just beginning their night's work.

Then they came upon Hyde Park. The gaslight of the street didn't reach far beyond the park's iron fencing, leaving the verdant depths in the dark.

Rather than continue on the road past the park, Butcher strode through Cumberland Gate and on into the darkness.

Wren supposed he should have guessed as much and followed him.

While Wren had never before personally availed himself of the many services offered by divers persons in Hyde Park by night, he'd heard all the rumours—not just of painted ladies but also of gentlemen seeking anonymous like-minded company. The Horse Guards in particular, with their barracks in Knightsbridge, had quite the reputation. And, as Wren stared at the shadowy outline of Butcher's feathered cap, he could well imagine the tall, brawny, self-assured stranger as a member of that particular crew. Such poise and carriage would serve a man well astride a warhorse.

Though, if that were the answer to Butcher's riddle, Wren wondered what deuced purpose the medieval costume served. If Butcher wasn't a soldier in the Horse Guards, perhaps he was auditioning for a role as an ornamental hermit in the park. Assuming he hadn't been hired on as such already—

Butcher threw his arm out to block Wren's path.

Wren stumbled to a halt and aimed a quizzical eyebrow up at him. Through the course of their journey through the park, his eyes had adjusted to the darkness, and he could just perceive the silvery outline of Butcher's profile. Butcher appeared stoic as ever, looking not at Wren but at something ahead of them on the path. Wren rolled his eyes and trained his gaze on the deeper shadows beneath the overhanging tree branches. At first he saw nothing. Then a thud resounded on the packed earth—a hoofbeat. The limbs of a dead tree emerged from the shadows—no, Wren realized, not leafless branches after all, but—

The antlers of a stag.

It stood far taller than a red or fallow deer; as tall as the draft geldings that pulled a brewer's dray, at least fourteen hands high at the shoulder, and with its noble head and many-pronged antlers climbing higher still. Perhaps the darkness made its shaggy coat look black as ink, rather than red or white-spotted fawn, but that didn't explain the thick mane of course fur hanging from its throat, tinged with gleaming grey like frost over heath.

As Wren stared, Butcher put up his palm before the beast. And to Wren's amazement, the stag bowed its head to nudge Butcher's hand. Butcher patted its broad, bovine nose, and the stag let him, tame as any fireside hound.

The stag startled Wren for many reasons. First, its monstrous size and apparently docile nature and Butcher's familiarity with it.

Second, not only was it out of season—Hyde Park being stocked with deer only during spring and summer, not autumn—it was neither a red deer nor a fallow deer, but some third, enormous, ethereal type he'd never beheld before. A type that retained its antlers well past the point where they ought to have fallen to the forest floor.

And third—

"Do you wish to ride ahead of me or behind?" asked Butcher.

Wren blinked at him. "Ride?"

Butcher waved a careless hand toward the stag, as if there were any doubt.

Wren's pulse fluttered in what he dared not acknowledge as excitement. The stag proved nothing. No matter how much Wren wished it could. He wondered what conspiracy the Restive Quills had concocted to acquire the beast. Perhaps Butcher was truly an eccentric aristocrat after all, the sort to not only keep his ancestral hold stocked with elk but also tame and ride them. And run around London dressed as a medieval highwayman. And hire himself out to literary clubs with grudges against former members.

The excuses were starting to sound weak even to Wren's own mind.

And the stag remained excruciatingly real.

"Behind," Wren decided. Better to cling to Butcher's shoulders than sit propped in front of him like a boy just learning to ride.

What other motivations Wren might have had for wanting the opportunity to cling to those broad-muscled shoulders, he pushed down into the darkest hollows of his heart.

Besides, he might never actually mount the stag. The beast had proved tame enough to approach, true, but that didn't mean it would suffer the indignity of conveying two grown men. Though it certainly looked big enough to do so if it wished.

Butcher, meanwhile, raised his wild brows at Wren's answer. Then he unpinned his cloak and swung it down off his broad shoulders.

"It'll be a chill night where we're headed," was the only explanation Butcher offered, along with his cloak.

After a moment's hesitation, Wren accepted it with an outstretched hand. The sheer heft of the cloak as Butcher dropped it into his grasp made him stumble forward. Yards upon yards of coarse black wool lined with untold silver-grey rabbit skins soft as velvet—altogether formed a substantial garment indeed. And, as Wren shrugged it over his own shoulders, it still carried the warmth and woodsmoke scent of Butcher himself.

Still, as Butcher stood a full head taller than him, Wren could only imagine how ludicrous he looked as the ragged hem of the cloak pooled around his ankles. No doubt the Restive Quills had all huddled in a nearby hedge to lampoon his novel costume. Wren pulled the cloak tighter around him as if it could shield him from their slings and arrows. He fiddled with the clasp—one of the ring and pin sort—in the dark.

Butcher closed the distance between them in a single stride. His fingertips brushed Wren's upon the clasp as he fastened it in two deft movements.

Wren swallowed hard—his throat had gone unaccountably dry—and murmured his thanks. He could just make out the flash of Butcher's smile in return.

Then Butcher turned to the stag, which had waited all the while with unprecedented patience, though it did nibble on the lower-hanging leaves overhead. This stopped as Butcher placed his palms on the beast's withers. He vaulted onto its back with astonishing agility for a man of his size.

Wren, who'd leapt back in anticipation of the stag bolting, stared in amazement as it did no such thing, but bore Butcher's weight with dignity.

Butcher nudged the stag's flanks with his boot-heels. It approached Wren at his urging.

As if he could perform the same acrobatic feats as Butcher.

Wren had ridden horses back when he and his father were still on speaking terms. More than a decade ago. Never bareback, though. And never deer. Much less a stag that stood over seven feet tall—not including the antlers.

Regardless, Wren would hardly give up without having a go at it.

Rather than come to a halt beside him, however, the stag continued on past him towards a looming shadow. Wren belatedly recognized it as a tree stump, cut off just above his own knees.

Wren required no further urging to clamber atop it.

Butcher bent down to offer Wren his hand. Wren clasped his forearm. Powerful sinews flexed beneath his fingertips, their might in no way disguised by the sleeve of Butcher's tunic. And the hand that grasped Wren's forearm in turn had a hold as strong as the Gordian knot. Wren braced his free palm against the wiry fur of the stag's back. He leapt—Butcher heaved—

And then he was up.

Wren glanced 'round from his new perch, breathless with exertion and wonder alike, sitting taller than he'd ever stood in all his days.

The stag's muscles shifted beneath him. Bereft of stirrups and not trusting the grip of his thighs, Wren's hands flailed to brace himself.

And landed on Butcher's shoulders.

They could land on little else, for Butcher sat so close to him, hardly a hair's breadth remained between Butcher's broad back and Wren's narrow chest. Wren's slender thighs aligned beneath Butcher's, and as for his fork and Butcher's fundament—well. The less said about that, the better. Still, Wren found it difficult to think of much else, with those massive shoulders clasped tight in his fingers and his face at the nape of Butcher's neck, inhaling his woodsmoke musk.

Butcher glanced back at Wren, but otherwise didn't so much as twitch beneath Wren's vise-grip. If Wren didn't know better, he'd think Butcher smiled at him. Doubtless the combination of fevered imagination and deep shadow had crafted the illusion.

Before Wren could apologize for the liberties he'd taken, Butcher spoke.

"Make no promises nor bargains. Consume neither food nor drink. Accept nothing, offer nothing. Shall we be off?"

Wren, still not quite daring to believe any of this was real, nodded.

Butcher's thighs clenched against the stag's flanks, and the stag leapt forward into the darkness.

Now Wren had no choice but to hold on for dear life to Butcher's shoulders, to clench his own thighs against Butcher's, and to roll his hips back and forth against Butcher's backside with every rise and plunge of the stag's galloping strides. He heard rather than saw the foliage flying past his face, a twig or two catching his cheek on the way. The cloak unfurled behind him like a banner in the wind.

Wren had just caught enough of his breath to consider asking where the Devil the stag was taking them when he glimpsed something at last on the path ahead.

A ring of pale mushrooms loomed stark against the black earth. They almost seemed to glow.

A fairy ring, Wren thought to himself. He had no time to think much else. In three bounding leaps, the stag had reached the ring.

Then it reared.

Wren lost his grip on Butcher's shoulders and seized his waist instead. Butcher, nothing daunted, took hold of the stag's antlers.

The stag sprang from its hind legs and charged down as if it meant to gore the earth headfirst.

Wren cried out and wrapped his arms tight around Butcher's waist, bracing for the impact.

None came.

CHAPTER FIVE

It felt as if all three of them—Butcher, Wren, and the stag—had plunged off the edge of a cliff. Not dashed against the earth but falling through it.

Wren had screwed his eyes shut in anticipation of the landing jolt. Cold wind struck his face like a crashing wave, and the shock of it forced his eyes open.

The fog of London had vanished. The full moon hung overhead in a crisp night sky full to bursting with twinkling stars, framed by the dark green points of enormous pines looming all around them. Wren could see the colour, truly, for the moon shone brighter than any gaslight, and it illuminated everything down to the lowest branches that still hung high above Wren's perch on the stag. Beneath these sat trunks wider than Wren was tall, surrounded by a carpet of ferns.

The stag, mid-leap when Wren had opened his eyes, now landed delicately on its fore-hooves and trotted to a halt.

"Where are we?" Wren whispered. His breath plumed in clouds of dragon smoke. He felt renewed gratitude for Butcher's cloak, warm and snug about his shoulders.

Butcher turned to catch Wren's eye. He put his finger to his lips, then cupped his hand behind his ear.

His pointed ear.

In the moonlight, and without his hood, Wren could see Butcher's ears quite clearly. Now there was no mistaking them for waxwork. He could see, as well, the black woollen tunic Butcher wore and how it clung to his muscular frame, tied off with a belted leather gyrdel at the waist and hanging down not much farther than that. Nothing covered Butcher's thighs save medieval hose, likewise black, and his black cavalier boots came up to his knees; a motley assortment of costuming eras in a monochromatic assembly.

Wren shut his mouth but kept on staring in wide-eyed wonder at his new surroundings. He'd never seen so many stars in his life. Had seen none, in fact, since he'd moved to London. The silence was new to him as well. Moreso than the muffled angles of Staple Inn, the forest had no wagons rattling endlessly over cobblestones, no people shouting, no bells ringing, none of the millions of incidental human sounds that tumbled all on top of each other every minute in the city. Just the rustling of pine needles in the wind.

Then he heard it.

An eerie sound, a howl that began low and swooped upward to end in a triumphant blast that echoed throughout the forest as if from miles off. A hunting horn.

Butcher took hold of the stag's antlers and dug his knees into its flanks. The stag leapt off once more, darting to and fro between the trees at harrowing speed, along no path Wren could perceive. He clung to Butcher's waist, his chest flush with Butcher's spine, the closest embrace he'd known in more years than he cared to count.

The horn resounded again. In its wake, Wren heard the thunder of beating hooves rumbling ever nearer. He thought he glimpsed shadows between the pines, mounted riders, as if their own reflection chased them.

Then the stag burst through the trees and into the throng.

A horde of hundreds surrounded them. Like leaping off a waterfall into flood-swollen torrents, the current of the pack swept up and swallowed the stag and its riders. Wren whirled his head 'round to glimpse them all—a grand host of elves in a staggering variety of costume, from Hellenic chitons to medieval armour, garments of rough hide and blood-stained fur, Tudor velvets and slashed doublets, bark and bone. Some rode, some ran, and some seemed to fly. A raven-haired elf-maiden's tunic looked half iridescent feathers and half torn leaves, her face smeared blue with woad and her white grin gleaming through it with wolfish fangs as she readied her twice-curved bow. Astride a grey horse rode a lady in a moon-white gown. Her hem trailed down past her steed's hooves and had dragged through enough muck and gore to rend it into lace-work tatters that flowed from white to pink to crimson-black. Another rider in sea-foam satin breeches and silk stockings would not have looked out of place in the court of George III—save for the spiderweb mask that obscured all but the knife-point tips of their blue ears. One hunter flitted along in a woollen cloak of mottled grey, storm-cloud on the left side and moonlight on the right, with a thick fur ruff. Grey tresses fluttered in the wind behind them, though their smooth face bespoke youth.

Wolf-hounds bayed and darted between hooves and boots. No, Wren realized, not just wolf-hounds, but true wolves the size of horses, their long maws snapping the air and their thick fur rippling in the wind. The smaller and more wiry frames of the wolf-hounds dashed about their larger friends with wagging tails. The crimson coat of a fox slipped amongst them, quick as a minnow in the overwhelming current. And some wolves... Wren blinked, but his vision remained unchanged, and so he felt forced to concede that some of the wolves had the shape of men and leapt up on two legs to throw back their heads and howl.

The werewolves were not the only hunters to straddle the worlds of men and beasts. Not every hoof belonged to a horse or hart. Merry fauns and sinister satyrs danced amidst the thundering hordes. Milk-white women with calf's ears and hollow backs ran on cloven hooves of gold. An immense broad-shouldered man with his blood bay coat descending into iridescent black at his hands, hooves, horns, and the tip of his tufted whip-cord tail, Wren knew in an instant for an incubus, though he'd never before seen his like or encountered his description. And, as Wren shot a second glance over his shoulder, he realized one figure he'd taken for a bearded archer on horseback was, in fact, a centaur.

All this wild abandon worthy of Hieronymus Bosch paled in comparison to the leader of the pack. At the helm of the hunt, astride the largest and fiercest wolf, rode a man who would have stood seven feet tall with both his heels on the ground. A pair of bear-skull pauldrons sat on his thick shoulders, while his grey beard, tinted green with moss, covered his thrice-broad chest like a pelt. Just as much hair trailed behind him, past his pointed ears and his antlers, which rivalled those of the stag Wren rode on even now. He gripped a cross-barbed spear in his right fist, and his left held a curling horn as long as a yardstick, from which he trumpeted the haunting howl that called the hunt to order.

It occurred to Wren, as he regarded that barbed spear and the sundry implements of the other hunters, that he didn't carry a weapon. Unless one counted the pen-knife in his waistcoat pocket, which Wren himself did not, and he doubted Butcher would either.

And what, Wren wondered but didn't dare ask aloud, was their prey?

A guttural, gurgling shriek rent the air. Wren whipped his head towards the sound—a horrible singular noise that echoed over the general cacophony of the wild hunt and seemed to come not from somewhere ahead of them, but from beside.

Butcher's thighs clenched atop Wren's. The stag darted off to the left, away from the pack and deeper into the forest.

Towards the dreadful cry.

Some other hunters seemed to have similar ideas, but the stag outstripped them all, darting nimbly through the dark, leaping over fallen logs and slipping under overhanging limbs. Wren, unable to see the path ahead, kept his narrow chest flush to Butcher's broad back, ducking when he ducked and dodging where he dodged. The hoots and horns of the hunt faded. Snapping twigs and rustling pine needles resounded in their stead. Then the babbling of running water, at first so faint that Wren assumed he imagined it, rose up louder and louder with every stride. Rapid tilts and plunges sent his heart into his throat and his stomach into knots. He tightened his arms around Butcher's lithe waist and tried to ignore how every leap brought his hips up against Butcher's backside.

A sudden stop almost sent Wren sprawling from the stag's back. He clung to his perch and found himself on the edge of a riverbank. The forest broke away, allowing the moonlight to illuminate a sheer drop-off carved out by the water in its spring swells. Now, with the first frost well past, the mountain springs had frozen up, and the river they fed had dwindled to a mere stream that wound its way through the wood some twelve feet below the rim of its flood-bank.

Wren smelled the reason for the stag's halting before he saw it, the scent of woodsmoke musk leaving him as he raised his head from the nape of Butcher's neck, replaced by a rank stench of stale urine, spoiled meat, and rotted blood. A glimpse down the steep bank into the riverbed destroyed any remaining doubt as to the source of the odour.

There, in a curved hollow of frozen mud beside the river's bend, stood a boar.

Until that moment, Wren had considered the wolves and steeds running in the wild hunt as the largest living creatures he'd ever seen. The boar dwarfed them. Indeed, it would have dwarfed any omnibus now rattling through London. A thick coat of stiff, wiry hair covered its mountainous bulk. Its natural colour Wren could not now discern; its lower half had turned grey with brackish filth, and its enormous hump and head looked as if bathed in pitch—but for the stench from which Wren felt forced to the sickening conclusion that the beast had wallowed in blood. Rivulets of fresher stuff spilled forth from its mouth between clusters of tusks—three to each side, the smallest as long as Wren's fore-arm and the largest half as long as his entire body, with the leftmost one broken off at its tip and cracked down to its base in the festering gum-line. Deep furrows of black rot stained with blood-red rust ran through the yellow ivory. And as he gazed on the monstrosity, Wren knew little of that blood was its own.

Butcher laid his hands on Wren's wrists and gently broke their embrace of his waist. Wren withdrew to give him freedom of movement. Butcher dismounted from the stag, a move which Wren thought foolish at best, until he realized they stood downwind of the horrible beast—and furthermore, the sound of the rushing water, diminished as it might be, proved enough to cover the sound of Butcher's boots landing on the blanket of dried pine needles.

"Stay mounted," he whispered to Wren. "The stag will bolt if the boar charges too near."

Wren nodded, though while he supposed the nimble stag would prove faster than the boar, he didn't feel entirely comfortable with leaving Butcher to his fate.

As Butcher crept towards the edge of the tree-line, Wren beheld his silhouette. Wrapping his cloak around Wren's shoulders had left him clothed in just tunic and hose. Belted around the waist, the tunic didn't fall far past Butcher's hips. At another time Wren might have appreciated the view; at present he fixated on the scabbards hanging on either side of Butcher's gyrdel. One held a dagger. The other appeared not quite so long as a sword and far more slender.

Neither seemed an adequate weapon against a beast of such monstrous size.

No sooner had Wren thought this than Butcher raised his arm into the lower reaches of the pine tree they sheltered beneath—dead, its branches stretched out like skeletal fingers in the moonlight—and seized a stout limb. A single wrench broke it off in his fist. His dagger flashed out of its sheath, and within the minute he'd trimmed off all vestigial twigs and whittled a point onto his own makeshift spear. Then, silent as a shadow, he slipped off beyond Wren's sight.

The boar, meanwhile, had pricked its ears at the echoing snap of the breaking branch and now snorted into the air, seeking the scent of what had made the sound. Its plough-share trotters carved deep furrows into the mud as it spun 'round in its search. Its ears swivelled in all directions. Yet it seemed it could not perceive Butcher—much as Wren had lost him in the shadows beneath the trees. He held his breath and tangled his fists in the stag's thick mane as he waited.

All at once the boar's nostrils flared. It reared, whirled, and charged the tree-line with a guttural roar.

Wren's heart leapt into his throat as he glimpsed a familiar silhouette darting behind the pines. The boar smashed into them a fraction of a second after. Wood cracked against tusks with a sound like cannon-fire. The trees swayed.

The stag shifted its stance beneath Wren but did not bolt. Wren's gaze flitted across the tree-line in a frantic search for any sign of Butcher. He'd almost given up hope when at last he spied him, limned in moonlight and crouching with makeshift spear in hand, a mere stone's throw in front of the boar. Only the tusks caught on half-shattered trunks prevented the boar from charging him. It yanked its head backward with violence and tore up the ground with its trotters in its efforts to break free, but its initial blow had embedded itself deep with the trees, and it stuck fast between two pines. All it could do was throw open its jaws and bellow in impotent rage.

And as it did so, Butcher sprang up and flung his spear down its throat.

A piercing shriek tore through the night. A horrible gurgling swallowed it up, but not before it set the hair of Wren's nape on end. The boar reared and, with a thunderous crash, succeeded, too late, in wrenching itself out of the trees.

The stag likewise reared at the sound. Wren seized it by the antlers to keep himself mounted. It snorted and dug its hooves into the dried needles but settled within the moment.

By then, Butcher had vanished again into the shadows of the forest.

The boar—still not dead, and not even dying, Wren realized with growing horror—staggered backward into the river-bed, taking the makeshift spear with it. One of the pines toppled into the mud in the boar's wake. The broken tip of a tusk gleamed amidst the shattered wood.

Beady black eyes rolled to whites Wren hadn't known the beast possessed. Blood dark as ichor dripped between tusks and the broken-off branch caught in the boar's throat.

The howl of the hunting horn echoed through the forest, so faint at first Wren thought it was the wind, but growing louder with every passing moment and bringing with it the thundering of a hundred hooves.

Whether it would arrive soon enough to finish off the boar, Wren knew not.

All he knew was the familiar snap of Butcher breaking another dead branch and the silver flash of his dagger not twelve yards distant.

With a gurgling bellow, the boar launched itself into the woods again —straight at where Wren had just espied Butcher.

Wren's warning shout died in his throat as an arrow pierced the boar's eye.

The boar reared, shrieking.

The elf-maiden astride a wolf dashed out of the forest and onto the riverbank. Her steed howled as she notched another arrow to her bow. A chorus of howls answered it. The thunderous approach of the hunt grew to a roar.

The boar whirled toward each fresh noise as it arose.

Which meant it faced away from the elf-maiden as she leapt off her steed and her wolf lunged for the boar's flank.

The boar reeled to combat the wolf. More wolves burst forth from upstream. They surrounded the boar and leapt at it from all directions. One made it onto the boar's back, sinking its teeth into the hairy hump over the shoulders and ripping its head back and forth. Another made for the boar's underbelly, but a swift turn caught it on the tusks and catapulted it across the riverbed. It struck the rocks on the opposite bank with a sickening crunch like snapping branches and fell down to lie very still.

The rest of the hunt surged in to take its place. The remaining wolves howled for blood and tore out the boar's flanks. Satyrs and centaurs hurled spears. The moth-like fairy with the fur ruff dove down on fluttering wings to inflict a thousand nicks with its glass dagger. Arrow after arrow flew from the elf-maiden's bow and dozens of others. The boar gave as good as it got—one tusk-gored steed fell shrieking beneath its trotters, the rider in the spiderweb mask barely escaping the same fate—and the snow underfoot turned to crimson mud.

Yet Wren couldn't focus on the chaos. His gaze kept flicking to the rim of the battlefield, the edge of the riverbank, the encircling tree-line.

The glint of moonlight off a blade's edge ignited a welcome spark of hope in his heart.

Butcher leapt from the darkness as if borne of shadow himself. In his fist he clenched a blade as slender as an icicle. He landed on the boar with all the agility and ferocity of a panther, bracing his limbs against its tusks as it shrieked and tossed its head. His blade found its sheath in the boar's remaining eye.

A gout of blood accompanied the horrible guttural scream that burst from the boar's throat. A terrible shudder ran through its bulk. Then it collapsed. Butcher rode it to the ground, alighting only when it lay still.

Cheers rang out from all corners as the hunt burst into jubilation at their victory. The wild rejoicing—mounts rearing, hunters leaping and whooping around the fallen boar, dances springing up to merry songs tripping off fae tongues—hid Butcher from Wren's sight.

More by instinct than design, Wren slipped from the stag's back and staggered out of the forest to the edge of the riverbed to peer down the embankment. At first he could glimpse nothing of Butcher amidst the confusing tumult. Then a tall dark figure strode forth from the fray. Strong hands held a delicate blade and wiped blood from silver on the tunic's hem. Glinting eyes gazed not down on the hands' work, but upward, searching the tree-line with an intensity that quickened Wren's pulse.

His heart hammered harder still when those dark eyes met his own and gleamed with unmistakable elation.

Butcher sheathed his blade and climbed the embankment in three long strides.

"Well done," Wren blurted as Butcher joined him.

The words hardly felt adequate to describe the courage and skill Butcher had displayed. Yet Butcher grinned down at him all the same. Wren noted his canines appeared more prominent than those of most mortal men. The pointed ears likewise drew his gaze again, if only for a moment before his interest came to what felt like its natural rest in Butcher's dark eyes focused so intently on his own face.

Wild impulses ran through Wren's mind. His fingers twitched with the repressed urge to seize those well-muscled shoulders in his hands. He bit his lip to quell the desire to take further liberties no decent gentleman would consider. As Butcher searched his face, his grin fading into a no-less-appreciative smile, Wren found he couldn't turn his mind from foolish thoughts without turning his head as well and so glanced away from Butcher and toward the hunt.

The rejoicing had only increased in the interim. Yet now, as Wren looked past the crowd around the fallen boar, he saw other figures in a more solemn gathering by the opposite bank. Some half-dozen wolves and werewolves attended the crumpled form tossed by the boar scant minutes earlier. One of the werewolves knelt beside the wounded wolf and cradled its head in its lap. Its sides heaved with laboured breaths. Wren, astonished it still breathed at all, felt his heart wrench in his chest at the sight.

"I know you said not to offer anything, but—" Wren dared to meet Butcher's gaze again. "Is there nothing to be done?"

Butcher studied Wren's face with an expression Wren couldn't quite read. "We may approach."

His words came low and gentle, rumbling forth from deep in his chest and resonating with the thrumming of Wren's own heart.

Wren nodded his assent. Butcher led him across the riverbed to where the wolves had gathered around their fallen pack-mate. Several turned at their arrival. One pinned its ears back and snarled. Another—a werewolf—didn't look much friendlier, standing a full head taller than Butcher with its arms cross over its barrel chest as it blocked their path.

Butcher halted a half-step ahead of Wren and held one arm out between Wren and the wolves.

"Your pardon," Butcher began, then continued in a language Wren didn't recognize, its words and tone both guttural and lyrical.

The werewolf cocked its head to one side as it listened. When Butcher had finished, it replied in a deeper and more growling version of the same tongue.

Butcher bowed. The werewolf nodded and made as if to turn away.

Wren put a hand on Butcher's arm. The other went to his own throat and tore his cravat from his collar.

"If they need a bandage," he explained as he shoved it into bewildered Butcher's palm. "Or a sling, or—something."

For a moment, Wren thought Butcher would refuse to pass it along. It certainly violated the rule against offerings. But then his fist closed over the cravat, and he turned to catch the werewolf's attention again. A much shorter conversation in the same unrecognizable language ensued.

At first the werewolf appeared irritated at the interruption, insomuch as Wren could read any expression in the canine face. Then, in slow increments, its flattened ears perked up, its lips relaxed their snarl, and at last, it uncrossed its brawny arms to take the cravat from Butcher's outstretched palm. It nodded to Butcher, and to Wren as well, and returned to its pack.

Butcher caught Wren's eye and jerked his head toward the tree-line across the riverbank. Wren followed him away.

"She says thanks," Butcher murmured before Wren could ask.

Wren stopped himself from questioning the pronoun. He knew little enough of human women. He could hardly expect to know a she-wolf on first sight, though now he knew better than to assume.

"You needn't fear for them," Butcher continued. "Wolves heal up almost as quick as fae."

A yelp came from behind them. Wren turned to see the wounded wolf staggering to its feet, supported by its fellows on either side, with more of its pack-mates leaping and yipping in victory. Its breath came hard, and its lumbering limp bore little resemblance to its once fleet pace, but it lived. A scarlet band had wrapped around its mid-section in the meantime. It took Wren a second glance to recognize his own formerly white cravat.

Cracks and crackling filled the air. Broken branches had piled around the boar, several of them on fire thanks to the efforts of a few industrious armoured fae still striking their chain-mail and swords with flint. Other more impish fellows perched on the corpse as if in imitation of the flock of ravens that had descended to begin their feast. The moth-like fairy in the mottled grey cloak seemed to delight in flitting through the embers flying up to join the stars.

The elf-maiden looked on from the fringe of the festivities with her bow held loose at her side as a mortal girl might hold a doll. She took note of Wren and Butcher as they passed by and inclined her head as if to invite them to join. Butcher shook his head in reply. She shrugged and turned away toward the other revellers.

Beyond the boar in a secluded curve of the riverbank, Wren espied the fairy in the spiderweb mask. A crimson stain had seeped through his seafoam-green waistcoat and spread all down his side. It didn't seem to concern him overmuch as he daubed at the darkest parts with a lace-edged silk handkerchief.

The stag awaited them at the forest's edge. Butcher swung himself up onto its back in the same swift leap as he'd done in Hyde Park. He held out his palm to Wren. His eyes danced with the gleam of the hundred thousand stars above. A shy smile tugged at the corner of his handsome mouth.

Wren's heart flung itself against his ribcage in its eagerness to join him. He settled for grasping that sinewy forearm and letting Butcher haul him up to sit beside him. His arms twined around Butcher's waist as naturally as ivy climbing the oak. The crest of his hip-bones jutted against the meat of Butcher's backside. His chin rested against the corded muscles of Butcher's shoulder. The exertion of the hunt had sharpened Butcher's scent, the woodsmoke musk rising above vanilla notes to mingle with the salt sweat of valiant feats. Neither absinthe nor opium could prove more intoxicating to Wren's senses than this. Something stirred within his atrophied heart, ancient embers breathed into renewed life by the exhilaration of the hunt and by Butcher's warm bulk in his arms.

Something stirred lower down as well. Wren tried to turn his mind to less tempting thoughts. The immediacy of Butcher's body against his own condemned such ventures to failure. He settled for hoping Butcher wouldn't notice his growing interest.

Then the thighs that overlapped Wren's own clenched against the stag's flanks, and they leapt forward into the night.

CHAPTER SIX

Shrike could hardly fail to notice the clerk's growing interest.

He'd taken him to join the Wild Hunt not just to prove the truth of his claims but likewise to prove his own martial skill and convince Lofthouse that, with his patronage, he was more than capable of achieving victory against the Holly King.

Now, with Lofthouse's arms wrapped around his waist like a second armoured gyrdel and the clerk's rigid interest thrust against his backside with every leap of the stag beneath them both, Shrike felt confident he'd surpassed his aim.

London had quieted considerably by the hour of their return to Hyde Park. The stag trotted to a halt beneath Achilles. Shrike slipped from its back and held out his arm to assist the clerk in following him down. No sooner had Lofthouse dismounted than he shrugged off Shrike's rabbit-fur cloak and returned it to him.

Shrike had admired the way his cloak looked with its furred bulk wrapped around the clerk's narrow shoulders. He felt almost sorry to have it returned. He resolved to fashion something like it for Lofthouse. Amongst other things. A thousand trinkets this mortal might have, if he could help Shrike survive the coming solstice. A thousand more, if he found Shrike as compelling as Shrike found him. Lofthouse's evident cock-stand on the path back to London seemed a promising indication, but it wasn't enough to merely possess desire. One must act on desire if one wished to achieve its prize. And for that, Shrike had patience enough to wait.

"You've convinced me," said Lofthouse.

Shrike allowed himself a victorious smile.

"I'll do what I can to assist you," Lofthouse continued, much to Shrike's satisfaction. "Though I know not how I might. For the moment, however, I must return to Staple Inn and to work in the morning—but if you would do me the honour of meeting me at the office after Mr Grigsby departs for the evening?"

"Aye," Shrike readily agreed.

Despite the fog hanging over the city, the clerk's eyes shone bright with excitement equal to Shrike's own, as if reflecting stars to match the constellations of freckles scattered across his sharp features. The ones on his curiously soft lips, in particular, drew Shrike's eye.

Lofthouse, gazing up at Shrike in turn, looked as if his mind entertained similar thoughts. For a moment, Shrike expected his idle desire might become decisive action.

But then a slight shudder ran through the clerk's frame, and with nothing more than a polite smile, he turned away and with a few swift strides vanished into the fog.

A delicate tapping sound roused Wren from dreams of wild woods and wilder company. He opened his eyes to find himself in bed.

The tapping sound persisted. Wren rubbed the last remnants of his dreams out of his eyes with the heel of his hand. He blinked stupidly at his room for a moment before he realized the tapping came from the door. The fog swirling past his window had bloomed full white with the risen sun. The fae hunt had been but a dream, and worse yet, it had kept him abed well past his usual pre-dawn waking hour.

And in the meantime, someone had not only got into the office, but up the stair to Wren's garret to tap upon his chamber door. He felt sure he'd locked up last night, and as only one person besides himself held a key...

Wren's heart plunged into his stomach, the horror of his situation like a bucket of ice-water upended over his head. He leapt out of bed and ran to the door—stopping just short of opening it, as he realized he wore only his nightshirt. He cleared his throat of its waking raps and called out, "Good morning, Mr Grigsby."

"Oh!" Mr Grigsby replied from the other side of the door. The tapping ceased. "Good morning, Lofthouse! Not ill, I hope?"

As always, no trace of sarcasm or ill-humour entered into Mr Grigsby's speech—though, considering his useless clerk had overslept by several hours and forced him to open up his own office, Wren thought him well entitled to a hint of exasperation, at least. Wren withheld a sigh and recited the falsehood Mr Grigsby had so obligingly laid out for him. "A touch out of sorts, sir, but I shall be downstairs shortly."

"And I'm very glad to hear it!" said Mr Grigsby, the only man in all of London who could utter the phrase with sincerity and conviction. "Though of course if you are feeling poorly, perhaps you'd better stay and rest. Should I send for a physician?"

"No need, sir," Wren hurried to dissuade him before the notion could take root. "I'm feeling much better already, thank you."

"Splendid! But don't over-exert yourself in rushing down, Lofthouse. I can manage well enough for the moment. Good morning!"

And with that, Mr Grigsby finally retreated downstairs.

Wren waited until the last audible footstep had echoed away into the muffled silence of Staple Inn. Only then did he collapse with his forehead against the door and give voice to a long-suffering groan. His dream had exhilarated him in the moment. Now, when it had all faded into bitter dregs that served only to remind him of his tedious, ceaseless, inescapable reality, the memory exhausted him.

Still, self-pity would change nothing. He forced himself upright from the door and staggered over to his wash-stand.

Running his hand through his hair as he went, his fingers caught on the strands. Puzzled, he tried to pull his hand away. It stuck fast, and took two attempts to free himself, taking more than a few hairs with it as it went. They clung to his palm along with the unknown sticky substance—some kind of resin, he thought as he squinted down at it. He saw not only his own chestnut hairs stuck there, but a few green needles as well.

Pine pitch.

Wren stared at his hand. There were no pines in London. Much less in his garret.

His dream was real.

The wild hunt was real.

Butcher was real.

Wren sat down hard on his bed and spent entirely too many minutes staring at his hand.

All Butcher spake of had been real, and furthermore, he had promised to meet with Wren again on the morrow.

And that morrow was today.

This thought, moreso than any thought about clerking or his duties towards Mr Grigsby, spurred Wren to action. It took some time to wash all the pine pitch out of his hair. To say nothing of combing out the multitude of tangles.

Fairy knots, Wren couldn't help thinking. Nor could he keep from smiling at the thought. He felt giddy as a schoolboy, his mood today as ebullient as his master's everyday—almost. It made him something of a dandy, for while he put on the same old black waistcoat, black frock coat, black trousers, and black neck-cloth (having surrendered his white cravat to the werewolves, and wasn't that something to consider), he did so with more care, smoothing out creases and wrinkles and picking out pine needles as he went.

All of which did make him arrive downstairs rather later than he'd promised Mr Grigsby. Late enough, in fact, for Mr Grigsby to have already put his own kettle on and set a cup of tea cool enough to drink on Wren's desk. Despite this, Mr Grigsby expressed only relief at Wren's entry.

Wren thanked his employer for his concern and sat down at his desk. Actually buckling down to work, however, proved nigh on impossible. After the exhilaration of the wild hunt, and with the promise of Butcher's return, Wren found it more difficult than ever before to settle into the mundane world of moving figures from one column to the next. A good man would strive to repay Mr Grigsby for his consideration and lenience by accomplishing more in the work day. As Wren filled the margins of his memorandum book with scribblings of pine trees and satyrs, he supposed he'd never been a particularly good man.

No sooner had Wren reached this conclusion than the downstairs bell rang.

Wren leapt up from his desk before Mr Grigsby could do more than open his mouth to request it of him. Mr Grigsby's mouth remained open in astonishment as Wren dashed past his desk for the door. And well might Mr Grigsby look astonished, for Wren didn't think he'd ever moved so rapidly in all his ten years of service to the man.

Wren paused at the door to catch his breath and give his nervous fingers one last dash through his hair. Then he took hold of the latch and swung the door inward with a very amiable and professional, "Good morning."

The figure on the stair was tall, dark, and broad-shouldered—but not Butcher. No feathered cap, no furred cloak, no highwayman's boots, no Venetian mask of black leather. Just a practical pair of laced shoes, trousers, waistcoat, and morning coat, all in sober brown, with a modest blue neck-tie the only spot of colour, and a soft crop of brown hair beneath a plain and practical beaver hat. The gentleman appeared to be in his early forties, with a solid build beneath his suit and a strong jaw beneath his sideburns, and as he swept the beaver from his head, the eyes he turned up at Wren precisely matched the shade of his blue neck-tie.

Wren caught himself before he let his face fall in disappointment—it wasn't the gentleman's fault he wasn't Butcher, after all—and as the gentleman reached the upper landing, Wren added, "How may I be of service, sir?"

A modest smile lit up the gentleman's features. Sober he might be, but by no means grave. "Mr John Tolhurst to see Mr Grigsby, if he's in."

Wren didn't have to glance back to know Mr Grigsby was, in both the literal sense and in the polite society definition of the phrase, "in" for the purpose of seeing visitors. Unlike some gentlemen of his profession, Mr Grigsby delighted in entertaining strangers. And while Wren kept a wary eye out for temperance campaigners and tract-leavers, this Tolhurst seemed like neither.

Besides, the name Tolhurst had a familiar ring to it.

Wren stepped back to allow the gentleman into the office, announcing as he did so, "Mr Tolhurst, sir."

Mr Grigsby had of course overheard everything that had passed in the doorway, but nevertheless he greeted the newcomer with all the merry enthusiasm of a country squire entertaining a guest in his manor. Tolhurst responded in kind with an indulgent smile and accepted Mr Grigsby's invitation to sit in Wren's chair.

"I'm afraid I have some questions of a delicate nature," Tolhurst said, with an apologetic glance at Wren.

"You may trust my clerk with your life," Mr Grigsby declared before Wren could make a silent retreat from the office.

Tolhurst relented with a chuckle. "Let us hope the stakes do not come to that! But yes, the subject is as dear to me as my own life. I must ask after my nephew—Mr Felix Knoll," he added, with another glance at Wren to show he spoke for his benefit.

And there, the final puzzle piece fell into place. Wren had read the name Tolhurst somewhere before, after all; in the last will and testament of Felix Knoll, senior, and on several financial documents pertaining to the case since then, though not many and not in recent years. A better clerk would have recognized the name from the start. Wren thought he deserved some leniency on account of Tolhurst being so unlike his nephew in every possible way—except for the eyes, which, Wren had to admit, shared that same curious shade of blue.

"I've heard tell of my nephew encountering some difficulty," Tolhurst continued. "A difficulty which he may have hoped to alleviate by visiting your office yesterday."

"While I'm touched by your tender concern," said Mr Grigsby, "I cannot divulge more than you've already heard."

"Nor would I ever ask you to break your confidence," Tolhurst hastened to add. "However, I only wish to know—is his need dire? Does he require my assistance to save him from his perils? I'd ask him directly, but you know as well as I the pride of a young man. Felix is no different in his obstinate quest for independence. A direct question from me would embarrass him, and it might shatter his trust in me beyond repair if I should overstep."

Wren tried very hard not to reflect on how Felix could piss away his annual allowance and still have concerned relations coming up out of the woodwork to look after him, like nursemaids tending a shrieking infant, while Wren himself could follow every rule save one and still find himself cast out on his arse.

"On that account, you may rest easy," said Mr Grigsby with a comforting smile. "His difficulty is of the most minor sort and will resolve itself with the coming of the new year."

Tolhurst mirrored Mr Grigsby's placid expression. "I'm most relieved to hear it." He hesitated, then added, "He said also that he attempted to draw on his trust and found it wanting."

Mr Grigsby's beatific smile altered not one jot.

Tolhurst had the decency to look abashed. "Is there nothing that may be done to enable him to withdraw the funds he requires this quarter?"

"I'm afraid not," Mr Grigsby told him, not unkindly. "But again, you may rest assured—the need is not dire. I daresay he will laugh about it if you question him on the subject in a year or so."

"As you say," Tolhurst replied with a laugh of his own. "Well do I remember my own foolish pursuits at his age and how important they seemed to me then! Do forgive my interruption, Mr Grigsby—I'll not intrude on your hospitality further. No, no, it's quite all right," he added, waving off Mr Grigsby's offer of tea. "I'm sure you've much to do, and no doubt Mr...?" He trailed off, looking to Wren with an expectant air.

"Lofthouse," Wren supplied.

"No doubt Mr Lofthouse wishes me out of your hair," Tolhurst finished, with a smile at Wren to show he meant no offence. "A pleasure to make your acquaintance, Mr Lofthouse—and a pleasure to see you again, Mr Grigsby."

With that, he donned his beaver hat, bid the pair of them good day, and showed himself out.

While Mr Grigsby might have wished Tolhurst could stay all afternoon, Wren didn't share in his sentiments. Particularly not today of all days, when anticipation of what the evening would hold frayed his nerves to their absolute limit. Though, he supposed as he returned to his desk, he ought to have thanked Tolhurst for breaking up the tedious hours 'til the work-day's end.

Despite Wren's hopes that Mr Grigsby would take it into his head to dine early this evening, Mr Grigsby departed at eight. Wren echoed his well-wishes and locked up behind him. Then he put the kettle on—for perhaps Butcher, unlike Tolhurst, would care for some refreshment—and settled in to wait.

One hour and three cups of tea later, Wren could no longer sit still. He got up to pace. From the window by his desk to the door, he could take six strides. From there to the back staircase that led up to his garret, another four, and then three more strides returned him to his desk.

An innumerable number of strides and several more cups of tea passed between the moment he began pacing and the moment the mantle clock struck nine. He tried sitting down at his desk again. Pen and paper occupied his hands, though his quaking fingers fumbled both, and his knee bounced with abandon.

The rattle of the door-latch at half-past the hour sent Wren leaping to his feet—but it was only Mr Grigsby returning from dinner. Wren gave a stiff smile as his employer bid him goodnight and headed up to his own rooms above the office. The moment Mr Grigsby vanished upstairs, Wren returned to his desk with renewed fervour.

By the time the clock struck eleven, Wren had finished filling his margins with jousting squirrels and snails and begun to wonder if something had happened to Butcher on the way to Mr Grigsby's chambers.

As the clock struck half-past the hour, however, it occurred to Wren that perhaps Butcher didn't intend to visit him after all.

The clock struck midnight. Wren conceded defeat. He blew out his candle and made for the stairs. As he ascended past Mr Grigsby's door and continued on up to his garret, he scolded himself for acting such a fool, like a love-lorn schoolboy awaiting notice from a senior classmate. Stifling a yawn, he withdrew his key from his trouser pocket to unlock the door to his room.

He opened the door to find a catastrophe.

Hundreds of papers lay strew about, blanketing the room in stark white spotted with the dark ink of Wren's pen-strokes like coal-dusted snowfall after a blizzard, forming drifts and mounds of Wren's darkest secrets. The illumination of this tragedy came not from moonbeams or candlelight, but from a flickering blue glow the size of a matchstick flame in the cupped palm of a broad-shouldered, slender-waisted shadow sitting hunched on his bed, with still more papers filling the lap, and a sheaf held up in a fist before the face.

Butcher.

CHAPTER
SEVEN

Wren stared in silent horror at Butcher. The fur-lined cloak lay flung over the foot-board. The highwayman boots sat on the floor amidst the snow drift secrets, one half-fallen over the other. The long-beaked Venetian leather mask and the peaked cap with its feather had tumbled onto the counterpane beside Butcher. Butcher himself, by the eerie blue light of his own fae lantern, appeared deep in concentration, his handsome brow furrowed, his full lips pursed, his dark eyes intent on the page he held up before him. He sat with his knees bent, one laid out on the bed and the other upraised, the hem of his tunic far too short to disguise what lay between them despite his woollen hose. A few strands of his black hair had come loose from the leather cord at the nape of his neck and now tumbled down over his high, sharp cheeks like ribbons of rain.

All this would have formed a composition of admirable beauty, had Butcher not held Wren's doom in his callused fingertips.

Wren recovered his voice. "How long have you been waiting?"

Butcher glanced up with such rapidity that it appeared as though he flickered rather than moved. His expression brightened as his eyes alighted on Wren—then his brow contracted at Wren's evident displeasure, despite Wren's efforts to keep his tone even and his face a blank mask. "Since nightfall."

Which had come at half-past six, meaning Butcher had hours to peruse every last piece of ill-advised literature Wren had penned throughout his career with Mr Grigsby. How foolish of him to assume the lock on his desk would prove sufficient to keep prying eyes at bay. Wren renewed his efforts at maintaining a casual tone. "Did you enjoy your reading?"

Butcher had the decency to look abashed—or so Wren thought, until he replied in a much-humbled voice, "I don't have my letters."

Wren felt rather abashed himself. He hadn't meant to shame the man for illiteracy.

"But," Butcher added, a faint smile returning to his handsome features, "I've much enjoyed your illuminations."

Wren hardly thought his doodling measured up to illuminated manuscripts, even if he did refer to his own illustrative scribbling as marginalia. And while he very much wanted to take the compliment in its intended spirit, he knew his drawings were just as incriminating as his writing.

Still, Butcher appeared more intrigued than disgusted.

Butcher rose from the bed with a shocking amount of grace for a man of his stature, his long limbs tangling and untangling themselves in a languid fluidity as he stretched. Wren found himself transfixed by the sight of him. Likewise transfixed by the tiny blue flame, which Butcher set down on the bed-post, where it neither fell nor burned through the wood, but continued to flicker and glow. A shuffling sound drew Wren's attention from it, and he belatedly saw Butcher had begun to collect the scattered papers.

Wren rushed to intercept him. "That's all right—I'll handle it."

Butcher paused, then handed his sheaves to Wren, who realized as he took them that Butcher had collected them in order.

"Your pardon," Butcher said. Then, "I was curious."

Curiosity killed the cat—but satisfaction brought it back. The childish rhyme rose unbidden to the forefront of Wren's mind. He dropped his gaze from Butcher's face to the top-most page in the stack, whereupon a slender and beautiful knight embraced a wild, bearded lord. The marginal illustration neatly summarized the entire manuscript. If Butcher had seen this and not been put off by it, then perhaps...? It seemed too much to hope for, and yet the existence of the fae realm had seemed just as impossible before Wren had visited it himself last night.

And wouldn't it be nice, for once, not to have to keep secrets?

"Well," said Wren, forcing a casual tone over his thunderous pulse. "What do the fae think of men who lie with men?"

The ensuing pause drew out into a lengthy silence as the two men stared each other down. Then, in a single stride, Butcher was upon him. Even barefoot, he towered over Wren. Near enough to fill Wren's lungs with his woodsmoke musk. Near enough for Wren to feel the heat of his body radiating through his woollen tunic.

And near enough for Butcher to raise his hand to Wren's jaw and gently lift his chin.

Wren's heart pounded in his ears. He gazed into those dark eyes, their depths glinting with warmth and curiosity like the night sky shot through with stars.

Then those eyes shut, and Butcher bent down, and Wren tilted his head to meet his kiss.

Wren hadn't received a kiss in more years than he cared to tell, though he'd imagined many. He could never have imagined this. Butcher's lips kindled the curious spark into a bonfire, which raged through Wren's heart as he opened his mouth to taste him, devour him, consume him as he felt himself consumed by the overwhelming flame of his own desire. He burned with need above and below and found himself clutching Butcher's arms with the grip of a drowning man. All too soon, however, his need for breath forced him to break away. He opened his eyes, gasping, and beheld Butcher gazing down on him with a fascination that matched his own passion.

"I think," Butcher murmured, "a man who lies with men is the sort of man I like."

No sooner had Shrike pronounced his preference than Lofthouse fell upon him anew. His small and slender frame seemed hardly able to contain the fury of his passion. It was all Shrike could do to keep hold of him as he took Shrike's face in both hands and all but devoured him. Shrike retaliated by seizing his neck-cloth and tearing free its knot. The collar and studs went with it, leaving the slender throat exposed. Shrike broke off from the embrace—shuddered in illicit pleasure at the moan that escaped the clerk—and kissed a bruise over the pulse leaping in the stark blue vein, much to Lofthouse's evident delight. Only a moment, and then lips found lips anew, as legs tangled and Shrike found solid proof of the clerk's enjoyment between his thighs. Very solid proof, indeed. Shrike let his hand fall to trace the rising shaft in admiration. Then, after a moment's fumbling amidst the woollen layers, Shrike found the fall-front of the trousers and slipped his hand inside.

Lofthouse broke away from the kiss with a gasp. "Wait!"

Shrike ceased. Withdrawing his hands from their work below the waist, he set them instead on the clerk's shoulders, as it seemed Lofthouse, on the brink of a swoon, lacked the strength to stand under his own power. It lasted but a moment, however, and with a firm shake of his head which sent his feathery locks scattering across his brow in a dishevelled look that quite became him, the clerk regained his firm stance. He stepped back from Shrike, who released him entire.

"Have I displeased you?" Shrike asked.

"What? No, no, not at all—quite the reverse—only—not here," said Lofthouse, running his hand through his hair again, as if he might find his composure there. "My employer is asleep just below us, and I cannot conceive of a worse place to be caught out if…"

Shrike furrowed his brow in confusion. "If what?"

"English law is not so forgiving as the fae," said Lofthouse. "At least not on the subject of sodomy."

This did nothing to dispel Shrike's confusion. He tilted his head to one side.

Lofthouse took this in with a glance and attempted another explanation. "Do you know what English law does to men who lie with men?"

Shrike shook his head.

"It hangs them," said Lofthouse.

Shrike stared at him.

Lofthouse averted his gaze. "The most recent execution was some ten years back. Two men—Pratt and Smith—caught together, tried, convicted, hanged." His jaw worked, clenching and unclenching, before he continued. "The penalties for mere indecent acts are less severe. Legally, at least. Socially the penalties are severe enough to drive a man to self-murder."

Shrike's initial shock, a mere spark when the explanation began, flared into indignation and ended in a blaze of outrage—anger at the injustice rather than the messenger, but anger all the same, enough to inspire one to take sword in hand and exact justice of one's own. He restrained himself to smouldering, though his voice hardened as he replied, "I should like to see them try to hang us."

Lofthouse glanced up in astonishment, which dissolved into a breathless huff of hollow laughter. "Well, I shouldn't like to see anything of the sort. Though I appreciate the sentiment."

Despite himself, a wry smile tugged at the corner of Shrike's mouth.

"Still," Lofthouse continued, "you see why it would prove inconvenient for me to be caught out with another man in the garret above my place of work. Not that I expect Mr Grigsby awake before dawn, but—" He broke off, conflicted desire twisting his porcelain features into stark shadows. He bit his lip in a manner that, in a different moment, might have tempted Shrike to kiss it. "You understand, don't you?"

"I do," said Shrike.

The relief that flickered across the clerk's handsome face proved ample balm. "That isn't to say we might not continue elsewhere—another time—if you're willing?"

"Most willing," Shrike replied, and dared express some of his own relief in a smirk.

The flash of a grin that answered him was worth a hundred blows. "Splendid. But, as for tonight, we'd best not go any further down that particular lane. And besides," Lofthouse added, "there's the matter of your predicament, which you came here to discuss."

If the threat of execution had not already sobered Shrike, the reminder of his impending duel did the trick.

Lofthouse gestured toward his desk. "Won't you sit down?"

Shrike would've liked to sit beside him on the bed but supposed that would prove too much temptation. He considered the desk and its chair. The desk appeared better suited to his height; he perched himself on the corner of it, with one leg drawn up beneath him.

Lofthouse regarded him with a curious expression, then pulled out the chair and sat down in it, gazing up at Shrike with an intensity that made it seem as if their perspectives were reversed. "When last we spoke, you said your queen had named you king, and this meant you must duel another king to the death on the winter solstice. Do I have the right of it thus far?"

"Aye," said Shrike.

"Why?" asked Lofthouse.

Shrike blinked at him, unable to stop himself from echoing, "Why?"

"Yes," said Lofthouse, as though his question weren't unprecedented. "Why did your queen name you king? Why does this mean you must duel another king? Why the winter solstice? And, for that matter, why to the death?"

Shrike shrugged. "I know not."

Bewilderment writ large on the clerk's handsome features. "Then why the deuce are you going along with it?"

"Because I must."

Lofthouse didn't appear convinced. "Tell me the whole of it—from the beginning."

"I know not how it began," said Shrike. "But I can tell you it has been so since well before I ever came to the Court of the Silver Wheel. Every year, the queen appoints an Oak King to rule from the Winter Solstice to the Summer Solstice, and a Holly King to reign from the Summer Solstice to the Winter Solstice. On the Winter Solstice, the Oak King slays the Holly King, ending winter and heralding the return of spring. Then the queen appoints a new Holly King, and on the Summer Solstice, this Holly King slays the Oak King, ending summer and heralding the impending autumn. Then the queen appoints a new Oak King, and so the Silver Wheel of the seasons continues turning."

"So this ritual honours the changing seasons?" said Lofthouse.

Shrike blinked at him. "It determines the changing seasons."

"What," Lofthouse scoffed, "so if the Oak King failed to kill the Holly King at the Winter Solstice, spring would never arrive?"

"Not until the queen appointed a new Oak King to try his luck at the Winter Solstice the following year. Assuming that Oak King didn't fail as well."

Lofthouse stared at him. "Has any Oak King ever failed to slay the Holly King before?"

"Aye."

"Some twenty-eight years ago, perhaps?" Lofthouse asked more hesitantly.

Shrike raised his brows, impressed at the accuracy of the clerk's estimation, particularly when one considered how little he knew of the fae realms. "Little more than a quarter-century ago, aye."

"1816," said Lofthouse. "The Year Without a Summer. Famine, riots, and the birth of a monster."

"It seems," Shrike concluded, "that the consequences proved more disastrous for the mortal realm than for the Court of the Silver Wheel."

"Indeed. And I don't think anyone should care to see their like again." Lofthouse absent-mindedly brought his hand to his mouth—still blushed pink from their frantic embrace mere moments past—then, catching Shrike's eye, seemed to recall himself and hurriedly dropped it to fold with its fellow in his lap. Ink had spattered over the knuckles much like the freckles on his face, Shrike noted, and the fingernails were bitten to the quick, the cuticles raw and red. Small wonder, given how he lived under the threat of execution for his very nature. It must weigh as heavily on his mind as the crown of the Oak King weighed on Shrike's brow. "So, we have established the stakes, personal and universal; you wish to survive the duel, and all wish not to see an endless winter. What role do you play within this Court of the Silver Wheel?"

Shrike, startled out of his own musing on how he'd like to kiss the ache from those much-abused fingertips, replied, "I am a knave."

"Yes," said Lofthouse, a hint of exasperation leaking into his tone. "But what does that mean?"

Never before had anyone tasked Shrike to define himself beyond a single word. After some contemplation, he said, "I may do as I like and answer to no court. And all may do as they like to me in turn, without fear of reprisal from any court."

Lofthouse's brow contracted beneath the careless chestnut lock that had fallen out of place when Shrike kissed him. "You don't answer to the Court of the Silver Wheel, then?"

"Not until his queen named me her Oak King."

"Why did she?"

"I know not," said Shrike. "As I've told you."

"Surely you have some idea."

Shrike levelled a blank look at him. "Do you know the mind of your queen?"

"Fair enough," Lofthouse admitted. "Let's set the why of it aside, then, and focus on the mechanics. How did your come to be crowned the Oak King?"

"I fought in her tournament," said Shrike.

"Why?"

Shrike, whose motives not one had bothered to enquire after in centuries, required a moment of reflection before he gave his answer. Lofthouse waited with quiet patience, the keen gaze of his dark eyes fixed on Shrike. Shrike found himself in surreptitious search for hints of the clerk's thoughts in his face even as he divulged his own.

"I've grown weary," Shrike said at last. "Weary of surviving as a target at which any wandering knight-errant might aim their lance with impunity. Or rather," he added, with a bitter smile that did little more than bare his teeth, "I tire of proving how far they've erred in assuming I would make easy prey. But moreso than that, I've spent centuries perfecting my craft, and seen little recognition for it. Then the Court of the Silver Wheel announced a tournament on the Autumnal Equinox in their queen's honour. Not only jousting, but a *mêlée*. Fae of all ranks could compete for her favour. Even knaves."

As Lofthouse listened, a gleam of intensity came into his eyes which

Shrine thought made his features still more compelling than before. "So you attempted to win her protection?"

"I thought I could display enough martial prowess to earn a knighthood. And then perhaps my craft could be seen on a wider stage. I won the mêlée, for all that was worth. But instead of knighting me..." Shrike's lip curled at the memory of her betrayal. "She declared me the Oak King."

"And effectively sentenced you to death," Lofthouse concluded. "Either on the Winter Solstice or the Summer."

Shrike admired how succinctly he'd put it. "Aye."

"And your sooth-saying led you to believe that I have a role to play in your victory."

"Aye," Shrike said again.

Lofthouse spent a moment in silent contemplation. He brought his fingertips to his mouth again, this time biting a cuticle before he caught himself and forced his hand back to his knee. Shrike's gaze lingered on his mouth, marking how the freckles scattered across his lips like constellations across the night sky. How dearly Shrike wished to kiss those stars.

"I won't deny this has been fascinating to hear," Lofthouse said, drawing Shrike's attention away from his desires. "But I still have no idea what part I might possibly play in it. Much less how I might render aid to your cause. Not that I don't wish to help you," he added quickly. "Truly, I do. But I'm at a loss as to what's expected of me."

"You're a clerk," said Shrike. "You have the gift of letters and an education in the mystic arts."

"The former, certainly," Lofthouse admitted. "The latter, however, remains to be seen."

"Perhaps the mere thought of you will inspire me to triumph."

That earned him a sharp glance.

Shrike smiled.

Lofthouse mirrored it in his own bashful way. "Tell me a little of the mystic arts, then. If I were some sort of warlock, how might I assist you?"

Shrike recalled all he knew of magic, which wasn't much. "A sigil of protection. Or an enchanted weapon. Or a geas that compelled me to win."

"I don't know that I've ever compelled anyone to do anything," said Lofthouse—which Shrike thought unlikely, given his unstudied natural charm. "And I'm certainly no weapon-smith. But let's say I could make a sigil of protection. How would I go about it?"

"You'd draw out the shape of it. Carve it into wood or stone, engrave it on silver or gold, scribe it on parchment with ink—or spit, or blood, or seed. A steed could be branded with a sigil that allows it to gallop tirelessly for nights on end. Bird skulls carved with runes and filled in with blood and ash become arrow-heads that always find their mark. A warrior who paints herself with woad before a fight may become ferocious and wash that ferocity away with the blood she spills and return from the battlefield serene."

"And what shape would a sigil of protection take?" Lofthouse pressed.

"Whatever shape you thought best suited to the magic you wished to do."

"The art favours improvisation, then?"

"It favours the intent of the practitioner."

The clerk considered the matter. Again his fingertips graced his mouth. "Spit, blood, and seed, you said, by which I must assume you mean…" A faint blush rose beneath his freckles.

A lazy smile wound its way up Shrike's cheek. "Aye."

Lofthouse cleared his throat. "Indeed. Well. That's certainly something to consider. When is the next holy day on the fae calendar?"

"Samhain," Shrike replied. "Halfway between the Autumnal Equinox and the Winter Solstice. And a full moon."

"Hallowe'en, you mean? All Hallow's Eve? When the veil between worlds is thinnest?"

Shrike didn't know about any of that, and said as much, but added he thought Samhain a suitably significant date for their intended ritual. "Shall I return for you then?"

"Yes—but not here. It wouldn't do for you to be seen hanging about. Perhaps I might meet you in Hyde Park. Beneath the statue of Achilles."

"The brawny fellow with sword and shield?" asked Shrike.

"And the fig-leaf." Shy amusement flickered across Lofthouse's star-speckled lips. "Yes, him. Would eight o' clock be a convenient hour?"

Shrike found most any hour convenient and said so.

"Very well. As for getting you out of here tonight," Lofthouse continued, hauling himself out of his chair, "I suppose there's nothing for it but to creep downstairs together so I may lock you out, thought it may take a mad dash if Mr Grigsby should wake—unless," Lofthouse broke off, shooting Shrike a suspicious glance. "How did you get in without our noticing?"

Shrike indulged in a self-satisfied smile and nodded toward the window.

Lofthouse cast his astonished look first at Shrike, then at the window, then back again. "And no one saw you?"

"The fog is very thick."

Lofthouse gave the window another considering look. "I suppose, then, if you've no objection to going out the same way you came in...?"

"None at all." Indeed, Shrike rather looked forward to the opportunity to display his acrobatic talent.

Lofthouse went to the window, unfastened the latch, and swung it out wide. A chill night breeze entered alongside a few wisps of curious fog. Lofthouse stepped back and shot Shrike an expectant, almost challenging look.

Shrike strode over to swing one leg out the window and balance on the ledge. He turned for one final glance back at his new comrade-in-arms. By the cold flickering light of fae flame, he beheld the dark eyes wide with wonder, the flush beneath the freckles, the chestnut locks and neck-cloth both askew after their frantic embrace. Impulse struck him. "Before I go—may I have something of yours?"

Suspicion clouded Lofthouse's brow. "That would depend on what it is."

"A kiss," said Shrike. "If you have one to spare."

A wry half-smile tugged at the corner of Lofthouse's perfect mouth. Then he glanced past Shrike to the night beyond the open window—moonless and impenetrable beneath the thick fog. Not even Shrike could see more than an ellspan beyond his own nose. Mortals had no hope of glimpsing what went on within an attic window.

Evidently Lofthouse drew the same conclusion, or perhaps he simply had more courage than most would credit him. Regardless, he approached the window.

The second embrace proved no less passionate than the first, and far more lingering. As Lofthouse withdrew, his wistful expression showed as much reluctance as Shrike felt in breaking off the embrace.

"'Til Samhain, then," said Shrike. "Fare thee well, Lofthouse."

And with a grin, he shoved off from the window-frame and fell backwards into the fog.

CHAPTER
EIGHT

Wren seized the window-frame and thrust his upper half out into the night where Butcher had gone. The fog swallowed up all trace of him. Wren doubted he could see his own hand if he waved it in front of his face, much less the cobblestones three storeys below.

As said thick, caustic, choking fog had begun seeping into the garret, Wren retreated and shut the window—though not without reluctance. He'd had half a mind to leap into the night after Butcher. Even now his heart flung itself at his ribs like a caged finch determined to escape. His fingers yet trembled with the thrill as he fumbled at the window lock. It took considerable resolve for him to shut the curtain.

The blue fae flame hovering over his quilt guttered and went out. Wren took this to mean Butcher had left Staple Inn. He lit a candle at his desk in its stead, though while a candle might replace the will-o'-th'-wisp, nothing could replace Butcher.

Wren sat down hard on the quilt where the fae flame had flickered—where Butcher himself had sprawled not an hour past.

Now alone, Wren brought his fingertips to his mouth to touch the ghost of Butcher's kiss. His lips yet tingled with it. So, too, did the mark blooming on his throat where Butcher had torn open his collar. The fury of Wren's repressed desires had overtaken him in the moment, had allowed him not only to submit to the embrace, but to return it in force. He knew he ought to feel appalled at his own audacity.

But rather than dread, his heart pounded with elation.

He'd long ago given up on his dreams of kissing another man, instead transferring his desires to the heroes and villains of his manuscripts and illustrations.

Until tonight.

When, incredibly, his first kiss in more years than he cared to count had exceeded all his considerable expectations.

He felt as if a decade's weight had lifted off his shoulder and made him a young university student again, his aspirations not yet snuffed out. Even now, with so long and grim a conversation between the first kiss and the last, the thought of either proved enough to stir Wren's prick to half-mast. Wren knew the recollection would drive him to onanism long before Samhain—likely more than once. For the moment, however, he would have to draw on twenty years of resolve to turn his mind towards more pressing needs.

The first order of business, after Butcher had vanished into the fog, was to find a new hiding place for his manuscripts. The desk had proved too obvious. It did, however, make a convenient perch for Wren to climb on as he stretched up into the rafters to search for someplace better. Unfortunately the stark white of the paper appeared far too visible against the dark wooden beams, no matter how deep a shadow he tucked them into. He went over the chimney brick-by-brick as he came down but found none loose. Only when he slid under his own bed to try stuffing the manuscripts between the ropes holding up his mattress did he discover, quite by accident, a solution. While crawling on his back, he struck his left elbow sharp against a floorboard and heard a curiously hollow thud. Despite the pain and numbness spreading down his arm to his fingertips, he felt along the edge of the board and, after much more crawling, writhing, cursing, and the retrieval of a letter-opener from his desk, pried it up. Beneath it lay the cross-boards supporting the floor above and ceiling below, and plenty of space between them—some six inches deep—more than enough room for his papers, which he stashed inside.

Dawn had broken by the time Wren finished hiding his sins. Which was just as well, as he didn't think he could sleep a wink after the night he'd had. The passing of a quarter-hour saw him scrubbed, brushed, and wearing a fresh shirt beneath his suit. In another quarter-hour he had tea boiling in the copper kettle downstairs and stood before the fire with bread on a toasting-fork in one hand and a pan of sausages in the other. His aborted educational career had taught him, amongst other things, the art of cookery outside of kitchens. By seven o' clock the first round of the penny post had arrived along with the morning edition of the *Times*. Wren arranged it on the breakfast tray alongside the buttered toast, tea, and sausages, and set the whole down on Mr Grigsby's desk. Five minutes later, punctual to the minute, Mr Grigsby himself descended the stair to the office.

"Good morning, Lofthouse!" Mr Grigsby said as he approached his desk, much like every other morning for the past decade. Today, however, he paused just before sitting down and shot Wren a questioning glance.

Wren froze. He kept his subservient mask on—barely—while panic raced through his mind. His heart stopped as he recalled the bruise Butcher had kissed onto his throat. He had thought his cravat covered it, but if it'd slipped since then—

"Are you feeling quite the thing, Lofthouse?" Mr Grigsby asked. He sounded more concerned than disapproving. Wren tried to take heart in that.

"Quite well, sir," Wren lied. "Thank you."

Mr Grigsby professed himself happy to hear it, adding, "It's only, if you'll forgive my saying so, you don't look as if you've slept well."

Wren had grown so accustomed to the blue bruises under his own eyes that he hadn't noticed they appeared much deeper than usual this morning. "Bit of a head-ache, sir. Gone now."

Mr Grigsby again declared his delight in learning this, and, more importantly, finally sat down and distracted himself with breakfast.

The rest of the day ran on in much the same manner as the thousands of unremarkable days that had passed before it—with the exception that Wren did a great deal more surreptitious scrawling in his notebook behind the stacks of ledgers, and towards a greater purpose. A multitude of potential magical sigils poured forth from his pen. Invented instructions for occult rituals flowed alongside them, his cramped hand producing increasingly arcane notes as he went. Amidst all of this occurred several attempted portraits of Butcher himself—tall, dark, and handsome—high cheekbones, aquiline nose, dagger-point ears—dark eyes in whose depths one could drown in and delight in drowning—sometimes in statuesque posture with an entirely invented sword such as appeared on the tombs of kings, and sometimes sprawled across gnarled tree-branches like Robin Hood with his shapely limbs displayed to their best effect, and sometimes brooding beneath his heavy cloak with its tattered edges like raven's feathers, but always invoking a spark of desire in Wren's heart.

Mr Grigsby could be counted on to notice none of this, for which he had Wren's silent and undying gratitude.

Thus the fortnight until Samhain flew by.

The morning of the final day of October dawned with the same dull grey fog that heralded every morning in London. Unlike most days, however, it did not rain, which Wren took as a sign of good fortune.

The hours crawled past. Wren drew many a marginal snail in between his clerking duties—light as ever—and his final, furtive designs for the Samhain ritual.

At eight o' clock, Mr Grigsby arose from his desk to go out to dinner. Wren tried to sound disinterested yet not ungrateful as he declined his master's customary invitation to join him. Inside, he felt as if a thousand fireflies flew through his blood. He thought only of dashing to Hyde Park the instant Mr Grigsby left the office.

But just as Mr Grigsby retrieved his walking-stick from the umbrella stand, the downstairs bell rang.

And all Wren's eager excitement withered into bitter anxiety.

"Goodness," Mr Grigsby remarked. "It's a very late hour for business. I hope nothing is amiss."

Wren withheld an irritated sigh as he shoved his sketches under an open ledger and tore himself away from his desk to answer the door. No doubt Felix had returned for a second attempt at an advance on his trust fund, or Tolhurst had come to hear another report on his nephew's affairs. Wren opened the door ready to suffer through either of these interruptions.

He had not prepared himself to come face-to-face with a girl.

She appeared just as surprised to encounter him. Her blue eyes widened, their colour enhanced by the blue of her morning dress and the matching ribbons in her bonnet, from which a few golden ringlets escaped to frame her milk-white face. She could not have seen more than sixteen summers—and all spent in luxury, judging by the lace trim on her hems and gloves.

Bizarre that a girl should venture into Staple Inn. Still more bizarre that she should come alone. Yet most bizarre of all—Wren thought he recognized her.

"Miss Fairfield?" Wren ventured.

Miss Flora Fairfield blinked back at him. "How...?"

"Mr Knoll carries your miniature," Wren hastened to explain. "He showed it to Mr Grigsby and myself shortly after its completion."

"Oh," she said.

It occurred to Wren that nobody carried his miniature for Miss Flora to acquaint herself with prior to this meeting. "Forgive me—Lofthouse, Mr Grigsby's clerk. At your service."

"Oh!" she said again, this time in recognition. "Yes, Mr Lofthouse— Mr Grigsby speaks very highly of you."

Wren could not fathom how.

"Miss Fairfield?" came Mr Grigsby's voice from within the office, and soon Mr Grigsby himself appeared over Wren's shoulder. "Bless my soul! What a pleasant surprise! Come in, come in—only," he added, blinking past Miss Flora into the empty stairwell, "surely you didn't come alone?"

"I must," Miss Flora replied with admirable composure as she crossed the threshold. "I had no other way to reach you. I didn't wish to put matters into writing, lest they fall into... other hands."

Mr Grigsby looked as confused by this as Wren felt. Yet he remained as amiable as ever as he ushered her into his chair and put the kettle on for tea. She perched on the edge of the seat and cast a wary look over the office as she untied her bonnet to reveal the same golden curls as her miniature portrait—though her rigid posture and unsmiling face, which accentuated all the hard lines of her shoulders and jaw, looked quite unlike her likeness. Wren had never expected to meet the girl in his life, but even so, she defied his expectations.

"Now, my dear!" Mr Grigsby said, just as if he addressed the meek and mild creature carried in Felix's locket and not the proud yet anxious young person seated before him. "Do tell us all we may do for you in your time of need."

She had, after all, come a rather long way to do so. Still, her eyes flicked toward Wren as she replied, "I would prefer to ask my questions in confidence."

"You may trust my clerk with your life," Mr Grigsby declared—again.

Wren, already halfway through his retreat to the staircase, turned on his heel and resumed standing by the mantle with his hands folded behind his back. Miss Flora glanced at him again. He ventured a comforting smile. She did not look comforted but made no further objection to his presence in the office and returned her gaze to Mr Grigsby.

"I wish to know," she began, her words halting with consideration, "whether or not my inheritance is dependent on my marrying Felix."

"Not at all," Mr Grigsby replied after a moment's stunned silence. "You shall come into it in full when your come of age—which you may do this very spring by marrying Mr Knoll, but of course, if you prefer to wait, then you shall have full use of it on your twenty-first birthday."

While this explanation was technically true, Wren privately supposed that what would actually come to pass was that Miss Flora's fortune would skip over her altogether and land straight in Felix's pockets—where it would pour out again like water through a sieve into the coffers of whichever gambling dens, whore-houses, and money-lenders he favoured. But Wren's opinion on the matter had not been asked, and so he did not give it out.

"Now, my dear," Mr Grigsby said to Miss Flora, his smile bespeaking his total ignorance of Wren's suppositions. "Is that all you wished to know?"

"Not quite," Miss Flora admitted. "Is it true that if I do not marry him, Felix will be ruined?"

"Goodness, what a question!" Mr Grigsby laughed, as much startled as amused. "My dear Miss Fairfield, whatever could have put such a notion into your head?"

Miss Flora did not answer him. Wren kept his own suspicions to himself. At length, Mr Grigsby's mirth subsided.

"In pecuniary terms, no," said Mr Grigsby. "He's as well-provided for as yourself."

Miss Flora looked as though she had some opinions of her own about whether or not she was well-provided for but kept these thoughts to herself.

"Though I daresay," Mr Grigsby continued, "it may ruin him in his heart, as it might ruin any man, to lose your affection."

A wan smile graced Miss Flora's pale lips.

"However," Mr Grigsby went on, "if your affection for him is not sufficient to permit you to marry, then you might do him the least harm by breaking off the engagement sooner rather than later."

Wren, surprised by the old bachelor's romantic acuity, gave Mr Grigsby a sharp glance. Mr Grigsby failed to notice it.

"Is that your advice, sir?" Miss Flora asked.

"It is," said Mr Grigsby. "Provided, of course, that you do not feel the affection for him that a bride ought to feel for her bridegroom. Better to have a small portion of misery now, in the breaking of an engagement, rather than to drag out a much larger portion of misery over the course of an unhappy marriage. Not that I mean to suggest you are miserable, or that your future together would prove certain misery," Mr Grigsby hastened to add. "I do not presume to know the mind of a young lady, much less how matters stand between you and Mr Knoll in particular. However, if you are uncertain as to the depth of your own feelings, I would suggest taking the matter up with the young gentleman himself."

Wren blinked at Mr Grigsby. Mr Grigsby continued to take no notice of his astonished clerk.

"Then," Miss Flora said, after considering Mr Grigsby's advice for many moments, "I have just one more question."

Mr Grigsby gave her such a look of solemn readiness that Wren might have had to disguise his laugh with a hasty cough if ten years in the man's service hadn't already inured him to Mr Grigsby's innate and guileless comedy.

"Do you know," Miss Flora asked, "where I might find a room to stay the night in London?"

A deafening silence thundered down on the office.

"Stay in London?" Mr Grigsby echoed after an excruciating pause.

"Yes," said Miss Flora, as if it were the most natural suggestion in the world for a girl of her station. "The hour draws late, and I don't think it wise for me to attempt to return to Miss Bailiwick's Academy this evening. Her wrath, I fear, is still too fresh. The storm ought to clear by morning, and when I return to Rochester tomorrow afternoon, her relief will render her much happier to see me than if I were to arrive on her doorstep after dinner tonight."

While Wren could not fault her reasoning, Mr Grigsby appeared quite at a loss. Another awkward pause ensued.

Wren cleared his throat.

Both Miss Flora and Mr Grigsby whirled to stare at him.

Wren put on an apologetic smile. "I meant to inform you earlier, sir, but as it so happens, this evening I intend to visit a friend, and do not expect to return before tomorrow morning. As such, I will make no use of my garret tonight. While it cannot offer accommodations of the standard to which Miss Fairfield is accustomed, perhaps it may prove a suitable solution for our present predicament?"

The awkward pause resumed.

"Visit a friend?" Mr Grigsby echoed. Then he clapped his hands in delight. "Splendid, Lofthouse! How wonderful—who is your friend? No, I mustn't press you, of course—only do give him my regards and hopes for many more such visits in the future. And how convenient for our purposes!" he added, seeming to at last recall Miss Flora's presence. "For, if you've no objections, Miss Fairfield...?"

"None at all," she said, her astonishment turned to repressed amusement at Mr Grigsby's reaction to Wren's scheme. Though, Wren noted, she didn't seem to mock Mr Grigsby so much as share in his good humour, or at least find her own joy in knowing he'd found his.

"Excellent," said Wren—and, for once, meant it. "Let me just tidy up a little and then I'll be out of your way. Good night, Miss Fairfield, Mr Grigsby."

Wren didn't wait for their reply before he dashed up the two flights to his garret. Within a quarter-hour he'd swept and dusted matters into some semblance of order. More importantly, he locked up his desk and ensured the worst of his creative efforts were hidden away in the hollow under the floorboards beneath his bed. He didn't think it would occur to Miss Flora to look for anything out of the ordinary. Still, he sprinkled some dust-sweepings over that particular corner to make it appear disused. Then, packing candles, tea-spoon, chalk, knife, matches, twine, pencils, and sketch-book into his satchel, he gave one final approving glance around the garret and fled downstairs. There he snatched up his hat and coat, handed his key over to a bewildered Miss Flora, and with a final good-night, vanished into the fog of Staple Inn.

Shrike waited beneath the statue of Achilles. He'd arrived at twilight and stood there ever since with his arms crossed as he leaned against the statue's plinth. Mortals flowed past him through the fog. Their gaze shot to his feathered cap and clung to his cloak, tunic, hose, and boots. The mortals who wore gowns and bonnets covered their gaping mouths with gloves or fluttering fans. Those who wore coats and trousers gawked with abandon. Most fell to whispering with their companions as they hurried on. Shrike paid them little heed. None of them were Lofthouse, and thus their opinions mattered not.

As the daylight dwindled, the gowns vanished, and most of the trousers passed through alone. They did not hurry on like those who'd come before. They wandered—meandered—sauntered, even—around the statue. Shrike wondered if the mortals had erected it as a holy site. Perhaps those who came after dark did so to pay tribute to the hero deified. Yet they did not seem interested in the statue itself.

If anything, they seemed very interested in Shrike.

The glances had changed from scandalized to intrigued. Their gaze lingered on him, running up and down the length of his figure, fixing not on the peak of his feathered cap or the fur trim of his cloak but on his visage and the point where his hosed joined in front just below the hem of his tunic. Shrike stared back at them in turn, which seemed more pleasing to them than otherwise, though they sauntered on without speaking to him.

One particular stranger in a blue coat, white trousers, and tall black boots passed Shrike by with a very interested glance indeed. And passed him again. And again, before turning back to lean against the plinth as well, an arm's-length away from where Shrike stood.

Shrike cast a sidelong look at the stranger. The stranger did not acknowledge it. Shrike returned his gaze to the fog, through which Lofthouse would soon arrive.

"It's a fine night."

Shrike glanced around to see who'd spoken. There was no one nearby save the stranger, who kept his eyes averted.

"Aye," said Shrike.

The stranger still didn't look at him, but a faint smile graced his lips. "Bit nippy, though."

As the season had in fact turned, and the Holly King's power waxed in both the fae and mortal realms, Shrike said again, "Aye."

The stranger stroked his chin in thought, almost as if to show off the strong cut of his jaw. "Could do with company to keep warm."

Shrike said nothing.

At last, the stranger turned his head to regard Shrike with an approving up-and-down look and a lackadaisical smile. "What say you and I take a stroll somewhere more accommodating?"

Ah. So this was the true purpose of the statue. Shrike felt rather foolish for not realizing it earlier. Still, he smiled as he replied, "You flatter me, sirrah. But my companionship is spoken for."

The stranger withdrew at once. "My apologies. Another time, then."

Shrike nodded farewell. The stranger tipped his hat

And soon enough, Shrike's patience was rewarded by Lofthouse emerging from the mist.

A grin came unbidden to Shrike's lips has he beheld the handsome clerk. The constellations of his freckles more than made up for the lack of stars in London's clouded night sky. Shrike pushed off from the plinth and strode to meet him.

"Butcher," said Lofthouse. He looked Shrike up and down as well, with as much or more interest as the passers-by had shown. He bit his freckled lip, and Shrike yearned for the opportunity to kiss him again. "Shall we be off?"

"Gladly."

Shrike turned to lead the way off the well-trod paths into the particular copse of saplings that held the mushroom ring. Lofthouse followed close behind. Shrike wished he could follow closer still.

"Where shall we go?" Shrike asked, halting at the rim of the ring.

Lofthouse's dark eyes gleamed with anticipation. "Someplace sacred yet secluded."

Shrike held out his hand. Lofthouse clasped it. His palms were not so rough as Shrike's, but his ring-finger bore the callus that bespoke his trade.

Lofthouse's hand clenched his. Shrike drew him close. Together they fell into the ring.

CHAPTER
NINE

Wren had stepped through the mushroom ring with Butcher half-expecting to find himself in the midst of the ancient pillars of Stonehenge. Instead, he opened his eyes to discover he and Butcher stood in a forest clearing. Dead leaves, twigs, and the flame-coloured remnants of withered ferns littered the ground, with living trees looming all around them. Not the mountainous pines of the Wild Hunt, nor the deliberately cultivated breeds of Hyde Park, but broad-leaf trees scattered around wherever their seeds had fallen and fought their way up through centuries to reach astounding heights. Of one thing Wren felt certain; he had arrived somewhere leagues away from London.

"Where are we?" Wren asked.

"Thynghowe," Butcher replied. "In Sherwood Forest."

"Sherwood?" Wren echoed, seizing on the detail he recognized. Then, "What is Thynghowe?"

Butcher cast a bemused look down at him. "It's the sacred meeting place of your ancestors."

"Well, they must have taken their secrets with them to their graves, for I've never heard of it." Wren cast another look about him at the stark white skeletal birches with golden foliage and the thick gnarled oaks with leaves in fiery shades of scarlet beneath the full moon. "It's beautiful, though."

Butcher's flickering smile appeared almost bashful.

Wren slung his bag off his shoulder and nestled it amidst the roots and against the broad trunk of an obliging oak. He wished he'd thought to bring a broom. By the moonlight he could just make out a few witches'-brooms in the upper branches of the birches—thick tangles of wild growth blooming pearl droplets of mistletoe—which, while boding well for the ritual he hoped to perform, would not prove much help in sweeping up the forest floor. He turned to Butcher. "We'll need to clear a space; about seven feet in diameter."

So saying, he scooped up a double-armful of dead leaves and hefted it to the outskirts of the clearing.

As he turned back for another load, he caught sight of Butcher vanishing off into the underbrush on the opposite side of the clearing.

Puzzled, Wren waited for him to return, but could not see him in the shadows beneath and between the trees. Nor, he realized, could he hear him, though the dried plant matter would have crackled and snapped beneath any other man's boots.

Still, wondering after him wouldn't get the work done, so Wren withheld a sigh to bend, gather, turn, and toss another armful of leaves.

A rustling sound came from behind him. Wren, fighting the natural panic one feels when one hears an unexpected noise alone in the forest at night, whirled towards it.

Butcher had reappeared with a stout fallen branch in hand. Its bare twigs formed a makeshift rake. He wielded it with the decisive ease of a harvester swinging a scythe, throwing his whole body into the motion from the twist of his waist to the toss of his shoulders. Each stroke scattered pounds of debris off into the shadowy underbrush and left only bare dirt in its wake. So intent was he on this work that for some moments it seemed he took no notice of Wren staring at him.

Then Wren, seeing how much more Butcher had cleared in much less time, hastened to catch him up, though his clerking arms could hardly do half so well. In the end, he tossed aside a quarter of the dead leaves, whilst Butcher swept away the remainder.

As he cast off his makeshift broom, the sheen of sweat on Butcher's brow glistened silver in the moonlight and only made him appear all the more handsome.

Wren, meanwhile, must have looked a wreck. At least he felt so as he shoved a sweaty hank of hair off his own forehead. He tore his gaze away from Butcher's compelling aspect and returned to his bag nestled in the oak roots.

From its leathery depths, he withdrew a knife. Not his penknife, but a Sheffield knife he'd picked up in the past fortnight. He'd have preferred a proper ceremonial dagger, but those were rather thin on the ground in London pawn shops and not likely to be acquired on a clerking salary. Still, its blade would serve, as would the ball of twine he also produced from his bag. He reached into the underbrush and snapped off a dead branch as thick as his thumb and set about hacking it into a stake—all the while conscious of how slapdash his efforts must seem compared to Butcher's swift and skilful crafting of the boar spear in the Wild Hunt, and keenly aware of Butcher's steady gaze on him at present. Despite this, Wren crafted a serviceable stake without taking off any of his own fingers, which he supposed counted as some sort of victory.

Then, working from half-remembered grammar school geometry, he cut a length of twine, tied one end to the handle of his knife and the other to the blunt end of the stake, and plunged the stake into the bare earth, stamping it twice with his heel to keep it in place. From that compass point he drew the twine taut and used the knife's blade to carve out a perfect circle in the dirt. At five equidistant points along this path he marked out connecting lines. He had practiced the design first with ink on scrap paper in the office, then on a larger scale in chalk on the floorboards of his garret, but never quite at the immense size he required now. Some quarter-hour later, he had completed his etching of Gawain's pentangle.

Perhaps it was the power of the pentangle—more likely the power of suggestion—but as the minutes passed, Wren felt more and more as though an aura of mysticism had descended on the surrounding forest.

If nothing else, Butcher appeared impressed with the completed pentangle.

Wren pulled one of the candles out of his satchel, uncertainty creeping over him as he regarded the desiccated undergrowth lying not so far beyond the outer reaches of the pentangle as he might have preferred. At Butcher's questioning glance, he admitted, "I'd thought to put a flame at each point, but I don't want to burn Robin Hood's hollow to cinders."

Butcher held out his hand for the candle.

Wren gave it over warily.

Butcher examined it close for a moment, then snapped his fingers above the wick. A blue matchstick-flame burst into existence and burned without heat.

"Perfect," Wren declared when he'd found his voice again. He fumbled in his bag for the tea-spoon. "Now, if we dig a shaft at each point..."

Butcher unsheathed his dagger and strode to the point opposite where Wren now stood. There he knelt, stabbed a hole in the dirt, and stuck the candle in halfway up its length.

"You're a quick study," Wren said as Butcher looked up at him.

Butcher grinned and held out his weathered palm for another candle.

In a few minutes, the five ignited points cast an eerie blue glow over the pentangle. Butcher's face lit from beneath ought to have appeared unsettling, but Wren found his chiselled features still more handsome than otherwise.

So handsome, in fact, that Wren quite forgot his purpose and only realized how long he'd been staring when Butcher arched a particularly angular eyebrow at him.

Wren cleared his throat. "I've devised two possible versions of the ritual. One of blood, and one of... seed."

Butcher looked neither confused nor displeased by this. If anything, he looked intrigued. Which was far better than Wren had dared hope for.

"Which would you prefer?" Wren asked with as much dignity as he could muster under the circumstances.

Butcher expression of intrigue turned wry. "Shall we combine them?"

Wren's pulse stuttered. "We might."

The wry expression became a smile that went straight through Wren like a bolt of lightning from his heart to his prick.

"In that case," said Wren, forcing a casual tone over his fluttering heart as he gestured to the pentangle, "we shall begin by lying down here."

Butcher cast a curious glance from Wren to the pentangle and back again. "If I might make a suggestion."

"By all means," said Wren.

Butcher spun his cloak off his shoulders and spread it out on the pentangle, creating a carpet of furs over the cold, hard ground.

Wren had to admit that seemed a much more sensible—and comfortable—prospect, and said so. He caught but a glimpse of the smirk Butcher cast him in reply before he forced himself to turn his attention downward to the matter of his own clothes. Shrugging off his frock coat did not go quite so smoothly as Butcher's sweeping gesture with his cloak. Likewise his fingers fumbled with his cravat, the buttons of his waistcoat and boots, and his trouser ties.

Butcher followed suit, tugging his tunic over his head.

Wren hadn't seen a bare male body other than his own in longer than he cared to remember. His gaze wandered over from his own fumbling buttons to drink in the sight of Butcher's undressing.

It did not disappoint.

In his medieval garb, Butcher had struck an imposing figure. This proved no less true as the clothes fell from his body. If anything, it seemed his tunic, cloak, and hose had disguised the true power of his muscular frame. His linen undershirt and brais gleamed silvery-cerulean with the moonlight above and blue flame below. Then these too peeled away. Corded sinews rippled beneath his sun-kissed skin, broadening his shoulders, knitting tight against his ribs and over his slender waist. His hose had done his strapping thighs no justice, and his well-turned calves would be better served in breeches and stockings, for any footman in livery would display them with pride. To say nothing of the two sharp lines that led from the crests of his hipbones down to a stalwart standard of true virility.

Yet Wren's eye caught details of still greater interest, for overlapping, tracing, and cross-hatching Butcher's handsome frame were innumerable scars. Punctures, slashes, and scrapes abounded, some puckering into the flesh beneath, some upraised like cords of hempen rope wrapped 'round the muscle, some as light and faint as pen-strokes flicking across a page. Wren found his attention drawn particularly to a long diagonal gash across Butcher's navel, from the crest of his left hip to his lowest floating rib on the opposing side, and to a sunken starburst puncture just below his left collarbone and above his heart.

Wren forced his gaze away from Butcher's bared skin and pulled his own under-shirt over his head, leaving himself naked in the literal as well as figurative sense. Butcher had liked him well enough in the garret, with all his clothes on, but what lay beneath Wren's own shirt couldn't prove anything other than disappointing. Ten years of clerking had certainly not improved his muscular definition. Except perhaps in the legs, which had their exercise in his walks—to meet the Restive Quills several times a week when he'd been a member, then to coffeehouses throughout London, and now to Hyde Park. The rest of him remained soft, and while he'd retained the generally slender shape of his youth, he grew softer still with every passing year. The slight pouch of his belly beneath the trail of hair from his navel on down paled in comparison to the taught skin over rigid flesh on Butcher.

But as Wren tugged his head free from the neck of his under-shirt and laid it aside with the rest of his clothes, he glanced up to find Butcher staring at him not with disappointment or disgust, but rather with increased interest.

Wren forced his nerves to steady despite the cold night air on his bare skin and the fluttering of his pulse. "Shall we begin?"

Butcher required no further prompting to stride forward and capture Wren's mouth in a hungry kiss.

If Wren had any lingering doubts of Butcher's desire for him, they vanished in that embrace. The taste of Butcher on his tongue, how greedily Butcher devoured him in turn, his woodsmoke musk filling

Wren's lungs, the clasp of those rough hands on his shoulders and waist, the stark contrast between the chill night air around him and the delicious warmth of bare skin against bare skin—all too much for Wren, and yet never enough, for he found himself ravenous for more, his hands clutching at Butcher's back to bring him closer, his nails digging into scarred skin. It felt as if a bonfire burned within Butcher's ribcage, the thrumming of his heart almost as rapid as Wren's own feverish pulse. Their legs tangled. Butcher's readily apparent stirring interest brushed against Wren's own, bringing their half-hard cocks to full attention. Wren shivered with everything but cold. Just when he thought he'd go mad from it, Butcher broke off their kiss to let him breathe.

"Wren," Wren blurted, gasping.

Butcher stared down at him. "What?"

"My name. It's Wren. Honest," he insisted as Butcher's expression only grew more bewildered. "My mother was fond of songbirds, and—well, that's not important. It's just, I wanted you to know my name, if we're to know each other in this way."

Butcher continued looking at him with an expression Wren had never before seen on his handsome features. Then, as a smile plucked at the corners of Butcher's lips, Wren recognized the look as one of wonder.

"Wren," Butcher repeated, giving the name a weight and reverence such as it had never had before. "It suits you."

"Thanks," Wren murmured, though the word felt inadequate.

Something seemed to trouble Butcher as well. A furrow had appeared between his brows. He looked not quite at Wren for a long moment, then returned to meet his gaze with his jaw set in determination. "Shrike."

"Shrike?" Wren echoed.

Butcher shivered as if someone had just danced over his grave. His arms convulsively clenched around Wren. Then he relaxed—by a concentrated effort, it seemed—with a wistful smile. "Few know it. But... you may call me by it, if you like. My fate is already in your hands."

It dawned on Wren that the fae held names dearer than mortal men.

"Does it pain you to hear it?"

"Not from your lips."

Wren couldn't help smiling at that.

Shrike kissed him again, and it took all Wren's resolve to remember their purpose this night. He guided them both down to lie on the spread cloak—Shrike beneath, and Wren above.

Wren straddled Shrike's hips with more confidence than he felt. The brush of his prick against Shrike's rigid length may as well have been a hammer striking an anvil, for it produced a like number of sparks behind Wren's eyes. He'd oft imagined such a night as this, but he'd never found the courage to make his dreams a reality.

Until now.

Now, Wren kissed along Shrike's jawline up to his ear. He nipped at the lobe—relished in the sharp gasp that resulted—then, on experimental instinct, licked its pointed tip.

A delicious shudder ran through Shrike's frame.

Wren bit down in earnest—but not before he whispered, "Shrike."

Shrike writhed beneath him with a deep groan that Wren felt as much as he heard vibrating through both their rib-cages. Then a hand tangled in his hair and pulled him down to join their lips anew.

Wren allowed himself to melt into Shrike's touch and go where he willed. As Shrike took them both in hand, the warmth and surety of his grip contrasted with the cold night air just as the soft underside of his cock against Wren's contrasted with the roughness of his palm. And as he stroked them both, building up rhythm until Wren's gasps matched his rapid pace, Wren found his hips grinding against Shrike's and thrusting into his fist, his hands clenching in Shrike's long hair—and even this seemed to delight Shrike, who bit his scarred lip and let his eyes fall shut as he gave.

"Shrike," Wren murmured into his mouth.

Shrike's breath hitched. His back arched off the cloak, and with a curious twist of his wrist that sent Wren spiralling into a delirium of pleasure, he brought them both to balance on the knife's-edge of ecstasy

—then, with a decisive stroke, he seized Wren in body and spirit both and dragged him alongside over the precipice to plunge into the fathomless euphoric sea.

Wren collapsed atop Shrike, a sailor shipwrecked on unfamiliar shores. Yet, as Shrike drew him into his embrace, he found those shores warm and inviting, strong arms clasping him in the tenderest hold, lulling him down into the delightful dreams of lotus-eaters.

And when kissing proved more than Wren could bear, he broke it off to find Shrike gazing up at him as if he saw something beautiful in the moonlight reflection of his eyes.

But Wren could not permit himself to bask in bliss. There remained a ritual to perform. He forced himself upright. Shrike's arms slipped from his shoulders as he went, Shrike himself seeming content regardless, though a faint grumble of protest emerged from his lips and tugged at Wren's heart.

With trembling hand, Wren picked up the knife.

Shrike opened his eyes. Yet he did nothing more than watch as Wren held the blade over him. He had expectation writ on his features without any trace of hesitation or fear. Whatever Wren intended, Shrike trusted him.

Wren only hoped he could prove worthy of that trust.

And so he brought the knife to his left hand and with its wicked point sliced into the tip of his middle finger.

Wren withheld a wince at the sting. Blood welled up in the wound, trickled down the blade, and dropped onto Shrike's bare chest.

The expectation in Shrike's eyes turned to open fascination.

Wren grit his teeth and bore down on the knife. He needed more than a paper-cut's worth of blood for his purposes. The wound split further. A steady stream of crimson pulsed forth. Wren ignored the throbbing pain and brought his bleeding hand to Shrike's chest.

Shrike didn't even flinch from Wren smearing blood over his scarred skin. It couldn't have been comfortable; the blood cooled rapidly as it leaked from the wound, and the teat between Wren's palm and Shrike's chest could hardly combat the chill night air. Still, Wren kept at it until he'd turned Shrike's bare skin into a scarlet canvas. Then he drew his hand down to where his and Shrike's seed had pooled together by Shrike's navel and dipped his fingertips into the silvery inkwell.

The shield of Gawain bore a gold pentangle on a red field. Wren's blood gleamed scarlet, and as he drew through it with his and Shrike's mingled seed, the tawny flesh of Shrike's bare chest shone through, creating the golden pentangle.

Throughout this ceremony, and despite Shrike's intrigued expression, Wren felt rather like a schoolboy scrawling skeletons in the margins of his Latin grammar. He knew nothing of magic. He had no idea what he was doing. It would never work. The moment he finished, Shrike would realize he'd allied himself with a fraud, and—

But as Wren connected the final point of the pentangle with the first, a jolt ran through him. From his fingertips all the way up his arm to the shoulder, to the nape of his neck and down his spine, an overwhelming sensation that drove the breath from his body and stopped his heart. It reached his navel, and lower still. His soft cock revived in an instant—Shrike's did the same beneath it—and from both shot twin pulses of seed as an orgasmic tide far beyond what he'd experienced mere minutes before crashed over him. A keening cry burst from his throat, the sound of it lost with the roar of blood in his ears. Shrike arched and writhed beneath him, lost in the same torrent. Then his strong hands seized Wren's shoulders in a convulsive grip, and Wren collapsed into his arms, their mouths meeting in a ravenous kiss that carried Wren on to oblivion.

When he returned to himself for the second time that night, Wren tasted blood. He ran his tongue over his lips in search of the wound. Though they felt bruised, he found no split in his flesh. He opened his eyes.

Shrike gazed back at him, their noses hardly an inch apart, their misty breath mingling. The dark pools of his half-lidded eyes reflected moon and stars alike. A soft smile tugged at his lips, which still bore the bite-marks Wren had wrought upon them.

Shame at his own feral nature burned in Wren's stomach—but

Shrike's low laughter dispelled it in the next instant. On impulse, Wren leaned in to kiss him, gentler than before. Shrike returned it with a satisfied hum that rumbled up from deep within his chest to resonate through Wren's own ribs. Wren had expected to encounter a cold and uncomfortable mess of blood and semen, but the sigil had vanished. As if by magic.

Because it was magic.

While Wren came to terms with this, Shrike reached across him to pull the edge of the fur-lined cloak up over his shoulders. Their legs tangled together within the cocoon warmed by the heat of their bodies. Shrike slung his arm over Wren's chest and pulled him into a hearty embrace.

"Did it work?" Wren asked.

Shrike raised his brows. "You cannot claim you felt nothing."

"No, indeed, I felt quite a bit," Wren admitted, and couldn't help smiling at Shrike's soft laugh in reply. "But did it work as intended? Do you feel stronger? Invulnerable?"

Shrike answered him with a long and lingering kiss. Wren's bruised lips ached deliciously.

"I feel," Shrike murmured when he broke away to let Wren breathe, "as if I could carve the Holly King's heart from his chest and eat it."

Shrike drew the clerk—Wren—nearer to him, drinking in the intoxicating scent of human exertion. Wren's spell-craft had succeeded far beyond Shrike's wildest hopes. Yet even without the sigil, Shrike would have considered the night well-spent. Wren nestled his head in the crook of Shrike's collar. Shrike inhaled his masculine musk and trace the curious curve of his ear.

"You've truly never crafted a sigil before?" Shrike murmured, hardly able to believe it.

"No," said Wren.

"I've never given a lover my true name before," Shrike confessed.

And though mortals gave away their names like trees shedding dead leaves, the reverent expression that broke over Wren's face showed he understood the gravity of what Shrike had given him.

Wary as Shrike had felt about it earlier, now that he'd done the thing, relief rather than dread suffused him. Wren had given over his own name freely, along with his body and his spell-craft. Wren had shed his own blood and spilled his seed to protect Shrike.

"You said it didn't hurt you to hear me speak your true name," said Wren. "But it could, couldn't it?"

"It could be used against me," Shrike admitted. Perhaps wiser fae than himself would leave the explanation at that, but if he trusted Wren with his name, he felt he could do no less than trust him with the whole truth of it. "One who knows it may command me."

"I've no wish to command anyone," said Wren. "Nor tell anyone else, either. It will never leave my lips for any ears save yours."

Shrike kissed him for it.

"Why did you tell me to call you Butcher?" Wren asked. He quickly added, "I know why you didn't give me your true name straight off. But why Butcher, specifically?"

"Because that's what folk call me," said Shrike. Nevermind why they did. "The Butcher of Blackthorn."

"Is that your trade?"

"Leather-working is my craft," said Shrike. "By necessity I'm a hunter and a warrior of no small skill. Both require me to carve meat from bone, and of all of these, Butcher sounds best with Blackthorn."

"And what is Blackthorn?"

"My brugh," Shrike replied. "In the fae realms."

"I'd like to see it," said Wren, to Shrike's surprise.

"I'd like to take you there," Shrike replied, and kissed him again to seal the promise.

Wren's eyes did not reopen after the kiss. He smiled instead, mumbled something, and insinuated himself into the bend of Shrike's arm, their legs entwining in the folds of the cloak.

"Wren?" Shrike murmured.

Wren stirred not, save for his low and steady breaths. Shrike didn't dare raise his voice further, lest he disturb the man's peace. He contented himself with running his idle fingers through Wren's soft chestnut locks, counting his freckles like stars, until Shrike, too, lapsed into slumber.

WINTER

CHAPTER TEN

Wren had drifted off to the hooting of owls in the trees above and the steady rumble of Shrike's breath through his own ribs as they lay thoroughly entwined within the warm folds of the fur-lined cloak.

Sharp birdsong forced his eyes open to behold the dawn creeping up over the canopy, illuminating the crimson and golden leaves like brilliant bursts of flame. Indeed, he fancied he could hear the fire crackling. The tip of his nose felt not unlike an icicle, but the rest of him remained quite snug within Shrike's cloak.

Shrike himself, however, had vanished.

The hollow he'd left behind in the cloak's folds remained warm and still held traces of his woodsmoke-vanilla musk. The scent of woodsmoke hung stronger in the air, as well, alongside the delicious smell of melting fat.

Wren sat up, bringing the cloak with him as he rose so as not to lose its vital warmth. He ran a hand through his hair and found it far more tangled than a typical night's sleep would allow. His breath formed plumes of vapour in the air before him as he glanced 'round to see where Shrike had gone.

Candles still stood at the five points of the pentangle. Between them, however, the ring that Wren had carved into the earth had grown over with white-capped mushrooms. The candles themselves had melted down as if true flame and not will-o'-th'-wisps had lit them the night before—though the wicks remained pristine.

Beyond the candles lay the source of woodsmoke scent and crackling noise alike, in the form of a brace of conies spit-roasting over a fire.

And as Wren stared at the unexpected breakfast, Shrike emerged from the trees carrying an armful of fallen firewood. A broad smile broke out over his handsome features as he caught sight of Wren awake.

"Good morrow," Wren ventured, his voice hoarse.

Shrike grinned and, dropping the wood into the fire on the way, bent to kiss him.

No breakfast before in Wren's whole life had ever tasted quite so satisfying as the roasted conies torn apart with hands and teeth whilst cocooned in the fur-lined cloak beside his newfound lover. Then, after performing his morning ablutions in a cold-running stream rather than an iced-over basin, Wren donned the trappings of society, stealing covetous glances all the while at Shrike's shirt, tunic, and hose. They returned to the ritual site and, joining hands, stepped through the toadstool ring.

Hyde Park had never before seemed so feeble and infirm as when contrasted against the ancient growth of Sherwood. Nor had London's acrid and omnipresent fog ever choked Wren so in the decade since he'd come to live in the city. He wondered how Shrike could stand it.

"May we meet again before Midwinter?" Wren asked.

Shrike gave him a wry smile. "I should very much like to."

Wren found himself biting his lip in reply. He recovered his senses and said, "I've a half-day on Saturdays and the whole day to myself on Sundays."

Shrike cocked his head to one side in thought. "Would you care to spend Saturday night with me on into Sunday morning?"

"Yes," Wren blurted almost before Shrike had finished speaking.

Shrike's smile broadened into a grin. "Then I shall meet you beneath Achilles."

"One o'clock," Wren agreed. Then, as he realized he'd never seen Shrike with a pocket-watch, added, "Just after mid-day."

From the gaze Shrike cast down upon him, Wren thought he'd have liked to seal the promise with a kiss. Instead he clasped Wren's hand between his own, his rough palms and strong grip infusing the gesture with as much passion as any wanton embrace. Wren, his heart thrumming with anticipation and bursting with desire, had almost enough nerve to throw caution to the wind and kiss him regardless—Hyde Park be damned.

But then Shrike released him and, with that wry smile Wren loved so well, fell back through the toadstool ring and vanished.

Lofthouse,
Gone to escort Miss Fairfield to Rochester. Don't expect my return before nightfall.
Warmest regards,
Mr Ephraim Grigsby, Esq.

Wren had suspected as much even before he'd picked up the note left on his desk. He felt more relieved than otherwise to find his employer and their unexpected guest gone when he returned to the office. For one, Mr Grigsby would never know that it'd taken Wren until half-past eleven to arrive at Staple Inn. For another, Miss Fairfield's absence meant Wren had no obstacle in dashing upstairs to confirm his hiding-place remained undisturbed.

The sight of his desk gave him the first inkling of alarm. Not ransacked, as Shrike had done, but nevertheless not quite put back the way Wren had left it. *Le Morte d'Arthur* and *Gawain and the Green Knight* had transposed their respective positions on the shelf, while *Ivanhoe* sprawled open across the blotter. His pen was out as well, set down neat beside the book. Atop the encounter between the Black Knight and the Friar lay a scrap of paper.

Wren ignored it for the moment, far more concerned with what lay under his bed. By throwing himself down on the floor he discovered the same layer of dust he'd left behind. Prying up the loose board with his pen-knife revealed his manuscripts had not altered by an inch.

Reassured that Miss Fairfield had not stumbled on his own body of work in her search for improving literature, Wren returned to his desk for the note. It ran on in a crabbed scrawl with the pen-strokes digging into the paper.

Mr Lofthouse,
Thank you for the use of your garret. My compliments to your literary tastes. Scott has proved a particular comfort for me.
Sincerely,
M. Fairfield.

Wren would not have expected such handwriting from a young lady. Particularly one of Miss Flora's background and education. Then again, he supposed he knew very little of young ladies and didn't give the matter any more thought than to smile and tuck the note away in the front cover of *Ivanhoe*.

Though he'd parted from Shrike on Friday morning and would reunite on the afternoon of that very Saturday, for Wren, the single night that lay between them felt as if it lasted a year and a day. The daylight hours he could bear, distracting himself with surreptitious sketches and, at times, even with actual work. But at night, after Mr Grigsby had returned from dinner and gone upstairs to bed, Wren had nothing to prevent his thoughts from running on in feverish imaginings of the fabled Blackthorn. He knew not when he dropped off at last. Only that when he awoke at daybreak tangled in his bedclothes like a firefly in a spider's web, he felt equal parts as exhausted as if he'd never slept and as fired up as when he'd spent whole nights drinking coffee in the company of the Restive Quills. He'd thought those nights wild, then. He'd never known what wildness was until he met Shrike.

Saturday morning, Wren accomplished little beyond increasingly intricate drawings of the Blackthorn of his dreams. A half-crumbled stone tower like a chessboard's rook with thorned vines rising up to reclaim its most ruined side; a ring of standing stones knotted together with walls of briars; a hill-fort wearing a coat of thorns like armour, the illustration cut away to reveal an interior as labyrinthine as any rabbit's warren. The stroke of twelve interrupted his attempt at rendering a castle with a moat full of brambles. He abandoned it with glee, hardly stopping to tuck it under a ledger before he dashed upstairs to retrieve his hat, coat, scarf, and satchel.

"Going out, Lofthouse?" Mr Grigsby asked, blinking in wonder as Wren thundered back downstairs and leapt for the door.

"Yes, sir," said Wren, catching the door-frame to halt his mad sprint. Though he feared the answer, he forced himself to ask, "Did you require me further, sir?"

"No, no, not at all," Mr Grigsby assured him. "Only idle curiosity. Good-day, Lofthouse!"

Wren wished him the same and vaulted down the stairs into the courtyard of Staple Inn.

His dash down Oxford Street saw him almost run down by an omnibus, much to the astonishment of a passing unfortunate. It mattered little to Wren. Only that it brought him nearer to Cumberland Gate, then through it, then down the paths to Achilles looming out of the fog.

Wren staggered to a halt, bracing both palms against the plinth and hanging his head down between them whilst he caught his breath.

"Hail and well met, fellow traveller."

Wren bolted upright and whirled to find Shrike standing before him, a handsome half-smile on his noble features.

"Hail," Wren heard himself reply, breathless for reasons beyond his mad sprint. His hand had fallen to the stitch in his side. He quickly shoved it into his trouser pocket instead. Foolish of him, perhaps, to attempt to hide his poor physical condition from a man to whom he'd bared his whole body not two days past, but his pride demanded the effort regardless. In stronger tones, he replied, "Shall we be off?"

Shrike nodded and turned to lead the way. Wren fell into step beside him. As they walked, they remained at arm's length. Wren found his gaze drawn again and again to the negative space between them. It felt as though an invisible barrier prevented their meeting. The barrier of polite society, perhaps, or the barrier of public opinion. Or the simple yet most effective barrier of English law, Wren concluded with no small bitterness. He wished he had the courage to surmount it. He'd had the man's cock in his hand the night before last, for Christ's sake, and yet now his heart pounded at the thought of merely brushing his fingertips against Shrike's knuckles. For over a decade Wren had deprived himself of another man's touch. Like a starved man, he'd grown inured to hunger pangs, but they did not die out, only slept. A taste of the barest morsel would have sufficed to reawaken every repressed ravenous impulse and render him insatiable. Even a feast such as he'd had on Samhain would not suffice to quell his desire now. He trembled at the temptation of Shrike so near to him.

But the tension between them found relief only when they stumbled on the mushroom ring, and Shrike reached out and grasped Wren's hand to guide him through it.

The warmth of his palm flowed through Wren's blood to overflow his heart. The intimacy of his rough fingers interlaced with Wren's own sent him shivering. Wren's eyes fluttered shut as they fell together hand-in-hand.

And when he opened them again, he found himself in another world altogether.

A forest more ancient than Sherwood loomed over him. Trees as broad as castle turrets towered above. Birches entwined with rowan, maple, elm, and oak, and breeds Wren couldn't begin to name, with sprays of emerald hemlock and the frosted wintergreen of spruce. Lichen and moss glowed green on their limbs and trunks, and amidst their roots, ferns unfurled from the carpet of fallen leaves.

Ruins stood among the trees. Latticed windows, their few remaining panes twinkling in the sunlight, hung in fragments of ancient walls. Crumbling staircases twisted upward, halting before they reached even the lowest of the overhanging branches, moss spilling down their steps in a waterfall of green. Arched doorways, Romanesque and Gothic alike, led to nowhere in all directions.

Or perhaps, Wren thought, considering how he'd arrived where he now stood, they led to everywhere.

Wren glanced down at where he and Shrike had entered the fae realm and beheld not the mushroom ring of Hyde Park but a stone wall. Centuries of fallen debris had packed firm to fill its once-fathomless plunge, leaving just a few inches of depth beneath its rim filled with ferns that seemed to bubble up like sea-foam.

Then Shrike, whose fingers still entwined with Wren's, pressed his hand, and Wren looked up at him to find a shy smile gracing his handsome features.

"Is this Blackthorn?" Wren asked.

"Not quite," Shrike replied. "We've some journeying yet to do."

A rare spark of courage ignited in Wren's heart. He withdrew his hand from Shrike's grasp.

And offered him his arm instead.

Shrike's smile broadened as he accepted the charge.

"Lead on," Wren said, his heart beating double as their entwined arms folded him closer still to Shrike's warmth.

Shrike did so.

Their passage through the enchanted wood—Wren couldn't conceive of it by any other description—was marked by silence. In contrast to the constant clatter and hum of London, the stillness of the wood was such that Wren could hear every fallen leaf shifting underfoot. The warbling notes of a thrush's song echoed clear as church-bells. All the while, Shrike strode on, each step swift and sure. Wren's eye continually wandered to his surroundings, but he always returned to Shrike's face. And when he did, he often caught Shrike glancing admiringly at him in turn.

Wren could have happily spent an eternity strolling arm-in-arm with Shrike. But at length, their trail brought them to an apparent impasse. A wall of thorns rose up before them, high as a house and almost too thick for the sun's rays to penetrate. Blackthorn trees had overgrown all other breeds. Here and there clusters of familiar purplish-black sloe berries belied the wicked points of the thorns surrounding them. Yet unlike the blackthorn bushes Wren had encountered in the mortal countryside, their leaves glistened burnt-black instead of green.

Shrike did not seem perturbed. Nor did it look as though he intended to alter their path by even a single step.

"How do we pass through the briars?" Wren asked.

Shrike gave him a bemused look. "I planted their seeds, tended their soil, and trained them up to grow into the shape they now hold. I know them, and they know me."

Wren didn't consider that much of an answer.

Until Shrike stepped forward and held out his hand—palm upraised, fingers relaxed, the way one might reach out to scratch the chin of a house-cat—and the briars withdrew like black lace curtains to reveal a flagstone path in the midst of the tree-roots blanketing the forest floor. The briars continued alongside it and overhead, forming a natural tunnel.

"Come," said Shrike, who'd already stepped up the path a ways and turned to offer his arm to Wren again. "They'll not harm you."

Wren blinked out of his stunned stupor and hastened to follow him.

The path wound through the briars until they opened into a meadow. Sunshine filtering down through the canopy above glistened off the babbling brook that ran behind a half-timbered, thatch-roofed cottage. A flock of chickens in motley feathers pecked their way across the yard in front of their own thatch-roofed coop, between three skeps with bees buzzing 'round. Flop-eared goats wandered amongst them, two chewing meditatively on the briars and one clambering atop the woodpile.

The walls of the cottage's single storey curved into squat turrets, and its slender windows resembled arrow slits. Thorns and ivy mingled in their upward climb towards its round chimney. They covered the door so completely that at first Wren thought the flagstone path led up to a wall.

As Shrike approached the door, the thorns withdrew, though the ivy remained. He reached out his hand as the last tendril unwound itself from the latch—tarnished copper, Wren realized, rather than wrought iron.

The latch clicked. The door swung inward to reveal impenetrable shadows. Boot-heels thudded against flagstone as Wren followed Shrike inside.

The thing which first caught Wren's eye was the enormous tree stump in the centre of the cottage. It ran as wide as Shrike was tall and had been cut off at the height of Shrike's waist. Its axe-hewn edges bore the polish of many decades' use. But what really drew Wren's attention, aside from its size, was that it'd been hollowed out down to its roots and fitted with copper piping leading up to a pair of faucets at its rim.

Above the stump, bundles hung from the rafters beneath the thatched roof. Dried lavender, chamomile, garlic, and sundry other herbs Wren' didn't recognize dangled amidst stoneware jugs and copper kettle and cauldron. As his eye followed one particular beam down from the roof's peak to the wall, he found sconces with beeswax candles over a broad hand-carved work-bench. Copper fastenings gleamed amidst sheets of vellum, scraps of leather, knives, chisels, needles, awls, ink-bottles, brushes, and wooden mallets. Several works-in-progress were laid out amongst the tools, but before Wren could move to examine them more closely, his eye fell upon a series of hooks along the wall. They had the shape of fish-hooks grown from thorns, and from them hung wool and linen garments alongside a padded tunic, an unstrung longbow and quiver, knives and short swords in tooled leather scabbards, and a cuirass, greaves, and bracers of boiled leather. Beside and beneath this open-air wardrobe lay a queer bed. Its round frame was woven from willow saplings to form a sort of enormous nest with a quilt of soft silver pelts.

A scraping sound tore Wren's fascinated gaze away from the rest of the room. Shrike bent before a stone hearth, stirring the banked charcoal out of the ashes and breathing life back into the flames. Warm flickering firelight washed over the room. As it went, it revealed a broken loaf of bread and the crumbled remnants of a piece of cheese on a baking slab beside the hearth.

"Did you build all this?" Wren asked when Shrike rose and set the poker aside. "The cottage and the work-bench and—everything?"

"Aye," Shrike replied. He sounded far from proud. Downright bashful.

Wren, who'd wrought nothing in his life with his own two hands, could hardly disguise the enthusiasm in his breathless exclamation. "Marvellous. Simply marvellous."

A shy smile broke over Shrike's handsome features. "You like it, then?"

"It's wonderful," Wren said.

For the first time in his life since his mother had passed, Wren felt as if he'd come home.

CHAPTER
ELEVEN

It was foolish to get attached to a mortal. Such ran the common wisdom, at least. Their lives proved too fleeting for true affection. Dally with them, by all means, but do not pin your hopes on them, lest you spend eternity mourning the loss of a mere flickering flash of a life. Or worse, let your own grief drag you down into their grave. After all, what was a mere thirty, fifty, seventy years when compared to the centuries any fae may live?

Any fae save the Oak King, who would die on this solstice or the next.

Yet as Shrike watched the wonder and delight steal over Wren's handsome face upon entering Blackthorn, he felt more certain than ever before that his attachment was well-placed.

Despite Shrike's evident poverty—no fae or human servants, and all he owned crafted by his own hands or bartered by such craft thereby for articles made by those no better off than himself—Wren seemed in no way daunted. Far from it. His excitement sparked through the air as he examined all Shrike had wrought.

"May I?" Wren asked, moving toward the work-bench.

Shrike granted him leave to examine it as he willed. Still, whenever Wren reached for a particular piece, he turned to Shrike again and waited for his nod before he picked up each with a delicate hand. Scores of oak leaves cut from leather lay scattered across the bench as if they'd fallen from the forest surrounding Blackthorn. Some joined together to adorn a pair of boiled leather pauldrons.

"For the Solstice?" Wren asked.

Shrike nodded.

Wren set them aside. His gaze fell on the other work in progress on the bench. Shrike held his breath as Wren lifted the palm-sized book, shrouded in a cover of soft suede that tapered off far beyond the borders of its pages to end in a stout knot. A smile wonderful to behold stole across Wren's speckled lips as he examined it.

"By Jove," Wren murmured, turning the blank pages with a gentle touch. "Is this vellum?"

"Aye," Shrike admitted, still somewhat stunned by his reaction. "I've not yet mastered wasp-work."

This confession did nothing to damper Wren's enthusiasm. "It's magnificent. I've never seen its like."

An unbidden smile came to Shrike's lips. "High praise from one of your talent."

This seemed to take Wren by surprise. "You flatter me."

"You forget I've held your work in my own hands. I know what praise it's worth."

Not the prettiest speech—Shrike didn't have a talent for pretty speeches—yet, judging by the roses that bloomed beneath Wren's freckles, it pleased him all the same.

"If that's so," said Wren, "then perhaps you'll consent to sit for a portrait?"

Shrike stared at him in frank amazement.

The rosy tinge in Wren's cheeks bloomed further. He fumbled for the clasp of his satchel and brought out a codex not unlike the manuscripts Shrike had found in his chamber in Staple Inn. Words tumbled from his tongue as he flipped through its pages. "That is to say, I brought my sketch-book and pencils to try and capture the imagery of the fae realms —I anticipated beauty, but this has surpassed all my wildest notions—

and, with your permission, I would like to preserve your likeness as well. I've tried already from memory, but—"

Wren thrust the open sketch-book at Shrike, who received it with reverence. Ink covered the pages like ivy creeping over a ruined castle and overwhelming its rigid stone with verdant growth. A dark figure shrouded in mystery appeared again and again. Here standing vigil beneath the shadow of colossal Achilles in Hyde Park, and with a frame comparing favourably against that mythic hero. There hunched over the corner table in the Green Man with a coffee cup before him and his eyes verily glowing beneath his hood. And there, perched on the window-sill of Wren's garret, long limbs bent sharp with lithe agility, a hawk-nosed profile with hair rendered in streams of ink that poured down to become a border of thorns across the bottom of the page. With astonishment, Shrike recognized himself many times over.

"I wanted to have something to remember you by until we might meet again," Wren continued. "After all, Felix carries a miniature of Miss Flora, even though they might visit each other whenever the whim strikes him."

"Aye," said Shrike, as if he'd ever heard of either person before and wasn't mesmerized by the depth of craft bent to capturing his own image.

"There's very little between Oxford and Rochester besides—what?" said Wren, glancing up at Shrike.

Shrike couldn't help smiling as he replied, "If you think me a worthy subject, then I'm honoured to appear in your pages."

"Oh." A shy answering smile alighted on Wren's bespeckled mouth. "Then—might we venture out-of-doors?"

The meadow surrounding the cottage seemed to impress Wren no less than the cottage itself had. His approving gaze fell in turn on the coop, the skeps, and the goats' shed. Even the garden delighted him, hidden as it was behind the cottage and fenced in with the same briars that protected all of Blackthorn. This late in the season, only turnips, beets, and fennel remained to be harvested. The scanty offerings did nothing to deter the goats in their efforts to reach the vegetables within.

"Are you not worried they'll gnaw through it?" Wren asked as he watched the goats crunch away at the thorns.

Shrike shook his head. "All they eat today will have grown back by tomorrow morn."

After looking over the whole of the yard, with particular attention to how the shafts of sunlight fell through the forest canopy above, Wren asked Shrike to assume a pose on the flat slab of worn boulder beside the waterfall where the stream passed through the wall of thorns into the brugh.

"However you feel most comfortable," Wren added, seeming to feel he owed Shrike some explanation for his direction. "You'll be sitting still for a long while, I fear."

Shrike, who had many a time stood motionless in the fork of a tree from dusk until dawn waiting for a particular hart to wander within range of his bow, doubted very much that anything Wren could ask of him in that regard would prove beyond his power to achieve. He sat on the rock in the same manner he'd sat on Wren's bed when he'd visited his garret. At Wren's gentle suggestion, he turned his face towards the stream and sunlight. Wren took up his own position some yards away from him across the stream. Fixing his eye on Shrike, he braced his sketch-book against his hip and began sketching in pencil.

The goats found all of this very interesting. Hawise, the fawn-coloured doe, left off gnawing the garden brambles to see if Shrike had tasty morsels to offer. Her kids, Meggy and Molle, ran to join her and discovered Shrike's seated pose made for a splendid climbing obstacle. The piebald doe, Etheldreda, wandered over to Wren and began investigating his pockets.

"No, no, nothing for you, I'm afraid," Wren told her, all politeness, before Shrike called her away. Turning to Shrike, he asked, "Are you all right over there?"

"Aye," Shrike answered—just as Molle used his shoulder as a spring-board to leap across the stream.

Wren laughed and returned to his sketching. Etheldreda and Hawise likewise returned to the garden bramble after they determined neither their master nor the stranger had carrots or pears for them. Meggy ran to join her mother, then moved on to chasing the chickens. Molle, exhausted by her acrobatic feats, fell asleep against Shrike's knee.

Remaining motionless proved no challenge to Shrike, despite the distraction of the goats. Yet he found himself challenged nonetheless.

While he had stayed still as a matter of course in hunts throughout the centuries, he had never been so watched as he was under Wren's steady and searching gaze. No one had ever looked at him for so long or with such eyes. Large and dark, their depths gleaming with curiosity and softened by something Shrike couldn't quite place. Their intensity, as they flicked over the length and breadth of his body, made him feel more naked in his tunic and hose than he'd ever felt in his bare skin.

Yet he did not feel judged. No hint of reproach ever appeared in Wren's eyes as they fixed on Shrike. Something else infused his gaze, something no less intense but far more enervating. Something that seemed to shine down on Shrike like the shafts of sunlight and illuminate him from within.

Admiration, Shrike realized. Appreciation. Affection.

No one had ever fixed such a gaze on Shrike before. He knew not how to answer it.

Drawing Shrike made Wren feel as much a sculptor as a draughtsman. Like Michelangelo revealing the angel trapped in the marble, as Wren's pencil traced Shrike's chiselled features and well-wrought frame onto the page, he found each stroke revealed something of the undercurrent of emotion flowing beneath the stoic exterior.

Englishmen were not particularly demonstrative as a rule, but Shrike's restraint, in Wren's opinion, exceeded even the reputation of the Queen's Guard. If placed in front of Buckingham Palace, he would make them appear positively effusive by contrast. While Wren and Shrike had shared a powerful and undeniable connexion on Samhain, a great deal about him remained a mystery to Wren. He knew his body—intimately—but his history, his habits, his thoughts and feelings were beyond all imagining.

Wren could piece together a few hints from Blackthorn. Shrike had already proved himself a hunter against the boar. His home showed him likewise to be an architect, a gardener, a craftsman, and a tender of flocks. Glimpses of a gentle nature broke through his stoic exterior as the infant goats clambered over his back. Every cracked smile in those handsome features struck Wren to his heart and warmed him as well as sunshine. Even Blackthorn itself proved nurturing despite its rough and tangled boundaries. Nuthatches and finches hopped amidst the sanctuary of the brambles, singing merrily without fear of hawk or owl.

It might prove a sanctuary for Wren, as well, from the suffocating society of London.

As the young goat settled down to sleep at Shrike's knee, Wren sketched it into his portrait. Likewise he added the soft and subtle smile that played about Shrike's lips and the dark lashes of his downcast eyes gazing fondly toward the peaceful innocent at his feet. The wretched coal-lump of Wren's heart stirred at the sight.

Wren felt loath to disturb a pose of such serenity. Yet his mind whirled with curiosity and unasked questions burned in his throat. All he'd seen within the cottage—the hollow tree-trunk with its copper taps, the nest of furs for a bed, the work-bench covered in leaves of leather, half-moon knives, and curious curving needles—provoked his imagination beyond restraint.

"Do you enjoy your craft?" Wren blurted.

Shrike glanced up with his eyes alone, his wide dark gaze darting to meet Wren's without disturbing so much as a hair on the rest of his person. Unearthly stillness suffused his whole form. It ought to have unsettled Wren. It thrilled him.

"What?" said Shrike. His lips hardly moved, yet his voice carried clear across the meadow to Wren's ear.

"The leather-work," Wren hastened to explain. "Do you enjoy it?"

Amusement gleamed in those dark eyes. "I'd not do it otherwise."

Wren found himself smiling in return. "Where did you learn it?"

Shrike looked as though he'd never been called to give such an answer before. "From my guardian. Long ago."

As Mr Grigsby was to Felix and Miss Flora. Wren had difficulty picturing Shrike's guardian as an awkward bachelor solicitor in Staple Inn. Some fae lord, surely. A squire of the forest. Or a huntsman.

"Guardian?" Wren echoed.

The light in Shrike's eyes dimmed somewhat. "Dead. Some centuries hence."

"My condolences," said Wren, more sincerely than he'd ever said it to a fellow Englishman, though even now the phrase felt inadequate.

Still, Shrike seemed to take it as Wren intended. The slightest of solemn smiles curled the corners of his mouth for a moment, and his eyes glanced away as if fixed on a distant past.

While Wren didn't wish to dwell on any subject which might give Shrike pain, his curiosity demanded he pursue the question. "What was he like?"

"A mortal," Shrike replied in his soft burr. "Called Larkin."

Shock halted the progress of Wren's pencil across the page. He glanced up sharp to meet Shrike's eye.

Shrike appeared as serene as ever, evidently unaware he'd said anything out of the ordinary.

Wren forced himself to continue drawing, though he couldn't keep from repeating, "A mortal?"

"A leather-worker," said Shrike. "One who'd escaped a failed uprising in the mortal realm. The king's men had slaughtered the leader of the rebellion in the midst of negotiations. Then they ran down every soul who'd dared follow him—and some who had not."

Something in the description recalled Wren's school-days; the hours spent memorizing the long list of English kings and the various risings and falls that saw them crowned and deposed. "Do you recall the rebel leader's name?"

"Tyler," said Shrike.

Wren stared at him. "Wat Tyler? The Peasants' Revolt?"

"He didn't call it that. But he'd followed Wat Tyler."

Wren continued staring. Astonishing enough to find Shrike's guardian had been a mere mortal. More astonishing still to realize he'd lived in the fourteenth century and had seen the days Wren had merely read of in Shakespeare's *Henriad* and Egan the Younger's radical novels.

"Larkin had fled across the countryside," Shrike went on. "More concerned with the knights gaining on him than the path ahead, he fell through a fairy ring. He stumbled through the forest—he knew not for how long—until he heard a child wailing and followed the sound until he stumbled upon me. I remember I had fallen out down from the tree. The other fledglings had pushed me out of the nest."

"The *other* fledglings?" Wren interrupted.

"Aye," said Shrike, confused by Wren's confusion.

Wren hesitated, not wishing to offend, before he ventured what felt like the obvious question. "Were you born a bird?"

Much to Wren's relief, Shrike didn't appear offended. Merely befuddled. "No."

"But you *were* born in a nest," said Wren. When Shrike confirmed this with a nod, Wren added, "From an egg?"

"Aye," Shrike said as if no one had ever questioned it before.

Wren supposed such circumstances were common in the fae realms. That conclusion didn't prevent his mind from reeling. "Do all fae come from eggs?"

"Some do. Others grow in flower buds, or on the under-sides of leaves, or beneath toadstools, or in hollow logs—or sometimes in bonfires or particularly sooty chimneys. And," Shrike added with a sceptical twist of his mouth, "some are born from other fae in the same manner kits come from vixens, or a fawn comes from a doe."

"Or as human babes come from human mothers," said Wren.

Shrike's eyes widened with dawning horror.

"Regardless," said Wren, who felt no more comfortable with the notion than Shrike evidently did. "You were born from an egg. Into a nest. Amidst other fledgling fae, who pushed you out of said nest."

"Aye." Shrike seemed glad for the opportunity to return his tale to its original course. "I wasn't badly hurt. Scratches and bruises. But it was the most I'd ever hurt in all my life up 'til then, and so I caterwauled fit to burst my lungs."

"Didn't anyone come down from the nest to find you?" Wren asked.

"No," said Shrike.

Initially, the revelation that some fae—including Shrike—grew from eggs had numbed Wren to the reality that fellow fae had shoved an infant Shrike out of the nest to fall from the tree-tops. Now he thought of the forest he'd seen along the path to Blackthorn and the canopy hundreds of feet overhead. The idea of any child suffering such a fall would distress even the hardest heart. To think of toddling Shrike crashing broken and bloody through all the branches to land on gnarled roots and cold dirt—it wrenched something within Wren he hadn't known he possessed.

"But Larkin did," Shrike added, as if to alleviate Wren's distress.

And Wren did have to admit it lightened his spirits to know someone had come to small Shrike's aid.

As each word fell from Shrike's lips, he seemed more at ease with speaking. A warm, deep, sonorous voice that Wren suspected hadn't seen so much use in centuries emerged—a slight break on certain words the sole remaining hint that it had lain silent for so long. "I heard him afore I saw him. He stumbled through the undergrowth with as much noise as the Wild Hunt. Yet he stood alone—a human man in simple garb, his face streaked with blood and a scythe in his hands. Not his own. He'd taken it up from a fallen comrade. Nonetheless, as he saw me, he halted. Any ferocity that had remained from the battle fled him in an instant. He tossed his scythe aside and gathered me up in his arms. I dried my tears on his tunic while he asked me questions few fae children could answer—where were my mother and father, and so forth. I think he believed me an orphan of the failed rising. Regardless, he assumed charge of me, set me on his shoulders and carried me away with him into the woods."

It'd been difficult at first for Wren to imagine the rough and hardy specimen of masculinity before him as a small and helpless creature. Yet Wren fancied he found echoes of that vulnerability in the warm depth of Shrike's dark eyes. He endeavoured to capture it in his sketch and thought at last he might meet with some success.

"I don't remember much of the first few seasons," Shrike went on. "He kept us fed by foraging and trapping game, kept us sheltered in wattle and daub. He taught me mortal stories and mortal songs. And as I grew older and became strong enough to be of real help to him, our means improved. Soon he taught me his trade, which I've kept up since. By the close of my first century, we—"

"We?" Wren echoed.

Shrike furrowed his brow, confused by his confusion again. "Larkin and I."

"After a century?" Wren protested. "How could a mortal man live so long?"

"Mortals do not succumb so readily in the fae realms."

"How old did he appear to you?"

Shrike shrugged. "Of middling age?"

"Like myself?" Wren pressed. "Or like Mr Grigsby?"

"Somewhere in between. Nearer to Mr Grigsby than to you."

Middle-aged after a century. Wren pondered the notion in silence, quite forgetting himself as he mused over its implications. The bleating of a goat recalled him to the present. "But to your story. A century after he found you."

"By then he'd met other fae and impressed on some of them his worth as a craftsman. While we belonged to no particular court—he swore he'd never serve another king so long as he drew breath—we traded our wares and kept up a more comfortable life than in our humbler beginnings. Our leather bartered livestock, grain, smithed goods. Anything we couldn't cultivate for ourselves from the forest's bounty. We were free-men, in Larkin's words. I think we might have remained happy in our own company for another century or more."

"But he passed on," Wren said when Shrike fell silent.

"Aye."

As the silence threatened to resume, Wren asked, "And who looked after you when he'd gone?"

The ghost of a wistful smile tugged at the corners of those handsome lips. "My own self."

A pang struck Wren's heart. He well knew what it was to be lonely. Except for Mr Grigsby, he'd lived in cold isolation ever since he'd left the Restive Quills. Now that Shrike had found him, however, he dared to believe his loneliness might abate. He only hoped Shrike might find the same relief in him. "If Larkin could see what you craft now, I think he'd feel very proud of his ward."

To Wren's astonishment, a rosy tint came to Shrike's swarthy visage. In his low burr, he replied, "Thank you."

Wren's mind continued on down the path of Shrike's craft to further muse on what he'd glimpsed in the cottage. "The leather armour is the work of your own hand, I presume? Will you wear it in the solstice duel?"

"Aye."

"Do all the fae wear leather armour? Does the Holly King?"

"Nay. He was a knight afore his queen crowned him. He has silver mail and plate yet."

Wren grew uneasy. "Should you not garb yourself alike, then? To make it a more even match?"

"I've never worn mail or plate. Less than two months' time is not much to learn to fight under their encumbrance."

Fair point, Wren supposed. "Best to trust in armour of your own making, then."

"And in you."

Wren's pencil ceased moving. "What?"

"Your sigil of protection," said Shrike, as though it were the most natural sentiment in the world. "I felt its potency. I know it will prove true."

Wren wished he could share in his certainty. While he, too, had felt the astounding magical effects of the sigil on Samhain, it still seemed impossible that something of his own making could withstand the test of the Winter Solstice.

"And I know," Shrike continued, another slight and becoming smile gracing his handsome features, "that a clever hand inscribed it."

Heat bloomed in Wren's face. He had to admit it felt rather inspiring to know Shrike thought so well of his work. While he might not consider his own hand particularly clever, as he laid down the final strokes of the portrait sketch, he thought he might have produced something clever at last, if only by choosing a worthy subject.

"Here you are," Wren declared, turning his sketch-book so Shrike might see.

Shrike cocked his head at the portrait. Then he rose from the stone and strode towards Wren. He took the sketch-book from Wren's hands with more reverence than Wren thought it deserved. Wren held his breath and awaited his opinion.

It'd been many years since Shrike had spoken so many words aloud at once. Few folk demanded his history, and of those few, he felt inclined to answer still fewer.

Yet when he sat before Wren, and Wren's gaze seemed to strip him down to his very bones, he found unspoken words rising up from deep within him and spilling over his lips as if desperate to be heard.

And as he beheld what Wren had wrought, it seemed those unspoken words had transformed into something beyond his imagination.

A figure sat on a mossy outcropping of rock beside a sparkling stream. It wore the tunic and hose Shrike recognized as his own, but their folds clung to flesh in a way that laid broad shoulders and lithe waist bare beneath the viewer's gaze despite the layers of wool. The waterfall and the figure's dark hair descended in the same straight lines, the latter framing a face slightly downcast, which rendered the sharp edges of the cheekbones in shadow and softened the sloe-eyes through sweeping lashes as they gazed at Molle, who curled asleep against the figure's boots. This sight seemed to provoke the enigmatic smile on the figure's full lips.

Throughout the centuries, Shrike had glimpsed his own reflection in still water and polished silver, but had never given his appearance much thought beyond his recognition of himself. To realize someone thought him handsome was astounding. To have Wren in particular think him handsome was wonderful. And to see himself through Wren's eyes, in the sketch Wren thrust upon him, was to see an aspect of himself he'd never before considered.

For the first time in all his centuries, he saw himself not as a hunter or a warrior or a killer…

But as a lover.

The beauty of the sketch, which even Shrike couldn't deny, he attributed to the skill of Wren's hand rather than his own appearance. And yet the portrait had an aura of authenticity. It seemed Wren had seen through Shrike to depths he hadn't realized he'd possessed. In wonder of the creator as well as the creation, Shrike looked up to meet the very eyes that had pierced him to his heart.

To his astonishment, Shrike found they held not the gleam of victory. Indeed, the concerned cant of Wren's brows suggested something had unsettled him, and his gaze flitted over Shrike's face with a look akin to fear.

"My apologies for my draughtsmanship," Wren said before Shrike could wonder aloud at what had disturbed him. "I practice as best I can in stolen moments from my work, but…"

Shrike realized his stunned silence had been mistaken for disapproval. He reached out his hand to touch Wren's cheek as he trailed off. His thumb traced across the freckles scattered over his lower lip. He bent to kiss him, Wren's lips parting beneath him as they met. A long minute passed before they broke away.

"You've done me better than I deserve," Shrike murmured against Wren's mouth.

Wren said nothing, but the way he threw his arms around Shrike's shoulders to drag him down into another embrace told Shrike he'd been understood.

CHAPTER
TWELVE

Staple Inn
London, England
December 20th, 1844

"Eager for Christmas, eh?" Mr Grigsby chuckled.

Wren, who'd been staring out the office window at the white fog fading into the black of night for almost three-quarters of an hour, flinched in surprise. "Pardon, sir?"

"Less than four days away," Mr Grigsby continued as if Wren had made a sensible reply.

Wren agreed that Christmas Eve was, in fact, three days out. This seemed to satisfy Mr Grigsby, who went back to his work with a smile after humming a few bars of *God Rest Ye Merry, Gentlemen*.

Wren returned to the window. The sun had set upon the shortest day of the year. Somewhere beyond London's blanket of fog lay the fae realms, where even now the Queen of the Court of the Silver Wheel made preparations for her twin champions to duel to the death. Wren had arranged to meet Shrike in Hyde Park at eleven. At midnight, the solstice duel would commence. Several excruciating hours lay ahead between now and then.

At half-past seven, Mr Grigsby rose from his desk and invited Wren to dine with him. Wren, his stomach in knots, declined. He still had his luncheon of bread and cheese tied up in a handkerchief in his desk. A nagging voice in the back of his mind told him he ought to eat, that the night's trials wouldn't go well on an empty stomach, but the first bite of bread had turned to ash on his tongue.

Ash tinged with blood.

Shrike was a warrior, Wren reminded himself, in skill if not in trade. And Wren had inscribed the pentangle of Gawain on him.

Still, the worry gnawed at his guts like a hound tearing through a rabbit.

Eight and nine o'clock chimed and went. At half-past the hour, Mr Grigsby returned from dinner and paused in the office just long enough to bid Wren a cheerful good-night before going up to bed.

Wren tried to occupy himself with the *Times* but fell to drawing in the margins. Sketches of fairies danced down the page on moth-wings. Daggers and arrows chased after them. The mantle-clock struck quarter-to-eleven.

Something thudded against the door.

Wren bolted upright from his hunch over his desk.

There came another thump and two more thuds, as if something had tried to knock.

Wren dashed to the door. "Butcher?"

The latch rattled in his hand as three more knocks pounded against the wood.

"Hold on," Wren told him—imagining a hundred disasters that must have befallen Shrike if he could not speak or ring a bell or open an unlocked door under his own power—and flung the door wide.

Felix Knoll slumped against the door-frame. His top hat had rolled away towards the staircase, leaving his blond curls rumpled. The left sleeve of his coat had slipped halfway down to his elbow, and his cravat hung untied in a way that created a whole new kind of knot. The stench of gin seeped into the office along with him.

Wren stared at him for a long and silent moment before he mustered the will to reply, "Good Lord."

This roused Felix enough to lift his head and blink—his eyelids not quite moving in tandem—at Wren. "Where's Grigsby?"

"Upstairs and asleep." Wren bit off the words, his already-strained nerves robbing him of patience.

Felix absorbed his information with a furrowed brow.

"Why are you here?" Wren asked.

"Went out with friends," said Felix. "Lost 'em."

Wren strongly suspected Felix's friends had lost him on purpose. "And so you come to Mr Grigsby to sober you up."

"He's a very sober man," Felix slurred.

Wren had to concur with that logic. And while he very much wanted to slam the door in Felix's face, he knew in his heart that Mr Grigsby, if he were here, would have welcomed the boy no matter his state of intoxication. Certainly with more concern for his well-being than Wren felt.

Against his better judgment, Wren held out his hand to Felix. "Come along, then. You'll be more comfortable sitting down than against the wall."

"On the contrary," Felix retorted, though he took Wren's arm and stumbled inside, "against a wall can prove very comfortable—in certain company."

Wren shot him a sharp glance at that, but the far-off expression on Felix's face bespoke wistful thoughts of all the unfortunate women Felix had known, rather than an attempt to ingratiate himself to Wren.

Felix slumped in Mr Grigsby's armchair while Wren broke off a strong portion of tea leaves into the copper kettle over the fire. Coffee would've been better, but Mr Grigsby found the stuff a touch too much for his old bones—his words, not Wren's. Wren had taken his coffee at night with the Restive Quills. They would hardly lend him a cup of it now.

The whistle of the kettle interrupted Wren's bitter musings. He poured the tea into two cups—chipped for himself and whole for Felix—and waited until ribbons of steam no longer rose from the tea-cups before handing Felix's over. Felix, in the midst of a mumbled rendition of a filthy song, accepted it with minimal sloshing. He even drank a few sips, though he pulled a spectacular face. Wren hid his bitter smile behind his own tea-cup.

The clock on the mantle chimed half-past eleven.

"Where are you staying in town?" Wren asked.

Felix, ever unhelpful, shrugged.

Wren suppressed any expression of his exasperation. The solstice duel lay barely an hour off. There were far more important things at stake than a single drunk toff. Yet Wren could hardly explain the true stakes to anyone. Especially not Felix. No matter whether or not he was too far gone to remember it in the morning.

"Mr Knoll," Wren began after some contemplation. "I'm afraid I cannot stay with you tonight. I have an urgent appointment this evening. However, if you'd like, you may make use of my rooms until you feel more yourself. Mr Grigsby will no doubt be very happy to see you when he wakes tomorrow morning."

Mercifully enough, Felix was drunk enough not to question an urgent appointment so late in the evening, yet not so drunk as not to understand the bulk of Wren's proposition. His brows knotted together as he slowly bobbed his head along with Wren's words. After Wren finished, it took him another moment to reply, "I follow you, Lofthouse."

"Splendid," Wren lied.

With that, he had only to scoop Felix out of the chair and haul him upstairs. Easier said than done, that, particularly for a man of Wren's stature, but he managed, no thanks to Felix's clumsy stumbling. As he leaned Felix against the wall at the top of the stair and unlocked the door to his garret, Wren tried not to think of the risk he undertook in allowing the prodigal son to sleep off his sins in his own bedroom. He consoled himself with the knowledge that his worst artistic ventures were tucked safely away under the loose floorboard beneath his bed; there was no reason Felix would bother looking under there for something he didn't know existed in the first place.

Besides, there was more at stake than Wren's literary sins. Shrike's very life, for one. The fate of the seasons, for another. Wren didn't think England could survive another year without a summer.

"All right, then?" Wren asked after he'd half-laid, half-dropped Felix onto his own mattress.

Felix blinked blearily around at his unfamiliar surroundings. "...All right."

"Jolly good. See you in the morning." Wren shut the door upon him without waiting for a reply.

Despite having locked up the office behind himself, Wren couldn't shake the anxiety gnawing at the back of his mind as he walked down Oxford Street. He resisted the urge to whirl 'round to see if anyone followed him. The hairs at the nape of his neck stood on end the whole way, though he turned up the collar of his frock coat to shield them from the wind. It did his heart a great deal of good to pass through Cumberland Gate and arrive at Achilles to see Shrike standing in the hero's shadow.

No sooner had Wren come within reach of him than Shrike shrugged off his coat and slung it around Wren's shoulders. The warm furs and familiar woodsmoke musk did much to calm his nerves. He chalked up his shivering to the weather as he watched his breath and Shrike's rise up to mingle with the fog.

"You're not cold?" he asked, as Shrike now stood defenceless against the elements.

Shrike shook his head, regarding Wren with a concerned cast to his noble brow. "Are you all right?"

"I'll be better when we're out of London," Wren lied.

To his relief, Shrike took him at his word.

They walked side-by-side at arm's length over the paths and through the trees. Wren would've liked to take Shrike by the arm or perhaps share the cloak between them, but he remained wary of prying eyes even after dark. Despite the warmth of the fur-lined hood, the hair on the nape of his neck still prickled.

Only when they came across the mushroom ring did Wren dare to grasp Shrike's hand, falling into his arms and through the fairy circle alike.

CHAPTER

THIRTEEN

The Court of the Silver Wheel
The Fae Realms
Winter Solstice

Returning to the fae realms gave Shrike a measure of relief on most nights—relief from the poisonous miasma of London's fog and from the bone-deep ache of the surrounding iron, if nothing else.

Tonight, however, while he breathed easier, and while the iron taint no longer dragged down his limbs, the true relief came from Wren's fingers interlaced with his own as they wandered together through the wood toward the Court of the Silver Wheel.

Traversing the forest with Wren felt like seeing the realm with new eyes. Wonder shone on his every feature, from the parting of his speckled lips to the gleam in his dark eyes with their pupils blown wide, to the quickening of his breath in plumes of astonished vapour. His sharp grin matched the knife-edge line of his jaw as he tilted his head back to stare at the bare grey branches and green needles hundreds of feet above them, exposing the swanlike curve of his throat. Shrike could've spent another century content in his company.

All too soon, however, the snow-muffled silence gave way to distant echoes of carousing. The trees thinned, and they came upon the tourney field of the Court of the Silver Wheel.

Shrike halted just short of the frost-limned grass. With great reluctance, he withdrew his arm from Wren's. Wren stepped back and moved as if to shrug off the cloak and return it to Shrike but stopped as Shrike caught his eye.

"From this," Shrike said, trailing his fingers along the hem of the fur-lined hood, "all shall know you are under my protection. None shall harm you, lest they incur my wrath. But—take care, nonetheless."

"I will if you will," Wren retorted.

Shrike laughed and bent to kiss him.

Wren balked.

Shrike withdrew at once, wondering what he'd done to displease him or what had happened to distress him.

Wren's eyes flew to the tourney field and the host of fae making merry just beyond the forest's edge. A few stragglers, a blue-horned faun and an ancient dryad among them, had turned away from the throng to gaze into the trees where Shrike and Wren now stood.

Too late, Shrike recalled that Wren hailed from a realm that had outlawed affection between men. Small wonder Wren should feel reluctant to embrace amidst the general throng.

Yet even as Shrike remembered this, something hardened in Wren's gaze, fear turning to determination. And it was Wren who leapt up to capture Shrike's face in his hands and give him a kiss worthy of a champion.

Breath demanded they break off long before Shrike felt ready to. He hardened his heart and turned to go.

Wren caught him by the arm.

Shrike halted and turned to gaze down on him.

"I have a favour to grant you," said Wren.

And before Shrike could do more than blink, Wren had pulled a fistful of something green out of his waistcoat pocket and pressed it into Shrike's palm. Silk, Shrike realized, shimmering smooth, still warm from Wren's own bodily heat, folded up so tight one might at first glance mistake it for a cluster of summer leaves, and of so bright a colour that it seemed the sun shone through its folds. He shook it out to reveal a scarf, its yellow-green body painted with a swirling ivy-leaf pattern in darker hues.

"I had supposed," Wren said, "that if green worked for Gawain's gyrdel, then..."

"It's perfect," Shrike replied.

A shy smile flickered across those beautiful bespeckled lips. Shrike bent to kiss them again, and Wren obliged him. Then he folded up the scarf and tucked it between his armour and his tunic—just over his heart.

For the first time, as Shrike strode off through the motley crowd, he did not venture forth alone.

Wren walked beside him.

Wren's freckled face remained a stoic mask save for his dark eyes flicking 'round in wide wonder. The crowd parted for them as they went. Each individual recognizing Shrike told their neighbours, sending up a tide of whispers to foretell his coming. They stood thickest at the rim of the duelling field to secure their view of the coming battle. Thereafter the crush abruptly ceased, none daring to step on the hallowed ground.

And on the edge of the field stood the queen's bower.

The knights circling the bower's roots withdrew as Shrike approached. Shrike halted some yards off. He shot Wren a speaking glance. Wren served him an understanding one in return. The handclasp they shared bespoke as much passion as any embrace. Then Shrike forced himself to release his grasp, to tear his gaze away from Wren's handsome upraised face and turn towards the queen.

The hemlock remained evergreen even on the darkest winter night of the year, though little moonlight filtered down into the bower through the branches overhead, laden as they were with sparkling snow. The mid-winter feast proved as abundant as the autumn harvest, though pomegranates and ghost-apples replaced peaches and blackberries. Courtiers gazed on Shrike with undisguised intrigue. He ignored them as he strode to the twin thrones on the balcony.

The queen's strawberry-gold hair, emerald eyes, and rosebud cheeks hadn't changed a whit since the equinox tournament. Nor had the small and knowing smile on her lips. She'd traded her grass-green gown for a silvery-blue as befit the season. In her lap she held a crown woven from oak branches, their scarlet leaves coming to sharp points and the acorns polished to a gleam.

The Holly King did not sit beside her, but rather stood behind his own throne, his blue knuckles clenched white on the back of it. Tendrils of frost spread from his fingertips over the wood. Instead of the suit of armour that befit his prior rank of knight, he wore just a chain-mail hauberk beneath his tabard. Holly berries shone bright as blood on his crown.

"Good morrow, my Oak King," said the queen. "We are gratified to gaze upon you. We had feared you might miss this day's ceremonies, for you've been so oft absent from court of late."

A cold smirk twisted the Holly King's lips. Shrike bared his teeth in a semblance of a grin.

"Kneel, my Oak King," the queen commanded. "Your coronation is nigh."

Shrike dropped to one knee and bowed his head. The queen's spider-silk gown whispered as she rose from her throne and approached him.

A moment after, the weight of the oaken crown settled on his brow.

Wren supposed he'd expected to find something akin to the tilting-yard of Templestowe where Ivanhoe had fought for Rebecca's honour. The queen, with her strawberry-golden hair and emerald-green eyes, bore little resemblance to the dark beauty of the virtuous Rebecca. At least none that Wren could see from his position beneath her bower, craning his neck up at her amidst the fae throng. Nor did she seem particularly persecuted by her court or in need of rescue by either her Oak or Holly King. Indeed her Saxon beauty appeared more akin to Rowena, noble and proud. Wren supposed if one were the sort of man to admire women, one might as well consider her worth dying for. He tore his eyes away from her piercing emerald gaze to regard her other champion—Shrike's fated opponent.

The Holly King was no Sir Brian du Bois-Guilbert, either. Frost covered his tabard like torn lace, and his pale blue flesh resembled no earthly complexion. His eyes shone as bright a crimson as the ruby berries on the wreath adorning his brow. He stood eye-to-eye with Shrike, which Wren misliked, having hoped the fight would prove more uneven in Shrike's favour.

Likewise, the dead and barren field held no lists for a joust. The coming duel would be fought on foot in hand-to-hand combat.

The general throng of fae had fixed curious eyes on Wren the moment he and Shrike had entered the court. Yet none approached. Either the memory of Shrike's arm in his, or his kiss upon Shrike's mouth, or the presence of Shrike's cloak around Wren's shoulders warned them all off.

While ice sheathed the barren branches overhead, and blue frost limned the dead grey grass underfoot, and Wren's breath turned to fog before him, and only Shrike's fur-lined cloak prevented his freezing, few fae appeared dressed for the weather. Indeed, a certain nymph with frost-veined wings seemed to thrive upon the cold, her laugh like the merry chime of icicles clinking together on the branches waving overhead. Fauns capered in breeches that covered just the thighs of their fur-tufted legs. A hulking ogre with a broken tush wore a shirt of flowing silk painted with poinsettia leaves. And then there was the raven-haired elf-maiden in a tunic of iridescent blue feathers, whom Wren thought he recognized as an archer from the Wild Hunt, gorging herself with a drinking horn in one hand and the leg of an enormous bird in the other. The only exception to the misrule seemed to be a small, slight figure flitting about in a mottled grey leather cloak—half storm-cloud and half moonlight—with a thick fur ruff. Wren followed their progress until his eyes fell upon a certain cluster of merriment.

Several blonde young women in peasant blouses had gathered around a fair-haired young man whose evening coat and top hat would not have looked out of place strolling through the West End. The ladies' low-cut necklines bared soft-sloping feminine shoulders and the swell of their bosoms. They created such an overt display of pastoral milk-maid fantasy that even Wren couldn't help taking notice of them. Having the sort of eye that wandered away from maiden's bosoms rather than towards them, Wren also noticed, as they lifted the hems of their skirts in cavorting, a glimpse or two of cloven hooves and a swish of something dun and tufted he thought might be a tail. When he at last tore his gaze away from these more interesting features, he noticed the young man glaring at him. Perhaps he thought Wren unwelcome competition for the ladies' attention. Or perhaps, Wren thought as he peered closer at the young man's face, he recognized him.

"The Oak King is crowned! The Oak King is crowned!"

The cry rippled through the crowd, jerking Wren's eye away from the gathered fae and up towards the queen's bower.

"Arise, my Oak King, and go forth in victory."

Shrike stood. He avoided the queen's gaze, instead alighting upon the Holly King. "Shall we?"

Another mirthless smile twisted the Holly King's blood-red gash of a mouth.

Shrike waited on the off chance that the Holly King would consult with his squire—a wiry sprite with tufted ears and a wine-stain birthmark blooming across the left side of their face—and don his customary suit of full plate.

But the Holly King merely strode past him to continue on through the feast-hall and down the spiralling stair out of the bower.

Shrike followed in his wake swift and silent as a shadow.

The throng hushed as the two kings entered the duelling field. Shrike searched the sea of faces for Wren. He did not find him. Other familiar faces emerged in his stead—the mottled moth from the Wild Hunt, and Nell. Shrike supposed he shouldn't feel surprised that those he ran with under the full moon would come to see how he fared in battle.

As the two kings reached the centre mark, the Holly King turned to cast one final glance back up at the queen's bower. The glimmer in his eyes froze before it ever reached his cheeks. He raised his two-handed longsword aloft in salute, then resheathed it, as to begin the fight fair.

Shrike did no such thing. Instead he cast his gaze over the crowd in a last desperate quest for Wren. He'd almost consigned himself to defeat when he spied him at last—a pale bespeckled face, chestnut locks tumbling in disarray over his brow, his dark eyes wide and deep with a longing that sang through Shrike's own heart.

Shrike vowed to return to his arms. Then put him from his mind for the remainder of the duel.

The herald—an apple-cheeked, toad-mouthed courtier in exquisite wasp-lace—called for the combatants to take their places marked on either side of a ring some three ells wide burned into the ground. He held up the queen's token between them. A scrap of emerald velvet, shimmering with sunbeams, a portent of the spring to come. Then he turned to the queen herself for the signal.

Shrike didn't bother glancing back at her bower.

She gave her sign regardless, for the herald dropped the token and leapt backwards out of the fray as it fluttered to the ground.

The moment the merest corner touched the dead grass, the peal of metal against metal rang out through the cold air as the Holly King unsheathed his longsword.

Shrike did the same with his arming sword an instant after. He had time to do little else before the first blow fell from the Holly King's blade and forced him to dive to the side. The blade sang as it cleaved the air by his head.

In its wake there came a sharp sting in the tip of Shrike's ear. Something cold trickled down its length.

First blood.

The crowd roared in approval.

While Shrike and the Holly King stood of a like height and swung with a like arm, the Holly King's two-handed longsword had far greater reach than Shrike's mere arming sword clenched in his left hand. Shrike couldn't hope to strike him without leaping into the longsword's range. He risked being cut down before he could ever land a hit.

Worse yet, the Holly King had trained as a knight under the full weight of plate for Shrike knew not how many decades. Perhaps even centuries. Had he worn such a suit of armour now, Shrike could've danced around him until his strength gave out and then darted in for a swift killing blow through his visor. Bereft of such protection, the Holly King had made himself all the stronger, all the faster, and all the more ready to run Shrike down. He could strike as swift as a falcon.

Shrike would just have to prove swifter.

No sooner had his first blow fallen than the Holly King shifted his grip on the hilt and brought it up and around for another swing at Shrike's head. Shrike fell into a crouch. The blade sliced through where his throat had been. He rolled aside, leaping up beside the Holly King.

And darted backward as the Holly King spun to attack him.

But not fast enough.

Crack!

The terrible impact rang out across the field like a thunderbolt cleaving a tree in twain.

Wren's hands flew to his mouth. The crowd leapt and cheered, surging in a bloodthirsty tide. The young man amidst the milkmaids let out a particularly gruesome guffaw. Wren didn't dare breathe. It seemed the world had ceased turning the instant the blow fell.

The sword had struck Shrike in the side. The Holly King's blade came away crimson. And the horrible noise, the crunch of metal against boiled leather and bone—

But Shrike rolled.

At first it seemed as though the force of the blow had thrown him aside, but as Wren watched him tumble, he realized Shrike had purposefully dodged. Not entirely, not quite fast enough for that, but dodged all the same, and when his feet came under him again he staggered upright.

And Wren's hopes rose with him.

Shrike lurched to his feet despite the agony in his side. On instinct, his free hand flew to the wound. His palm braced against his side to hold his guts in place. Blood, cooling quick in the wintry night, trickled out between his fingers.

But nothing more.

The Holly King wasted a fraction of a second staring down at Shrike in as much bewilderment as Shrike stared up at him. Then he raised his longsword over his head for another chop.

Shrike leapt out of the way. Pain tore through his side as he went, radiating up to his arm and down to his hip. Worth it, though, to escape. The longsword buried its blade in the frozen dirt where his body had lain not a half-second earlier.

In the instant it took the Holly King to rip his longsword out of the ground, Shrike dared a glance down at himself, pulling his hand away from the wound for a moment. Bleeding, yes—but not spilling out entrails in his wake. And the stabbing pains in his side with every gasp bespoke cracked ribs rather than broken ones. He could feel the difference, having suffered both several times over the centuries.

A blow like that should have felled him like an oak beneath an axe. Instead it had glanced off his flesh, leaving the most minor possible injuries under the circumstances.

Wren's pentangle ward had worked.

Just as Shrike had known it would.

A wild grin twisted its way up Shrike's cheek. It remained as he sprang forward to thrust his sword's-point through the Holly King's eye.

The Holly King evidently did not expect agility from a foe who by all rights ought to have lain dead at his feet. As such, he almost parried too late. But parry he did. The cross-guard of the longsword caught the arming sword's point before it could reach its mark. A twist of the Holly King's wrists drove Shrike's blade upright and tangled the two swords together at the hilt.

Shrike held his ground, but with the Holly King's two-handed grip against his single arm, both blades began to inch towards him. Shrike's free hand fell from his wound to his belt.

Frost crept up the hilt of the Holly King's sword and spread to Shrike's own blade. His fingertips stung with cold. Then they began to numb.

With a flick of his wrist, Shrike unsheathed his misericord and plunged it into the Holly King's left side. Its point—sharp and slender as a needle—found its mark between the links in the chain. What strength remained in his arm drove it in to the hilt.

The Holly King staggered. His blade scraped against Shrike's sword. But he did not fall.

"Well, knave?" the Holly King spat. Flecks of blood gleamed on the frozen ground as round and full as the ruby berries adorning the wreath on his brow. "Do you suppose her hearth will warm you as it has warmed me? Are you eager to cut short your life's thread for a chance to lay your head in her lap? I tell you, you are but the latest corpse to plough that field, and a thousand corpses shall plough on in your wake. Her embrace will last for a moment—your doom, forever!"

"I care not," Shrike replied.

The Holly King sneered. "You care not for your fate?"

"No," said Shrike. "I care not for her."

The crimson eyes flew wide—and fixed upon forever as Shrike twisted his misericord in the Holly King's heart.

The multitude exploded in a roar of victory. No cry could escape Wren's throat with his heart stuck in it. Nor could any exclamation express the overwhelming wave of relief that crashed over him as Shrike withdrew his deadly blade, untangled his sword, and stepped back to let the Holly King fall to the frost-covered ground, dead.

Shrike had won. Shrike had lived. Shrike had survived.

Wren felt as if his heart would burst with joy.

Shrike staggered towards the edge of the duelling field. Strands of dark hair clung to his high cheekbones and noble brow, where frozen sweat glistened amidst flecks of the Holly King's blood. His sword sang out as he slipped it back into his sheath, and the hand that had held it went to the wound in his side. In his other hand, he still gripped the slender blade that had spelled the Holly King's ruin. Plumes of vapour escaped his clenched jaw like dragon's breath. Despite his wound, he stood tall and proud as the oak itself, a king victorious. All the while, his dark eyes searched the crowd in aimless confusion.

Wren knew the futility of calling out for him amidst the cacophony. Instead, he elbowed his way past a green-bearded brute who turned as if to strike him down for his impertinence, then paled at the sight of Shrike's cloak over Wren's shoulders and hastened to make way before them. Their flight rippled through the crowd, parting as more of the fae realized with whom they stood in company, and soon Wren had a clear path ahead to the duelling field.

Just as Shrike's eyes found him at last.

Wren ran to him.

The rush of victory left Shrike wanting. While he took hard-earned pride in slaying the Holly King, the approval of the multitude rang hollow in his ears. Only one individual mattered to him in that moment—and never before had he so longed to see him. Survival demanded celebration; wounds be damned.

And then, when Shrike had resigned himself to carving through the crowd to find the man he wanted, the throng parted to reveal a singular figure dashing towards him.

Shrike dropped his misericord and threw his arms wide just as Wren crashed into him.

CHAPTER
FOURTEEN

For Shrike, the pain of split flesh and cracked ribs felt well worthwhile to have Wren's arms flung around his shoulders and those beautiful bespeckled lips open beneath his own. His hands clenched in Wren's cravat, slippery with gore, streaking scarlet in their wake.

The roar of the crowd filled his ears. Whether in approval of his victory or his embrace, he knew not. Nor did he care. He had Wren. He needed naught else.

"My lord?"

An unwelcome voice pierced the general tumult, sounding nearer than Shrike had expected. He broke away from Wren with great reluctance and turned to find the queen's toad-mouthed herald had returned with a half-dozen of her knights.

The herald bowed. "May I offer you our congratulations upon your triumph. Her majesty commends your courage."

Shrike stared at the herald, then glanced back at the queen's bower. He could just make out her figure standing at the prow of her balcony. Her white hands braced against its scale-barked rail as she leaned out towards him.

"I thank her majesty for her consideration," Shrike forced out as he returned his attention to the herald. "With her permission, I would withdraw from the field."

"But of course!" said the herald with a great twirling of hands.

Shrike served him a nod, then at last turned to Wren, still in his arms. Wren looked rather bewildered at the exchange. Shrike could hardly blame him.

"Do you wish to remain?" Shrike asked in a low voice. Low enough that the herald would have to venture much nearer to overhear, and as they had remained at arm's length from him, Shrike doubted they wanted to come within range of his sword, with a half-dozen knights or no. "There will be a great revel. Feasting. Dancing."

Wren looked not at the herald, nor the knights, nor the queen, nor the wild throng already rejoicing all around them. Instead his eyes searched Shrike's, then dropped to the wound in Shrike's side. "I think we've more pressing concerns."

Shrike could have danced upon such a wound if Wren had asked it of him. But truth told, he felt some measure of relief.

"Do the fae have surgeons?" Wren asked abruptly.

Shrike blinked down at him. "Chirurgeons, d'you mean?"

"Yes," Wren replied after a moment's pause. "Who do you go to when you're wounded?"

"No one," said Shrike. "I come home to myself and do what I can."

Wren appeared far more aghast than Shrike thought warranted. "You can't mean to stitch yourself up."

"I've done it afore." Shrike shrugged, wincing as it pulled at his wounds. "I'll do it again."

Wren hardly looked convinced. He set his jaw as if he meant to argue the point, but with a sigh, he replied, "Very well. Blackthorn, then, I suppose."

Shrike smiled and took his proffered arm to lead him from the battlefield, ignoring the astonished expression of the toad-faced herald in their wake.

The crowd parted for them. Like the herald, few dared approach. Some swerved into view with flagons and horns filled with wine, proffering toasts with the victor, but a glance from Shrike set them back on their heels, and they satisfied themselves with drinking to him rather than with him.

Soon enough, though not so soon as Shrike might've liked, he and Wren reached the forest's edge and plunged into it down quieter paths towards Blackthorn. Despite his wounds, the long walk felt shorter with Wren at his side. Only the occasional hoot of an owl broke the snow-muffled silence of that wintry night.

Blackthorn's briars withdrew from Shrike's approach much as the revelling crowd had done in the Court of the Silver Wheel not more than an hour past. He staggered across the cottage threshold and leaned one hand against the wall beside the hearth to catch his breath. Before he could bend down for the poker, Wren had snatched it up and stirred the fire to life again.

Shrike left him to it and began unbuckling his armour. He gently tugged Wren's favour out of its place over his heart, winding it around the hilt of his sword for safe-keeping, and set both aside as he shed his boiled leather. Blood had soaked into his gambeson and tunic beneath and dried into a dark crust. Peeling it off tore into his wound afresh, but Shrike had grown inured to such pain over the centuries.

A sharp gasp made Shrike jerk his head up to regard Wren, who'd gone quite pale.

"Are you hurt?" Shrike asked, a bolt of panic in his tone turning the question into a demand. If any of the Court had laid a hand upon Wren, he'd flay them for boot-leather.

Wren gave a strangled scoff. "Am I hurt? Look at you!"

Shrike glanced down at himself again. The black crust of dried blood over the blue-bruised lips of the wound did not appear too grave. The fresher stuff oozing through looked worse than it felt. The glistening scarlet of scored muscle under the skin gave him some pause, but the blade had not carved through to the vitals beneath. He lifted his eyes to direct another questioning look at Wren. "I'm alive, thanks to your sigil."

Wren somehow turned a shade paler. "It doesn't seem like it worked at all."

Shrike gestured along the length of the slice and withheld a wince as the motion pulled at the wound. "His blow ought to have cleaved me in half. It hardly broke the skin."

Wren barked out a hollow and disbelieving laugh.

Shrike dropped his gaze to the wound, considering. "Though I suppose there's no way to tell if the sigil or the token saved me."

"You're saved," Wren said firmly. "That's what matters. And if you think I had something to do with it beyond pure luck, now's not the time to argue it. What do you have to fix yourself up with?"

Shrike, who'd spent centuries doing all for himself, took a moment to answer. "Bring me that chest beneath the window."

Wren leapt to fetch it. It was a stout thing carved from oak, fastened and hinged with leather straps, no longer than Shrike's forearm in any direction. He'd crafted it himself some two centuries ago, though he'd had to replace the leather straps within the last decade and its contents still more recently. Bottles of white vinegar, honey, wormwood, rose and lavender water slotted into compartments beside silver needles, knives, and tweezers, spools of silk thread and catgut. Linen towels lay folded beneath long strips of linen bandages wound into a ball like yarn. A satchel of dried willow bark cushioned several dried poppy pods.

"You're as well-supplied as any surgeon," said Wren, a hint of admiration leaking into his dry tone. He picked up the green bottle with a crude image of a snail etched into the side. "What's this?"

"Snail oil," said Shrike.

"What." The disbelief in Wren's voice removed all trace of a question.

"It's good for burns," Shrike explained.

Wren did not appear convinced.

Shrike didn't feel the need to convince him at that particular moment. "Hand me that vinegar jug. And the linen."

Wren did so.

Shrike uncorked the jug with his teeth.

"Wait," said Wren as Shrike moved to splash the vinegar onto his wound.

Shrike paused mid-gesture, keeping the jug suspended at an angle despite the burning pain in his side. He shot Wren a questioning look.

"Let me do it," said Wren.

Shrike considered the insistent tone in Wren's voice and the determined set of his jaw. He weighed this against the cold blood trickling down his side, the sharp stab of his cracked ribs with every breath, the ache settling into his back and arms as the fury of the fight wore off, and the burning throb of his wound. After a moment, he returned the linen and vinegar to Wren's keeping.

"This might go easier if you sit down," Wren pointed out.

Shrike conceded the point and settled himself on the rim of the hollow-stump tub.

Wren did not flinch from his duty. The vinegar splashed over Shrike's side, colder than his blood, burning as it cleansed his wounded flesh. Shrike withheld a hiss of pain. It stung, true, but no worse than the initial blow—indeed, a good deal less. And it needed doing. He didn't want to give Wren any indication to cease, however involuntary.

Another splash of vinegar went over the linen towel in Wren's hand. Shrike braced himself for the second round of cleansing.

But Wren's touch as he daubed at the wound astonished Shrike with its delicacy. Small, swift, sure strokes. Effective without being abrasive. And tender in such a way that touched Shrike's heart as well as his wound. It had been too long since someone had treated his flesh as something worth protecting rather than an obstacle to overcome.

Some minutes later, Wren tossed the soiled linen aside.

Shrike held out his hand. "Needle and thread."

Wren balked, but Shrike did not have to ask him twice. Though he did watch in open horror mixed with fascination as Shrike, having threaded the silver needle with silk, pinched the lips of the wound together and punctured his skin over and over to pull the thread through and close the bloody gash. It hurt, as it always did, yet it had never before occurred to Shrike that such hurt could mean anything to anyone—never mind how much it seemed to mean to Wren, whose brow grew still more furrowed and whose lips pressed into a thin white line.

Still, Wren said nothing.

Shrike knotted the silk with fingers that had just begun to tremble.

No sooner had he finished than Wren plucked the silver knife out of the medicine chest and cut the cord without Shrike having to say a word. Likewise, Wren remained silent as he took up another linen towel and daubed away the beads of sweat that had gathered on Shrike's temples.

"There's a hand-broom on the sill," Shrike forced out between clenched teeth. "Spin the cobwebs down from the rafters—if you can reach...?" he added, as it occurred to him Wren stood a full head shorter.

After a searching glance 'round the cottage, Wren's eyes caught on the broom across the way and the cobwebs above, and he leapt to retrieve both. His whole body stretched taut as a strung bow to bring the willow-and-lavender bristles to the cobwebs. A deft flick of his wrist gathered more than enough for Shrike's purposes. Wren returned to Shrike's side looking no less sceptical than when he began. His brow grew still more arched as Shrike plucked the cobwebs from the bristles and packed them against the wound.

"It staunches blood," Shrike explained.

This raised still more questions in Wren's face, but he voiced none of them as he picked up the roll of linen and began winding it around Shrike's waist. The bandages pulled taut, bracing against the wound and the cracked ribs alike. Wren's touch, however, remained gentle. Silver scissors clipped the linen off the roll, and delicate fingers tucked the bandage-end into its own folds to keep it in place.

His work done, Wren's eyes fell to Shrike's scars with a renewed interest that Shrike found unnerving—particularly when combined with his furrowed brow and the hard line of his mouth. His gentle hands reached out for Shrike again, his fingertips alighting on the pale starburst just beneath Shrike's left collarbone and over his heart, left behind by an errant arrow in the Wild Hunt some decades ago.

For a moment, Shrike wondered if the scars disgusted Wren, whose own freckled flesh remained miraculously unmarred.

Then Wren bent his head to press a reverent kiss to the scar.

Warmth suffused Shrike's heart. He slipped his fingertips beneath Wren's chin and tilted his face upward to kiss him more thoroughly.

"Will you lie with me?" Shrike murmured against Wren's lips when they broke apart for breath. "I'm yet wild with victory."

Doubtless Wren could feel as much for himself, so near as he now perched—and Shrike felt his desire in return, stirring to life beneath the layers of wool between them.

Yet still Wren hesitated. "I don't want to hurt you."

"Nothing could soothe my wounds more than your touch," Shrike replied.

Wren gave a breathless laugh against Shrike's cheek. "Doubtful. But if you're certain I won't do you harm…"

Shrike answered him with another kiss, long and deep and languid.

"The Oxford rub," Wren broke off to gasp. In response to Shrike's puzzled expression, he added, "Between the thighs."

Shrike grinned. "How sweet to die betwixt those thighs."

Wren scoffed, but did so with a smile.

Having already stripped to the waist, it was a simple matter for Shrike to divest himself of his hose. Wren's garments proved more complicated. Much had changed in mortal fashion over the centuries, but in the months since Samhain, Shrike had ample opportunity to gain familiarity with their fastenings and became quite adept in unbuttoning, untying, and stripping away waistcoat, trousers, shirt, and small-clothes to bare Wren's beauty.

And it was beauty, indeed.

Wren's slender clothed silhouette belied the strapping frame beneath. The arms that twined around Shrike clutched him close with powerful sinews. Laughing dark eyes grew darker still, fluttering shut as Shrike's fingertips traced the delicate curve of his ear. Speckled lips plucked into a shy smile, then fell open in a gasp before Wren bit them to suppress further outburst. Shrike could restrain himself no longer and caressed his jawline to coax him into another kiss. He could never tire of this, the taste of Wren on his tongue, the weight of him in his arms, how the lightest touch or the faintest breath could draw forth a paroxysm of pleasure from his mortal lover.

Lying down beside him on the bed, Wren drew Shrike close before turning 'round, nestling his back against Shrike's front. His freckles fell like a mantle over his shoulders, their breadth once disguised by the heavy woollen coat, now revealed to sharp contrast with his soft and slender waist.

Shrike wrapped his arms around that same waist, trailing his fingers through the soft hair over Wren's navel and on down to where his prick now stirred. All the while he pressed fervent kisses to the nape of Wren's neck, tracing the freckled constellations with his lips, and delighted in the choked-off gasps and bitten-back moans Wren made in reply.

Then Wren reached behind to take Shrike's cock-stand and guide it between his own supple thighs. Wren's legs closed over Shrike like a vise. Shrike rolled his hips, unable to restrain a groan as he slid through the delicious grip. His own hand closed over Wren's prick like the hilt of a well-balanced blade. A twist of his wrist brought forth drops of seed. A bruising kiss to Wren's throat provoked a hushed exclamation.

"Shrike!"

The particular exquisite ecstasy of his true name in his lover's voice —a pleasure Shrike, like most fae, had denied himself until now—broke over him and left him gasping in its wake. Each blissful breath punctuated by the stabbing pain of cracked ribs already on the mend. The contrast only served to heighten the sensation. With his cock clenched tight between Wren's thighs, Wren clutched close in his embrace, Wren's prick pulsing in his palm, seed spilling over through his fingers, and his true name on Wren's lips, Shrike could last but mere moments. With a final frantic thrust, he followed Wren over the brink to plunge down into the dark and soothing waters of oblivion.

"Lofthouse!" cried Mr Grigsby. "I was just about to send the Horse Guards out in search of you!"

Wren froze on the office threshold. About an hour ago he'd awoken in Shrike's arms to find the sun nearly at its mid-day crest. His pocket-watch confirmed the wretched hour and sent him into a frenzy of ablutions and scrambling for his clothes. Shrike roused halfway through this chaotic process and assisted not only in providing some much-needed calm but also in retrieving scattered pieces of Wren's ensemble from about the cottage. He suggested breakfast, as well, but though Wren's stomach growled to life at the thought of black pudding, eggs, bread, and cheese, they simply didn't have time to spare. So Shrike had taken him out to the fairy ring in the forest and leapt through it with him to Hyde Park. While Wren didn't dare embrace him as he so dearly wished to, their parting handclasp lingered, and carried with it all the longing of Wren's heart. Only the promise to meet again on Boxing Day gave him the strength to let go.

It occurred to Wren as he half-walked, half-ran down Oxford Street that he hadn't even taken a moment to ask after Shrike's duelling wound, much less clean and re-dress it. In attempting to straddle two realms' worth of responsibilities, he'd failed them both.

At present, Wren wondered if Mr Grigsby had intended a deliberate hint in saying he would ask the Horse Guards in particular to find him. He pushed his anxieties down to reply in an almost normal tone, "I beg your pardon, sir. I was out visiting a friend and quite forgot the time. It won't happen again."

But Mr Grigsby's astonishment at Wren's entrance had already dissolved into his customary good humour, and he chuckled as he replied, "I should hope not!"

Still, Wren hesitated in the doorway. A glance around the office showed no sign of Felix Knoll, hung-over or otherwise. Mr Grigsby would only have known Wren was gone, rather than simply having a lie-in, if he had climbed up to the garret to see for himself—and in doing so, he could hardly have avoided discovering Felix in Wren's bed. Unless Felix had arisen and shown himself out before Mr Grigsby awoke, which, given Felix's condition the previous night, Wren thought unlikely in the extreme. At length he dared to enquire, "Has Mr Knoll graced us with his presence this morning?"

Mr Grigsby appeared puzzled but by no means concerned. "Not yet, no. Were we expecting him?"

"Not by appointment," Wren hastened to say, lest Mr Grigsby think he'd forgotten to mark it down in the office diary. "Only I met him in town last night, and he mentioned he might visit us on the morrow."

Mr Grigsby brightened. "Wouldn't that be a nice surprise! Still, I suppose he is very busy visiting his friends, and we mustn't expect he'd find the time to do more than pop his head in, if at all."

Wren agreed—aloud, if not in his heart—that a visit from Felix could prove nothing short of wonderful. He further begged Mr Grigsby's pardon again whilst he went to his room to fetch a fresh pen-knife. Mr Grigsby cheerfully waved him off.

It took a great deal of concentrated effort for Wren to prevent himself from dashing up the stair. Still moreso when he reached the first landing and looked up to find his garret door a half-inch ajar.

Wren crept up the last few steps and nudged the door open with his fingertips. It creaked inward, revealing the untouched desk with its chair pushed in, the wash-stand in disarray, and the much-rumpled bed devoid of Felix.

This mystery did not hold Wren's attention for long. His foremost concern remained beneath the floorboards. He kicked his door shut behind him and dove under the bed to check his hidden nook.

Every page remained just as Wren had left it.

Wren indulged in a deep sigh of relief as he hauled himself upright and dusted off his knees. Liberated of his most pressing anxiety, he took a second glance at the mess Felix had left in his wake. The bedclothes had dragged halfway across the floor, and the fine blond hairs stuck to Wren's straight-razor combined with the layer of scum in the wash-basin suggested Felix had made himself quite at home.

Trust Felix not to bother making up the bed, Wren supposed, though he'd have thought they taught boys better than that at Eton. Still, he had to admire Felix's industry in getting up before Mr Grigsby. Particularly when one considered the state of intoxication in which Wren had put him to bed. No doubt Felix had wanted to escape without any lowly witnesses to his shame. A twisted part of Wren wished Mr Grigsby had stumbled upon Felix that morning, if only to show Mr Grigsby just how his golden boy spent the funds kept in trust for him.

Without proof, however, Wren could do nothing. So he returned downstairs and settled in to work with Mr Grigsby as if Felix had never stayed the night and Wren himself had never visited the fae realm.

Over Christmas, Wren could not escape Mr Grigsby's company. Mr Grigsby himself took both the Eve and the Day off. Unlike most gentlemen of his profession, he extended this holiday to his clerk, as well. However, as Mr Grigsby himself had no near relations or close friends to spend it with, he invited Wren to enjoy Christmas with him. And as Wren was no longer welcome in the company of his near relations or close friends, he had no excuse to demur.

Wren knew he ought to feel far more grateful for Mr Grigsby's generosity—for Mr Grigsby neither pleaded with him to accept, nor lorded it over him afterward. And he did grant Boxing Day to Wren in its entirety.

Nevertheless, Wren found it tiresome to match Mr Grigsby's holiday cheer when he felt so little of it himself. Particularly this year of all years, when Wren not only had, for once, a dear friend with whom he might spend a holiday, but also knew that while Mr Grigsby smiled and hummed carols to himself as he carved up the roast goose—ordered in advance from Mr Grigsby's favourite inn across the way—said friend lay alone and wounded far beyond Wren's reach.

Never mind that Shrike had assured Wren of the injury's insignificance and of his own fae resilience. Never mind that Shrike had stitched himself up for decades if not centuries before Wren came along. Never mind the myriad scars that bespoke how Shrike had already survived wounds just as bad or worse than the one he received in the solstice duel. Wren's heart bled for him regardless—as did his cuticles, gnawed raw in what few moments he could spare out of Mr Grigsby's sight.

Despite all this, Wren survived Christmas without giving Mr Grigsby any hint as to his own misery or Shrike's plight.

Boxing Day dawned as bright and clear as any day could in the midst of London's fog-smothered winter. Wren bolted out of bed with the sunrise, though he'd hardly slept, and hastily made himself ready to go out, packing up his satchel with leftover Christmas pudding and laudanum. Then he dashed downstairs, his mind already flown far from the confines of Staple Inn and off to the fae realms—to the blackthorn brugh—to Shrike's warm and welcome embrace.

Which made it particularly irritating when the door-bell rang.

Wren swore a vicious oath under his breath. Mr Grigsby wasn't even awake yet—which made the unknown visitor Wren's problem, holiday or no holiday. Whatever idiot had decided Boxing Day was a day for seeking legal counsel at the crack of dawn, Wren could hardly escape the office without encountering them along the way. He didn't have Shrike's talent for leaping out of windows.

Before Wren could bring himself to submit to his fate and unlock the door, much less open it, a hail of blows fell upon it from the other side.

"Mr Grigsby?" a man's voice cried out. "Mr Grigsby! Open up, I beg you! Something terrible has occurred!"

The voice sounded genuinely distressed as well as familiar, and this familiarity prompted Wren to unlock the door.

Tolhurst burst through it.

CHAPTER
FIFTEEN

Wren, too startled to do more than leap backward, gaped at Tolhurst. Gone was the sober gentleman Wren had met in autumn. Flecks of shaving foam stuck behind his jaw and below his ear; his left shoe had come unlaced; his modest blue necktie hung rumpled and half-undone from his collar; his beaver hat perched precariously askew until he swept it off his head, whereupon his hair stood up at all angles in its wake; and deep shadows underscored his bulging eyes.

Tolhurst's wild gaze locked with Wren's. "Is my nephew here?"

"No," Wren answered, mere surprise curdling into genuine alarm. "Why? What's going on?"

"I expected him for Christmas, but he never arrived." Tolhurst peered past Wren into the darker corners of the office, as if he expected Felix to jump out of them and reveal himself. "If he hasn't come here then I fear the worst has come to pass."

Wren could think of a few more likely places in London to find Felix than Mr Grigsby's office. None appropriate to divulge to Tolhurst if they hadn't occurred to him already. He tried a more sedate suggestion. "Perhaps he's spent the holiday with a university friend."

"I've just come from Oxford," Tolhurst said almost before Wren had finished speaking. "His intimate friends said they all came down to the city on Saturday for an evening's entertainment. They parted ways afterward. No one's seen him since."

Saturday the twentieth. Wren knew someone who'd seen Felix since then, all right. Though he could hardly explain why, after letting a drunken Felix into his garret, he'd then left him alone in such a state and told no one of it when Felix had up and vanished by the next morning.

Yet it wasn't the thought of trying to explain his own indecent adventures in the fae realms that gave Wren pause. No, it was the dim recollection of a blond young gentleman whose black tailcoat and top hat had appeared so out-of-place amidst the pseudo-medieval garb of his fellow revellers at the solstice duel.

"Lofthouse?" came Mr Grigsby's curious call from the stairwell. The gentleman himself followed soon after. In his haste to dress he appeared almost as dishevelled as Tolhurst, though far less distressed. His creased brow of confusion lifted in surprise upon sighting their visitor. "Oh! Good morning, Mr Tolhurst! What brings you to our humble doorstep today?"

Tolhurst explained his concerns in full, to Mr Grigsby's increasing alarm.

"He must be found without delay!" Mr Grigsby declared when Tolhurst had arrived at a breathless finish. "But do sit down a moment whilst we form a plan of action. Lofthouse, if you would—?"

Wren had already pulled out his own desk chair for Tolhurst to sit in and put the copper kettle on for tea. Mr Grigsby thanked him. Tolhurst did not, though doubtless he had more pressing matters on his mind.

"You've done very well so far in eliminating possibilities," Mr Grigsby assured Tolhurst as the latter sank down in Wren's chair with a hollow look. "And a great deal more than anyone could expect a single man to accomplish alone. Mr Knoll is fortunate to have such a devoted uncle as yourself."

Wren noted that Mr Grigsby did not suggest calling up the Horse Guards in search of Felix.

"Thank you," Tolhurst replied, his words clipped. "But I fear it has not been enough."

Mr Grigsby, his eyes brimming with unsinkable optimism, opened his mouth to counter Tolhurst's despair.

Wren cleared his throat.

Both gentlemen turned their heads to regard him.

"Is it possible, Mr Tolhurst," Wren ventured in his most careful tone, "that Mr Knoll may yet attempt to meet you at your lodgings in Rochester?"

Tolhurst considered him with a curious furrow in his brow.

"Why, Lofthouse is quite right!" cried Mr Grigsby. "Yes, we should hope that Mr Knoll is doing his best to find his way home, just as we shall do our utmost to find him."

The weariness in Tolhurst's aspect grew still more pronounced.

Wren hastened to reach his point before Mr Grigsby could pontificate further. "It may prove more expedient to have you wait for him there, while his friends likewise await him in Oxford, and Mr Grigsby remains ready to receive him here. That way, no matter where he may choose to seek shelter, he may be assured of a warm reception."

"And who should go out in search of him, if I do not?" asked Tolhurst, doing a better job than most men at disguising his impatience with the half-cocked notions of an upstart clerk.

"I shall," said Wren.

Tolhurst, for the first time since Wren denied any knowledge of Felix's whereabouts, gazed upon him with something approaching interest.

"I'm well used to walking throughout the city," Wren continued, as Mr Grigsby seemed on the verge of interjection. "I'm familiar with its by-ways and bolt-holes. I'm prepared to examine it minutely, street by street, from sun-up to sun-down. And if, Heaven forbid, my own search proves unsuccessful, I can bring our case to the Bow Street Runners—with your permission, Mr Tolhurst," he added in his most respectful tone.

"What a splendid notion, Lofthouse!" said Mr Grigsby.

Wren noted how Mr Grigsby made no mention of the fact that today was supposed to be a holiday for him—then put that disappointment from his thoughts as he fixed his attention on Tolhurst, who seemed to require another moment to turn the proposal over in his mind.

"If you were to undertake such a charge," Tolhurst said at last, his words well-measured, "I would be indebted to you, Mr Lofthouse."

"Excellent," said Wren, striding in for the door. "Then I should set off without delay."

"But to where, Lofthouse?" Mr Grigsby called after him. "It wouldn't do for us to lose you, too!"

Wren paused halfway across the threshold, his hand upon the door-latch. "I'll start in Hyde Park and work my way out from there."

Mr Grigsby looked as if he wanted to question why Wren would choose Hyde Park in particular as his starting point. Tolhurst looked as if he knew exactly why a young gentleman of means might lose himself in Hyde Park, and it came as no surprise to him that his nephew had gone astray in that particular direction—though the firm line of his mouth suggested he wished Wren wouldn't say so aloud.

Before either man could question him further, Wren shut the door on them both and ran.

Oxford Street at dawn in midwinter meant a treacherous layer of ice upon the cobblestones gaining slush with every wagon-wheel that rattled over it. Even wrapped up in scarf, gloves, and overcoat, Wren felt the chill nipping at him. He dove into the crowded fog, lurching, slipping, and sliding alongside horses and carriages alike. His legs went wholly out from under him just once, whereupon he seized a lamp-post to keep from sprawling and hauled himself upright to press on.

At last he reached Cumberland Gate. A few moments after, Achilles loomed through the fog.

And in his shadow stood Shrike.

Wren's heart leapt to see him. He'd not caught sight of Wren yet; his dark eyes remained fixed on some point in the fog beyond Wren's own vision, putting him in profile which displayed his strong jaw, high cheekbones, and noble brow to great effect, and with the hood of his cloak down, the bulk of its furred folds added to the already-impressive breadth of his shoulders. His statuesque frame seemed to outstrip the monument he stood beneath.

Yet, Wren realized as he drew nearer, Shrike did not stand, but rather leaned back to brace his shoulders against Achilles' base, his arms crossed over his chest beneath his cloak. Perhaps he had assumed a casual pose—or perhaps he felt too weak to stand under his own power. Perhaps his jaw appeared strong because he clenched it in pain.

Wren dashed to him.

This motion at last drew Shrike's attention. His dark and brooding gaze lit up with a grin, and he pushed off from the plinth to greet Wren with a warm handclasp.

"Are you all right?" Wren asked.

Shrike appeared bemused. "Well enough. And you?"

"Your wound," Wren continued, ignoring the question. "Does it pain you at all? I've brought medicine," he added, releasing Shrike's hand to dive into his satchel for the laudanum.

"A dull ache," Shrike answered him, still looking confused.

Wren halted with his hand clenched around the laudanum bottle in his bag. "Your bones broke."

"Almost a week ago, aye. They're not fully healed, I admit, but the pains are not sharp."

Wren hesitated, then dropped the laudanum back into his satchel and withdrew his hand, letting it fall to his side useless. "If you're certain."

"I am," said Shrike. Then, with a wry smile, he added, "You may see for yourself when we've returned to Blackthorn."

Wren would have liked nothing better than to strip Shrike down. Unfortunately more pressing matters demanded his attention.

Shrike knit his brow at Wren's hesitation. "What else troubles you?"

"Felix Knoll is missing."

"What is Felix Knoll?"

"A young gentleman determined to waste all the gifts life has seen fit to grant him," Wren replied before he could stop himself.

Shrike tilted his head to the side.

"One of Mr Grigsby's wards," Wren explained. "He has inherited a great sum, held in trust until he takes his degree from university and attains his majority. And he is engaged to Miss Flora, in accordance with the wishes of both their late fathers."

"What does he look like?" Shrike asked.

Wren supposed he ought to have started with that. "Blond hair, blue eyes, milky complexion. Handsome," he added, trying not to let bitterness seep into his tone.

Recognition dawned in Shrike's dark eyes. "The boy who visited your master the afternoon before we rode in the Wild Hunt."

"Yes," Wren said. Then, "How do you know that? He left well before you arrived."

"I saw him through the window."

Wren caught his counter-argument upon his tongue as he recalled something about that afternoon he'd almost forgotten. "Did you perchance strike the window?"

"The glass looked far clearer than any I'd seen in my last visit to the city," Shrike said, colour blooming in his high cheeks.

Wren wondered aloud exactly when Shrike had planned to tell him he could transform into a bird.

Shrike cleared his throat and continued. "It's unfortunate that this Felix should have golden hair. Some fae are particularly fond of that shade."

"Like yourself?" Wren heard himself ask before he could think better of it.

Shrike blinked down at him. Then he raised his hand to Wren's own chestnut locks and ran his fingers through a few strands that had evidently tumbled loose over Wren's temple, smoothing them back into place, and twining them between his fingertips.

Wren knew he ought to catch his wrist and remind him where they stood—though he could see no one near them, and surely no one could perceive them in turn through the pea soup fog that blanketed the park. His heart hammered in his chest, in fear and desire both. Yet he said nothing.

Shrike let his hand fall. "No. You?"

Wren, who'd known he asked a stupid question even as it fell out of his mouth, still felt some relief at his answer. To know magical compulsion alone was not responsible for Shrike's interest in him despite natural inclination. He replied in kind. "Not particularly. But you believe Felix's hair colour may mark him out for danger amongst the fae?"

"Perhaps," said Shrike. "If he has encountered any fae besides myself."

"I think I saw him in the Court of the Silver Wheel," Wren confessed. "Amongst the revellers during the solstice duel."

Shrike frowned. "In whose company?"

"Women," said Wren. "Blondes, mostly. Only their ears hung down like a goat's, and they danced on cloven hooves. And I think I saw a tufted tail, as well."

"Huldra," said Shrike.

Wren shot him a startled look. "Do you know them?"

"I know of them," Shrike said in a none-too-encouraging tone.

"What about them?" Wren pressed. "Are they dangerous?"

"All fae are dangerous when they wish to be." Something of Wren's frustration with so vague an answer must have shown in his features, for Shrike quickly added, "The huldra pose a peril unique to their kind. They delight in revels and never tire of them, but will continue on well past the exhaustion of other folk."

"Which must make them the most obnoxious sort of neighbours," said Wren. "But I hardly see the danger in it."

"They will dance until their partner's feet are cracked and bloodied—and then dance on. They will embrace until their lover collapses in their arms—and then abandon them. Some say they feed upon it, that to throw themselves into the throng revitalizes them even as others are drained to death. Others say the draining itself is how they draw their strength."

"A succubus," Wren concluded.

"Some are called so," Shrike admitted. "Though they come in many forms and are called many things. It's wiser to ask the individual which title they feel most suits them. The ones who appear as you described—the milkmaids with bell ears, cloven hooves, and tufted tails—are most often called huldra."

Old ballads and folk tales flickered through Wren's mind. Fae capturing mortals to exhaust and kill them with their revels was a story as old as the hills. Yet he recalled nothing about cloven hooves, which seemed a vital detail to leave out. "Are they the only fae who dance mortals to death?"

"No," said Shrike. "But they are the only fae who embrace fae to death."

"You said fae could only truly die if they lose all will to live," Wren replied uneasily.

"There comes a moment where exhaustion grows so great that one would do anything for rest—even if it meant one must rest eternally."

Wren stared at him.

"Though," Shrike added, "there are some who know what the huldra are capable of, and seek them out for the pleasure of their company."

Wren made no effort to disguise his incredulity. "The pleasure of dancing to death?"

A spark of amusement lit up Shrike's eyes. "More for the embracing than the dancing."

"Oh." Wren supposed he ought to have guessed as much. An uncomfortable suspicion likewise grew in his mind, that Shrike might have first-hand knowledge of why and how the huldra's charms proved so appealing to more adventurous fae. Wren shoved the thought to the back of his mind for the moment; it wasn't as though it were any of his business, and besides, they had more pressing matters to hand. "Whereas a mortal may not hope to survive the draining."

"Aye. Which bodes ill for the fate of your Felix."

"He's not my Felix," Wren hurried to say. "He's his own Felix. Or Miss Flora's Felix, I suppose. And Tolhurst's, and perhaps Mr Grigsby's as well."

Shrike raised an eyebrow. "And thus your master charges you with securing his Felix's return?"

"Yes," Wren replied with hesitation. "That is to say, he very much wishes for Felix's safe return, but he has no idea I might know where Felix has gone. He's only sent me out to look for him."

"And you wish for his safe return as well?" Shrike asked.

Wren levelled a considering look at Shrike. He'd spoken not in the tone of one attempting to impart moral lessons through the Socratic method, but in the tone of one who wanted to understand what the shape of such morality might look like. It did not unnerve Wren as much as he supposed it ought.

"It would serve Felix right, and solve a number of other smaller problems besides, if he got himself drained to death by faeries," Wren admitted at last.

"Yet you come to me in search of him."

The "why" went unspoken. Wren answered it anyway. "Because his absence distresses his uncle and Mr Grigsby. And more importantly, it spells Miss Flora's ruin."

Shrike cocked his head to one side in the manner of a puzzled songbird.

"Felix is her betrothed," Wren explained.

"She is fond of him?" Shrike asked.

"Whether she is fond of him or not, a missing *fiancé* would make life rather difficult for her. A broken engagement would be bad enough, but if he is missing, she must either wait for his return or risk his unexpected arrival interrupting her marriage to another man. As it is unlikely any man will want to risk the awkwardness of a possible *fiancé* returning to claim what was promised to him, she will be condemned to wait—and likely die an unhappy spinster."

"Unless we retrieve him from the huldra," Shrike concluded.

"Yes," said Wren, giving in to his conscience with great reluctance. "Could you track him the way you found me? Or the Restive Quills? Acorns and knuckle-bones?"

"I could," said Shrike. "But if you saw him in the company of huldra, then it may be quicker to go to them at once."

"You know where they are?" Wren asked, careful to keep any note of suspicion from his tone. Judging by Shrike's expression, he half-succeeded.

"I know the lands from whence they hail," Shrike admitted. "And from there, we may trace their path."

"Oh," said Wren.

A wry smile tugged at the corner of Shrike's lips. "Shall we?"

CHAPTER

SIXTEEN

Upon leaping through the fairy ring, Wren found himself in a valley of snow-drifts limned in dark pines beneath a star-studded night sky. The moonlight sparkled across the snow in a fashion which might have appealed to Wren's Romantic sense of natural beauty if he hadn't instantly sunk up to his knees in it.

Shrike stared down at him in bewilderment from an even greater height than ever before—for he had not sunk into the snow an inch. Seeing Wren's predicament, however, he at once swept his cloak off his shoulders and settled it around Wren's. It did nothing to lift Wren out of the snow, but its fur-lined depths nevertheless proved a welcome shield against the biting wind.

Wren glanced 'round, shivering beneath Shrike's cloak, his breath escaping in plumes of steam as if he were a racing locomotive. "The huldra live out here?"

"No," Shrike answered him, still appearing puzzled by Wren's sunken position. "In their brugh."

Before Wren could make further enquiries, Shrike reached down under Wren's arms and plucked him up out of the snow as if he weighed no more than a quill. He set him down at once beside him atop the snow. Wren began slowly sinking again, much to Shrike's evident confusion.

"And where is their brugh?" Wren asked with what dregs remained of his dignity.

Shrike finally tore his gaze away from Wren to consider the surrounding terrain. Silence settled around them like snowfall, broken by howling wind. Just as Wren's patience reached its breaking point, Shrike put one forefinger to his lips and with the other pointed to a pale grey spot upon the white field.

Wren squinted at the spot.

The spot hopped nearer.

As the spot approached them, further details emerged to Wren's inferior human eyes. He beheld an animal no larger than a bread-box. It had the antlers of a stag, the wings of a pheasant, and the body and head of a fluffy white rabbit.

"What," Wren whispered, "is that?"

"Wulpertinger," said Shrike, as though that were a word.

The wulpertinger continued advancing towards them. Unlike Wren, it did not sink a single inch into the snow. When it drew but a stone's throw away, it paused and sat up on its haunches. Its little black rabbit's nose twitched as it regarded them.

"There is a pocket inside my cloak," Shrike murmured so low Wren almost didn't hear him. "By your left hand."

Wren fumbled through the cloak's folds. As his numb fingers slipped through the rabbit-fur lining, he keenly felt the wulpertinger's stare upon him. He hoped the creature took no offense. Thus distracted, it took him by surprise when his hand plunged into a pocket full of notions. By touch he recognized the fortune-telling knucklebones, a thimble, several rings, a fragment of leather cord, a pair of scissors small enough to fit into his palm, and a songbird's skull, amidst a dozen other unknown oddments and ends. He wondered what, out of all of this, Shrike wanted him to pull from this tiny treasure trove. Just when he opened his lips on the verge of asking this question, his fingertips fell on something smooth and round, capped at one end and tapered at the other.

An acorn.

Wren withdrew it from the pocket and held it out to the wulpertinger. Under other circumstances he would have knelt to make his offering. At present, with himself sunken into the snow and the wulpertinger sitting atop it, he hardly had to bend forward to bow.

The wulpertinger closed the distance between them in a few gentle hops. It stretched out its neck, its wings unfurling with the strain, and took the acorn between its teeth. Then it hopped out of reach again and turned its back to munch the treat.

Wren waited, glancing at Shrike to see if this had all gone as he expected. Shrike's expression remained unreadable in its stoicism. Still, Wren took heart that he seemed neither surprised nor disappointed.

The wulpertinger began hopping away.

Shrike strode off after it. Wren struggled to forge his own path ahead through the snow. After a few paces, Shrike halted and peered 'round. When his eyes found Wren, he looked startled to see how far Wren had fallen behind. He quickly turned and made his way back to him.

The wulpertinger hopped on ahead, heedless of Wren's plight.

"Don't worry about me," said Wren as Shrike appeared ready to hoist him out of the snow again. "Let's just keep moving. I'll catch you up."

Shrike glanced behind Wren at the deep trench his shambling steps had carved in the snow, but said nothing and led on, which earned him Wren's undying gratitude.

The cloak trailed along, buoyed by the snow-drifts and doing nothing to keep warm any part of Wren below his thighs. While he could keep his arms comfortable by wrapping his hands in the furred folds and tucking them close to his chest, his toes went numb within minutes, and his shins stung with cold.

Shrike strode on, as Wren had asked him to, but hung back from the wulpertinger and more than once cast a surreptitious glance behind, as if to assure himself that Wren hadn't vanished into the snow entirely.

And though Wren's legs and nose remained bitterly cold, each backwards glance from Shrike warmed his heart.

Still, Wren felt a great deal of relief when he glanced up from his miserable trudging to find a mound had appeared on the frozen field with several streams of smoke spiralling up from it.

Where there was smoke, there must be fire, and Wren redoubled his march in the hopes of reaching it before frost-bite set in. When he opened his mouth to ask Shrike if this was the fabled brugh, the wind dove down his throat, making his lungs seize up with cold and choking him as surely as if it had closed its fist 'round his neck.

Shrike glanced back again and, realizing Wren's distress, bolted back for him. This time Wren offered no resistance as Shrike hauled him up out of the snow.

"I'm fine," Wren tried to say. It came out as a weak wheeze.

Shrike took Wren's arm and twined it with his own. "Lean on me."

His warmth had always felt welcome to Wren, but never moreso than now. It seemed a bonfire burned beneath Shrike's skin as Wren draped himself against his much taller frame. Wren basked in all the heat he could soak up through the layers of linen and wool between them and cursed the wind for robbing him of what little he could retain.

Thus, Shrike half-carried him the remaining distance to the mound, where the wulpertinger waited on its haunches, preening its feathers.

"You have our thanks, friend," Shrike said when they halted before it.

The wulpertinger scratched itself behind an ear with its hind leg, then hopped away.

Through the side of the hill.

Wren blinked. No hole had appeared, no snow had shifted. The mound appeared as smooth and unbroken as ever. He pushed off from Shrike and reached out his hand to the hillside.

It, too, passed through the snow.

Nothing wet or cold met his touch. Rather, it felt as if he held his hand before a blazing hearth. Warmth suffused his fingertips, frozen nerves searing to life. A hiss of pain escaped his clenched jaw.

Shrike caught him as he fell back. They shared a glance—Shrike concerned, Wren reassuring—then together, with Wren leaning heavily upon Shrike, they strode forth through the hillside.

Wren found himself in a mead-hall worthy of *Beowulf* and full to bursting with fae.

The cold brightness of the sunlight striking snow had vanished. Golden firelight replaced it, from the candles set into roots growing from the beams and peat overhead and from the blazing bonfire rimmed with rough-hewn stones in the centre of the hall. Scores upon scores of fae danced 'round it, casting devilish shadows on the earthen walls; Wren supposed the hall's warmth came as much from their exertion as from the bonfire. Music rang throughout the hall. The merry and curious combination of flue, fiddle, drum, and instruments unknown set a frantic pace which sang straight through Wren's heart and bid him dance. The strings in particular seemed to shriek for joy. The savoury aroma of roasting meat hung in the air, combined with the spiced-honey scent of mead flowing into drinking horns.

As Wren's sight adjusted to his surroundings, he spied the wulpertinger hopping away from him towards a cluster of fae in a particular secluded alcove of the cavern. It halted at a pair of cloven hooves peeking out from beneath the ragged hem of a patchwork gown of leather and pelts. Wren glanced up to see a strong-jawed woman with a crown of thistle and harebells nestled amidst her broad and many-pointed antlers. She sat on a throne of black walnut carved with knotwork serpents and dancing wolves. An enormous long-furred grey cat curled on her lap. The fae flanking her stood, sat, or sprawled across bearskins heaped in piles around her. Whether guards or courtiers, Wren couldn't say—they had too much mirth for the former and too many armaments for the latter.

Shrike strode past Wren to kneel before the throne. Wren followed suit. The furred folds of Shrike's cloak all but swallowed him up as he dropped to one knee.

"The Court of Hidden Folk bids the Oak King welcome," said the antlered woman.

Shrike's head shot up.

The antlered woman smiled. "Don't be so astonished. Word of your coronation has spread far beyond the Court of the Silver Wheel."

Her gaze slid towards Wren, and he realized her mottled green eyes had horizontal slits for pupils.

"My companion," Shrike said before Wren could explain himself. "Called Lofthouse."

My companion. Despite the dire circumstance, Wren's heart fluttered to hear Shrike introduce him as such.

"Well met... Lofthouse," the antlered woman said, her smile growing wryer. She returned her attention to Shrike. "To what do we owe the honour of your presence?"

"Mistress of Revels," said Shrike, bowing his head again. "We seek a mortal youth amongst your company. Blond of hair, blue of eye, bereft of courtesy."

Wren stifled a snort of laughter. Several of the guards, or courtiers, laughed outright.

The Mistress of Revels's smile became a grin, revealing twin fangs on either side of her incisors. "I believe we have such a mortal youth among us tonight. You are welcome to join our throng in search of him. We grant you our hospitality."

Shrike bowed again and thanked her. At a casual gesture of her hand, he rose. His fingertips brushed Wren's shoulder to guide him up beside him.

Wren laid a hand on Shrike's arm and summoned all his courage to step forward into the throng.

A passing faun carried an oaken cask on one shoulder to a trio of raucous revellers holding out empty drinking horns. They weren't alone. Mead and wine alike poured forth from every corner. Other fae bore upturned shields laden with roast haunches of venison, pomegranates broken open to reveal their ruby splendour, raw chunks of honeycomb golden and dripping. None of the fae serving seemed to be servants. Far from it. Those who beckoned for the feast soon turned 'round and passed it along to their fellows with their own hands. For all the motley forms around him, Wren could perceive no distinction of rank, save for the Mistress of Revels.

Nor did they feast on food and drink alone. Some of the folk made a decadent meal of each other, as well. As Wren threaded his way through the crowd, drawing ever nearer to the whirling figures dancing 'round the fire, he realized many of those on the fringes of the fray were twining arms across each other's shoulders and bestowing kisses on collars, throats, mouths—and further still. A particular pair of satyrs caught Wren's eye. One stood with his back braced against the pelt-covered earthen wall, his head thrown back and mouth agape in ecstasy. The other knelt before him and took him into his mouth.

"Do you see Felix?" Shrike asked.

Wren broke off staring. "What? No, not yet. Wait—" he added, catching sight of something over Shrike's shoulder.

A glint of gold amidst dark furs.

"There he is," Wren said, standing on his toes to bring his lips nearer to Shrike's ear. "In the corner. Do you see him?"

Shrike nodded as his eyes found where Wren dared not point.

Felix lounged on a pile of pelts by the fire. Huldra swarmed him. His coat had vanished, and his waistcoat seemed about to suffer the same fate, given the intensity with which one particularly industrious huldra tugged at its buttons. Another, not patient enough to wait for her friend to finish her work, had started in on his shirt. They already had the fall-front of his trousers open and his shirt-tails pulled out. Felix neither aided nor prohibited their efforts. His head lolled across the furs to catch the lips of still another huldra as her arms wrapped around his shoulders, his cravat lying across his collarbone in a crumpled wreck. A fourth huldra hiked up her skirts—revealing the tufted end of her tail swishing to-and-fro like a cat's—to straddle him. As she did so, she turned away from the rest of the party. No fabric lay beneath the laces of her bodice, and between the golden ribbons Wren glimpsed the cavernous hollow of her back, a dark void despite the warm fire and candle-light throughout the long-house.

Wren moved to cross the dance floor.

A huldra blocked his path. Her costume bore greater resemblance to the Mistress of Revels than to the milkmaids crawling over Felix, with her face painted with woad and her dark hair braided back. Her fearsome face split into a sharp-toothed grin. "Will you not dance, my lord?"

"No, thank you," Wren replied automatically.

Her eyes slid over to Shrike and ran him up and down, but he only shook his head.

"May we pass?" Wren asked, as she didn't seem inclined to move out of the way.

"I'm afraid not," she replied, her smile growing more mischievous. "As newcomers to our brugh, I cannot let you cross without dancing—and one cannot dance without a partner."

More huldra and other fae turned towards her as she spoke. By the time she'd finished, many had halted their pursuits to gather and gawk with intense interest at Shrike and Wren. If this unnerved Shrike, Wren found no sign of it in his stoic face. Wren, meanwhile, felt as if they could all see his pulse leaping in his throat. The heat of the so many bodied gathered so near dizzied him. He'd felt his garb insufficient for the blizzard without, but his wool suit was far too much for the orgy within.

"But how fortunate for you!" the huldra continued. "We've many eager dancers amongst us—you need only speak your preference. Or point," she added with another smirk, "if your reserve overpowers your speech."

A maiden with cloven hooves peeking out from beneath the hem of her skirt put her hand on her ample hip and cocked her head at Wren as he glanced past her. A flaming redhead with antlers growing from their temples and freckles spattered across their bare shoulders winked at him. A lithe faun with ram's horns coiled in his curls caught Wren's eye and smiled. Wren found himself mirroring the expression and, with more effort than he'd expected to expend, turned his gaze toward Shrike.

Shrike likewise glanced over the crowd of waiting dancers. His profile looked severe and handsome as ever, though Wren noted a hard swallow traveling down his throat as his eye fell on a strapping incubus.

"Butcher," said Wren.

Shrike's gaze snapped to meet his in an instant.

Wren swept the cloak out of the way with his left arm, held his right hand up to Shrike, and bowed. "Will you do me the honour of this dance?"

Gasps and whispers sprung up all around them.

Wren dared to glance up from beneath his lashes and found Shrike's grin gleaming above him.

"Aye," Shrike replied, and heartily clasped Wren's hand.

Wren used the handclasp to draw himself upright and draw Shrike flush to him, chest to chest. Whispers grew louder, interspersed with titters and hushed exclamations of frustration, amusement, and wonder. Yet none moved to stop them. Wren kept his own gaze fixed on Shrike's dark and beautiful eyes.

"Would you be willing to withdraw as I advance?" Wren asked. The feeling had just returned to his legs after trudging through the snow. He hoped their strength would soon follow.

Shrike had strength enough for two, and more besides. A shy smile crossed his handsome lips and sent flutters through Wren's heart. He nodded.

Wren took a deep breath and plunged them both into the dance.

A blue roan incubus bent his horned head over a long box-shaped fiddle laid across his lap. His dark hair fell like sheets of rain over his face as the curved bow leapt and dove between his splayed thighs. Beside him, a brawny huldra draped in furs beat a skin-drum, and a faun played pan-pipes that seemed to scream with wild joy.

Their music bore little resemblance to the tinny tepid tinkling of the piano-forte at school, where Wren had learnt the quadrille and cotillion from a rheumatic dancing master amidst a dozen other boys who made no secret of their disdain for the practice. Wren, who even then understood he enjoyed dancing with his fellows far more than he ought, had all-but-trembled with repressed elation, stumbling through steps he knew by rote rather than following the notes and rhythm of the song.

But now, in the company of satyrs and incubi, he need not hide his desires.

And to dance with Shrike was to know desire, indeed.

The damp and trembling hand of a boy had been replaced by the firm, warm grasp of a man. Shrike's fingers threaded through Wren's own, the caress of his rough palms and calloused knuckles sending sparks up Wren's arm to ignite his heart. His woodsmoke and vanilla musk lent welcome familiarity to the strange scent of their surroundings. Despite the wild throng whirling 'round them, Wren found his gaze did not stray from the dark eyes looking down into his own.

Wren abandoned any attempt at quadrille or cotillion. They hadn't enough couples joining them to accomplish either—at least, none Wren thought would know the steps—and besides, Wren had no wish to relinquish Shrike to another partner. Instead, he found himself flowing from step to step, each quicker and more daring than the last, until he whirled in a joyous tempest of his own making, and Shrike sailed through alongside.

While Shrike might have had no formal dance training, he possessed a great deal of natural grace, which more than made up for Wren's lack of the latter and abundance of the former. The frantic fiddle and shrieking pan-pipes sang through Wren, demanding he leap to meet their peaks and valleys. The ceaseless skin-drum quickened to match the feverish pulse of his own heart. The queer and unfamiliar music played on his nerves in ways the tinkling piano-forte could never imagine.

For a moment, he could even forget he'd come here to rescue the most undeserving cad in all the realms.

And yet Felix remained.

"There," Shrike murmured, glancing towards something over Wren's shoulder. His voice carried through the noise of the music and the crowd to Wren's ear like the call of a hawk over the moors.

Wren spun them both—an entirely natural movement, yet another thread in the weaving dance—and tore his gaze away from Shrike's face to look where he'd indicated with the jut of his jaw.

Felix looked not as Wren had remembered. Nor did he look quite as Wren had thought when he first glimpsed him across the mead-hall. While he wore a sanguine expression as the huldra insinuated themselves into his eager embrace, his hollow cheeks and sunken eyes belonged to a consumptive. The torn buttons of his shirt revealed not just collar-bone but breast-bone and ribs as though many months starved. Indeed, Felix almost unhinged his jaw beneath the huldra's kiss, as if he intended to swallow her whole to sate his hunger.

Some selfish impulse within Wren bade him ignore Felix's plight and dance on. But as Shrike's steps slowed, Wren let them come to a halt, and with considerable effort he forced himself to withdraw from Shrike and let him remain out of reach as they went to meet Felix.

Felix, in the midst of entertaining the huldra who straddled his hips, seemed not to notice their approach.

Wren cleared his throat. "Mr Knoll."

Felix neither opened his eyes nor disentangled his lips from the huldra.

"Mr Knoll," Wren repeated a little louder.

Felix moaned into the huldra's mouth and put his fingers around her wrist to slide her hand beneath the fall-front of his trousers.

"Felix," Wren barked.

The huldra glanced up sharp, breaking off her kiss to do so. Felix groaned and tried to pull her down again, but she held him off with one palm planted on his all-too-visible sternum..

"Your friend wants you," she said, her indefinable accent lending a husky timbre to her words.

Felix followed her line of sight to Wren. His dreamy smile dropped into a sneer. "Lofthouse. What're you doing here?"

"I could ask the same of you," Wren replied before he could stop himself. As Felix opened his mouth to retort, he quickly added, "Neither of us should be here. We're leaving. Now."

The huldra obligingly withdrew from her prey.

Felix, however, gave a half-shouldered shrug. His clavicle appeared as if it would burst through his skin like an iron bar through parchment. "Go, then. I'll not stop you."

"You're coming with us," said Wren.

Felix rolled his eyes. It seemed as if it cost him a great deal of effort to summon the strength to do so. "Make me."

Wren, who had crossed realms to retrieve the delinquent spendthrift, found himself bereft of patience. As such, he did what he had oft wanted to do in the years since Felix had come under Mr Grigsby's guardianship. His hand shot out and seized Felix by his mangled shirt-collar.

To Wren's astonishment, Felix weighed on his arm as insubstantial as a wicker poppet. He'd meant to drag him upright, yes—but he'd never expected to succeed in the attempt, having assumed Felix would prove both a literal and figurative anchor to drag him down. Yet a swift clench sufficed to bring them nose-to-nose. The fetid wine-soaked breath that poured from Felix's mouth soon gave Wren cause to regret this.

Felix, meanwhile, looked no less astonished than Wren. Yet he mounted no resistance. His head lolled against his own shoulder as his blue eyes flew wide.

"Must you take him?" one of the huldra asked, her voice languid and low in a way Wren suspected had more effect on other gentlemen.

"He makes a fine feast for us," the other huldra added, taking Felix by the wrist. "But we fear he may prove too much for mortal maidens' appetites."

Wren did not divulge how sincerely he shared their satirical concerns. Nor how much he thought Felix deserved such a fate. He wondered if perhaps this was why they'd chosen Felix in particular; perhaps something in the way Felix had approached them at the solstice duel had given offence, and this was how they chose to exact their vengeance, not only on their own behalf but on behalf of all the fairer sex.

"Regardless," Shrike rumbled overhead as Wren struggled to say, convincingly, that he truly wanted Felix returned to the mortal realm. "He is required elsewhere."

Both huldra gave Shrike an appraising look, then exchanged a speaking glance between them.

Whispers and murmurs rose up on all sides. Wren realized the music had faded off into silence. He glanced 'round and saw that those who'd danced and feasted moments before had halted all their merriment to stare back at him and Shrike. Satyrs, fauns, incubi, succubi, and huldra alike drifted towards them.

Then the sea of fae-folk parted, and through their midst came the Mistress of Revels. Seated on her throne, she'd seemed a formidable presence. Now, striding towards them, Wren realized she stood eye-to-eye with Shrike—taller, if one included her antlers—and her sleeveless gown displayed sinewy strength that put Wren's own arms to shame. She halted a single stride away from Shrike and Wren.

"Mistress," said Shrike. He gestured to Felix slumped on Wren's shoulder. "By your leave, we would bring this boy back with us to the mortal realm."

Her mottled green eyes flicked from Shrike to Wren and back again. "With what shall you ransom him, Oak King?"

"I am a leather-worker," said Shrike. "A crafter of no small skill. Armour, tack, scabbards, belts, satchels, quivers—name it, and it shall be yours, by my hand."

The Mistress of Revels tilted her head at him. "While your craft is not without its charms, we find your company more charming still. Perhaps, since you deprive us of a guest, you would yourselves return again?"

Shrike glanced to Wren. Wren, with Felix's dead weight heavy on his shoulder, gave the barest hint of a nod in reply.

"For one night," said Shrike.

"After Midsummer," added Wren.

Murmurs of intrigue rippled through the throng. Shrike shot Wren a look of knowing approval. Wren's cheeks glowed.

The Mistress of Revels smiled. "A bold promise, indeed. Though I suppose we should expect as much from the Butcher of Blackthorn."

The huldra who'd held Felix's wrist released it as if she were dropping refuse onto East End cobblestones.

"Do with him as you will my lord," she said, lowering her gaze in a manner which seemed more coy than reverent.

Shrike thanked her with a nod and slung Felix's free arm over his broad shoulders.

The crowd withdrew to carve a path through the long-house before them. Wren found himself confronted with the same wide-eyed wondrous gaze he'd cast over the throng, now returned to him a hundredfold. He fixed his own eyes above all their heads and horns to look past them towards the hide-covered passage in the hillside.

From the first step it became apparent that Felix would prove no asset to his own rescue. Whether due to his desire to remain with the huldra or due to his withered strength after so long spent in their embrace, his legs dragged across the dirt floor as Shrike and Wren strode forth. By the time they crossed the long-house, he had slumped altogether. Wren only knew he yet lived by taking out his pocket-watch and holding its crystal face up against Felix's lips to see his breath's fog on it.

"If he cannot walk," Wren began.

Shrike required no further suggestion before he seized Felix about the waist and slung him across his own shoulders like a slaughtered stag.

"That'll do," Wren said, astonishment forcing the words from his lips. "Except," he added, as he realized with no small amount of resignation what part he must take in the matter, and slipped Shrike's cloak off his own shoulders.

Whether or not Felix deserved its warmth was immaterial. He couldn't survive the frozen walk without it. Wren set his jaw and threw the cloak over Felix and Shrike alike. With the lump of Felix's body beneath it, the hem rode up to Shrike's calves, and Felix's unconscious face remained just visible over Shrike's shoulder beneath the hood.

Wren shoved his hands into his pockets and staggered forth into the biting wind.

CHAPTER

SEVENTEEN

"By Jove!" Mr Grigsby cried. "Our dear Mr Knoll!"

Wren forced a smile as Mr Grigsby all but fell over himself to make way for the motley trio to enter the office. Shrike still carried Felix on his shoulders—had carried him all the way across the snow through the wood and into the fairy circle to Hyde Park, then up Oxford Street, without a moment's rest nor a single syllable of complaint. The journey, according to Wren's pocket-watch, had taken hours. It felt like days. Night had fallen by the time they reached Staple Inn.

Mr Grigsby had evidently spent the intervening hours pacing, given the wrinkles in the rug upon their arrival and the breathless state in which he'd answered the door. A full cup of tea on his desk emitted no steam. Wren wondered how long it'd sat there, unheeded.

"Shall we take Mr Knoll upstairs, sir?" Wren asked, forcing a chipper tone. As much as he would have preferred to dump Felix onto the floor before the fire, he didn't think Mr Grigsby would agree. Nor did Wren think Felix capable of sitting upright under his own in either of the office chairs. Nothing for it but to put him to bed, and the only free bed in the office belonged to Wren.

"Yes, of course," said Mr Grigsby, indicating the stairway with an open palm. "Right this way, Mr—Mr Butcher, if I do recall correctly?"

Shrike appeared no less astonished than Wren to find Mr Grigsby had remembered his name. After a stunned silence, he replied, "Aye."

Mr Grigsby's customary smile returned, if only for a moment.

Wren led them all upstairs and unlocked the garret door. He had no time to even think of the manuscripts under the floor, much less spirit them away into his satchel. Then Shrike brought Felix in and laid him down on the bed more gently than he deserved, and Mr Grigsby rushed in after them. Wren's relief rivalled Mr Grigsby's, if only to see Shrike relieved of his burden. Shrike appeared none the worse for it save a few beads of exertion across his brow. Still, Wren thought of the awful wound, and the cracked ribs besides, all hidden beneath his tunic.

"But what has happened to him?" Mr Grigsby asked, laying his wizened hand on Felix's brow. "Where did you find him?"

"Somewhere he oughtn't have been," Wren said, which was true enough.

Mr Grigsby took in Felix's torpor and wasted appearance and formed his own conclusions. "Not opium, surely...?"

"No," Wren quickly corrected him. The last thing Felix needed was for his well-meaning guardian to shove a handful of charcoal down his throat. "No, I don't think so. Only quite exhausted. I don't think he's eaten or slept since the twenty-first."

"My word!" Mr Grigsby breathed. "Well, we have him safe at last, and will soon have him on the mend, too. Though I should like to send for Dr Hitchingham."

Wren supposed there wasn't any harm in that. "I'll go out for him straight away, sir."

"And of course Mr Tolhurst must be informed of the good news," Mr Grigsby added.

Wren, in the midst of shaking the snow out of his scarf before he wrapped it around his neck again, paused long enough to say, "I'll go on to Rochester from Dr Hitchingham's."

"And," said Mr Grigsby, turning to Shrike, "I cannot thank you enough, Mr Butcher, for your assistance in this matter."

Shrike, in the midst of settling his cloak around his own shoulders once more, paused for a moment before murmuring that it was nothing.

Wren would have liked to point out that carrying a thirteen-stone man on one's back over hill and dale through the snow and up two flights of stairs was certainly not nothing, and particularly not nothing when one was wounded.

Instead he took the task Mr Grigsby had set him as an opportunity to escape the office altogether, with Shrike by his side once more.

"Dr Hitchingham?" Shrike asked as he followed Wren out of the office to Staple Inn's courtyard.

"An old acquaintance of Mr Grigsby," Wren explained. "He bleeds his patients more often than I'd think prudent, but then again I'm not a doctor, and I don't suppose it will do Felix much harm. His chambers aren't far off from here. You don't have to come along, if you'd rather not."

Shrike halted in confusion. "Would you prefer I didn't?"

Wren stopped as well, glancing up sharp at Shrike. "What? No, of course not, I'm happy to have you along, it's just—your wound."

Shrike fixed him with a puzzled look. Almost a full week had passed since the Winter Solstice. He'd taken out the stitches days ago. The wound itself had well scabbed over, and while his cracked ribs had protested vehemently throughout his rescue of Felix, he didn't think he'd come into any danger of re-injuring himself. Still, Wren's concern touched him deeply and sent a sympathetic ache through his heart. "It's healed."

Wren didn't seem to hear him. "And you've gone so far for Felix already, and over such terrain—"

"I didn't do it for him."

Wren faltered. A blush rose in cheeks. Shrike cherished it.

"It's after dark already," Wren said when he'd collected himself. "You must be exhausted."

"Are you?" asked Shrike.

"That doesn't matter."

Shrike paused, unnerved by how casually those words left Wren's tongue. "It matters to me."

Wren appeared more surprised by that than Shrike thought warranted, though the ghost of a smile flickered across his speckled lips. "Then you understand my concern for you in turn."

"I've endured worse."

Wren did not appear comforted.

"Come," said Shrike. "Our quest is not yet ended, and I'll not abandon you before I've seen it through."

This, at last, provoked the shy smile Shrike loved so well.

They walked on. As Wren had promised, the physician's office wasn't far off from Staple Inn. Soon they stopped before a particular edifice.

Wren made for the front steps, then paused and glanced back at Shrike close behind. He looked him over from head to foot and said, "Perhaps it might be best for you to wait outside."

Shrike glanced down at his own person, taking in the garb that looked nothing like anything worn by any of the mortals they'd passed along the way. Indeed, Shrike's cloak, tunic, and hose had already caught the eye of many strangers, and his peaked and feathered cap had seemed to raise particular ire. "Aye."

Still, Wren hesitated. "Will you be all right?"

Shrike found himself smiling. He'd never had a lover worry after him so before. "I'll be fine."

Wren returned his smile and went up to the office.

Shrike folded his arms across his chest, leaned back against the wall, and settled in to wait.

Despite Wren's absence, Shrike did not wait alone. London's streets bustled with mortal undertakings long after nightfall. A lamp-lighter, doing what little he could to combat the fog, gawked at Shrike as he passed by. Shrike gawked back. A crossing-sweeper kept sneaking amused glances at him. Shrike shared their mirth. A lady in garish costume ambled past once or twice in no evident hurry and with many a lingering look over Shrike's figure. Shrike tipped his hat to her, which earned him a smile before she moved on to more lucrative hunting grounds.

Just as the office door opened and Wren stepped down into the street to rejoin him.

"What of Dr Hitchingham?" Shrike asked as Wren emerged alone from the physician's edifice.

"Dr Hitchingham will be along shortly," Wren said. "He didn't like my coming in—think he was about to close up shop for the night—but when I mentioned a young man of considerable means had collapsed from exhaustion in Mr Grigsby's office, he reversed his attitude. Though I think the mention of Felix's wealth moved him more than his symptoms."

Shrike agreed.

"Regardless," Wren continued, "he knows the way and doesn't need us to guide him, so we're free to go on to Rochester."

"Then let's be off," said Shrike when Wren made no immediate move towards setting out.

"It's thirty miles to Rochester," Wren explained after some hesitation. "Ten hours by foot."

"Ah," said Shrike.

"If we've any luck," said Wren, "we may catch a farmer's cart on its way out of town and convince them to take us along."

Shrike could tell Wren did not consider such a prospect likely. "If I may propose another solution."

"By all means," said Wren.

"I could find us a steed in the park."

The excited gleam in Wren's eyes tempered with hesitance. "Folk might look askance at two men astride a stag in Rochester."

"I could find us a horse, if you prefer."

"Could you indeed?" said Wren.

He spoke in a tone of such wonder that Shrike felt all the more determined to impress him with success.

Wren did not realize the implications of Shrike's plan until they stood together before the Horse Guards' barracks in Knightsbridge.

"When you said you could *find* a horse," he ventured in a low voice, "I believe you meant to say you could *steal* one."

Shrike appeared bemused by the distinction. "Aye."

As a gentleman, Wren ought to have objected to embarking upon criminal enterprise. Instead his pulse quickened as he developed a wry smile to match Shrike's own. "Then, by all means, lead on."

Shrike's faint blue will-o'-th'-wisp lit their creeping path through the fog. The patrol around the barracks appeared as intermittent shadows weaving through the grey. None seemed to note Shrike or Wren's presence, and small wonder, when the flickering yellow gas flames did not penetrate more than an arm's length beyond the lamp-posts.

If the stable door had any lock, Shrike's deft fingers disposed of it before Wren ever perceived it. And then they stood inside, cold wind replaced by animal warmth well-insulated with hay.

Dozens of horses stood on the straw-covered floor; most asleep, some roused by Wren and Shrike's geldings, and none particularly concerned with the ghostly light flickering over them.

Bold as anyone pleased, Shrike strode down between their lines, casting appraising glances over each horse in turn. He halted by one particular steed, sleek black like all the rest.

Wren had just begun marvelling at the ease of their passage into the cavalry barracks when the golden light of a lamp burst into the stable, banishing the pale blue spark.

Shrike dove behind a bale of hay. His tumbling appeared remarkable no less for its agility as for its occurring in total silence. Wren scrambled to follow him with far less grace.

"Who's there?" a gruff voice called. "Show yourselves!"

Wren looked to Shrike for guidance.

To his astonishment, Shrike rose and strode out to stand in the lantern's light.

The guard stood almost as tall as Shrike. He looked to be in his early thirties, with a strong chin, blue eyes, and a waxed moustache. His blue coat hung well on his broad shoulders, and his white trousers and gleaming black riding boots clung to his brawny thighs and well-turned calves. He appeared no less surprised than Wren felt to see Shrike approach. But as he held up his lantern to cast its light across Shrike's face, his shock faded into a wry smile. "Well, halloa there! Changed your mind, have you?"

"Perhaps." Shrike glanced back where Wren yet crouched in the darkness. "It depends on the opinion of my friend."

Wren supposed that was his cue and unbent his aching knees to join him in the limelight.

The guard took it well, all things considered.

"We require a steed," said Shrike.

"I'll bet you do," the guard replied with a smirk.

Wren's bewildered gaze flitted between the two of them. He knew well the reputation of the Horse Guards—and so, it seemed, did Shrike. Still, Wren thought better than to voice his confusion. Instead, he put on a lofty tone and asked Shrike, "This is the fellow of whom you spoke?"

Shrike, who'd told Wren less than nothing about any horse guard, nodded.

Wren would certainly demand the whole tale from him—but in due time. He turned to the guard. "I see you're everything he claimed and more."

The guard's smirk broadened into a grin. "That I am."

Wren decided to take a gamble. "Would you walk with me a while? I should like to know a little more of you before I give my opinion."

The guard raised his brows. "Most toffs take me or leave me."

"I'm no toff," Wren replied—which was true enough. And indeed, he'd never felt less like a gentleman than he did at this very moment.

The guard chuckled. "Come along, then."

As the guard turned to lead the way out of the stable, Wren cast a speaking glance at Shrike, hoping he understood what Wren meant to accomplish by distracting the guard. Shrike returned him the barest hint of a nod and more than a hint of a smile. Only when Wren had passed over the threshold out into the fog did he catch in the corner of his eye the blue spark of the will-o'-th'-wisp and Shrike's long shadow moving towards the horse.

The guard, his attention on the path from the barracks to Hyde Park, noticed none of it. Nor did his patrolling comrades raise any alarm as their silhouettes flitted by through the fog. Wren hardly dared breathe, much less speak, until the cobblestones beneath his boots became clipped grass and trees outnumbered lamp-posts. Shadow felt safer than light for a man of his predilections.

"Fine night," the guard remarked in a low voice as they meandered through the darkness. Fog and foliage alike muffled the city's incessant noise almost as well as the curious nook of Staple Inn.

"It is," Wren forced himself to agree. His panicked pulse had only increased its frantic pace in the interim since his discovery in the stable. He shoved his hands into his coat pockets to disguise their trembling. Untold nights he'd spent in furtive self-abuse at the thought of what a moment like this might feel like. Now it'd come upon him and he hadn't the faintest idea what to do with it.

The guard strolled along oblivious to Wren's internal torment. Or perhaps quite aware of it, but better prepared to weather a nervous wreck. After all, if one believed the Horse Guards' reputation, then Wren could hardly be the first nervous john that this particular guard had ever encountered. Wren envied him his experience and the courage required to attain it. He couldn't see much of the guard at present, save for his strapping frame, but he recalled his features from their brief introduction in the stables, and from the tone of his voice he could well imagine the handsome smile now upon them.

"What shall I call you?" Wren asked, the fae custom oddly fitting for an anonymous tryst.

"My friends call me Jack," the guard replied with casual cheer. "And yourself?"

Wren, who'd used but one pseudonym since his resignation from the Restive Quills, blurted, "Gawain."

Jack took it in stride. "Welsh?"

"On my mother's side," Wren admitted, for that much was true.

Jack seemed pleased. "What did your friend tell you of me?"

"We intend to ride out this evening," Wren said after some consideration. "He said we might find a suitable steed here."

To Wren's relief, Jack laughed. "That's one way of putting it."

Silence fell. Wren, having as little gift for conversation as for flirtation, concocted and discarded a half-dozen phrases to break it before he settled on, "Do you often find the opportunity for steeple-chasing? Or does the guard keep you too occupied for sport?"

"A man after my own heart," Jack replied, as if their talk had never lulled, and continued discoursing his opinions on racing and horse-flesh and asking after Wren's own thoughts on all matters equestrian, for some time.

The path Jack struck through the darkness twisted and turned. Wren gave up trying to keep track of where it went, trusting that Jack did not intend to murder him, and if worse came to worst the sun would rise eventually and show him where he stood. Then, as the conversation came to its natural end, the golden glow of gas-light faded through the fog, and Wren realized they'd returned to where they'd begun; in the trees on the border of the park, just behind the stables of the Knightsbridge barracks.

Jack turned to Wren with a look of wordless enquiry.

"You've been... very good company," Wren said, because he had. "I don't think we'll dally further tonight, but if my friend and I might return?"

"You might," said Jack with understandable wariness.

Wren held out his hand. Jack clasped it. His expression brightened as he felt the shillings Wren pressed into his palm. They broke off, and Jack's hand returned to his pocket in a smooth and well-practised gesture, without the slightest hint of silver in the gas-light.

"Until we meet again," said Wren.

Jack tipped his hat and vanished into the barracks.

Wren shoved his hands back into his pockets and tried very hard to look far less nervous than he felt waiting for Shrike to reappear. Minutes passed uncounted whilst he steadfastly ignored his pocket-watch.

A sparrow trilled somewhere in the darkness. Wren didn't give it much thought, until he recalled that very few sparrows remained awake past sunset. Then he whirled—which must have looked very foolish to any horse guards yet watching him—and peered into the foggy night as though he could see his hand in front of his face.

The sparrow trilled again from behind him and to the left. Wren stepped towards the noise, which brought him into a copse of trees. A will-o'-th'-wisp sparked to life not a stone's throw away, and there, illuminated by the flickering blue light cradled in his palm, stood Wren's whistling Shrike. There remained, however, neither hide nor hair of a horse in sight.

"So," said Wren, drawing near. "A horse guard."

"Forgive me," said Shrike.

Wren's heart stopped. All his worst suspicions had come true in two simple words.

Shrike continued. "I didn't expect to find a mortal in the stable at this hour. I'd have warned you otherwise. Though you contrived well upon instinct."

Wren ignored the praise. "He seemed to know you."

Shrike raised his brows. Wren could've kicked himself. He hadn't intended to sound accusatory. He wished he hadn't said anything at all.

"We met in passing beneath Achilles on Samhain," said Shrike. "He offered companionship. I declined."

Wren's heart eased as the missing pieces slotted into place. "So when he saw you in the stable, he assumed you'd changed your mind about his offer."

A small smile graced Shrike's noble mouth. "Aye."

"He didn't seem much put off by seeing me with you," Wren added.

"I'd refused him on the grounds that my heart lay in another's hands."

"Oh," said Wren.

Shrike's bashful smile increased. Wren couldn't help returning it. Only the presence of the horse guards in the barracks close by prevented Wren from kissing Shrike there and then. He satisfied the urge by clasping Shrike's hand instead. He delighted in the warmth of the weathered palm as calloused, clever fingers wove between his own.

"And the horse?" Wren asked, eager to be out of the city.

"Soon," said Shrike.

Wren knit his brow. If Shrike hadn't stolen a steed whilst Wren flirted with the guard, then he knew not how else he might have spent the time. Or why he required Wren's diversion in the first place.

Just as Wren opened his mouth to voice his doubts, a soft thumping sound came from the direction of the barracks. The noise continued, growing louder, drawing nearer, a steady rhythm one might march to.

Hoof-beats.

The thumping turned to crunching of dead twigs and leaves underfoot. Then the horse's black head emerged from the grey fog, as if formed from it. Its ears pricked up and swivelled towards Shrike. A few more hoof-beats closed the distance between them, and it butted its nose against Shrike's chest. Shrike stroked its neck whilst Wren stared.

"His name is Rainscald," Shrike told Wren, as if that explained everything. "He has agreed to carry us to Rochester for the sake of adventure."

"Right," said Wren. "Of course."

Shrike smiled and without further ado mounted their steed in a single swift leap. Impressive enough under normal circumstances. Doubly so when Rainscald wore neither saddle nor bridle. To say nothing of Shrike's injuries. Wren supposed Shrike required no tack, if the experience with the stag were any indication.

As he'd done with the stag, Shrike bent to offer Wren his hand. Wren hopped up behind him with half as much ease and far less grace, but succeeded in attaining and keeping his seat, which was more than he'd expected. He wrapped his arms around Shrike's waist and leaned his head against his shoulder, revelling in his warmth and the simple comfort of being near to him.

Then Shrike's knees clenched against Rainscald's flanks and they dashed off into the night.

CHAPTER

EIGHTEEN

The clatter of hooves over cobblestones filled Shrike's ears as Rainscald galloped away from Knightsbridge and over the Thames. Soon, however, he twisted his hands in the gelding's mane to rein him in. As Shrike did not have an enchanted bridle, spurs, whip, shoes, or saddle that might enable Rainscald to gallop thirty miles without exhaustion, it would be wiser to alternate between trotting and walking to Rochester. The thundering hoof-beats died away into a dull pattering. It grew duller still as they left the city's paving stones behind for roads of packed dirt.

The further they ventured from the city centre, the easier horse, mortal, and fae alike breathed. No longer did caustic fog burn Shrike's lungs, or iron ache weigh down his limbs. Just Wren's head against his shoulder, Wren's arms around his waist, and Wren's breaths low and steady in his ear. On any other night, nothing could have made Shrike more content. Certainly Wren had earned his rest. Yet this night demanded far more of them both.

"Wren," said Shrike.

With a groan, Wren lifted his head from Shrike's shoulder. "What?"

"Some centuries have passed since last I wandered these roads."

"Are you lost?" Wren asked in the rough voice of one not quite roused from his drowsy state.

"Not yet," Shrike admitted. "I've ridden from London to Rochester once or twice, but I've never been to Tolhurst."

Wren straightened up with a stifled yawn. "We're on the right track. But I don't know how much longer I can stay awake."

Shrike could hardly blame him after all they'd been through since yesterday. "Shall we stop and rest awhile?"

"No, we haven't the time. Talk to me."

Shrike didn't think he had words enough to fill an hour, much less a night.

"Or rather," Wren added, as the silence became telling, "keep me talking. Ask me something."

Shrike would have liked to hear Wren expound on a myriad of subjects, but one particular question had remained foremost in his mind throughout their adventure. "Why does Felix vex you so?"

"You should know," Wren replied. "You've met him."

Shrike laughed.

Wren shared his mirth, though it faded as he elaborated on his point. "I came into Mr Grigsby's employment after my father cut me off and threw me out."

The remnants of Shrike's laughter died in his throat.

"My literary-minded acquaintances formed the Restive Quills in our sophomore year," Wren continued. "We collaborated on many a foolish publication—they all as authors and myself as a sometime-author, more often illustrator to their works. Among them I had a particular friend. John Vincent. Rather more than a friend," Wren added. His words emerged in a peculiar pattern, halting and hesitant for a phrase or two, then surging forth in a rush as if he could no longer contain them. "Enough so that I produced a great many sketches of him. Portraits at first. Then more elaborate costumed poses and scenes for illustrations. And then... nude studies. And in such a position as to leave no mistake of just how close we had grown."

A silence fell. Shrike waited patiently for the tale to continue. When the silence grew tense, he realized Wren was waiting to see how he took it. He wondered if Wren expected jealousy. Shrike felt none. Likewise he wondered if Wren might ask him to pose for something similar, and why he hadn't already. Bashful, perhaps. A fond smile tugged at the corner of Shrike's mouth as he replied, "I see."

A slight sigh of relief escaped Wren's lips to ghost over Shrike's ear. "In my third year at university, I came home for Christmas and, foolishly, brought my artistic efforts along to occupy myself during what had always proved a very dreary holiday. Unfortunately my father, for the first time since I'd failed to grow up into a strapping sportsman, chose to take an interest in my work. I'd left the library for but a moment to fetch a composition I'd forgotten in my chambers. In that moment, he entered the library for the first time in over a decade. And in doing so, he saw what I'd been working on."

"Ah," Shrike said as his heart plunged into his stomach.

"Indeed. As you might well imagine, he did not see its artistic merit. He said if that was all I'd learnt at university, then he'd not pay a penny more for it. And threw me out of his household besides."

The light and sarcastic tone of Wren's retelling did not quite disguise the undercurrent of pain in his voice. It made Shrike's heart ache.

"With nowhere else to turn," Wren continued, "I recalled a distant bachelor cousin of my mother, who kept chambers in London. I walked from Norfolk to Staple Inn and threw myself on the mercies of one Mr Ephraim Grigsby, Esquire. I told him my father disapproved of my artistic ambitions, without specifying which details had proved so objectionable. Mr Grigsby, as it so happened, was extraordinarily sympathetic to my plight—far moreso than I deserved, if I may be perfectly frank—and took me on as his clerk. The Restive Quills allowed me to remain a member even after I'd been forced to withdraw from university itself. At first they lauded me for my courageous defiance. They felt delighted to create in the company of one who'd truly suffered for his art as they all wished to do. But as the years passed, they took their degrees. Then they found honest employment in banks and counting-houses and shipping firms. And little by little it happened that I remained one of the few to continue producing new works. They lost their admiration for flouting convention. I kept on until my position as an outsider amongst supposed outsiders became too apparent to ignore." Wren fell silent, then said, "Are you familiar with the tale of Gawain and the Green Knight?"

The sudden change in subject didn't give Shrike much pause. He found it more concerning to think on what great exhaustion must have made Wren's mind wander. Still, by Wren's own word, there was nothing he could do for it at present, save to keep Wren talking. "I've not heard it. Though I'm eager to hear you tell it."

Shrike could hear the smile in Wren's voice as he began. "One Christmas, the Green Knight came to Camelot and issued a challenge to all King Arthur's knights. Any knight could strike him a blow, and he would strike them the same blow back with his axe in a year and a day. Sir Gawain accepted the challenged and decapitated the Green Knight with a single stroke of his sword. However, his victory proved short-lived. The Green Knight picked up his head, set it back on his shoulders, and declared he would meet Gawain in a year and a day at the Green Chapel. I don't know how common such occurrences are in the fae realms, but here in England I can tell you most men stay down when their heads are off."

Shrike chuckled.

Wren spoke on. "Though unnerved, Gawain felt honour-bound to fulfil his vow. He spent much of the ensuing year searching in vain for some treasure or trick that might allow him to survive the coming blow from the Green Knight's axe."

Privately, Shrike thought Gawain's quest would have proved more successful by far if he'd had a Wren of his own by his side.

Wren continued his tale. "At length Gawain resolved to face his fate and turned his path towards the Green Chapel. Three days before the year and a day was up, he stumbled upon a castle. It belonged to Lord and Lady Bertilak, who welcomed him as a guest. Lord Bertilak offered Gawain a wager. For the coming three days, Lord Bertilak would go out hunting each morning and return each evening to surrender his kill to Gawain. In return, Gawain would remain in the castle and surrender to Lord Bertilak whatever he caught there. You'd think Gawain would've had his fill of wagers by then, but I digress—he accepted the lord's challenge.

"At dawn, Lord Bertilak rode out to hunt deer. Gawain waited for his return. And as he waited, Lady Bertilak approached him. She demanded he lie with her. He refused, as it would break both his chivalric oath and his duty to her lord as a guest in their castle. She replied that he was her guest as well as her husband's and to refuse her would offend them both. Caught between opposing fealties, Gawain relented and asked if a kiss would suffice. She agreed, and a kiss was shared between them.

"That evening, when Lord Bertilak returned and gave Gawain his venison, Gawain kissed him." Wren paused, adding dryly, "Perhaps you can see where in particular this tale piqued my interest."

Shrike laughed.

With a smile in his voice, Wren continued. "However, Gawain neglected to explain from whom he'd acquired the kiss, and Lord Bertilak did not ask.

"The next dawn, Lord Bertilak rode out to hunt a boar. Again, Gawain waited for his return. And again, Lady Bertilak approached him and demanded he lie with her. Gawain refused on the same grounds as before and again offered to receive her kiss instead. Lady Bertilak relented and kissed him. That evening, Lord Bertilak returned and gave Gawain the boar's head on a pike, and Gawain gave Lord Bertilak another kiss.

"On the dawn of the third day, Lord Bertilak rode out to hunt a fox. Gawain awaited his return. Lady Bertilak demanded Gawain lie with her. As before, he refused. This time, however, she offered another enticement; she would give Gawain her green gyrdel. The gyrdel, she claimed, was enchanted, and whoever wore it would survive any blow struck against them. Given what Gawain had to face at the Green Chapel on the morrow, you can imagine his temptation. Yet still he resisted her advance and would only consent to a kiss—alongside accepting her gift of the gyrdel.

"At last the morning arrived where Gawain would have to go to the Green Chapel and meet his fate. He set out alone from Castle Bertilak wearing Lady Bertilak's gyrdel beneath his tabard. But when he arrived at the Green Chapel, he found Lord Bertilak waiting there for him. And in short order Lord Bertilak revealed he'd been the Green Knight all along.

"Gawain knelt and waited to receive the Green Knight's blow. The axe blade came down on his neck—but he escaped with a mere nick of the nape. This bewildered the Green Knight. That is, until Gawain, overcome by guilt, confessed he'd taken not only kisses from his lordship's lady but her magic gyrdel as well. The Green Knight, amused rather than outraged, laughed heartily—for all this had been his design from the beginning, to teach the knights of Camelot a valuable lesson. What the deuce that lesson was supposed to be, no one's quite puzzled out in the intervening centuries since the poem was set down, but regardless, the knights of Camelot wore green sashes in remembrance of it ever after."

"Quite a story," Shrike said when the ensuing silence made it plain the tale had reached its end.

"It's not the elegant telling it ought to have," said Wren, "but thank you all the same. The poem languished in a medieval manuscript for centuries. Some five years back, Sir Frederick Madden put out a printed edition. I, being altogether mad for chivalric romance after *Le Morte d'Arthur* and *Ivanhoe,* snapped it up with my savings. I devoured it all the more greedily when I hit upon the first kiss between Gawain and Lord Bertilak. There'd been suggestions of such things in my earlier readings, the sworn comradeship between knights and all that, but never anything so set down in black-and-white as this. You can well suspect how such a tale set fire to my imagination. I illustrated what I considered the most interesting aspects of the story and brought my sketches to show off at the very next meeting of the Restive Quills."

Shrike wished he might see those illustrations for himself. But before he could express his wish aloud, Wren spoke on.

"You perceive my folly," Wren continued. "Giddy with the delight of discovery, I did not. In the privacy of a coffeehouse's back-room, I laid out my drawings. I expected they would receive, if not a warm reception, then one of polite interest, as my illustrations of my fellow members' works had gone over well in the past. But from the deafening silence of my audience, I knew I had erred."

Rainscald's ears flicked back and forth as Shrike's hands clenched in his mane.

"Vincent spoke up first," said Wren. "He declared I had missed the point of the poem entirely. It was a celebration of Courtly Love, a pure and chivalrous affection that lives in the soul rather than in the flesh. The kiss between Gawain and the Green Knight was a kiss between brothers-in-arms. To believe otherwise, one must possess a prurient mind, incapable of comprehending the sublime nature of chaste love. He bade me return to my scribbling and leave literary interpretation to those who'd actually taken a degree at university."

A hiss escaped Shrike's clenched teeth.

"When he had finished," Wren continued, "the others took up his cause. They contributed nothing novel to the argument. Merely making the same point again and again in stupider terms. I hardly heard them. All my thoughts remained fixed on Vincent. Vincent, who'd oft pressed his lips to mine in stolen moments in shadows at university. Kisses which evidently meant nothing."

Shrike couldn't fathom a man who could kiss Wren and feel naught.

"I made no mention of this aloud," Wren added. "Nor did I ask them how, if Gawain gave the lord the same kiss as the lady, why then the kiss between the lady and Gawain held the threat and promise of erotic possibility—it being such a kiss as might stand in for carnal knowledge —whilst the kiss between Gawain and the lord did not. Cowardice held my tongue. Instead I gathered my illustrations with what remained of my dignity and departed the Restive Quills forevermore. Vincent married within the year. Some among their number had already done so; many more did afterward. Fewer left off patronizing unfortunates in Whitechapel. A better man than I might pity their wives. My literary compatriots, who but five years hence were all afire to become the next Byron or Blake, now sought the domestic bliss of Dickens. Something a bachelor of my inclinations can never hope to achieve."

Shrike knew nothing of Dickens or their domestic bliss. Yet he hoped he might achieve something akin to the peace and tranquillity of hearth and home with Wren.

"But I digress," Wren continued regardless of Shrike's private musings. "There is no measure to which I might dilute myself that will make my essence palatable to society. Whereas Felix," Wren added, his words dripping with disdain, "no matter the depraved depths of his debts or vices, may count upon finding himself accepted and admired wherever he goes, simply because he fits the mould of what society thinks a gentleman ought to be. Everyone bends over backwards to grant him second chances, to shield him from the consequences of his actions—and here I am!" Wren choked out a mirthless laugh. "Rescuing him! After he spurned my efforts to sober him up and sleep off his stupor somewhere safe—he follows me to the fae realms like a sneak-thief, dishonours his *fiancée* by consorting with other women, falls prey to their trap—and just when it seems like he might receive his comeuppance, I rescue him again! And why do I do it? Because he is everything my father is, and everything I ought to be—and so the world loves him, and so I must pretend to do so as well, though I loathe him more than all the world."

Silence fell in the wake of this outburst, broken only by the steady and gentle plodding of Rainscald's hooves.

"Not that I'm bitter," Wren added dryly.

Shrike chuckled despite himself. Wren joined in after.

"Forgive me," said Wren when the dregs of mirth had subsided. "This must all seem the peak of pettiness."

"Not on your part," said Shrike.

"No?" Wren sounded surprised. Shrike couldn't account for why.

"It's an injustice," Shrike said when it became evident Wren required an explanation from him. "Your king's law is cruel and absurd. The Restive Quills are fools. And as you said before—I have met Felix and found him wanting in any admirable trait."

A bark of laughter escaped Wren.

Shrike couldn't help smiling as he replied, "I spake true."

"I know. It's just—you're the first person I've ever heard say anything of the like." A pause ensued. It lasted long enough that Shrike thought Wren might have fallen asleep after all. Then, in a voice muffled against the fur lining of Shrike's hood, Wren added, "Thank you."

Shrike hardly thought his words warranted any thanks but knew it wouldn't do any good to say so. He replied instead, "Think nothing of it."

They reached Rochester just before dawn.

"Here," Wren croaked, hoarse from a night spent in story-telling. "To the left. It's just down this way."

Shrike patted Rainscald's neck, and the gelding obligingly turned where Wren had indicated. Soon they stood in front of Tolhurst's lodgings. Wren dismounted with less grace than he would've preferred to display, his legs numbed by trudging through the snow and riding alike. Shrike swung off his perch with a dancer's poise and hastened to steady Wren on his feet.

"I'm fine," Wren said in answer to the deep furrow of concern between Shrike's brows. "Just tired."

Shrike did not appear convinced but nevertheless followed Wren up to the front door. Wren rapped the knocker. He didn't have much hope for a speedy reply, given the hour, but no sooner had he turned away to say so to Shrike than the door burst open behind him.

"Lofthouse?" Tolhurst said, glancing rapidly between Shrike and Wren. A salt-and-pepper scruff had grown over his cheeks in the hours since Wren had last seen him. The bruising beneath his eyes had deepened to match Wren's own. And, unless Wren was quite mistaken, if he had slept at all he'd done so in the very same clothes in which he'd visited Staple Inn. "Have you found him?"

"Yes," said Wren. "He's with Mr Grigsby, and Dr Hitchingham attending."

"Is he—?" Tolhurst cut himself off, seemingly unable to voice his worst fears.

"He's not well," Wren admitted, as that seemed safe enough to say. "We're prepared to bring you to him, if you're ready."

Tolhurst gave Shrike a sceptical glance.

Belatedly, Wren realized how shocking Shrike must appear to him. While Wren had long since grown accustomed to the medieval garb and imposing figure of his beloved, and Mr Grigsby would cheerfully wave off any oddity if it came with Wren's recommendation, the same could not be expected of anyone else in England.

"My associate, Mr Butcher," Wren said. "Butcher, may I present Mr Tolhurst."

"Associate?" Tolhurst echoed as he mechanically shook Shrike's hand.

"An actor by trade," Wren explained. "And one whose skills proved crucial to Mr Knoll's safe return."

Tolhurst appeared a fraction more at ease with his information. To Shrike, he said, "Then I'm honoured to make your acquaintance, sir. Now, by all means, let us go to my nephew."

Rainscald had wandered off by the time Wren, Shrike, and Tolhurst ventured out into the night. Shrike didn't seem concerned for his fate. Wren supposed the horse would find its own way back to Knightsbridge. All the better for Wren, who no longer had to explain how he and Shrike had come by the horse or how they had ridden it thirty miles with neither saddle nor bridle.

The night-mail coach had rattled into Rochester in the interim. Wren caught it in the street outside Cemetery Gate and arranged passage back into London. The ensuing ride passed in tense silence. Wren hardly felt free to speak to Shrike with Tolhurst present, and it seemed Tolhurst felt likewise disinclined to voice his own thoughts in front of Mr Grigsby's clerk's bizarre friend. Tolhurst fixed his gaze out the window, through which nothing could be seen save darkness, though it turned more and more to the sooty grey of fog the nearer the coach drew to London. His jaw clenched and unclenched. Doubtless, Wren thought, his nephew's condition preoccupied him. Mr Grigsby would have said something bright and chipper to reassure Tolhurst. Wren, who'd trudged through thigh-deep snow, scampered all over London, and stolen a horse by flirting with a soldier, without so much as a crust of bread, a sip of water, or a wink of sleep, found he had nothing more to offer. It took every ounce of self-restraint remaining just to keep himself from leaning against Shrike on the coach seat beside him.

The first inklings of dawn had just begun to filter down through the fog when the coach reached London. Never before had Wren felt so glad to see Mr Grigsby's face as when they all arrived at last in Staple Inn and the door flew open to greet them.

Mr Grigsby ushered Tolhurst upstairs to his nephew. Wren took advantage of their absence to collapse into his desk chair. Shrike strode toward him, hand outstretched. Wren stayed him with a glance—half warning, half desperation—and Shrike settled his hand on the back of Wren's chair rather than on his shoulder, where his warmth might have suffused and soothed Wren's aching muscles.

"You should go," Wren forced himself to say. "While they're distracted. Before they start asking questions."

Shrike gazed down at him a moment longer with an expression no less handsome for its mournful cast. Still, he nodded his assent and turned to go.

"Wait," Wren blurted, his exhausted mind belatedly recalling what he'd nearly forgotten.

Shrike halted, looking somewhere between confused and concerned.

But before he could enquire, Wren had already dived into his satchel and fished out the laudanum.

"It's for easing pain," Wren explained as Shrike studied the bottle. "Just a drop or two mixed into drink. Any more and it becomes deadly poison."

"Such is the way of all medicine," Shrike murmured.

Wren held it out to him. Shrike took it. His fingertips brushed Wren's knuckles. The touch sent a shiver across Wren's skin. He wanted nothing more than to reach for Shrike, to seize his cloak and drag him down into an embrace, throw his arms about his shoulders and collapse into him.

Instead, Wren dropped his hand to the arm of his chair and clenched it hard.

Shrike's eyes followed the gesture. He tucked the laudanum into the folds of his cloak and said, "Whenever you can get away..."

"I will run to you," Wren finished for him.

A faint smile tugged at the corner of Shrike's lips. "Go to Achilles. I will be there."

The thought of Shrike waiting for him night after night, when he might not arrive for weeks, only made Wren's heart ache all the more. Yet, selfish though it was, he nodded.

Shrike left.

Wren sat staring at the closed door for many minutes after. He could barely keep his eyelids open, much less crawl up out of his chair and climb the two flights of stairs to his bed to dote on the prodigal invalid with Tolhurst, Mr Grigsby, and Dr Hitchingham. Even if he'd had the strength to move, he lacked the will.

"Lofthouse!" cried Mr Grigsby.

Wren bolted upright as if struck by lightning. "Yes, sir?"

Mr Grigsby leaned into the office from the bottom of the staircase. "Splendid news—Dr Hitchingham declares our dear Mr Knoll is on the mend."

"Wonderful," Wren deadpanned.

Mr Grigsby's smile turned apologetic. "However, as Mr Knoll is quite weakened by his ordeal…"

Wren hesitated. "What exactly was Mr Knoll's ordeal, sir?"

Mr Grigsby blinked at him. "Good heavens. I thought you knew."

Wren shook his head. Far easier to lie without words.

"Well!" said Mr Grigsby. "Mr Knoll says he can recall nothing between his parting from his friends in town and waking in your bed. I suppose the only hint we might have is where he was found—where did you find him, Lofthouse?"

"Hyde Park."

Mr Grigsby's astonishment did not abate.

"We found him in a copse of trees," Wren added, thinking of the mushroom ring. "Unconscious. I don't know how long he lay there—days, possibly. It wasn't a place one could see from the path. We only stumbled across him by chance, systematically tramping over the whole park."

"By Jove," Mr Grigsby murmured.

Wren wished he did not believe the lie so readily, even if it was half-true.

"A very good thing you stumbled across him, indeed!" Mr Grigsby concluded, his satisfied smile returning. It faded a little as he continued. "But as I've said, given Mr Knoll's delicate condition, Dr Hitchingham strongly advises against moving him until his strength returns."

Wren did not realize it was possible for his blood to run any colder.

"And so," Mr Grigsby went on, "I hope you might not mind it overmuch if Mr Knoll remains in your garret until such a time as Dr Hitchingham believes him recovered enough to go to Rochester and convalesce in his uncle's household."

"Not at all, sir." The words fell from Wren's lips like stones.

In Mr Grigsby's defence, he did look very sorry about it. "We cannot thank you enough for your assistance in this matter, Lofthouse. Nor your friend—" Mr Grigsby peered around the otherwise empty office, evidently just noticing Shrike had vanished.

"Butcher had a pressing engagement," said Wren. "Though he gives Mr Knoll his best wishes for a full recovery."

"How very good of him! Please, give him my regards the very next time you see him."

Wren swore he would do so. "Will Mr Tolhurst be staying, as well?"

"Yes, at the Red Lion—though I expect most of his hours will be spent with his nephew."

Wren hadn't the funds to do likewise, even if he had the inclination. "If I may make a suggestion, sir."

Mr Grigsby bid him do so.

"Perhaps," said Wren, careful to disguise his more bitter feelings with rote adherence to etiquette, "if it would not prove inconvenient to you, I might find lodging with a friend in the city until Mr Knoll is well enough to go with his uncle."

"What a splendid notion!" said Mr Grigsby, as Wren had known he would. "Yes, that would do nicely, I think."

Wren managed a faint smile. "Is there anything else you require of me, sir?"

"Nothing particular, Lofthouse," Mr Grigsby said, raising Wren's hopes only to dash them in the next instant by adding, "Only, mind the office while I see to Mr Knoll."

"With pleasure, sir," Wren forced out.

Mr Grigsby smiled and vanished away upstairs again.

Wren stretched out an aching arm towards a random ledger to throw open across his desk whilst he tried very hard not to think about how not only Felix, but Tolhurst, Dr Hitchingham, and Mr Grigsby himself now lurked over his most incriminating manuscripts and would continue to do so for the foreseeable future. He hadn't the concentration to do more than stare down at the blurred and warping columns of accounts laid out before him. Twelve hours passed by in this aimless pursuit, interrupted on occasion by Mr Grigsby popping downstairs to ask Wren to run a script over to the chemist or to carry a message to Dr Hitchingham's household or to order and retrieve dinner from the Red Lion. Wren accomplished all this in a dull haze not unlike the fog hanging over the whole city. Only the chime of eight o' clock roused him from his stupor.

"If you've quite finished with me, sir," Wren said, hat and coat already donned and one hand upon the latch.

Mr Grigsby replied in the affirmative and had hardly got out his good-night before Wren all-but-fell through the door and down the stair into the foggy night.

Whilst his heart wished to run, his exhausted legs staggered and stumbled over the cobblestones of Oxford Street. Every step burned as if he dragged his boots through molten lead. Still, he told himself, every step brought him nearer to Cumberland Gate. Then, nearer to Achilles. And then, at last arriving, he beheld the familiar long shadow, the feathered hat, the furred hood, and the noble profile of his own dear Shrike.

Wren collapsed—not into Shrike's arms as he so desperately yearned to, but against the plinth. He waved off Shrike, who'd moved as if to catch him. Shrike halted just short of doing so. Between the fog and the darkness, Wren could perceive little of his expression, but his silhouette moved with the hesitation of grave concern.

"I'm fine," Wren said, though the words emerged muffled. "We'd best be off—there's nothing to do be done for it in London."

Shrike waited with an air of worried anticipation as Wren dragged himself upright and pushed off toward the mushroom ring. Even in the dark, by now Wren knew the path as well as if it were carved into his heart. Shrike fell into step beside him.

The very instant Wren passed through the ring, Shrike fell upon him. The furred cloak swept off Shrike's shoulders and onto Wren's. Shrike's arms swiftly followed, wrapping around Wren in an embraced that warmed his body alongside his heart and lifted him from his slumped and shambling posture, and began half-carrying Wren through the wood.

Wren felt as though he ought to protest on behalf of his dignity, if nothing else, but found he lacked the strength to do more than insinuate himself further into Shrike's grasp. He let his eyes fall shut and leaned against Shrike's warm bulk to keep himself upright. His legs staggered mechanically along with Shrike's stronger strides—though, Wren noted even through the fog of exhaustion in his mind, Shrike seemed to take much shorter steps than his long legs would otherwise make.

The wintry wood proved not quite so cold as the realm of the huldra, but colder than London, and it seeped through Wren's boots and trousers to rob him of his strength. He knew not how long they walked. Then, all at once, warmth washed over him, and he opened his eyes to find himself in Blackthorn's cottage, with Shrike lowering him to the bed.

Wren, conscious of London's soot and slush on his clothes, attempted to protest.

Shrike shushed him—gently—and went to shut the door.

Wren struggled upright and fumbled at his waistcoat buttons with fingers that could no longer feel. The hearth-fire crackled as Shrike rekindled it. Then Shrike himself returned and deftly slid his hands beneath Wren's to do what Wren could not.

With a defeated sigh, Wren let his arms drop limp to his sides, moving only as needed to assist Shrike in withdrawing limbs from sleeves. Every layer removed seemed to take some of the cold with it, until Shrike had him down to his small-clothes—and then out of those, as well. Wren shivered, but not for long, as Shrike drew the furs over him. Then, after a moment's parting, which Wren protested with a feeble mutter, Shrike returned to sleep beneath the furs beside Wren, as naked as himself.

Shrike curled his body around Wren, his chest flush against Wren's back, his heartbeat reverberating through Wren's own ribcage, their legs entangling as he pressed his lips to the nape of Wren's neck. Wren would have liked to roll over and make good use of their mutual nakedness, but all too soon the sleep he'd put off for so long washed over him.

Some hours later, Wren opened his eyes to sunshine streaming through the high round window and Shrike's arms enfolding him still.

"Good morrow," Shrike murmured into his ear, a delicious rumble that left Wren hungry for more.

Wren twisted 'round to claim his mouth in a kiss. As their thighs tangled together, he felt Shrike rise to still greater wakefulness against him. He slipped a hand down between them to take both cocks in his fist. With Shrike's lips on his collar and throat, it took mere moments to bring them both to bliss. Wren collapsed against Shrike's broad chest in complete contentment.

Shrike stroked stray locks of hair back from his brow and rumbled something low over his head.

Wren raised his gaze to meet him. "What?"

A shy smile of soft wonder played across Shrike's handsome features. "A brugh full of huldra, and still you chose me."

Wren found himself smiling in return. "Quite a feather in your cap, that."

Shrike laughed.

Emboldened, Wren voiced a question that had shadowed the back of his mind ever since they'd entered the fae mead-hall.

"The male huldra. The... huldrus?" Wren guessed.

Bemused, Shrike gently corrected him. "Huldrekall."

"Yes. Huldrekall." Funnily enough, the pronunciation wasn't the most difficult part of the question Wren wished to pose. "Have you ever... embraced one?"

The bemused smile faded somewhat. "Sometimes. After Wild Hunts. Not often, and not recently."

Wren swallowed hard. "Would you care to do so again?"

Shrike raised his brows. "Would you?"

"I asked you first."

Shrike gazed down at him as if he could read his thoughts if only he considered them long enough. At length, he replied, "Not without you."

Relief forced a laugh out of Wren. "Same answer."

Shrike returned his mirth and added an embrace of his own besides, to which Wren submitted gladly.

CHAPTER
NINETEEN

Felix remained in Wren's garret for the rest of December and the entire month of January.

As one might imagine, this circumstance gave Wren no small measure of irritation. For one, to have his sanctuary invaded and occupied by his greatest foe would provoke simmering rage in any man. For another, having Felix, Tolhurst, Mr Grigsby, and Dr Hitchingham lingering above his most indecent manuscripts, perpetually on the brink of discovery, did nothing to soothe Wren's constant anxiety.

On the few occasions Wren did go up to see to the patient—never of his own accord, but at the request of Mr Grigsby or Tolhurst—he didn't dare so much as glance at the floorboards, much less the particular hollow beneath his bed. He reminded himself that none of the gentlemen would have any reason to search the room. Felix could not even raise himself up on his elbows; crawling under the bed must prove quite beyond his strength. And the other gentlemen were too preoccupied with the invalid to investigate their surroundings.

However, Felix's presence in his bed did give Wren the perfect excuse to spend every single night from the end of December to the beginning of February in a fairy-tale cottage with his handsome and affectionate lover, which made it somewhat easier for Wren to keep his complaints to himself when he returned to the office each morning.

On one particular afternoon, as Wren brought the tea-tray upstairs for the invalid, he overheard Tolhurst speaking with Mr Grigsby. Rather than burst into the garret and interrupt their conversation, Wren waited in silence in the stairway, the tea-tray weighing heavier and heavier on his arms with every passing moment. Though Dr Hitchingham ordered the door kept shut, lest an errant draught do the invalid an ill turn, the wood proved not so thick as to prevent Wren from catching what words passed between his employer and the invalid's uncle.

"...visit his friends in the city often?" Tolhurst asked.

"Oh, yes!" Mr Grigsby replied. "Lofthouse has a wide circle of acquaintance, and they meet quite regularly."

"In the evening?" Tolhurst continued.

Mr Grigsby chuckled. "I'm afraid poor Lofthouse has few other hours to himself in my employ."

"In Hyde Park?" Tolhurst pressed.

It took Wren a great deal of self-command to not drop the tea-tray.

"Of all the parks," said Mr Grigsby, "it is the most convenient to Staple Inn."

Tolhurst hesitated.

Wren held his breath.

"Is Mr Lofthouse," Tolhurst said, drawing out the words with uncertainty, "perhaps, a Chartist?"

Wren indulged in a silent and full-bodied sigh of relief.

Mr Grigsby laughed. "Bless me, Mr Tolhurst, I've never asked him!"

As Tolhurst then deftly turned the conversation towards punting, Wren deemed it safe at last to open the door and interrupt them.

On another afternoon, whereupon Mr Grigsby had to visit Rochester to reassure Miss Flora of her *fiancé*'s imminent recovery, Dr Hitchingham had to minister to another patient, and Tolhurst had to see to other business in the city, it fell to Wren to attend the invalid. Felix had not yet awoken when the last of these gentlemen departed at half-past noon.

Not knowing when Felix would awaken or the gentlemen would return, Wren wasted another quarter-hour attempting to gather the courage to crawl under his bed and retrieve his manuscripts. He'd just bent to one knee to peer beneath the bed-frame when Felix groaned.

Wren leapt to his feet, grabbed *Ivanhoe* off his desk, and fell back into his chair to adopt a lounging pose of indifference. His unseeing eyes flew back and forth across the page in a parody of reading.

Felix grumbled, smacked his lips, lolled his head across the pillow, and at last opened his eyes. Wren watched all this in his peripheral vision, only raising his gaze from the book when Felix yawned and struggled up onto his elbows.

Wren snapped his book shut. "Good morning, sir."

"Where's my uncle?" Felix demanded in an insolent drawl.

In a voice dulled by disinterest, Wren replied, "He had an appointment elsewhere in the city. We expect him back in time for tea."

"An appointment? Is that what he told you?"

Rather than point out no one had told him anything, but had left it to each other to pass on to him over his head, Wren said nothing.

Felix continued on without him. "Don't suppose he said with whom?"

"No," Wren answered in perfect honesty.

Felix didn't seem surprised. "Gone to meet Woodbridge, I expect. A dear friend of his, old Woodbridge."

Wren neither recognized the name nor had any comment on the observation.

"Grigsby out as well?" Felix asked.

"Mr Grigsby has gone to inform Miss Flora that you are out of danger."

"And the doctor?"

"Has other patients."

This last remarked veered near enough to insolence to make Felix narrow his eyes. "What did you tell Grigsby about where you'd found me?"

Wren had dreaded this. He almost didn't want to know how much, if anything, Felix remembered of his adventures in the fae realms. "I told him I found you in Hyde Park."

"I suppose that's true enough," Felix muttered. "For him, at least. No doubt my uncle's already guessed the truth."

"The truth?" Wren echoed before he could stop himself.

"Oh, he's well familiar with my habits," Felix replied airily.

Wren doubted Tolhurst had much familiarity with the huldra, but said nothing.

Felix heaved a sigh. "I suppose I ought to thank you for rescuing me from that nunnery."

Wren stared at him. He couldn't tell if Felix had built upon his own lie, or if the young man genuinely believed he'd been saved from a mere mortal brothel. If Felix remembered nothing, far be it from Wren to remind him. But if Felix remembered everything, then Wren didn't think he could stand it. The fae realms had become his haven from the worst aspects of English society—Felix included. And if Felix knew, then he might tell others. Or hold the threat of telling others over Wren's head. Wren had expected blackmail to befall him for most of his adult life. Still, being blackmailed specifically regarding the fae was certainly a novel fear.

Wren didn't dare ask Felix anything outright, lest he show his hand, or worse yet, trigger the full recollection. In a carefully indifferent voice, he remarked, "And I suppose you've learnt your lesson."

Felix gave a derisive snort. "What's for breakfast?"

Wren supposed reformation had been rather too much to hope for. He set about making tea and toast for the invalid—about which Felix had many complaints, until Wren pointed out that the only alternative, under doctor's orders, was beef tea. This didn't shut Felix up by any means, but it did convince him to clear his plate.

After breakfast he asked for a newspaper. Wren gave him Mr Grigsby's copy of the *Times*. Felix then promptly fell asleep with it open over his face.

Wren spent another quarter-hour watching him, marking his deep and steady breaths for any change which might indicate a return to wakefulness. When nothing of the like occurred, and Felix seemed only more asleep than ever before, Wren dropped to his knees and crawled under his bed. With one leg still protruding out into the room behind him, he worked his pen-knife out of his waistcoat pocket to pry up the loose floorboard.

Then the door creaked open.

"Lofthouse?"

Wren jerked up and banged his head against the underside of the bed-frame. He bit back an oath and scrambled out from beneath the bed still clutching his pen-knife.

Mr Grigsby stood on the threshold. From behind him Miss Flora peered over his left shoulder into the room, whilst Tolhurst took the right. Three pairs of eyes fixed expressions of mixed confusion and incredulity on Wren, lingering on his dusty knees and elbows.

"Forgive me, sir," Wren forced out, though all his worst anxieties had come to roost in his garret. Holding up the article in question, he added, "I dropped my pen-knife and it slid under the bed."

Mr Grigsby appeared bemused. Miss Flora looked indifferent. And Tolhurst wore an aspect of unmistakable disapproval.

This last in particular riled up Wren's indignation. He stood in his own damned room, after all, which he'd given up to the ingrate invalid without complaint. He had every right to crawl into whichever corners of it he damned well pleased. But, mindful of his position and his cowardice alike, he bit his tongue.

"And how fares our dear Mr Knoll?" asked Mr Grigsby, stepping into the garret.

Mr Grigsby's entrance allowed both Miss Flora and Tolhurst to come in as well, with Tolhurst slipping past him and Wren alike to reach Felix's bedside.

Wren glanced back at the invalid, who through some miracle slumbered on despite the absurd circumstances. "Quite well, sir. Very peaceful. He woke up soon after you left and took his breakfast before dropping off again."

"Splendid," said Mr Grigsby. "Then you may leave him in the tender care of Mr Tolhurst and Miss Fairfield. Come along, Lofthouse."

So saying, Mr Grigsby turned to go out again. But before he could take one step down the stair, Miss Flora's voice rang out clear as church-bells.

"If it pleases you, sir, I'd like to request that Mr Lofthouse remain for a moment. I have some particular questions for him regarding Felix's rescue."

Mr Grigsby appeared no less bewildered by this announcement. Tolhurst looked almost as perturbed as Wren felt.

Yet, as Mr Grigsby's creature, Wren could reply in no other way but, "Of course, Miss Fairfield."

And so Mr Grigsby went downstairs alone.

Wren pulled his desk chair back into place so Miss Flora might take her ease at her betrothed's bedside. She thanked him and sat down. Then, as Tolhurst stepped forward to stand by her, she beckoned Wren closer in his stead. Wren shot Tolhurst an apologetic glance and went to meet her—against his better judgment. He'd dreaded this interrogation from the moment Mr Grigsby declared Felix must stay in his garret. Mr Grigsby might believe any wild tale Wren chose to tell him, but Miss Flora, in Wren's short acquaintance with her, had given him a far more canny impression. To say nothing of Tolhurst's suspicions already raised against him.

Miss Flora kept her gaze on Felix's sleeping face as she asked, "Where did you find him?"

"In Hyde Park," Wren answered. He caught Tolhurst's look of alarm in the corner of his eye, but ignored it. While a gentleman might understand the connotations of such a place, a young lady of Miss Flora's breeding would not.

Indeed, Miss Flora seemed hardly perturbed. "And what became of him to reduce him to this state?"

"I must confess I know not," Wren lied. More truthfully, he added, "Dr Hitchingham believes that, after his friends abandoned him, he became lost in the fog. In attempting to reach Staple Inn and take refuge with Mr Grigsby, he wandered by accident into Hyde Park. It was a very cold night. Hypothermia brings on grave confusion and eventually drags its victims down into a deep sleep. In such a trance, and exposed to the elements for three days, the cold consumed him and left him in the condition you now see before you."

The story had so many holes that it more resembled a fisherman's net than a tightly woven narrative. Miss Flora might prick her needle into any one of them and unravel the whole.

Yet, to Wren's growing astonishment, she did not. Instead she asked him when he thought Felix might be well (not for some weeks yet), how often he had awoken (once or twice a day but not for very long), whether he had ever asked after her (several times, according to Mr Grigsby—and while Wren had never heard it himself, he didn't think it pertinent for Miss Flora to know that), and if he would be well enough to marry in June as they'd planned (on this point, Wren demurred).

Each question came more tepid and toothless than the last. Not once did she look at Wren whilst he answered. At first she kept her eyes on Felix's face. Then, as the interview continued, her gaze drifted away across the room towards Tolhurst.

Tolhurst, meanwhile, had kept his attention fixed on her.

Wren wouldn't have noticed under normal circumstances. Standing between the two of them, however, he could hardly avoid it. It seemed as if Tolhurst's eyes burned into him in their efforts to reach her.

But her answering glances remained hard and cold.

At length, Miss Flora announced her curiosity satisfied. Wren bowed and turned to go. Then, to the surprise of Wren and Tolhurst both, she rose from her seat to follow him.

"I'm sure I do the invalid more ill than good by chattering over him," she explained in response to their mutual curiosity. "Pray don't trouble yourself, Mr Tolhurst—my guardian is more than capable of arranging my return to Rochester."

Indeed, he was. And throughout the remaining weeks, Miss Flora never returned to visit her betrothed in Staple Inn.

And on the very last day of January—not a minute too soon, by Wren's reckoning—Dr Hitchingham declared Felix had progressed from an invalid state to convalescence and could remove to his uncle's rooms in Rochester without fear of relapse.

The first of February fell on a Saturday, which for Wren meant a half-day's work before he could escape to Hyde Park and realms beyond. Tolhurst and Mr Grigsby waited until Felix roused himself at half-past ten, then bundled him up and piled all three gentlemen into a hired coach to bring him to Rochester.

The instant the coach pulled out of Staple Inn, Wren dropped his smile and his waving hand alike to sprint upstairs to his garret. His heart hammered as he threw himself under the bed.

The loose floorboard had fallen pried-up beside its proper place, the hollow beneath it an empty void.

SPRING

CHAPTER
TWENTY

Wren stared into the empty void where his life's work had once lain.

A similar void opened in his chest. Just a tear at first, a single broken thread in the weave of his soul, but rapidly unravelling into a gaping crevasse into which all certainties capsized and were lost.

Wren plunged his arm into the floor up to the elbow. His fingernails scraped against the bare wood in a desperate grab for all that wasn't there. He probed every corner, every crack, hoping against hope the pages had somehow slipped between the floorboards and fallen out of sight.

He hoped in vain.

Wren lurched to his feet, cracking his skull against the bed-frame as he went. A glance over the garret showed him nothing. His fingers shook at his sides with a horrible prickling sensation that crept up his arms to the nape of his neck. In desperation he shoved his hands beneath the mattress and flipped it over onto the floor. No pages fluttered down alongside it. Not even when he tore the bedclothes off and tossed them. His desk likewise held nothing save what inconsequential papers he'd locked into it himself. The drawers pulled out and thrown to the floor had no manuscripts hidden behind or beneath where they'd lain. No book he opened and shook out let fall any pages that did not belong to it. He tossed them all aside as well and stood staring at the wreckage he'd made. His breath came hard, and his heart hammered at his throat and pounded in his ears fit to burst his skull.

His manuscripts were gone. All of them—gone.

And any of the five people who'd been in his garret in the last month could have taken them.

The thought that Mr Grigsby might have discovered them gave Wren a faint spark of hope at first—only for rational thought to smother it an instant after. If Mr Grigsby had at last found Wren's body of creative work after so many years of earnest enquiry, Wren would be the first to hear of it. The brilliance of Mr Grigsby's initial delight would be matched only by the depths of despair that would descend on him when he actually examined the contents and realized what manner of wretched creature he'd harboured all these years. As Wren had heard nothing from Mr Grigsby on the matter, it could not be Mr Grigsby who had his manuscripts.

Besides, given his rheumatism, Wren very much doubted Mr Grigsby could crawl beneath the bed to find them in the first place. Dr Hitchingham likewise lacked both the agility required to discover the manuscripts and any motive to seek them out. He hadn't even been present when Wren had been caught out crawling under the bed with poor excuses.

Which left Felix, Tolhurst, and Miss Flora.

Felix had not left the garret since his arrival at the end of December. When his strength had returned, sheer ennui might have prompted him to search the room for something, anything, to occupy his mind. And the manuscripts beneath the floorboards would certainly have given him a great deal to think over.

Tolhurst had spent almost as much time in the garret as Felix. Miss Flora had visited the garret only once, but in that short time she—alongside Tolhurst and Mr Grigsby—had witnessed Wren himself sprawled half-under the bed in a posture which could not appear anything short of suspicious. Perhaps enough so to arouse even her curiosity.

And all three of these persons were either on their way to Rochester or waiting there already.

Wren stared at the wreckage he'd made of his garret. Then a second whirlwind ensued as he whipped it back into some passing semblance of order. The mantle-clock struck twelve as he dashed down the stairs and out of the office altogether.

Not since before the Winter Solstice had Shrike taken up his post beneath Achilles during daylight hours. It didn't make much difference. Despite the lengthening of days as the Silver Wheel turned toward the Vernal Equinox, patches of snow yet covered the grass of Hyde Park, and precious little sunshine filtered down through the thick blanket of eternal fog. The most prominent change came in the form of the mortals passing by. Glove-covered gasps and stark stares replaced the subtle sidelong appreciation of twilight glances. Shrike smirked at some and, at the gawking of one particularly boggled young lady, touched the brim of his hat. He took offense at none. Only one mortal's opinion mattered to Shrike.

And that very mortal approached him now.

A spark of delight ignited in Shrike's chest at the sight of Wren dashing toward him. But as Wren drew nearer, that delight turned to cold dread.

Wren did not run with eagerness to meet him.

He ran as if pursued.

Mid-stride, wind whipped the hat from his head. Despite the evident shock of on-lookers, he made no move to snatch it from the air as it fell, nor to chase after and retrieve it. He seemed not to notice it had gone at all. His sweat-streaked chestnut locks flew like moulting feathers in the breeze. His already-pale face had turned a sickly milk-white beneath the scattered freckles. Every panicked gasp bared his teeth. His eyes rolled white like a hart ridden down by the Wild Hunt.

Shrike knew such a look well. He saw it often enough in the eyes of quarry he himself had slain.

Beneath the folds of his cloak, Shrike dropped a hand to the hilt of his misericord. It would fly from its sheath in an instant. Another blink would see it in the throat of whoever dared threaten his Wren.

But first, he would see Wren to safety.

On instinct, Shrike reached to catch Wren as he stumbled to a halt before him.

Wren darted out of his grasp. It seemed as though he would bash himself against the statue's plinth—then he threw out his hands and struck the stone with his palms instead.

Too late, Shrike recalled how the mortals of London viewed intimate touch between men. Against his wont, he forced his hands to retreat beneath his cloak, rather than throw it over Wren's shoulders and whisk him away to the haven of Blackthorn. He could only watch, helpless, as Wren shuddered and gasped to catch his breath.

"What pursues you?" Shrike asked, keeping his voice low lest whatever harried Wren might overhear.

"What?" Wren blinked up at him in confusion, his eyes yet wide with terror. "No, nothing pursues me."

"Then why—"

"My manuscripts. They've gone missing. Stolen from my garret."

The horror of this struck Shrike like a lance through his chest. Not just the danger to Wren, but the tragedy of losing his life's work. More than anything, he wanted to embrace Wren and shield him from peril. Yet he could not.

"By whom?" Shrike asked, a certain suspicion in mind already.

"Felix," Wren snarled with a violence that surprised Shrike, though the name itself did not. In more subdued tones, Wren added, "Or Tolhurst. Or Miss Flora. One of the three has taken them, and I know not which."

Having met Felix and Tolhurst, however briefly, Shrike reasoned he could dispatch them without much effort. He could take both of them on at once if it came down to it. Miss Flora remained an unknown quantity, but Shrike felt no aversion to making the attempt on Wren's behalf.

"But," Wren continued, oblivious to Shrike's resolve, "I know where they must have hidden them—to a point. We must get to Rochester without delay. Miss Flora is there already, and Felix and Tolhurst are on their way. We need Rainscald—"

"No," said Shrike. Even at a breakneck gallop, no mortal horse could suffice.

Fresh horror dawned in Wren's eyes. It vanished an instant after beneath the stoic mask he wore in London, but not before the sight struck another blow to Shrike's heart. "Some other horse, then, or—"

Shrike hastened to explain. "There may yet be a faster way."

The fear fell away from Wren's features. Granite resolve remained. "Then by all means guide me to it."

First, Shrike went to where Wren's hat still lay, having rolled some distance off the path. Handing it back to Wren was not the same as laying a hand on his shoulder, but it was as close as he might come to comfort whilst they remained in London.

Then they were off to the toadstool ring.

Shrike did not run, but his long legs carried him further with every stride than many of the mortals ambling past. Wren had to trot beside to keep pace. Yet he made not a whisper of complaint, and as Shrike glanced down to see how he fared, he found his sharp jaw set in grim determination.

Rochester had changed much in the intervening centuries, but from Shrike's brief sojourn there in midwinter, he had found it not yet so iron-choked as London. What he would attempt would pain him, yes, but it was nothing to what Wren suffered now. And Shrike would hap'ly endure far worse if it spared his Wren from further harm.

They reached the toadstool ring in the secluded copse. Shrike halted before it and held out his upraised palm to Wren.

Wren's eyes darted 'round—though Shrike knew they remained unnoticed by the other mortals in the park—before he dared to grasp Shrike's hand.

And Shrike pulled them both down into the ring.

Traveling between the fae realms, or even the fae and mortal realms, in Shrike's experience, was a simple matter of following the natural currents of the boundless ocean and drifting downstream to one's destination.

Navigating the realm between realms from London to Rochester, one choked with iron and the other well on its way to the same fate, was not quite so straight-forward.

Rather than slipping smoothly amidst warm and gentle waves, Shrike plunged through ice into frigid depths. The shock of cold drove the breath from his body, and though he did not need it, he felt the want of it keenly, his lungs starving for air he could not gather. His flesh numbed, then froze, then burned. Fish-hook snares of broken ethereal ice tore him open as he clawed his way through, fighting against the current, drowning in total darkness.

Yet amidst the fathomless void of the icy sea, a point of warmth and familiarity remained to anchor him.

Wren's hand clasped in his own.

As his flailing limbs struck a barrier, Shrike knew it would lead to his salvation. He drew back his fist and struck it. It spider-webbed beneath his raw knuckles and shattered. Shrike plunged his arm through the hole, breaking off larger and larger pieces, widening it enough to fit his shoulder, then his chest, then the whole of him, pulling Wren through after.

All at once the waves broke over his face and he gasped the iron-tinged air of Rochester.

The stone rim of a well loomed above him. He threw his arm out to grasp its edge and haul himself and Wren both out. Wren seemed to come alive in his grasp and scrambled up with admirable agility for a mortal. Shrike followed, ready to catch him if he should fall.

He needn't have worried. Wren landed on his feet.

Shrike, meanwhile, did not leap over the rim as he intended, but rather collapsed onto the dirt beside it, the back of his skull thudding against the outer wall of the well.

Shrike and Wren had both emerged dry as dust despite the water rippling in the well below. Nor had any ethereal injuries followed Shrike into the mortal realm. Still, his head swam. His raw throat drew ragged breaths. An ache had bloomed deep within his bones and threatened to make his limbs tremble. He forced his eyes to focus on his surroundings.

He found himself in a stable-yard, bereft of mortals apart from Wren. A few scattered horses stood about munching hay and gazing over them both with disinterest. The sun shone brighter than it had in London. Even so, Shrike could tell its position remained unchanged. Scarcely a blink had passed whilst he struggled to drag them both through the portal. It had felt like eons.

Shrike looked to Wren to see how he fared. Mortal, and unused to journeying between the realms, it could hardly have been easy for him.

Yet Wren appeared not half so harrowed as Shrike felt. He gazed down at Shrike with a perplexed expression.

"Are you all right?" Shrike rasped.

Wren stared at him. "Are *you*?"

"Aye," Shrike lied. The resilience of mortals in the face of iron never ceased to amaze him. With Wren's example before him, he could hardly do less. He braced his trembling palms against the well and struggled to shove himself upright.

Wren hastened to his side. His soft hands proved their strength as he grasped Shrike's forearms and hauled him to his feet.

Shrike clutched the rim of the well and gathered his breath. Dark spots flitted in the corners of his eyes. His legs, not quite recovered from the numb shock of the journey, burst into pins-and-needles beneath him. Still, he stood.

As quickly as he'd approached when Shrike first faltered, Wren retreated an arm's-length away—the customary distance between them whenever they met in the mortal realm. The pained expression on his handsome features suggested it cost him a great deal to do so.

"I'm all right," Shrike assured him. "Let's be off."

Wren didn't look as though he believed him but set his jaw regardless.

The path out of the stable-yard led into a quiet by-street. Once Shrike had overcome the initial shock of his arrival, he found it easier to breathe in Rochester than in London. A smaller town with fewer mortals meant far less iron surrounded him.

Yet despite how few mortals wandered Rochester's roads, Shrike caught far more astonished glances from those he passed.

Shrike supposed it better the strangers fixed their gaze on him rather than on Wren. If their memories filled with Shrike's striking appearance, they would hardly recall the comparatively plain figure of Wren beside him. Thus, Wren might pass almost unnoticed in Shrike's shadow. All the better for the surreptitious work yet before them.

Meanwhile Shrike could not keep his own gaze from returning again and again to Wren. Not just for the simple pleasure of gazing at Wren's beautiful bespeckled face. Wren did not meet his gaze, nor the gaping gawk of any of those who stared as Shrike passed by. Yet Shrike noted how again and again Wren stretched his fingers at his sides to prevent their forming into fists. Shrike could almost feel the nervous energy sparking off his small form.

Wren's determined march kept up a pace that Shrike, his long stride hindered by his weakened state, found difficult to match. The cathedral steeple loomed over the town and drew closer and closer with every step. Then they turned a corner and came to High Street, where Cemetery Gate arched astride the road.

"Tolhurst first, then Miss Flora," Wren explained, though Shrike had never intended to question him.

At Shrike's nod, Wren trotted ahead to the door in the southern leg of the arch. He paused on the step and glanced surreptitiously up and down the street.

"Shall I keep watch?" Shrike murmured, having caught him up by then and shielding him from view with his own cloaked bulk.

Wren hesitated before replying in an undertone, "If it's all the same to you, I'd prefer you by my side."

Shrike's heart yearned for nothing more.

Wren clenched and unclenched his fists at his sides. Then he raised his arm, hesitated, and lightly rapped his knuckles against the door.

No answer came.

Another minute passed in silence before Wren put his fingertips to the iron latch. It clattered beneath his hand, and the door swung a few inches inward. Wren flinched from it, then set his jaw again and pushed the door fully open.

A dark and narrow stair loomed before them. Worn patterned carpet lay over the warped wooden steps. Simple iron sconces with unlit candles flanked the upper and lower landings. Another door stood at the top.

With a final glance up and down the street, Wren passed over the threshold and indicated for Shrike to follow him up the stair.

"I suppose," Wren said over his shoulder in a low tone, "I oughtn't be surprised it's not locked during the day, even if he has gone out. There are perhaps twelve persons in Rochester, and they all attend the same church."

Shrike chuckled. Wren shot him a wan smile.

They reached the upper landing. Wren knocked again. No one answered. Yet the second door proved not so unlocked as the first. Wren swore a blistering oath. He began patting down his coat, waistcoat, and trousers alike. These efforts produced a button-hook, but this didn't satisfy him.

"Have you anything like a hairpin?" he asked Shrike. "Something long and thin, like a needle or—"

Shrike dipped his hand into his cloak pocket and produced a silver awl.

Wren raised an eyebrow. "That'll do."

Shrike dropped the awl into Wren's outstretched palm. Wren crouched before the lock.

"I required the contents of my father's wine-cellar to survive the holidays at home during my university years," Wren explained as he probed the mechanism with button-hook and awl. "Neither he nor his butler felt inclined to furnish me with the key."

Shrike, to whom it had not occurred to demand an explanation for such fortuitous skill in night-work, cocked his head as he watched Wren's progress against the lock.

After a considerable amount of rattling, a decisive click resounded through the hall. Wren's shoulders slumped in a sigh of relief. He rose to his feet and turned the knob.

Sunshine poured into the stair as Wren opened the door. The room within was warm and bright. A merry crimson carpet lay across the floorboards, and the mantle above the fireplace held a porcelain vase filled with golden aconite blooms. Glass-fronted shelves held a multitude of bound tomes along one wall. A window in the wall opposite looked out over High Street and the bridge over the River Medway beyond.

A desk stood between the window and the fireplace. It appeared much like the one Shrike had found in Wren's garret, except its brass fittings shone brighter, its gleaming wood bore more intricate carvings and flourishes, and it had a horseshoe-ring of small drawers surrounding its writing surface instead of the myriad pigeon-holes into which Wren stuffed his papers.

Wren fell upon these drawers at once. The shrill scrape of wood-against-wood rang in Shrike's ears as Wren yanked each open in turn, flicking through their contents with furtive rapidity and cursing under his breath as he failed to find what he wanted. One particular drawer, however, did not open. To this Wren applied button-hook and awl.

Shrike left him to it. His own hands itched to prove some aid to Wren's cause, and so he turned to the remainder of the room. Running his fingertips over the chimney-bricks in search of loose mortar turned up nothing. Likewise the hearthstones beneath revealed no secrets. Flipping and shaking the rug proved fruitless. None of the floorboards rang hollow under his boot-heels.

But through an open doorway in the far corner of the room, he glimpsed the corner of a bed. And so he crept onward.

The bedroom appeared as warm and bright as the parlour. The bed lay between a wash-stand and a chest of drawers. Shrike considered the quilted counter-pane for a long moment, wondering if he ought to rip its seams to see if Tolhurst had sewn Wren's manuscripts into the patches. However, as he laid his hands on it, he felt not crisp or crumpled paper but mere feathers beneath the fabric. He settled for merely stripping the bed and flipping the mattress. These efforts revealed nothing.

Shrike turned to the chest of drawers. Scarves and handkerchiefs abounded in the upper, whilst shirts, trousers, waistcoats, and small-clothes dominated the lower. In the very bottom drawer, however, after Shrike had tossed out the linen bed-clothes, he found something.

A cache of papers lay beneath all.

Shrike snatched them up—only for the thrill of victory to vanish as his eyes fell on unfamiliar scrawls. Nothing he now held looked like Wren's handiwork. Most of it took the form of random dots laid out over parallel lines. The only drawing in the bunch was a sketch of a young woman, fair-haired and vacant-eyed, with her figure warped by the artist's unskilled hand and a face that, if it reflected reality, marked her out as a most unfortunate creature.

Still, while the scribbles meant nothing to Shrike, they might yet mean something to Wren, and so Shrike brought them out with him when he returned to the parlour.

Wren, meanwhile, had made great progress against the desk and book-cases. The glass-fronts had divulged their tomes onto the carpet to lie gaping open in piles. Every desk drawer was out and spilled over onto the floor, where Wren now sat sorting the contents into neat stacks, his speckled brow stormy with intense concentration. At Shrike's entrance he glanced up. His gaze flew to meet Shrike's own, then darted to the papers Shrike held before him. At once the storm on his brow broke out into a sunshine smile of sheer relief.

Shrike's heart broke to see it.

Wren leapt to his feet. The papers surrounding him scattered like wind-tossed snow. "You've found them?"

Shrike cursed himself for having raised Wren's hopes. "No. Something else."

The shattered expression passed over Wren's face for the merest instant, yet its ache lingered in Shrike's heart. He took the paper from Shrike's outstretched hand with a weary look and glanced over the pages. They rustled as he flipped through them.

"What are they?" Shrike asked.

"Sheet music," Wren said, turning the pages to show Shrike the dots along bars. His brow furrowed when he came to the portrait.

"And the maiden?" Shrike asked.

"I'm very much afraid it's supposed to be Miss Flora." Wren twisted his mouth to one side as he considered the sketch. "I can't make out the signature, though I wouldn't expect much better from Felix. If Tolhurst did it himself, he oughtn't abandon his musical career."

"Could we use it to bargain for the return of your own manuscripts?"

Wren blinked. "Now there's a thought. But, no. I'd feel ashamed to hang this in a gallery, certainly, but it's nothing Tolhurst or Felix might lose their liberty over."

"There is nothing in the desk, then."

"Nothing, save a collection of receipts and correspondence even more meticulously organized than Mr Grigsby's records. Very bland receipts and correspondence, at that. Tolhurst has never spent a penny that he didn't earn and never upon anything he need blush at. He's even kept note of Felix's accounts," Wren added with a raised eyebrow. "Not surprising, given he's almost as much his nephew's guardian as Mr Grigsby is. Matches our own records down to the last decimal. I've never met a more boring person in the flesh or by proxy."

Shrike could hardly disagree.

"Which doesn't necessarily mean Tolhurst doesn't have my manuscripts," Wren continued. "It could mean he only stole them this morning and is still transporting them here along with his nephew. Or perhaps he stole them a month ago and ever since has carried them on his person whenever he goes out. Which in my opinion would be the height of foolish daring, but I suppose a man such as he has very little to fear from society."

"He will have a great deal to fear from me if he has stolen from you," said Shrike.

Wren's eyes flew wide. Yet a smile flickered at the corner of his bespeckled lips. Shrike should have liked to kiss it, if they stood in Blackthorn and not in Rochester. And unless he mistook the gleam in Wren's gaze, Wren wished for the same.

Still, the ghost of Wren's delight remained on his face even as his voice resumed its disinterested drone. "More likely—to my mind, at least—it is Felix who has the papers and has taken them with him just his morning as he departed Staple Inn. But we cannot know for certain until he arrives. In the meantime, we must eliminate all remaining possibility."

"Miss Flora," said Shrike.

"Exactly so." Wren glanced over the papers he'd scattered across the floor. "After we restore order."

Putting the room to rights, a more sombre and less frantic task than searching it, took the better part of an hour.

"We may hope," Wren said as he shut the door on their handiwork, "that Tolhurst is too preoccupied with his nephew to notice his rooms are unlocked. Or, if he does notice, he will assume he forgot to lock them in his haste to reach London."

"Where does Miss Flora reside?" Shrike asked, following Wren down the dark stair and into High Street.

"Mrs Bailiwick's Academy," Wren answered him. "It's not far. Just a few streets over. Although..." he added, with a wary glance back at Shrike which travelled from the peak of his feathered hat to the hem of his furred cloak.

Shrike took his meaning. "Are you prepared to face Miss Flora alone?"

Wren seemed bemused by his concern. "I've met her before and emerged unscathed."

"Then perhaps," Shrike suggested, "I might keep watch for Tolhurst's return."

CHAPTER
TWENTY-ONE

The housemaid who answered the door-bell looked as if Wren were the first gentleman she'd seen in all her days. She didn't appear any less astonished when Wren told her he'd come to see Miss Flora Fairfield. She left him standing on the doorstep whilst she went to see if Miss Flora was "in." Some quarter of an hour later she returned and led him in to a very rosy little front parlour and instructed him to wait before she left him alone again. Wren spent another quarter of an hour casting a dubious eye over the flocked golden damask wallpaper, the delicate white lace antimacassars laid out over the backs of armchairs that had evidently never known the grease of a gentleman's hair, and the myriad framed examples of young ladies' samplers, watercolours, and pencil-sketch portraits rendered in varying levels of skill. He had just determined one particular watercolour depicted a horse—and not, as he had at first surmised, a very unfortunate and lumpy hound—when the parlour door opened again.

The voluminous lace-flounced tartan cake of a gown that swept over the threshold did not carry Miss Flora along with it. Instead Wren found himself under the stern gaze of a woman whose greying hair tucked beneath her starched white cap bespoke her middling years and widowed status.

"Mrs Bailiwick, I presume?" said Wren.

She looked him up and down with an audible sniff.

"Mr Lofthouse, at your service," Wren added with a bow. "Clerk to Mr Grigsby."

Her formidable scowl relaxed by fractions. "So you are here to see our Miss Fairfield on behalf of her guardian."

"Yes," Wren lied. "Do forgive the short notice. Mr Grigsby is accompanying Mr Tolhurst and Mr Knoll to Rochester today, and they sent me on in advance of the invalid to bring Miss Fairfield the glad tidings."

Mrs Bailiwick brightened considerably. "Glad tidings indeed, if our dear Mr Tolhurst is returned at last! We've so missed our marvellous music master. And I daresay Miss Fairfield shall be as happy to hear of his return as that of her fiancé—for, indeed, Mr Tolhurst has doted on her ever since she entered our academy."

"Has he," said Wren, more out of politeness than any real interest. As Mr Grigsby's clerk, he'd assisted him in choosing his ward's education, and therefore knew very well that Tolhurst had been the music and dancing master of Mrs Bailiwick's Academy for many years. Long before Miss Flora had arrived at the tender age of eleven. Small wonder that the man should take an interest in his nephew's betrothed. "Most attentive of him."

"I'm certain you found him thus in London whilst he tended to his nephew," said Mrs Bailiwick with a satisfied smile. "They may as well be family already—Miss Fairfield and Mr Tolhurst, I mean," she added with another bizarre trill.

Wren forced a smile. "I should like to inform Miss Fairfield without delay—and, with your permission, in privacy. I'm afraid I must bring her some dreadful dull matters of business as well as joy."

A hint of suspicion returned to Mrs Bailiwick's gaze, but she nevertheless replied, "I suppose we might. Let me collect her for you. She's in her French lessons at present."

For a third time, Wren found himself left to his own devices in the academy. Yet he didn't feel entirely alone. Mrs Bailiwick had left the door ajar in her departure. Through it, Wren glimpsed certain tittering figures peeking 'round the corner at the end of the hall, darting out of sight when he turned his head fully towards them. As much as he would've liked to attribute this phenomenon to the fae, he suspected his masculine presence had excited the curiosity of the two dozen young ladies who lived cloistered as nuns save for Mr Tolhurst's tutelage. He ignored them and pretended to study the artworks on the parlour walls. At third glance, he thought the horse might be an unfortunate hound after all.

"Mr Lofthouse."

Wren turned to find Miss Flora standing on the threshold. She appeared not so astonished to see him as Wren might have expected. On the contrary, she seemed almost annoyed. The same housemaid who'd let Wren into the academy—with eyes and hair alike a deep mahogany shade, and rosebud lips parted in wonder—peered in at him over Miss Flora's shoulder.

"Miss Fairfield," Wren replied, avoiding the housemaid's gaze. "I'm happy to report that your *fiancé* is *en route* to his uncle's house here in Rochester for his convalescence."

Miss Flora served him a blank stare. In a tone flatter even than Wren's own, she replied, "I'm equally delighted to hear it. Though I do wonder at Mr Grigsby sending you ahead of them all this way just to tell me."

Wren, having no explanation, cleared his throat. His mind had raced in panic all the way from his garret to Cemetery Gate to the academy. The rote script of polite formalities had carried him into the academy itself and through conversation with Mrs Bailiwick. Now, face-to-face with one who might have glimpsed the most unfettered fantasies he'd ever set down in ink, he found the cold fire of fear returning to his veins. In a voice far calmer than he felt, he added, "There is another matter, as well."

"I wish you would name it," said Miss Flora.

Wren let his eyes flick over to the housemaid, who yet remained standing just behind Miss Flora, before returning his attention to Miss Flora herself. "I would prefer to state my business in confidence."

A faint smile ghosted across the corners of Miss Flora's lips. "You may trust Sukie with your life."

The ironic echo did not escape Wren. "Very well. Do allow me to apologize for any inconvenience my visit may incur."

"If you were my only gentleman caller, Mr Lofthouse, I should scarcely have any inconveniences whatsoever."

Wren stared at her. She'd spoken her words with nothing approaching affection. Indeed, her dry tone came very near to bitterness. Given their brief acquaintance, he didn't think she could have any reason to grow fond of him in particular. And so he felt forced to conclude she spoke not from any favour toward him but from a distinct lack of favour towards her other gentleman caller. With Felix as her betrothed, Wren could hardly blame her—though her candour surprised him. Still, good manners demanded he force out, "You flatter me, Miss Fairfield."

"I do not," she returned, no less blunt than before.

Wren thought it prudent to come straight to the point. "I regret as well that I must come to you with ill tidings. Certain papers have vanished from Mr Grigsby's office in Staple Inn."

Miss Flora raised her brows.

Wren didn't glance at Sukie, no matter how much his nerves compelled him to do so. Bad enough to have to phrase his enquiries so as not to arouse Miss Flora's suspicions. He had no idea how to handle a housemaid. His father's household had employed footmen, and what few maids assisted the housekeeper and cook had remained almost invisible—to him, at least. He forced his mind to his present difficulties and made a game attempt. "Have you heard anything—perhaps from Mr Knoll himself or from Mr Tolhurst—of any suspicious persons lurking around Staple Inn in recent weeks? Or noticed anything strange yourself on your own visit there?"

Miss Flora looked as if the strangest thing she'd noticed was Wren standing before her now. Yet all she said was, "I have not."

Wren supposed that had been rather too much to hope for. Still, "If you should recall anything of the sort in the future, may I ask that you write and tell me of it?"

"Write to you," Miss Flora echoed, "and not to Mr Grigsby?"

Wren's intended speech died on his tongue.

Miss Flora studied his face with eyes that suddenly seemed all too canny. "Would I be correct in presuming Mr Grigsby is not yet informed of the loss of these certain papers?"

Too late, Wren realized everything he'd let slip despite his efforts at subterfuge. Miss Flora had proved more astute by half than he'd given her credit for. As he watched her expression, willing his own into an impassive mask, he thought he detected the wisp of a smile in her eyes. Yet, to his surprise, it did not seem an unkind smile. He dared not look at Sukie.

"If at all possible," Wren said after a moment's contemplation, "I should like to recover the papers without causing Mr Grigsby undue distress."

Not, technically speaking, a lie.

Miss Flora fixed him with a gaze that made him feel as if he were an object in a still-life watercolour exercise. A stick of goat willow in a vase, perhaps, or a stuffed goldfinch chained to its perch. She continued to study him for a long while before she spoke. "I appreciate your taking me into your confidence, Mr Lofthouse. Perhaps I might one day return the favour."

Wren managed to disguise his astonishment—barely. He couldn't begin to fathom what secrets a young lady like her could possibly have.

"For today, however," Miss Flora continued as if she hadn't said anything at all alarming, "I have some particular questions for you regarding the trust left to me by my family."

"I shall do my able best to answer them," Wren replied when he'd recovered his composure. He could do little else.

"How much may I withdraw from my trust before I attain my majority by either reaching my twenty-first birthday or by marrying?"

Wren attempted to disguise his bewilderment as he named the sum.

Miss Flora didn't seem satisfied with the answer. "And is there no way to withdraw anything further?"

"I'm afraid not," said Wren, his unease only growing. Her questions reminded him all too well of Felix's repeated visits to Staple Inn.

First and foremost, Wren was Mr Grigsby's clerk. As such, he was beholden to the same confidences as Mr Grigsby. Both Felix and Miss

Flora were Mr Grigsby's wards, which meant, amongst other things, that Mr Grigsby would consider their interests as secrets to be guarded with his life. Just as Mr Grigsby couldn't communicate anything specific about Felix's finances to his Uncle Tolhurst, nor could Mr Grigsby tell Miss Flora anything about Felix's finances—or tell Felix anything about hers.

However, at present, if Miss Flora intended to bankrupt herself to rescue her profligate betrothed, that action would have grave consequences for her own fortunes. And Mr Grigsby, with her best interests at heart both professionally and personally, would do everything in his power to dissuade her from such a disaster. Nor could Wren, as Mr Grigsby's clerk, do anything less.

Yet how to do so without breaking both his own and his master's confidence with Felix—particularly when Miss Flora insisted on having her favourite housemaid stand witness to their meeting?

Wren attempted a delicate enquiry. "Mr Knoll has told you how he stands with his own trust?"

"He has not told me of his debts himself, if that's what you're asking," said Miss Flora. "But I have heard of them. To my knowledge, they are considerable."

This revelation made Wren's position a great deal less awkward. "If you're intending to wipe out his debts with your own fortune—"

"I am not."

Wren, who'd been on the brink of warning her against that action, choked on his own admonition. "Then, if I may be so bold as to ask, what are your intentions?"

"You may ask as boldly as you please, Mr Lofthouse. Whether or not you shall receive an answer is another matter altogether."

An astonished laugh escaped Wren. He hastily turned it into a cough, which allowed him to compose himself beneath his handkerchief.

"I hope you won't think me too forward," Wren ventured after he recovered his breath, "if I remind you it is within your power to break off the engagement, for whatever reason, whenever you see fit, and with your guardian's complete confidence."

Miss Flora said nothing.

In gentler tones, Wren added, "Even such infamy as a broken engagement may be lived down in time."

Miss Flora shot him a disdainful look. "Have you lived down such infamy, Mr Lofthouse?"

"I haven't," Wren admitted. Though, if whoever now held his manuscripts should bring them to light, he would have to live down far worse infamy than Miss Flora might ever encounter in all her days.

A faint curl came to Miss Flora's lip. "While I admit I have not quite the regard for Felix that a wife ought to have for her husband, it is advantageous to me to remain engaged. For many reasons. Not the least of which is, a betrothal does a great deal to discourage other would-be suitors."

Wren thought that last remark rather pointed at him in particular. While his very nature made him no danger to her in that regard, he could hardly tell her so. And so he said nothing.

"Is that all you wished to discuss with me, Mr Lofthouse?" Miss Flora asked coolly.

It wasn't all he wished to discuss—not by half—yet courtesy compelled him to reply, "If you have no further need of me."

"I have not." Miss Flora curtsied. "Good day, sir."

Wren bowed to her in turn and showed himself out.

Rochester Castle had far fewer defences than most castles Shrike had encountered in the fae realms. No archers stood ready on its battlements. No enchanted statues recited riddles to ensnare the unwary traveller. The gardens between the gate and the keep held neither brambles nor thorns nor a single poisonous petal, nor did the ivy crawling over the walls wraps its tendrils 'round Shrike's limbs. Not even a token labyrinth lay within.

All the better for Shrike.

While a few mortals stared at his passing as he strode through Rochester's streets, none moved to prevent him from entering the castle gate, crossing its garden, and reaching the keep.

The ruined state of the castle likewise proved no barrier to him.

Shrike might have flown to his perch in the north-west tower, had the passage through the path of iron not left him muddled. As such, he went by foot. The wooden floors and rafters of the keep had long ago crumbled into dust. The stone spiral staircases within the walls looked as if they would soon follow, but for the moment they held strong beneath Shrike's boots. He had oft climbed far more treacherous cliff-faces in pursuit of his quarry.

And when he at last ascended to the top of the north-west tower, he could see clear over the castle walls and the sundry houses of Rochester to the bridge spanning the River Medway.

On this bridge he trained his eye.

Before he and Wren had parted, less than an hour hence, he had asked Wren what sort of horses drew the carriage bearing Felix away from Staple Inn, so he might watch for them and thus mark Felix's arrival. Wren confessed he hadn't thought to commit the horses to memory before the carriage left Staple Inn, but upon racking his recollections, he supposed one of them had a white blaze down its nose. Furthermore, he added, Mr Grigsby or Tolhurst would likely be riding alongside the coachman outside of the carriage itself.

Shrike felt confident he could spot a horse's blaze from a clear mile off, and had said so, which provoked a smile from Wren.

Then Wren had gone off to the academy, and now Shrike stood alone in the castle tower.

According to Wren's estimation, it would take six or seven hours for the carriage to travel from London to Rochester. It'd started out late, around eleven, and would therefore probably arrive well into the evening. Most of the intervening hours had already burned away in turning over Tolhurst's rooms. The sun had passed its zenith long ago, and its gentle decline towards the western horizon began to turn the sky's hue from pale grey to faint heather as dusk drew on.

Many unremarkable coaches and wagons rattled over the River Medway in the meantime. Shrike, who'd waited for weeks in far less hospitable circumstances for far more dangerous prey, nevertheless clenched his jaw as he watched the bridge. His own hide wasn't in peril.

Something nearer and dearer to his own heart lay at stake. And as minutes passed with no relief in sight, he found his patience rapidly waning. Every wrong carriage rolling across the bridge seemed to rattle its wheel-rims against the nerves of his teeth.

Then, like a silver fox darting out of the underbrush to race through fallen crimson leaves, a drop of white appeared at the north-western end of the bridge.

Shrike surged upright. The horse with a blaze, just as Wren had described, drew a carriage along the straight line of the bridge. No coursing hare or leaping hart moved in so predictable a pattern. Nor did any forest offer so clear a shot as Shrike now had from the castle tower. If Nell had stood from this very vantage point, she could have shot the horses dead—four arrows, one clean through the eye of each beast—and seized the coach, taking its passengers hostage to ransom back Wren's manuscripts.

But Shrike didn't carry his longbow in the mortal realm. He had only his blades, which would do little from this distance. Nor did he think Wren wished him to spill blood, or to do anything else which might draw more eyes than his garb already had.

And so he watched and waited as the white-blaze horse and its fellows drew the carriage on.

At length they alighted on the south-eastern bank and entered Rochester proper. When it vanished between the houses, Shrike began his descent from the tower. Even with the ache of iron in his bones he climbed with greater agility than the carriage-wheels rolled. Mere minutes found him striding once again across the castle garden and outside its walls. He slipped through the streets to an alcove between two particular houses where he could flatten himself into the shadows whilst watching Cemetery Gate.

The coach had halted beneath the gatehouse arch. The round figure of Mr Grigsby appeared in conversation with the coachman. From behind the open door of the coach came Tolhurst, who reached back in from whence he'd come to retrieve his nephew. Felix looked less frail than Shrike had seen him last, though no better tempered. He leaned heavily on his uncle's arm and shuffled into the gatehouse. Mr Grigsby followed soon after. The coachman flicked the reins, and the coach lurched off down the street again.

Shrike might not have had his bow to hand, but he could made do with his blades. Felix, weak to begin with and weaker still after his ordeal with the huldra, would hardly pose a threat. Tolhurst was of bulkier build, but Shrike doubted he was any better-trained than his nephew in the art of combat. Still, some harm might come to Mr Grigsby in the attempt, which would distress Wren. And the whole incident would prove difficult to explain to mortal satisfaction.

And so, rather than mount an attack on Cemetery Gate, and against his better judgment, Shrike withdrew to the cathedral.

Shrike didn't visit mortal temples often. Most of what he knew of them came from Larkin's tales of the world he'd left behind. As such, he found Rochester Cathedral fit his expectations. It was one of the peaked and pointed sort, with windows like spearheads and filigree like a thousand daggers, rather than domes supported by ribbed columns. The only rounded arch, to his eye, sat over the westward entrance. Rows on rows of carved figures filled this arch, with still more flanking the doorway. Shrike recognized an ox, a lion, and an eagle among them, though the more numerous mortals represented remained strangers to him.

Passing through them, Shrike entered a grand hall with a vaulted ceiling high above. Stained glass windows and alcoved statues depicted still more figures of worship, none of which Shrike could name, nor did he care to. He cared only for the mortal flesh-and-blood man who awaited him.

Wren appeared very much like his namesake, so small and solemn in the enormous hall, standing in his severe garb with his hands folded behind his back and his eyes fixed above. He took no notice of Shrike's approach. Not even when Shrike halted beside him to follow his gaze to the face carved in the joint where six of the ceiling's ribs crossed.

It was the first familiar thing—besides Wren—that Shrike had seen since he entered the cathedral. Centuries had worn smooth the finer details of the carving, but he could not mistake the vines pouring forth from its gaping maw. The green man. An aspect of the Oak King, and yet another reminder of his own destiny as decreed by the Queen of the Court of the Silver Wheel.

Shrike cleared his throat.

Wren leapt and whirled.

Shrike raised his hands in surrender. "Forgive me—I didn't mean to affright you."

But the moment Wren's eyes alighted on Shrike's face, his heart-wrenching look of fear had changed to one of determination. "Felix has arrived?"

"Aye," Shrike admitted, and told him all he'd seen. "What of Miss Flora?"

Wren grimaced. "I'm afraid I rather showed my hand with her. Still, she had but one opportunity to steal the manuscripts—and not a very convenient opportunity at that. If by some chance my papers are in her possession, I can only assume she must hold them at Felix's behest. Overall I think it much more likely that the manuscripts are now in Cemetery Gate, having arrived alongside Felix. We cannot now search with both Tolhurst and Felix in—"

Wren's speech cut off as suddenly as if his throat were slit. His eyes widened and fixed on some point over Shrike's shoulder.

Shrike turned, one hand on the pommel of his dagger whilst the other held his cloak out to shield Wren from the view of whatever now pursued them.

A mortal man of middling age, black-robed and white-collared, had entered the cathedral from the doorway beneath the organ-pipes. He wore a curious expression and ambled towards Shrike and Wren with his hands folded before him.

"Let's be off," Wren said in that queer clipped tone he took on whenever he and Shrike stood together in mortal view.

Shrike relaxed his warrior stance and followed Wren's swift yet measured retreat.

Wren didn't say a word all the way from the cathedral down the winding pathways of Rochester. Only when they reached the stable-yard and found themselves alone—save the horses—did he pause and turn to Shrike.

"Forgive me," said Wren, surprising him. "I ought to have asked before we started out, but, are you recovered enough to make the journey back?"

"To leave iron behind altogether is far easier than going from iron to iron."

Wren didn't appear as though he entirely believed him, but nodded nevertheless. He joined Shrike in climbing the well to balance on its rim. Shrike held out his hand. Wren clasped it.

And together they leapt down into the unfathomable depths of the sea between realms.

The crumbling ruins of the Grove of Gates had never before seemed quite so welcoming as they did now. The moment their boot-heels struck solid ground, Wren cleaved to Shrike, using their clasped hands to twine their arms together and urge him on with the same fevered pace he'd kept up all day.

"On the subject of the missing papers," Wren said as if their discussion had never cut off. "If Tolhurst doesn't have them, and Miss Flora doesn't have them, then Felix must have them. Secreted somewhere on his person or in his baggage. It's a small enough packet. He could hide it in a few issues of *Master Humphrey's Clock*. Lord knows Mr Grigsby has enough of them about the office. He'd be only too happy to lend them out."

Shrike supposed Wren would know his master's habits well enough.

Wren spoke on, words falling from his lips in an ever-rising torrent. "Felix isn't high-minded enough—or moral enough, for that matter—to take my manuscripts to the magistrate. More likely he's keeping them as collateral against the next unreasonable request he intends to make of his trust. As such, I'll have some warning of his intentions until he reveals all and ruins me."

"And you are content to wait for him to make the first move," Shrike concluded as Wren fell silent.

Wren grimaced again. "I haven't any choice otherwise."

"You could leave."

Wren ceased walking. Shrike, entangled arm-in-arm with him, likewise stumbled to a halt. Wren stared up at him in confusion which Shrike knew must mirror what Wren saw on his own face.

"Leave?" Wren echoed. "Impossible. I cannot."

"Why not?"

"Mr Grigsby is entirely and utterly dependent on me. He's treated me far better than anyone else in all of England—far better than I deserve—and while I might not deserve his kindness, I will do my damnedest to repay it. I'll not abandon him."

"If Mr Grigsby is so fond of you," Shrike reasoned, "and so dependent on you, surely he would not wish to see you in chains."

"No," Wren conceded. "I suppose he would not. Though he wouldn't like to employ a sodomite, either. I doubt he'd feel half so fond of me if he knew me for what I truly am."

"Has he said so?" If he had, Shrike would have strong words with him, if not strong blows.

"He needn't say a word," Wren replied, taking no notice of Shrike's resolve. "Every gentleman in London thinks it."

"Then I have a quarrel with every gentleman in London."

Wren stared at Shrike. Then a startled laugh burst from his throat. "If anyone could succeed in such a venture, I daresay it would be you."

Shrike found himself smiling in return. If you're determined to wait until Felix attacks—"

"Which I am."

"Then when he does," Shrike continued, "know you may seek sanctuary in Blackthorn. Its paths are ever open to you."

This seemed to astonish Wren, though the wistful smile it provoked on his bespeckled lips bespoke how well it pleased him.

"Should you ever find yourself in peril in the mortal realm," Shrike added, "call for me by my true name, and I shall come to your aid."

Wren's smile grew fonder still, though he replied, "You must think me ridiculous."

"Wherefore?" Shrike asked, bewildered anew.

"It's the height of foolishness for me to complain of what fate might befall me in London, knowing what you must grapple with come the Summer Solstice."

How bizarre, Shrike thought, for Wren to worry after him who had proved over and again his prowess on the battlefield and who bore Wren's own sigil of protection, when Wren himself stood defenceless against the thousand slings and arrows of the mortal realm. Yet it warmed Shrike's heart nonetheless in a manner he could never have anticipated. He found himself smiling. "Come the solstice, with you at my side, I can claim nothing less than victory."

CHAPTER
TWENTY-TWO

The moon hung bright above the fae realms as Wren and Shrike passed through the briars on the path to Blackthorn. They walked along arm-in-arm in companionable silence, Wren's mind yet preoccupied with the loss of his manuscripts to an unknown hand. So much so that he noticed nothing amiss until Shrike came to a sudden halt. Wren hadn't even realized Shrike had drawn his sword until he saw the moonlight glinting off its edge.

"What," Wren started to ask, but stopped as he saw what had given Shrike pause.

In the arrow-slit window of the cottage flickered a faint candlelight.

"Trouble?" Wren whispered with more courage than he felt.

Shrike shook his head. His arm slipped from Wren's grasp. He strode up to the door and pushed it open.

There at Shrike's work-bench, by the light of a beeswax candle, sat the elf-maiden archer of the Wild Hunt, with her raven hair braided with feathers and her high cheekbones bereft of the woad she'd worn against the monstrous boar. Or rather, she sprawled, for the tunic and hose she wore in place of a bodice and skirt allowed her to put her boot-heel up on the corner of the work-bench whilst she flung her arm over the back of the chair in a posture of perfect casual indifference, making herself as much at home as Wren had felt when first he came upon Blackthorn.

Shrike dropped his sword-arm to his side. "Nell."

"Butcher," the elf-maiden replied. "No one has seen you since the solstice."

"You see me now," said Shrike.

To Wren's astonishment, Nell laughed. And to Wren's further astonishment, Shrike smiled with her and sheathed his blade.

"What shall I call your companion?" Nell asked.

Shrike shot an enquiring look over his shoulder at Wren.

Wren stepped out of Shrike's shadow. "Lofthouse, Miss Nell."

"Lofthouse," she echoed with another smile. "Just Nell, an' it so please you."

"What brings you to Blackthorn?" Shrike asked, shutting the door behind them.

"Imbolc and Ostara," she replied.

Wren, bewildered, watched Shrike nod as if she'd said something sensible.

"I'm afraid I must disappoint you for Imbolc," Shrike said. "What did you hope for on Ostara?"

Nell pulled a face. "Don't know. Rather hoped you might come up with something. And don't say a raven."

"Pardon me," Wren interrupted with a bravery he'd never felt in any withdrawing room. "Who, pray tell, are Imbolc and Ostara?"

Both fae turned to look at him; Shrike in confusion, Nell in bemusement.

"Forgive me," Shrike said and looked as if he meant it. "Imbolc is the mid-point between the Winter Solstice and Ostara, marked by fire. This year it falls upon a full moon."

"Which makes for a particularly auspicious hunt," Nell added.

"And Ostara?" asked Wren.

"The Vernal Equinox," said Shrike. "Whereupon votive offerings are made to the tree of mask to provoke the budding of new growth."

"What sort of offerings?" asked Wren.

"Masks," Nell said dryly.

Wren supposed he ought to have surmised as much for himself.

"And your Butcher," Nell added with a jerk of her chin towards Shrike, "makes the finest masks in all the realms."

Shrike looked as though he would disagree but said nothing.

"Which is why I've come to commission one," Nell concluded. "And to congratulate you on your victory in the solstice duel. And I'd also intended to enquire what has occupied you so to keep you from the hunt since before Samhain... but," she added, her gaze sliding to Wren, "I think I already know the answer to that."

Wren's blood ran cold. His face fell into the same impassive mask he wore in London. He didn't dare look at Shrike, lest he reveal more than he already had. All this in the space of a blink and upon instinct.

Yet, he forcibly reminded himself even as his heart pounded in his throat, the fae held no law against men with men. Nor did their customs look askance at such practices. Indeed, Nell made her guess with a glance of amusement rather than disapproval or derision.

Or at least she had. Now, thanks to Wren's panicked silence stretching into a far-too-long moment, her wry smile had frozen into uncomfortable confusion. Her eyes went to Shrike. Wren found the courage to follow them.

Shrike, whose brow had furrowed in concern—not at Nell, but at Wren.

But before Wren could blurt something to break the awkward pause, Shrike turned to Nell.

"Truly it does my heart good to see you," Shrike said. "On another eve I would bid you stay, but the day's trials have brought us low."

Nell dropped her boot-heels to the floor and sat up straight. In a light voice that nevertheless retained a wary edge, she replied, "I suppose that's what provoked you to greet me with a drawn blade."

Shrike gave her a brisk nod.

Nell stood up altogether and arranged her cloak about her shoulders. "Pray, don't let me add to your distress. Only," she continued, swinging her quiver and unstrung bow onto her back, "if it is something which might be alleviated by a well-aimed arrow..."

A fond half-smile tugged at the corner of Shrike's mouth. "I will send for you."

Nell returned his smile and served Wren a bow that would do any courtier proud. "Are you sure you won't join the hunt tomorrow? You should be most welcome—both of you," she added, turning her wry smile upon Wren.

Shrike shook his head.

"Another eve, then," Nell concluded, nothing daunted. She nodded to Wren. "Well met, Lofthouse."

And with that, she threw her hood up and vanished out the door into the night.

In her wake Wren's mind felt full to bursting with questions he dared not ask out of common courtesy.

Shrike, however, seemed in no way burdened by society's expectations. He turned to Wren with an apologetic cast to his handsome features. "Forgive me—she is an old friend and has little patience for courtly conversation."

"Nothing to forgive," Wren hastened to reply. His mind still reeled. He'd assume Nell and Shrike were cousins, if not siblings. They didn't seem like lovers—even if Shrike's blade bent towards the fairer sex, Nell appeared to bear little regard for men—and in English society, only blood relation could explain such close comfort between a gentleman and a lady. Yet he did not stand upon English soil now. "She seems... very capable."

A breathless laugh escaped Shrike. "That she is, indeed."

"How did she pass through the briars?"

"She is a friend and ally, and so the briars part for her. Just as they part for you."

"They part for me?" Wren echoed. All this time he'd assumed he gained passage through them due to Shrike's presence alongside him.

Shrike looked almost as bewildered as Wren felt. "Of course."

"Oh." Warmth suffused Wren's heart and rose in his cheeks. He cleared his throat. "So it isn't just anyone who might wander through the mushroom ring and find us."

"No," said Shrike.

Uneasiness came over Wren. "Though Felix did follow us on the Winter Solstice…"

"Not to Blackthorn," said Shrike.

Wren fought to keep his rising panic at the notion out of his tone. "But if he did—"

"He cannot," Shrike interrupted him gently.

"Yes, the briars, I understand," Wren admitted with impatience. "But he need not follow us so far as to the cottage to know where we go and to surmise what we do. It's only a stone's throw from the well, after all."

"No it isn't."

Wren stared at him in frank disbelief. "We walked it ourselves not an hour hence."

"If you know the way to Blackthorn," said Shrike, "then the path is very short. If you don't know the way to Blackthorn, then the path is very long."

Wren continued staring as he pondered this riddle. "It's magic, then?"

"Enchanted, aye."

In retrospect, Wren supposed he ought to have supposed it himself. "So when you say he *cannot* follow us, you are speaking literally."

"Aye," said Shrike, with evident relief that Wren had understood him at last. "We would vanish into the woods before his eyes the moment we left the Grove of Gates."

Wren filed away this information with far more interest than he'd ever filed accounts for Mr Grigsby. "Then, if none but friends may enter Blackthorn, why did you draw your sword when you found someone already in the cottage?"

To Wren's surprise, Shrike appeared chastened by the question. He glanced away and hesitated, the silence broken only by the slight clink of his sword in its scabbard as his fingers played upon the pommel. When he met Wren's gaze again, the fathomless depths of his dark eyes shone soft with reverence. In a much-abashed tone, he replied, "I have far more to lose now than ever I had before."

To be wanted was one thing. To be cherished and defended was another. To be loved… Wren dared not think so far as that. But nevertheless his heart sang with the knowledge that Shrike considered him worthy of protection, and that the loss of Wren would pain Shrike as much as the loss of Shrike would pain Wren.

No words seemed sufficient to express even a fraction of what Wren felt. As such, he abandoned language entirely. Instead he reached out his hand to Shrike's scarred cheek, turning his face so he might capture his mouth in a kiss.

Shrike's fervour for defending Wren was well-matched by the passion with which he returned the kiss as Wren guided them both toward the bed.

The next morning, Sunday, dawned bright and clear. Frost crept across the narrow window-panes in delicate spirals and Wren's breath left his lips in plumes of vapour. Shrike rolled out of bed and stirred the hearth-fire out of the ashes. Then he returned to warm Wren with his embrace. Wren drifted off again.

A gentle repetitive tapping roused him a second time. He blinked his eyes open to find Shrike had vanished from the still-warm hollow beside him, and the sunbeams had travelled across the bed-furs to his face. It was still morning, according to his pocket-watch laid out atop his neatly folded clothes. And the tapping sound, he discovered as he glanced over the cottage to find where Shrike had gone, came from Shrike himself, bent over his work-bench as he plied a wooden mallet and bronze spike to leather.

Wren wrapped himself in a pelt moreso for warmth than for modesty and wandered over. As he approached, Shrike turned his head over his shoulder to regard him—Wren supposed his footsteps must sound as loud as galloping hooves to fae ears— and shot him a smile so handsome and gentle that Wren could hardly do otherwise than bend to kiss it.

"Masks for Ostara?" Wren murmured when the kiss broke at last, peering over Shrike's shoulder at the leather laid out before him.

"Aye." Shrike idly picked up a particular scrap of leather cut in the swooping webs of a bat's wing and began worrying it betwixt his thumb and forefinger. The spike lying atop its fellows, Wren now realized, had a broad rounded end, which when hammered into the leather created a thin burnished surface to stretch between the long and slender lines that marked the bat's bones. Several bat-wings already lay across the bench. Many more than a single bat would require. "For Nell."

Bats were certainly not ravens, Wren had to admit. Beyond the bat-wings he espied other works-in-progress. Two round green glass lenses sat atop three long triangular leather tapers. Several rolls of vellum pale as moonlight lay beside half-moon knives and a scalpel with a blade as small as a thorn. A pile of pointed oak leaves—which Wren only realised after several moment's study were cut from leather and not plucked from a branch—were raked into the far corner of the bench. And in the other corner, stretched atop a polished wooden block-head, sat a mask with feathered wings outstretched on either side and a wide round mouth like a Roman font, but not yet any holes to see through.

"What will you make of that one?" Wren asked, gesturing to the mask without eyes.

Shrike returned him a puzzled glance. "It's finished."

"Oh," Wren replied as if he understood. "And the others?"

Shrike rolled his broad shoulders in a stretch that drew far more of Wren's attention than he probably intended. "Finished for the moment. You must be hungry. I know I am. The hens and goats have already broken their fast."

Honey and goat cheese melted over toast tasted all the sweeter and all the richer to Wren for being wrought by Shrike's deft hands. To have Shrike's company, to lean against his warm bulk and to have those same clever fingers brush against his own as their shared their repast, nourished Wren's soul as well as his body. Falling into step beside Shrike as he tended his flocks felt as natural as breathing.

And when Shrike returned to the masks afterward, Wren took up his sketch-book to preserve what had already begun to assume the shape of a treasured memory.

The sheer strength of Shrike's frame proved itself through his strapping shoulders and sinewy arms. To Wren, he appeared all the more breath-taking when he bent over work so fine and delicate as plying the merest sliver of a blade to the thin sheet of pale white hart's hide and slicing the leather into lace. Rough yet gentle hands, whose touch could make Wren tremble, now split a slender piece of wire in twain—a boar bristle, Shrike explained when he caught Wren's curious gaze—and wound with catgut for needle and thread to piece together a patchwork harlequin who would've been the envy of all in Venice's Carnivale. Wren felt his pencil scribblings hardly did justice to the man he knew and loved. Still, as the house passed in comfortable silence, he filled his sketch-book's pages with his attempts to capture the knife's-edge balance between brutish brawn and elfin grace.

When the golden afternoon faded into rosy sunset, Shrike rose and stretched with a deep groan that rumbled through Wren's own ribcage. A knowing glance from those dark eyes was all the invitation Wren required to follow Shrike out of the cottage and through the wall of thorns to stroll arm-in-arm through the tranquil twilight of the fae wood.

Wren's breath mingled with the mist roiling through the trees in the chill night air. Yet, as Shrike enfolded them both in his cloak, a warmth to rival a bonfire seeped in through Wren's veins to his heart. To wander so entwined with Shrike and watch the moon-rise through the bare branches of the fae forest left Wren with a sense of serenity he almost believed might persevere even after he returned to Staple Inn.

"When will Nell return for her mask?" Wren asked as he ambled alongside Shrike.

"She won't," Shrike replied. "I'll deliver it to her at the Moon Market. Along with the others."

The mere mention of the fabled Moon Market sent a thrill through the withered husk of Wren's cynical heart. "When?"

"Under the last half-moon before Ostara."

"May I come along?"

Shrike glanced sharply down at him, and even in the dim silvery moonlight Wren could read the astonished cant of his brows.

Hot shame rose in Wren's cheeks. "Forgive me—that was rather too forward on my part."

"Nothing to forgive." A sly and handsome smile graced Shrike's otherwise stoic features. "I like you forward."

The heat in Wren's face assumed an entirely different character as he found an answering smile tugging at his own lips.

"And," Shrike added, his arm twining 'round Wren's waist as naturally as ivy encircling a castle tower, "I'd be glad of your company in the Moon Market."

Such was Wren's delight, both in the woods beneath the moon and nestled in the cottage beside Shrike soon after, that he could almost forget what awaited him in the mortal realm.

Morning dawned—Monday, as Wren called it—and Wren himself departed Blackthorn to return to Staple Inn.

Whilst Wren toiled in the mortal realm, Shrike remained behind to work on his craft for Ostara.

For a few hours, at least.

At length, however, when he'd stitched together every oak-leaf and burnished every bat-wing and sewed the green glass lenses into their long leather snout, he arose from his bench, wrapped his cloak 'round his shoulders, and set off out of the briar to the Grove of Gates.

Before he dove into the portal, he slipped into his more feathery form, and flew rather than crawled out of the stable-yard well into Rochester.

The horses took little notice of his appearance. The mortal stable-hands noticed even less. Shrike swooped past all of them and flitted down the by-streets toward Cemetery Gate.

Smoke drifted from the chimney at the top of the gate, which prevented Shrike from diving down it to search as thoroughly as he wished. Still, he could perch on the window-sill and peer in through the latticed glass as he'd done in Staple Inn so many months ago.

A gap between the curtains allowed sunlight to stream in across the bed wherein lay Felix, his blond curls tousled, his hollow cheek propped up in his palm, and his blue eyes cast down into a book. Though, Shrike noted, Felix's eye did not travel back and forth across the page as Wren's did when he read from his romances. Several other books and papers lay scattered over the rumpled bed-clothes. None resembled Wren's missing manuscripts. Felix's chest rose and fell in a heavy sigh as he turned the page with a careless flick of his hand.

Shrike hopped along the windowsill to find a more opportune vantage point. Most of the room remained as he'd seen it when he'd overturned it in his hunt. Now, however, a trunk sat at the foot of the bed, its lid open to reveal a surfeit of white linen shirts and silk handkerchiefs in many hues. Perhaps Wren's manuscripts lay beneath them. If so, Felix was careless beyond measure—yet Shrike hardly expected more from him.

A latch clicked. A hinge creaked. The bedroom door swung into view. From behind it emerged Tolhurst carrying a tray laden with teapot and cups. Wren had brought similar pieces to Blackthorn over the course of his evening visits.

Tolhurst laid the tea-things out for his nephew with almost as much care as Wren had done for Shrike. Felix received them with far less gratitude than Shrike had felt. Tolhurst, all smiles, spoke too softly for Shrike to hear from the other side of the glass with feathers over his ears. Felix likewise muttered his replies with a disinterested scowl.

Then Tolhurst, still smiling, turned away from his nephew toward the window.

Shrike braced himself to take wing.

But Tolhurst took no notice of the little bird perched on the windowsill as the threw the curtains wide—much to his nephew's chagrin.

"...ghost in the castle," Tolhurst concluded, his speech becoming clearer to Shrike as he drew nearer to the window.

Felix, one arm thrown over his eyes to block the sunlight, made a reply Shrike couldn't hear.

"A medieval spirit haunting the ruin," Tolhurst continued as he tied back the curtains. Perhaps he hoped his nephew would benefit from the sight of the quaint town and its surrounding countryside. Shrike doubted Felix, who according to Wren loved nothing more than urban vice, would find much to sustain him in Rochester. "Sighted in the tower the very day you arrived. Not a knight—a yeoman in a furred cloak and feathered cap. Perhaps some poor soul murdered in the siege. Or more likely a trick of the light. Still, you cannot now say nothing of interest has occurred in Rochester this week!"

Shrike couldn't catch Felix's reply. He doubted it came in the affirmative.

His nephew's poor attitude did not deter Tolhurst's smile as he returned to the bedside. From the nightstand he took up a small bottle. While shrike couldn't read the letters printed on the paper label, he recognized the shape and pattern as something like the laudanum Wren had left for him after the Winter Solstice. Tolhurst dispensed several drops into a teacup, poured tea over it, and passed it to his nephew, who drank the resulting concoction with a grimace. Shrike couldn't blame him. Tolhurst had given Felix a far greater dose than Wren had given Shrike. The tincture couldn't taste anything short of bitter. Shrike supposed mortals, being weaker, required more medicine than fae to withstand the trials of a misadventure like Felix had endured in the Court of Hidden Folk.

As Felix sipped his uncle's brew, Tolhurst looked to the books scattered across the counterpane. He picked up one in particular, examined its spine, then flipped it over to leaf through its pages. His brows rose. He closed the book and set it down again with a few words Shrike couldn't make out. Whatever they were, Felix rolled his eyes at them.

Tolhurst took up another book from the nightstand and held it out to Felix. After a long moment, Felix accepted it in the manner of one accepting the gift of a live viper or a dead rat. Tolhurst seemed accustomed to this as well, for his nephew's reluctance did nothing to strike the beatific smile from his otherwise unremarkable features. With a few words more—to which Felix did not reply—Tolhurst left the room and shut the door after him.

With the nephew now free from his uncle's scrutiny, Shrike eagerly awaited any hint of where Felix had hidden Wren's manuscripts.

Felix continued glaring down at the book Tolhurst had given him.

Shrike, ever seeking a better vantage point to examine the room, flitted from one end of the window-sill to the other.

Felix's head shot up like a hart who'd caught the hunter's scent. His ice-blue eyes fixed on Shrike. With greater speed and strength than Shrike would have assumed possible given his weakened state, Felix drew back his arm and hurled the book at the window.

Shrike leapt off the sill just as the book's spine struck the glazing bars. A single pane cracked. Through it, as Shrike fluttered 'round the window, he glimpsed the gold embossing in the book's leather cover. While he could not read the letters along its spine, he recognized the symbol on its front—a cross like those adorning certain points in the cathedral.

It seemed prudent for the moment to abandon Felix to his dissipation. Shrike swooped away beneath the Gatehouse arch to the other side of Tolhurst's rooms. The window he found there looked in on the front chamber with the hearth. The desk stood beneath that very window. Tolhurst sat at it now. He had his head bent over neat stacks of papers, absorbed in concentration. Either he had not heard his nephew's outburst, or he had already heard so many similar outbursts that the latest one did not prove worthy of his attention.

Shrike likewise took a great interest in the papers. But no sooner had he alighted on the windowsill than he realized they were not Wren's manuscripts. They were simply more of the same dots arranged on rows he'd found on his first search of the gatehouse. Evidently they formed the bulk of Tolhurst's craft. For a music master, as Wren claimed Tolhurst was, Shrike saw precious little evidence of music and heard still less.

Chimes echoing from the cathedral bells drew Shrike's notice to how near the sun had sunk toward the horizon. He took wing again, this time north-west, and kept on over and past the River Medway. London lay scarcely thirty miles off by the crow road—as Nell so oft said—and a shrike might fly just as swift. Certain it was easier than navigating the sea between realms from iron to iron again.

Shrike reached Hyde Park just as crimson sunset began turning to purple twilight. The copse of trees surrounding the toadstool ring sufficed to disguise his transformation from prying mortal eyes. Then he stretched his legs and strode to Achilles to await his Wren.

Only to find his Wren awaited him.

Like in the cathedral, Wren didn't notice Shrike's approach. Shrike supposed the encroaching darkness and eternal fog didn't help matters. He cleared his throat as he drew up to the statue.

Wren flinched—then relaxed as his eyes fell on Shrike and welcome relief broke out across his freckled features. "There you are! I was worried something had happened."

"No," Shrike said honestly. "Nothing happened."

Wren took up his rapid pace toward the toadstool ring. Shrike fell into step beside him—at arm's length. Though their eyes met many times, as Shrike didn't like to take his eyes off Wren now that he might have his fill of the sight of him, and Wren kept stealing glances back, they didn't speak again until they'd fallen through the realms-between-realms and stood in the Grove of Gates.

"What kept you?" Wren asked in a tone of curiosity rather than accusation.

Shrike told him all he'd seen, or failed to see, in Rochester. They set out for Blackthorn as he spoke.

"What might Felix read to incur his uncle's disapproval?" Shrike asked at the conclusion of his tale.

"Anything," Wren replied. "Most likely a French novel. Or perhaps *Fanny Hill*. No doubt Tolhurst would prefer *Pamela*. But to return to the beginning—you say you flew through Rochester?"

"Aye," said Shrike.

"And no one remarked on the oddity of a man flying down the street?" Wren pressed.

"I was not in the shape of a man."

Wren's stare did not grow any less bewildered. "What shape were you in, exactly?"

Words seemed to fail them both. Shrike thought it better to show him. The space of a wink saw him in his feathered form.

As did Wren.

"Oh," said Wren, gazing down in amazement at Shrike. "I see."

Shrike flew up to perch on his shoulder.

Wren smiled and reached out to gingerly stroke the feathers on Shrike's head. "Like when you encountered our window in Staple Inn."

Shrike chirruped, leapt off, and changed back into a grinning man.

Wren closed the distance between them and took Shrike's face in his hands.

Bending down to kiss him felt like falling into flight.

CHAPTER
TWENTY-THREE

The eve of the Moon Market fell crisp and clear. Dusk had just begun to creep over Blackthorn when Shrike gathered his masks into his satchel and led Wren out of the cottage into the surrounding woods. As the half-moon rose, the bare branches above crossed over it like cracks in porcelain. Wind sighed through them, fallen leaves rustled underfoot, and the hoot of an owl echoed from the ever-deepening darkness betwixt and beyond the trees. For many minutes, as Wren strode arm-in-arm with Shrike, these were the only sounds to reach his ears.

Then came the voices.

Wren thought he imagined them at first—his feverish anticipation heightening every snapping branch and rustling breeze into some hidden significance—but with each step, the voices grew louder, more distinct, and more divers. The rattle of wagon-wheels over tree-roots alongside the thud of hoof-beats, jingling bells, and even the trill of a wild fiddle joined the distant murmur rising and ebbing with the passions of speakers yet unseen.

The silvery moonlight deepened the shadows where it couldn't yet reach, and it was with difficulty Wren could even perceive his own hand held out before him.

Yet as he glanced up to seek Shrike's gaze, he could not mistake his smile.

And just when the darkness reached its deepest hue, still more lights joined the moon and stars reflected in Shrike's eyes.

Wren whipped his head 'round to the trees again. The once-impenetrable shadows now danced with specks of violet, blue, and green. The soft yet brilliant glow given off by each will-o'-th'-wisp put all of Vauxhall Gardens to shame. And the shadows cast by the figures wandering amidst them looked far more intriguing—to Wren's eye, at least—than any mortal who strolled down Mayfair.

And in another stride, Wren found himself amongst them.

Even in the dead of winter, the archaic winding pathways overgrown with tree-roots and ferns and faintly glowing toadstools far outshone the beauty of any well-ordered arboretum. The mossy trunks became tent-poles for the booths of fae mongers. Their awnings—some striped canvases that wouldn't look out of place in Rag Fair, some tanned and stretched beast hides, some massive cobwebs glistening with dew, and some entire embroidered tapestries seemingly pulled straight down from castle walls—hung from the otherwise bare branches crossing overhead to form the roof of this natural arcade.

Some peddlers Wren recognized, by court if not by individual. A herd of huldra in their pastoral milk-maid garb had set up a booth overflowing with milk and honey. The sidelong glances they cast his way made him uneasy. He wondered if they were the self-same huldra who'd stolen Felix away, and if so, if they resented him for snatching Felix back. All the fairer sex were equally inscrutable to Wren, be they fae or mortal, but even he couldn't help noticing how the huldra's eyes followed Shrike as he and Wren passed by their booth.

And still others seemed to recognize Wren, as well.

A trio of fae had thrown up a tent made from handkerchiefs of every hue, some silken, others cotton, and still others so threadbare Wren couldn't identify their make, stitched together into an enormous patchwork quilt of all colours. Beneath the canopy of handkerchiefs, enormous clay vessels huddled together. Wren had never before seen amphorae outside of the British Museum. Certain Classicist acquaintances in the Restive Quills would have given their eye-teeth for such a glimpse as Wren had now.

The hawkers of these wares likewise drew his attention. A willowy figure with sticks tangled in their long grey hair moved with astonishing speed given their apparent age as they dipped a copper ladle into the open mouth of a pithos thrice their own size to dispense wine into the waiting wooden bowl of a tusked fae leaning over the branch that served as their bar. At least Wren assumed it was wine. It certainly had the colour of it—a deep, dark shade of purpled crimson that rivalled the best bottled Burgundy in his father's cellar. A woman who would have towered over Shrike, and whose arms put beer-barrels to shame, proved her strength in hauling the amphorae hither-and-thither as custom demanded. The third peddler, a young man who looked unremarkable save for the dark-stained cravat he'd tied 'round his throat, caught Wren's eye as Wren stared.

Wren hastened to look away, lest the young man take offense.

But before he could, the young man flashed a smile filled with fangs and, to Wren's surprise, gave him a jaunty wave as if greeting a friend from across a pub.

Wren, confused, nevertheless raised his arm to return the gesture.

This appeared to satisfy the young man, who went back to assisting his compatriots.

Yet while each of the three peddlers bore very little resemblance to either of their partners, Wren realized one common trait among them. They all had rounded ears.

"Are they mortals?" Wren murmured, drawing Shrike's attention to the particular booth with a hand on his arm and a nod of his head.

Shrike followed Wren's gaze and replied, "For another fortnight, at least."

Wren didn't take his meaning. He dared another glimpse at the peddlers in an attempt to glean the truth. His eye fell again to the stained cravat. A ruddy stain, he noted, and an old one at that, half washed out in blotches. Wine, probably. Or perhaps blood. Though the throat beneath it didn't seem to bear any scars. And yet the cravat looked familiar. Wren owned a half-dozen like it himself, he supposed. What might happen in a fortnight to make its wearer no longer mortal, he couldn't fathom. He caught Shrike's eye again with his own brow knit in confusion.

Shrike held his gaze, then glanced away, significantly, upwards past the skeletal canopy to the shining half-moon hanging overhead.

Wren stared at the half-moon—which, in a fortnight, would wax full.

The familiar cravat was his own, given to a wounded werewolf so many months ago.

Before he could think better of it, Wren whipped his head 'round again to gawk at the wine-bearers. None seemed to pay him any mind. The young man—the werewolf—with Wren's blood-stained cravat on his throat had engaged another customer in smiling conversation. No hint to his true lupine nature save his sharp teeth.

Then Shrike's palm settled gently onto the small of Wren's back, and Wren took the hint to move along.

Walking together in the fae realm afforded Wren and Shrike the opportunity for open and silent communication between them. They could speak with touches and glances as well as words. Wren's eyes—and indeed, his hands—might linger as long as they liked on his beloved's form. The fae held no malice towards his wanton affection. Wren basked in this newfound freedom. Yet the presence of the werewolves conjured questions.

"Are there mortals in the market?" Wren asked Shrike in a low tone as they rejoined the current of the crowd. "Besides myself, I mean."

"The blacksmith," said Shrike.

"*The* blacksmith?" Wren echoed.

"Aye." Shrike's mouth formed a grim line.

The thought of what other sorts of mortals might carve out their lives in the fae realms set Wren's mind afire with curiosity. He looked sharp in search of a stall filled with iron. "And where is his booth?"

"She has no booth."

Wren fixed Shrike with his full astonished attention. "She?"

"She doesn't bring her wares to market," Shrike explained. "Iron makes folk uneasy. She walks through when it pleases her and settles her accounts with those who owe her. Most are indebted to her for years yet. It takes several harvests to pay for something of her make."

"And if someone wants to commission her anew?" Wren asked.

"She's easy enough to find in a crowd. Folk give her a wide berth."

"Out of respect," Wren hypothesized.

Shrike gave a one-shouldered shrug. "Or fear."

Wren glanced 'round to see if the fae crowd avoided any particular person in their midst. While many clustered at booths and many more streamed between the trees, he found no one whom they dared not bump elbows with.

Save Shrike and himself.

"Where is your booth set?" Wren asked.

"I've none," Shrike answered him.

"Then how will you dole out your masks?"

"I'll go from booth to booth myself, for most. Others I'll find amidst the crowd."

"Like the blacksmith," Wren concluded.

"Aye."

Wren caught Shrike's gaze and held it in expectation.

Bewilderment flickered through Shrike's eyes for a moment before he drew the same conclusion as Wren. He didn't seem to take any satisfaction in it. If anything given how he shifted his gaze, Wren supposed him embarrassed. Trust Shrike to remain modest despite the evident strength of his reputation amongst the fae host.

Shrike strode past many a peddler which drew Wren's attention. A fae with tufted ears had filled their booth with every sort of stringed instrument imaginable—many beyond Wren's imagination—and demonstrated a dulcimer for another fae with damselfly wings. The resulting tune tugged at something within Wren he hadn't realized had been left wanting his whole life. Shrike's hand on the small of his back kept him moving along, past another booth piled high with armour and armaments, some gleaming, some rusted, and others with fresh scarlet spatter glistening amidst the silver. But not until they reached a particular painted wagon did Shrike halt his stride.

The first thing that caught Wren's eye was not the goods proffered, but the seller. Specifically, the seller's eyes. They were not an unusual shade, nor an unusual shape. There were, however, six of them; two on the brow, and two high on the cheek, with the more typical pair arranged between. Wren hadn't felt afraid for his own sake before in the fae realms—how could he, when Shrike stood at his side—but nonetheless a cold spike of alarm drove through him as he locked eyes with too-many-eyes and watched them blink out of turn. Then they turned away to barter with a fox-tailed fae. Wren, no longer pinned down by the tripled stare, found himself able to breathe again and to notice other details about the peddler. Such as their spindly limbs with too many joints shifting beneath their tunic sleeves. Or the stringy green hair hanging down over their pointed ears.

Wren forced his gaze away from the fae altogether. Their wagon proved almost as interesting and far less alarming. Wine-red pomegranates spilled forth from wicker bushel baskets, alongside heart-shaped persimmons and tangerines and something that looked rather like a tangerine except as small as an olive and—if Wren were to believe the example set by the fox-tailed fae who bartered for a palmful ahead of them—they were to be eaten whole, rind and all.

As the fox-tailed fae wandered off eating their prize, the peddler turned their peculiar gaze on Shrike. Shrike dug into his satchel and brought forth the eyeless mask. In exchange, the many-eyed fae gave him three pomegranates that, while plump and bright, seemed hardly sufficient payment for the quality of Shrike's craftsmanship.

Yet Shrike slipped them into his satchel with a nod of thanks and continued on his way. Wren followed him and tried to ignore the feeling of six eyes watching his retreat.

Shrike next halted before a stall both formed from and filled with beast pelts. The furs presented for sale included at least one tiger, as Wren assumed from its fire-and-coal striped hide, and several shaggy bears, though others proved more difficult to identify. One particular specimen that began with feathers, continued into fur, and ended with scales gave him considerable pause. Some were merely skins tanned into leather.

The fae who hung the skins from the branches was a peculiar little creature with a tufted tail and a hat with a wide brim that flopped down over their face. They greeted Shrike with a queer chirruping sound. Shrike gave them the patchwork mask. They took it from him without handing over anything in return. Shrike didn't seem to expect it of them. He took his leave with a nod. Wren followed suit.

"Do they not pay you for the masks?" Wren asked when he thought they'd passed out of earshot.

"They do," said Shrike.

"They didn't just now," Wren pointed out. "Are the masks given out on credit? Or have they paid in advance?"

"The masks will grant me their service for a year and a day."

"Which begins tonight," Wren concluded. "For the pomegranates, at least."

Shrike smiled. He brought forth one of the pomegranates from his satchel. A swift twist of his strong hands sufficed to break its ring and reveal the glistening jewels within. He held it out to Wren.

Wren accepted with unaccountable fluttering in his heart. He plucked out one particular fruit and popped it into his mouth. It burst all the sweeter for Shrike having given it to him. "And what will you receive for the patchwork mask?"

"The services of the tannery. For a year and a day I may leave my hunted hides in a particular hollow stump and expect to find them returned there cured. The air of Blackthorn has improved much since we came to that arrangement."

Wren, who had the misfortune to walk through the reek of a tannery once or twice in his time in London, readily agreed. "Why a year and a day? Why not simply a year?"

"Most contracts run thus in the fae realms. They have done so for centuries. I know not why."

"I suppose," Wren conceded, "it's no more odd than a Bond Street tailor giving his price in guineas rather than pounds."

Shrike furrowed his brow in confusion.

"A guinea is worth one pound and one shilling," Wren explained.

"Ah," said Shrike, though he didn't quite look satisfied, and indeed appeared as if he might enquire further.

Before he could, a sudden silence descended on all the Moon Market like a fog falling over a moor.

Wren feared he'd done something to try the patience of the gathered fae. But a glance across the mute crowd showed no eyes fixed on him in turn. Some, he noted, looked to Shrike.

Most looked down the winded wooded market path to a figure which loomed over all.

A grey horse, some fourteen hands high, strode through the crowd, at a languid yet deliberate pace despite the lack of reins. Its rider was a lady whose gown fell like a waterfall over her steed's flanks, whereupon its moon-white folds faded to a blush, then crimson, and finally, as it dragged over the moss and tree-roots beneath her, to a dark ragged hem like lace burnt black. Even Wren, who did not oft take note of women's beauty, felt awe-struck by her ethereal grace.

The grey horse halted before Shrike.

Shrike inclined his head in the barest nod.

The lady returned the gesture.

From his satchel, Shrike drew out the cut-filigree mask of white hart's hide. He held it up toward her. Her silvery hair spilled over her shoulders as she bent to receive it with hands whose fingertips hardly peeked out from beneath the lily-throated sleeves of her gown.

Then she arose. Without any other sign from her that Wren could perceive, her steed resumed its slow and steady pace. She departed as silently as she had arrived, continuing on in the same direction as she had begun to pass through all the market and vanish into the mist with as much substance as a ghost.

Gradually the crowd stirred in her wake until the raucous bustle she had interrupted returned. Only Wren and Shrike remained still and silent together.

"Who was that?" Wren whispered when the pale lady had disappeared from view.

"Lady Aethelthryth," Shrike replied in a murmur. "Of the Court of Bells and Candles."

"And what does she grant you in return?" Wren asked.

"She has promised to grant me a boon and given me leave to name it. I know not yet what shape it shall take."

"What has she granted you in prior years?"

"Nothing," said Shrike. "I've never before made her a mask."

"Then word of your craftsmanship must have spread in the past year," said Wren, unable to hide the pride in his voice.

Shrike's return smile appeared more wistful than proud. "Methinks she is enchanted with the novelty of having her mask made by the Oak King."

Before Wren could dispute that point, a cry rose up from the milling crowd.

"Oi, Butcher!"

Both Shrike and Wren whirled toward the shout.

A glass-blower's booth stood across the way. A small ceramic furnace nestled amongst the particular copse of trees which formed their stall. The fire burning within it appeared unlike any Wren had ever seen before. Glowing ribbons swirled through each other in an ever-twisting living knot whose pale hues shimmered between lavender and sea-foam. It etched a similar pattern onto the globs of molten glass thrust into it, and as the fae tending it withdrew the long pipe to blow out its shape into a rounded bottle, the pattern spread out like frost across a window-pane and continued to shift long after the bottle itself had cooled into its final shape.

Then a figure melted out of the shadows cast by the curious flames. From the flickering depths, Nell strode forth to meet them.

"Hunting you out of a crowd is oft more trouble than this," she observed, glancing between Shrike and Wren. She wore the same garb—tunic, hose, boots, and all—as she had when Wren had met her, and the same knowing smile as well.

"You had some luck to aid you," Shrike replied with a significant look to where Lady Aethelthryth had vanished.

"P'rhaps." Nell put a hand on her hip and cast an equally significant look at Shrike's satchel.

Shrike seemed well-practiced in taking her hints. He opened his satchel and drew out the bat-winged mask.

Nell took it from him. As she experimentally flapped its jointed leather wings, her smile changed from sardonic to sincere. When she glanced up again, pure delight gleamed in her eyes. "It's certainly not a raven."

Shrike seemed pleased with this assessment. "Have you seen the ambassador this night?"

This enquiry didn't appear to baffle Nell even half so much as it baffled Wren.

"No," she replied. "Though doubtless I'll meet with him in the next hunt. Will you?"

"I cannot say for certain." Shrike held out the beaked mask with the glass eyes. "If you would be so kind."

Nell arched one eyebrow so high Wren assumed she meant to refuse, but then the wry half-smile twisted her mouth, and she took the mask from Shrike.

"When will you rejoin us," she said, tossing the mask from hand to hand with the ease of a juggler, "if not before Ostara?"

"I know not," said Shrike. He didn't seem overmuch troubled by it.

"But you will rejoin us," Nell pressed.

"Aye," Shrike conceded.

Nell seemed satisfied. She nodded to Shrike, then gave Wren a bow whose sweeping arms appeared somewhat mocking. With that, she turned away from them both and vanished into the streaming crowd.

"What masks remain?" Wren asked Shrike.

"None but one," Shrike replied.

"And for whom?"

Shrike glanced over Wren's head at the surrounding crowd.

Wren turned to follow his eye.

A rag-and-bone seller across the way boasted a mighty stack of blood-stained broadsides several feet taller and many years older than

Wren himself. The piles of bones surrounding it proved even more varied.

The booth beside the rag-and-bone seller held still greater interest for Wren. Enough clockwork to keep all of London in time whirred and ticked together in a profusion of brass. Yet while a great many pocket-watches hung from the surrounding branches, they were outnumbered by the multitude of queer instruments Wren couldn't recognize. And what watch-faces he did see didn't seem to keep the same twelve hours as his own watch. One particular delicate contraption of minuscule glass globes suspended in concentric wires seemed to track the phases of the moon. The purpose of the clockwork fish with shimmering brass scales swimming up and down inside the confines of a bell jar, Wren couldn't begin to fathom.

Between the two booths wandered a fae who might have looked almost human, save their pointed ears, their iridescent blue-black-violet feathers instead of hair, and the glistening membrane sliding sideways across their eyes beneath their lids every time they blinked.

But when Wren turned back to Shrike, he found Shrike gazing down at him and him alone.

"Follow me," said Shrike, and strode off.

Wren followed him. It wasn't difficult. Shrike carved a path through the crowd as a sickle through wheat. Fae fell away before his steps, leaving plenty of room for Wren to scurry along in his wake. Their stares made the nape of his neck prickle. He ignored it.

Shrike led the way all through the winding arcade of the Moon Market. The tapestries and awnings and flickering will-o'-th'-wisps dwindled as they went. Then they ceased altogether, and Wren and Shrike stood alone in the dark forest beneath the cracked-porcelain moon.

Only the distant echoes of the market's din broke through the wintry silence. Wren peered into the shadows, straining his eyes to see what fae would emerge to claim Shrike's final mask.

The slight creak of leather against leather reached Wren's ear. He whirled towards it. Silver streams of moonlight limned Shrike beside him and showed his satchel open, with his hand delving into it. He withdrew the final mask still wrapped in its protective cloth. His deft fingers plucked away the folds to reveal a face formed of ivy, with vines pouring forth from its eyes and mouth. Only Wren's prior knowledge of Shrike's craft gave any hint of its leather construction, for his eyes beheld delicate pointed leaves glistening faintly green, indistinguishable from those running over the tree-roots beneath his tread.

And Shrike held it out to Wren.

Wren stared up at him in disbelief. "For me?"

Shrike smiled.

Wren took the mask with reverence. It seemed almost too beautiful to behold, much less grasp in his own unworthy hands. To think Shrike had crafted it for him in particular...

"Thank you," Wren said, though the words hardly felt sufficient.

All the moreso when he glanced up to find Shrike delving into his satchel once again. He withdrew another parcel. This time, he held it out to Wren still swathed in a protective layer of silk.

Wren handed back his mask for Shrike to hold as he took the second parcel in bewilderment. "What's this?"

Shrike gave him a look that bade him unwrap it.

The silk alone was precious. What lay beneath it proved far more precious still. The smooth fabric flowed across Wren's palms and gave way to leather of equal softness, gathered together in an intricate Celtic knot at one end, and falling away into a hem like the ragged edge of autumn leaves. Over-turned, its folds parted to reveal a cunningly-crafted tome as tall as Wren's hand and as thick as his thumb. Its blank pages fluttered in the evening breeze.

Only then did Wren recognize what he held. He'd never seen its like outside of antiquarian collections, and even amongst those it proved rare indeed. A gyrdel-book of the kind which might have hung from the belt of a medieval monk in the days of knights. For Wren, a sketch-book in a leather shroud. Except its pages didn't bear the rough texture of rag-paper. Beneath Wren's fingertips, they felt soft and smooth as moonbeams.

"Vellum?" Wren breathed, hardly able to believe it. He glanced up at

Shrike again just in time to see him affirm his guess with a solemn nod. "When did you make this?"

Shrike's modest smile appeared all the more handsome by silvery moonlight. "While you were in London."

Wren hardly knew how to even begin thanking him. The sheer beauty of the craft took his breath away.

So it seemed only fitting to seize the front of Shrike's tunic and pull him down for a kiss to take his breath away in turn.

CHAPTER
TWENTY-FOUR

The Vernal Equinox fell on a Friday, which made matters not quite as convenient as Wren might have hoped.

"A holiday?" Mr Grigsby echoed when Wren finally screwed up the courage to ask him about it on Thursday morning.

"If it wouldn't be too much trouble, sir," said Wren.

"No trouble at all! You've done so much for us all winter long, Lofthouse—it's high time you had a spring holiday."

Privately, Wren very much agreed. Aloud, he demurred.

"Nonsense," Mr Grigsby said over him. "A holiday you deserve, and a holiday you shall have. When we part tonight, don't let me see you again before Monday morning."

In the face of that, Wren could do little more than acquiesce.

That evening, Achilles watched over him as he met Shrike in Hyde Park and continued on at arm's length to the mushroom ring. They returned to Blackthorn, where, despite the sturdy warmth of Shrike's embrace, Wren found himself hardly able to sleep. His nerves remained afire with eager anticipation. Like a child counting the minutes until Christmas morning, though no Christmas he could recall from his own childhood had ever promised so much delight as any day with Shrike.

Dawn arrived. Wren and Shrike broke their fast in the customary fashion. Then Wren took up his Green Man mask. It appeared beautiful as ever, Shrike's craftsmanship evident in the burnished point of each leaf and the curl of every vine.

"It seems a shame," Wren said as Shrike shrugged on his cloak. "To toss it aside after wearing it but the once."

Shrike appeared bemused. "If you like it so well, I'll make you another."

"You needn't," Wren hastened to say. "Unless, of course, you wish to."

"Your wish is mine," Shrike replied with his small, bashful, handsome smile.

Wren couldn't help but return it. He raised his mask to his face as much to hide his glowing cheeks as to test its fit.

The mask fit his face as if tendrils of true ivy had grown over his bones. Inside, it felt soft and smooth and warm against his skin. Crafted by hands that by know knew his features as well as their own. Peering out through its eyes limned his vision in verdant growth, all the world framed in by bending branches. He turned this gaze on Shrike and found it suited him well.

Shrike, meanwhile, had donned his antlered oaken mask. While it hid certain handsome features, the warmth of Shrike's dark eyes shone through the shadows cast by the leather as he smiled.

The path through the woods from Blackthorn Briar to the gathering place of Ostara celebrants echoed with trills of birdsong. The merry whistles increased the further along Wren and Shrike went down the winding way. Wren's anticipation heightened with every step.

Then all at once the forest fell away to reveal a glistening glade.

Its span rivalled the breadth of the tourney field of the Court of the Silver Wheel. A massive beech tree, its trunk gnarled and burled and its branches stout and curving in all directions, stood proud in the midst of the host of fae already gathered. It would take a score of fae joining hands to encircle its roots. Indeed, some seemed determined to try, as they clustered 'round it. Others flocked together in smaller congregations throughout the meadow, dancing, drinking, laughing, and performing arcane rites Wren felt all too eager to examine more closely.

"Where is Nell?" Wren asked, his arm thoroughly entangled with Shrike's as they strode out into the meadow. "Do you think she's arrived?"

Shrike tilted his head toward a particular corner of the meadow. Wren squinted. There, amidst a picnic of pomegranates and wine strewn over mossy stones, a half-dozen nymphs in pale gauzy chitons lounged tittering around a singular dark-haired feathery figure in tunic and hose and bat-winged mask. Nell, Wren concluded, had not only arrived but already staked her claim on the hearts of a bouquet of beauty which even Wren's own biased eye couldn't fail to appreciate.

"Ah," said Wren.

"Aye," replied Shrike.

Wren's gaze flitted over the masked crowd in search of other examples of Shrike's handiwork. He thought it best to leave Nell to her amusements. It seemed Shrike thought likewise, as he strode through the crowd on a meandering course which allowed Wren to soak up all the bizarre sights his feverish dreams could never have imagined.

A faun frolicked past on prancing hooves. The eyes and mouth of their wood-carved mask were all perfectly round, its surface mottled like tree-bark, and they played a jaunty melody on a hornpipe as they went. A pair of fae danced to his tune; they wore helms of knights so rusted full of holes they appeared as lacework, one in green-tarnished copper, the other in black-tarnished silver. Following their path led Wren's eye to a circle of fae seated on the ground before a pile of eggs—speckled quail, robin blue, pale green duck.

Among these fae Wren recognized a mask of Shrike's make in the patchwork leather mask with button eyes. Its wearer plucked an egg from the pile and pierced its shell with a pin before blowing out the innards into shallow dark-glazed bowls. They bent to examine the resulting patterns; what conclusions they drew from them, Wren couldn't fathom.

The other gathered fae, who had evidently already enacted this very ritual, carved and painted their hollowed eggs and strung them through with strands of hair plucked from their own heads. The mask of one had clockwork features which whirred and spun together to form a brass imitation of a fae smile that moved as the wearer spoke. Another wore a cracked doll's face which appeared porcelain at first, but at second glance Wren thought might be egg-shell. The third wore a goat's skull bleached white with the sun save for the blackened spatter of dried blood across its ivory brow.

The current of the crowd ebbed before Shrike as he and Wren strode on through the revelry. The variety of masks did not abate—one of feathered wings which seemed about to flutter off the wearer's face; another of rose-vines with the mouth ringed in thorns; a veil of chain rings woven so fine as to flow like folds of silk over the wearer's cheeks; a mask of glass blown so thin it appeared as little more than a sheen of dew on the wearer's skin. Rising above the tumult of gaiety rode a pale woman on a grey horse. Wren recognized Lady Aethelthryth, though the white hart hide of her lacework mask had crusted over crimson since he'd seen it last.

Wren's heart leapt to recognize another of Shrike's make in the beaked plague doctor's mask with the bottle-end green eyes. He had expected to find it on an imposing figure, one of Shrike's own height or more, something to loom over all like the spectre of Poe's Red Death. To his astonishment, the wearer appeared no taller than himself, though the rest of their costume satisfied Wren's desire for the dramatic. A voluminous black hooded robe obscured any hint of their shape, like shadow over shadow, and from the sleeves falling like sheets of rain over their hands, only a slender silver-capped walking stick protruded. Despite this encumbrance, the plague doctor wove their way through the crowd with sprightly animation and twirled their arms in apparent delight at the sight of Shrike and Wren going past.

The plague doctor was not alone in taking notice. While Wren gawked at his fellow revellers, many more eyes gazed back at him. He could not quite deny his initial spark of alarm at attracting attention—as he strode arm-in-arm with Shrike through the wide open meadow with neither tree nor shrub to shelter them from judgment—but as before, in the Wild Hunt and the Moon Market and the Court of Hidden Folk, the fae gazed on him not with censure or derision. Some of their glances appeared admiring. A few Wren thought held the gleam of jealousy.

Most, by far, fixed him with eager and open curiosity. A certain delight in discovery ran throughout the fae realms like a golden thread winding through a tapestry. And on this particular occasion, they delighted in discovering the Oak King arm-in-arm with his mortal paramour wearing beautiful masks crafted by his own clever hands.

As Shrike and Wren's amiable ambling drew them nearer to the sacred tree, Wren caught sight of the leather patchwork button-eyed mask again. Its wearer carried strings of blown eggs decorated in intricate patterns, and as Wren watched, tied them on to the slender tips of the lowest-hanging twigs. Wren paused to observe their work and by so doing drew Shrike's attention to it.

"And when shall we make our own votive offering?" Wren asked.

"After the dance," Shrike replied. "If you'll join me in it."

Wren turned to him with brow raised. "Are you asking, my lord?"

Shrike wore the small, shy, handsome smile that Wren loved so well. "An' it so please you."

Wren grinned.

They did not have long to wait. Above the general murmur of the crowd the strains of the hornpipe grew louder, and a jaunty fiddle and chiming tambourine soon rose to join its song. Folk turned away from idle conversation towards the tree looming over all.

Shrike held out his hand to Wren.

And, as he had wished to do so many times over in Hyde Park, Wren accepted his handclasp.

The warm rough palm laid against his own as if, like pages from a book, they were meant to nestle together for centuries, with their interlaced fingers as binding. Wren had lost count of how oft he touched Shrike whilst in the fae realms. Every instance gave him the same thrill settling into comfort, like a wave crashing over the shore followed by the gentle lapping of the tide. How happily Wren could sink beneath that sea and sleep in bliss.

But the masked dance was no Vienna waltz.

As Wren took Shrike's hand, so too did other revellers, hand-over-hand-over-hand until a loose chain of fae began to encircle the massive, gnarled cluster of roots at the base of the mighty tree. Despite the wild and unconventional appearance of the throng, Wren recognized the form as the beginnings of a country dance. He expected Nell and her nymphs to appear beside Shrike and himself to complete the ring. But they appeared on the far side of the circle, and other fae seemed reluctant to approach Shrike, bound by the same wary awe as the crowds of the Moon Market. At length, just when Wren thought the chain must break, two bold souls stepped forward. The one who grasped Wren's free hand wore a fox-faced mask carved of wood, and while it disguised her visage, her pastoral garb, cloven hooves, and tufted tail marked her out as one of the huldra. A creature with a frame as small as a child's took Shrike's hand on the opposing side, yet Wren noted the grey beard trailing out from beneath their golden sun mask with sparkling sapphire *cloisonné* surrounding the eyes.

No sooner had all hands clasped than the dance began. The steps proved simple enough; a winding spiral grapevine that sent Wren stepping sideways across the tree-roots, his boot-heels fitting into the hollows between them. Wren had attended a few country assemblies in his youth—however unwillingly—yet he felt far more at ease amidst the fae, where his blood seemed to sing in his veins at the bidding of the fiddle and flute and tambourine. Shrike and the huldra released him to spin, a move he followed a half-second behind, but no matter, as he reunited with them all with backs to the tree, and on and on in the ever-winding chain of masks, faster and faster, whirling with the rising shriek of the fiddle until, with one final desperate trill, the song ceased, and the dancers with it.

Wren turned to find Shrike removing his own mask and hastened to follow suit.

A pang of regret struck Wren's heart as he tied the leather cord of his mask 'round the branch. His recollection of Shrike's promise to craft him another soon soothed it away—less so for the mask itself and more for the thought of wearing his beloved's handiwork on his unworthy frame.

Thus freed of his burden, Wren stepped back from the tree and glanced over his fellow Bacchantes in search of Shrike. He did not find him at first sight, though he did find his handiwork in evidence all throughout the throng. There was the many-eyed fae with their eyeless mask strung up amidst twigs which greatly resembled their own limbs. There were Nell and her accompanying nymphs with their masks strung together in a garland of daisies—Nell's at the centre—to drape across the barren branches. There was Lady Aethelthryth astride her grey steed reaching up to tie the delicate ribbons of her crimson-encrusted leather lacework to a far higher perch than anyone else could hope to attain.

And nearer to hand stood the plague doctor in their voluminous black robes and the long-beaked mask with bottle-green glass eyes.

The plague doctor threw back their hood to reveal shoulder-length silver hair tied in a loose queue at the nape of the neck. They shrugged off their black robe to uncover satin breeches, silk stockings, an embroidered waistcoat with at least a hundred minuscule buttons running down its front, and a frock coat in the same style with voluminous skirts, all in a particular shade of green like sunlight seen through the under-sides of leaves in summer. Then they took their leather mask by the beak and lifted it from their head. Beneath it lay thousands of silvery silken threads crossed over each other into a tightly-woven mask.

With a jolt, Wren recognized the spiderweb fae from the Wild Hunt.

Oblivious to Wren's gawking, the spiderweb fae hung his leather-beaked mask on the end of a barren branch and folded his black robe over the limb behind it, as if to dress the branch up as a writhing shadow serpent with glass eyes of glittering green. He clutched his cane in slender kid-gloved hands—a cane which Wren belatedly realized was not a cane at all, but the scabbard of a rapier. This he buckled on to a slender belt strung across his narrow chest to hang down at his waist so his palm might naturally come to rest on the pommel.

And, just as naturally, Shrike's palm came to rest on the small of Wren's back.

Wren smiled despite his distraction. He turned to regard the welcome sight of Shrike's dark eyes gazing down on him. Such a gaze pulled Wren in as the moon pulled the tides and seemed to bid him lift his own face up to meet Shrike's in a kiss. A call which sorely tempted Wren, and even in the midst of a crowd, here in the fae realms he felt almost free enough to respond to it.

Almost.

"Hail and well met, Butcher! Lofthouse!"

Both Shrike and Wren whirled towards the now-familiar call. Emerging from the current of the crowd, like Venus rising from the foam, came Nell, flanked by a pair of attending nymphs. She draped one arm around the first nymph's shoulders and nestled the other around the second nymph's waist. With her bat-winged mask relinquished to the tree Wren could see she bore a most satisfied grin, and the nymphs for their part appeared equally content to share her company.

"Nell," Shrike replied, sounding not in the least surprised to find her thus.

Nell raised her brow at the nymph to her left. The nymph lifted her free arm, which held a wine-bottle. A pale green liquid sloshed within.

"A toast," Nell said as the nymph held the bottle out to Shrike. "To the new season and the Oak King."

"To the new season," Shrike conceded, accepting the bottle from the nymph with a nod of thanks. He took a swig, and Wren took no small pleasure in watching the swallow travel down his long and slender throat—a throat which begged for bruised kisses—as he threw his head back.

Shrike made as if to return the bottle to the nymph but paused as he caught Wren's expectant eye. After a moment's hesitation, he offered it to Wren.

Wren received it from him and tossed back a swallow. He braced for a burn like the gin he and the Restive Quills had found themselves reduced to drinking after Oxford.

Instead he encountered the bubbles of champagne.

It tasted of honey and star-anise and something more Wren couldn't quite discern. It tasted the same way the fiddle had echoed through the Court of Hidden Folk, as if the wine had bubbled forth from the mountain's depths and shrieked in wild abandon as it danced down waterfalls into the bottle and would continue on dancing through his veins.

The taste lingered on his tongue. He lowered the bottle to find Nell, the nymphs, and Shrike all staring at him—Nell and the nymphs with varying degrees of curiosity, Shrike with something that bordered on concern.

"Not bad," Wren blurted, and found his words hoarse. As if he'd spent the night previous carousing and then drunkenly singing *Twa Corbies* and *Three Ravens* in an alternating loop to compare the lyrics until he'd utterly lost his voice and thoroughly annoyed his friends. Not that such a thing had ever happened before. Certainly not at Oxford.

Nell laughed and accepted the bottle back from him.

"We should withdraw," said Shrike, surprising Wren.

"What for?" Wren asked.

"To make way for the second round of the dance."

"You've brought a blade," Nell interjected. "Shall you not join us? Or have you had your surfeit of dancing?"

"It's a dance of swords," Shrike explained in the face of Wren's evident confusion.

"And Butcher cuts quite the handsome figure in it," Nell added. "For those who admire such things."

Perhaps it was the fae wine. Regardless, Wren heard himself declare, "I should like to see it."

Shrike shot him an astonished glance.

Wren, his head full of Yorkshire Morris dancing and the memory of how Shrike had looked with a sword in his hand, met his gaze steadily. "If you're willing."

The rosy hue returned to Shrike's high cheekbones alongside his shy smile. "I'm willing, an' it so please you."

Nell grinned. "You're an excellent influence on him, Lofthouse."

And with a cheery wave, she strolled off, nymphs in tow.

No sooner had she passed out of earshot than Wren developed second thoughts. "There's no danger in it, is there?"

"None aim to wound," Shrike replied.

That wasn't quite what Wren had asked, but he supposed the answer would suffice.

Shrike drew out his sword. The blade glistened. Wren had watched him sharpen it on one Sunday afternoon, sitting on the rock by the stream, his hair falling to frame his face as he bent to ply the whetstone.

Shrike looked no less handsome now, holding it forth with far greater strength of arm than Wren himself could boast.

Over Shrike's broad shoulders Wren espied other fae unsheathing their blades. Several bore silver similar to Shrike's. Some, however, had weapons of more peculiar make—a bronze gladius pitted and tarnished with barnacles clinging to its hilt; a flamberge whose waving edge seemed to flicker with its own inner candle flame; a longsword of polished wood with dried vines curling down its length; a scimitar whose smooth and gleaming milk-white edge looked uncomfortably as if it were carved of bone; and a blade of pale translucent blue that might have been either glass or ice. The only sword-dancer Wren recognized, apart from Shrike, was the spiderweb fae, who drew out a slender silver rapier from its cane-sheath.

All the while, as the dancers drew their weapons and assumed their positions, unarmed fae withdrew from the tree. Wren followed suit and perched at the rim of the crowd near enough to watch Shrike's performance with eager and hungry gaze.

Shrike did not disappoint.

The music of the fiddle and flute rekindled. The sword-wielding fae gathered in groups of five. Each raised their blade in their left hand. At the first beat of the tambourine, two blades crossed, the others following one-by-one in time with the song's rhythm. When all swords had crossed, the dancers spun like the spokes of a wheel, and each five-spoked wheel in turn began to whirl around the tree.

Then, as the fiddle unleashed a joyous shriek, the wheels burst. Swords uncrossed and lashed out anew to strike each other in time with the beating of the tambourine. The rhythm increased in rapidity and the sword-wielders redoubled their efforts to match it with thrusts and parries enough to dizzy any mortal fencing master. Over, beneath, and between these blows the wielders danced, Shrike amongst them.

Every glimpse of Shrike made Wren's heart sing. His strapping frame bent and leapt in serpentine patterns to avoid the crashing blades, his dark locks trailing behind him in narrow escape, his own arming-sword in constant motion to deflect the others' strikes.

Wren held his breath as he beheld Shrike flip backwards over the curving moon-white bone scimitar and the rippling flamberge. His form plunged beneath the sea of blades.

And did not emerge again.

The bow slashed across the fiddle. The music ceased, and with it, the dance.

Wren's heart remained in his throat.

The dancers broke their wheels and withdrew. As they did so, they revealed the rising form of Shrike. The writhing Gordian knot of swords had come together across his body. His broad chest heaved beneath five blades—his own among them—crossed to form a star. Beads of sweat glistened on his brow. A smile graced his handsome lips, and a mischievous gleam lit his dark eyes. The points of the bronze gladius and the ice-glass sword lay on either side of his throat.

The waiting crowd erupted into cheers. Wren drew breath for what felt like the first time.

The dancers uncrossed their blades and exchanged bows. When the dance had ceased, Shrike's wheel had halted a stone's throw from Wren. As such, when the dancers began to rejoin the throng, and the throng in turn flowed in to reclaim them as the tide reclaims the waves it sends to shore, the ensuing chaos hid Shrike from Wren's sight once again. Even standing on his toes did not afford him a view of Shrike, Nell, or any other recognizable figure.

Save for the spiderweb fae.

The spiderweb fae had joined an entirely different wheel from Shrike's and had wound up quite near to Wren indeed by the dance's end. Unlike all the other dancers, the spiderweb fae now wandered the crowd alone, unacknowledged by any of the other folk.

Perhaps it was because fae society had fewer restrictions, with folk of all sexes mingling in conversation, feasting, and dance. Or perhaps it was because the fae held no prejudices against men of Wren's predilections. Or perhaps it was something in the fae liquor Nell had provided. Whatever the reason, Wren found himself drawn more towards strangers rather than shying away as he would have done in London.

And, as the spiderweb fae stood alone rather than mingling with the throng, like a wallflower at a country dance, Wren thought it only polite to bridge the expanse between them.

Layer upon layer of cobwebbing, like so much lace, built up the diaphanous material of the spiderweb fae's mask into something stiff and opaque that shone silver-white in the rays of the full moon. It covered everything from the hairline down to the sharp curving tip of a beak which Wren suspected ran somewhat longer than the actual nose beneath—though, given what he'd seen thus far of the fae, he supposed he couldn't make too many assumptions. On either side he could just make out the tips of two pointed ears, which matched the pointed chin and full lips in their deep shade of iridescent indigo. The French heels of the silver shoes added some three inches or more to his height, which allowed him to stand eye-to-eye with Wren. The eyes were likewise blue, but icy pale, which made the cat-slit pupils all the more apparent. These eyes slid toward Wren as he approached and widened when they met his gaze.

"Good evening," Wren said, and hoped his words sounded polite rather than presumptuous.

The spiderweb fae blinked. For a moment, Wren feared he'd given offence. Then, to Wren's astonishment, the dark blue lips parted in a delighted grin.

"Hail and well met, fellow traveller!" said the spiderweb fae, his voice ebullient and bright. He gave a court bow worthy of Versailles yet performed with far greater grace than any mortal courtier could accomplish, equal parts elegant and ornate. Somehow the bend of his waist, the dip of his knee, and the twirl of his hand did not seem in excess, as it might have done on an Englishman.

Wren bowed far more simply in return.

"I believe I've glimpsed you once before," the spiderweb fae continued. "In the Wild Hunt? By the Oak King's side?"

"You're familiar with the Oak King?" asked Wren.

"Moreso this year than any other. But less so than yourself, I should think."

Wren privately conceded the point. Aloud, he said, "What familiarity did you have with past Oak Kings? If it's not too bold of me to ask," he added hurriedly.

"None too bold in the least!" the spiderweb fae assured him with another wrist-twirling wave. "But I'm afraid my answer will disappoint you. I've enjoyed no familiarity whatsoever with the Oak Kings of the past. I'm merely a visitor to the Court of the Silver Wheel, and an infrequent visitor at that. Urgent matters at Midwinter prevented my attending even this most recent solstice duel, for which I must express my most profound regrets. However, it makes me newly determined to satisfy my curiosity regarding the Midsummer contest. I am more concerned in its outcome than otherwise—however slight my acquaintance with the reigning Oak King."

"And for which outcome do you wish?" Wren asked.

The spiderweb fae blinked at him. "For his victory, of course."

"Oh." Wren hadn't dared to hope to find another besides himself—and perhaps Nell—who wished for Shrike's victory. "Then I'd be delighted to pass along your well-wishes."

"Would you indeed?" said the spiderweb fae, sounding rather delighted himself. "You honour me, m'lord."

"Not at all," Wren assured him in the polite formula he'd uttered so often in London society. Only after the words left his lips did his ears perceive the honorific the spiderweb fae had applied to him. It gave him considerable pause. While Wren was a gentleman by birth, he was by no means an aristocrat, and had certainly fallen far below the station of his father the squire. He found himself quite at a loss for words to explain the title the spiderweb fae had thrust upon him.

"Pray forgive my prattling on," the spiderweb fae continued, evidently oblivious to the confusion he'd caused Wren. "I've not had the opportunity for conversation in some time."

"Oh?" The startled syllable escaped Wren's lips before he could think better of it. The spiderweb fae seemed quite at home conversing with strangers. Not at all like one who had avoided society—or, Wren realized as he considered the matter, perhaps one whom society had avoided.

The spiderweb fae opened his mouth as if to say more. Then his cat-slit eyes flicked away from Wren's face to fix on a point over Wren's shoulder. They widened, and his jaw shut with a sharp click.

Wren whirled to find Shrike swiftly approaching through the already-parted crowd. While the sight of him warmed his heart, Wren could see how, with his stormy aspect, bold strides, and billowing black cloak, Shrike might strike an imposing figure to those who knew him not so well. But Wren knew the furrow in Shrike's brow bespoke mild concern rather than ill temper.

"Hail and well met, m'lord!" trilled the spiderweb fae, drawing Wren's attention again.

"Hail," Shrike echoed warily. As he drew up to join their conversation, he laid a heavy palm on Wren's shoulder. His touch felt warm and familiar, yet Wren couldn't help but notice an undercurrent of urgency in the gesture.

"I cannot praise enough the mask you crafted for me this season," the spiderweb fae continued. "And what a bounty it is to have the opportunity to tell you so in person."

"You have my thanks," said Shrike.

"And your friend has proved delightful company this eve," the spiderweb fairy went on with a nod towards Wren. "Pray, allow me to withdraw so you might enjoy his companionship yourself. Goodnight, and good morrow!"

"Goodnight," said Shrike.

The spiderweb fae gave another flourishing bow, deeper still than the one he'd given to Wren, and whirled away to vanish into the throng.

The instant he did so, Shrike swept over Wren like a dark tide. His cloak billowed 'round them both as Shrike's hands slipped beneath Wren's coat to swiftly and gently brush over his shoulders, waist, and heart. Before Wren could do more than balk in bewilderment, Shrike's hands rose to cradle his jaw, and while his rough thumb traced Wren's cheek with tenderness, his palms tilted Wren's face in a peculiar manner that Wren could only conclude was meant to examine his throat.

"Are you all right?" Shrike asked, his words low and urgent.

"Yes," Wren answered with some impatience. He wrapped his own fingers around Shrike's wrists to halt their bizarre ministrations. "Why shouldn't I be?"

Shrike offered no resistance as Wren pulled his hands away to rest on Wren's shoulders. "Do you know to whom you spoke?"

"I saw him in the Wild Hunt before. And I saw him tonight wearing a mask made by your hand. Beyond that, I know nothing of him."

"Did he give his reason for approaching you?" Shrike pressed.

"On the contrary, I approached him."

Shrike's eyes widened.

"You needn't look so shocked," Wren added. "I found myself bereft of company, saw he stood likewise, and struck up a conversation to pass the time whilst I awaited your return. He behaved a perfect gentleman throughout."

Shrike broke his stunned silence to reply, "I would expect nothing less of him."

"Then pray tell me what vexes you."

Despite this extraordinarily reasonable request, Shrike remained silent.

Wren's unease only grew. "He commissioned his mask from you. What payment did you arrange?"

"He is connected to a certain fabric-seller," Shrike admitted. "I cannot yet make my own wools and linens, much less silks and velvets."

"He must do so very well indeed to earn such a mask as you've crafted for him. And to earn your silence, besides. Did you make his cobweb mask as well?"

"No." This time, Shrike's answer came far more quickly. "It's the customary garb of his court."

"And pray tell, what court is that?"

"He hails from the Court of Spindles," Shrike said at last, adding, "An infamous realm of betrayal and dread."

"Oh." Wren felt rather as though Shrike had up-ended a pitcher of ice water over his head. The spiderweb fae hadn't seemed the least bit dreadful, but Wren supposed that was where the betrayal came into play.

"Some call him the ambassador," Shrike continued. "I believe it's meant in jest. More likely he is an exile. Whether the Court of Spindles banished him or he escaped of his own accord, I cannot say, though I'm inclined to think the latter."

"On what evidence?"

"The knowledge that the Court of Spindles is far more likely to eliminate offenders than release them from their snares."

"And what role did he play in such a court?" Wren asked.

"No one knows for certain. There are many rumours, each more absurd than the last. Given his finesse in the Wild Hunt, I would hazard he was an assassin for an aristocratic bloodline."

"An assassin?" Wren echoed, his whisper cracking halfway through the word.

"Or trained in that art," Shrike added. "Which it is said the nobility may do to give purpose to their superfluous heirs. He's certainly skilled with a blade. Regardless of his role within the Court of Spindles, he commands respect without it, all through the realms."

Wren recalled how the other fae had given the ambassador an even wider berth than they gave Shrike. A berth which had extended to encompass Wren whilst he stood in conversation with him. And Wren had thought the fellow merely an awkward wallflower.

"But he has not harmed you?" Shrike said, his urgent tone startling Wren out of his reflections.

"No," Wren answered honestly. "Would you expect him to? Does he make sport of hunting mortals?"

"One never knows quite what to expect of him. Though I'll admit I've not heard tell of him killing mortals."

"Then what made you fear for me in his company?"

Shrike looked at Wren as if he thought Wren already knew the answer.

And after some reflection, which brought unaccountable heat to Wren's face, Wren realized he did. "Oh."

Shrike shot him a self-deprecating smile. "Forgive me."

Wren, far too wrapped up in the knowledge that Shrike considered him someone precious and worthy of his protection—and perhaps also under the haze of fae wine—didn't think Shrike had done anything to require his forgiveness. "Only if you'll dance with me."

Wren wouldn't have blamed Shrike for feeling sick of dancing with him by now. Yet Shrike's shy smile bespoke as much delight at the prospect as when they'd first begun. His strong arms wound their way around Wren's frame to carry him off to rejoin the throng, and for a blissful evening, Wren forgot all the gloom that awaited him in London.

CHAPTER
TWENTY-FIVE

Shrike awoke with a headache.

The dull throbbing concentrated on two particular points on either side of his brow, just ahead of his temples. Still half-asleep, he groaned and raised his hand to rub the soreness away.

The brush of his fingertips felt like tonguing the raw nerve of a broken tooth

Shrike bit off an oath and snatched his hand back.

"What?" Wren murmured, rolling over to wakefulness beside him. His blearing blinking eyes fixed on Shrike's face and flew wide.

"What do you see?" asked Shrike.

"Did you hit your head?" Wren asked in return, still staring. "Twice?"

"Tell me what you see," said Shrike.

Wren grimaced. "It looks like a pair of bone-spurs scabbed over with lint."

Shrike stared back at him.

"Is that normal?" asked Wren.

"Not for me."

"But for others?" Wren supplied when Shrike failed to say anything more.

"Aye," Shrike admitted. "For huldrekall and certain other fae. And bucks."

"Bucks?" Wren echoed.

Shrike shrugged it off and sat up. The room tilted. He grit his teeth through it and stood. He ignored the leaden feeling in his limbs as he performed his morning ablutions and dragged on his tunic and hose. More than once he caught Wren watching him warily out of the corner of his eye, but neither spoke.

Not 'til Shrike went out, and the sunlight piercing his eyes alongside the slight breeze hammering against his raw brow combined to collapse him against the door-frame.

Wren's cry of alarm rang in Shrike's ears as he attempted to master himself. Then a strong grip took him by the shoulders. He let Wren half-carry him back to the bed, though he would only deign to sit on it rather than lie down. He didn't open his eyes again until he heard the door shut against the sun.

A scraping sound across the room announced Wren had gone for the medicine chest. Bottles and vials clinked as he searched through it. He withdrew the same potion—laudanum, he'd called it—that he'd given Shrike after the Winter Solstice. Then he plucked the copper kettle down from its hook on the rafters and filled it at the tap in the hollow stump. The hearth-fire rekindled as he raked the ashes, and soon he had the kettle whistling over it. He returned to Shrike with a hand-thrown mug of tea. The soothing scent of lavender wafted up on the steam.

Shrike took it with no small gratitude and sipped. The sweet flavour of honey almost disguised an unfamiliar bitter note. Shrike supposed that belonged to the laudanum. And as he continued sipping, the throbbing pain in his brow dwindled and dwindled, until the last dregs reduced it to a dull twinge.

Wren, meanwhile, rummaged through his satchel. From its depths he produced a hand-mirror and held it out to Shrike.

Shrike took it. Throughout his centuries he'd heard of mirrors in stories and songs and glimpsed them in the hands of fae and mortal gentry. Then Wren had brought his to Blackthorn—a plain thing, he'd called it when he caught Shrike staring, merely a palm-sized circle of silvered glass set in an oaken frame and handle. Shrike had watched him ply his razor with it many a morn.

But he'd never held it in his own hand until now.

His face looked rather like it had in reflections of still water and in Wren's sketches. There were but two difference—the bulbous, velvet-covered sprouts of a pair of antlers, one on either side of his brow.

"Ah," said Shrike.

"You don't seem terribly surprised," said Wren.

"It's a bit early for the first tines to split off," Shrike admitted. He gingerly touched the tips of the new prongs, then pulled his fingers away with a hiss of pain.

"So," Wren said, filling Shrike's mug again—minus the laudanum—and pouring another for himself. "Antlers."

"Aye," Shrike replied.

"And this has never happened to you before?"

"Never."

"So you don't know how long they'll take to grow in. Or how broad they'll be when they do."

"No," Shrike admitted. Then, "Do you mind them?"

Wren looked at him as though he'd just asked something absurd. "I mind the pain they've caused you."

Shrike chuckled into his tea.

"But, no," Wren added with a smile of his own. "I don't mind them."

Shrike supposed he ought to have surmised as much, given Wren's reaction to the Court of Hidden Folk, but it still relieved him to hear the answer.

"Do you?" Wren asked. "Mind them, I mean."

Shrike shrugged. "They're coming in whether I mind them or not."

Wren blinked. "Fair enough."

Shrike's head-ache ebbed and flowed throughout the day. Sometimes just the barest whisper of pain and sometimes pulsing in agony with his heart-beat. He accomplished not half so much as he would have liked. When it peaked and he found he could bear no more, Wren put him back to bed. A warm clout soaked in chamomile tea over his eyes allowed him to catch some quiet rest, if not sleep.

The next morning, Shrike arose almost as exhausted as when he'd drifted off. A gentle probing of his antlers told him they'd grown out by another inch overnight. More worrisome was the look of alarm Wren cast upon him. In response to Shrike's enquiring glance, Wren handed him the mirror.

Something had indeed changed in his reflection beyond the growth of his antlers. Deep blue bruises encircled his eyes, and his cheeks had hollowed.

"Is *that* normal?" Wren asked as Shrike passed the mirror back to him.

"It's something I ought to have expected," Shrike admitted.

"Temporary?" Wren pressed.

"I believe so."

Wren didn't appear in the least bit appeased. "You look as bad as Felix after his adventure with the huldra. Though," he added, "I'd have much preferred to host you in my garret."

"I'm all right," Shrike insisted. "Just tired."

"Go back to sleep, then."

Shrike shook his head, wincing as the pain throbbed through his brow. "Can't. Too much to tend to."

"What needs doing?" Wren asked with the attitude of one who intended to do it all himself.

Shrike hesitated. "Nothing I can't manage on my own."

Wren crossed his arms and raised his brows.

"Tending the hens," Shrike relented. "And the goats."

"And?" Wren prompted when Shrike fell silent.

Shrike gestured to his antlers. "That's all that can't wait for these to finish growing in."

Wren cracked a wry smile that did much to lift Shrike's spirits. "Fair enough."

While Shrike wasn't feeling up to performing his own labours, he did succeed in following Wren out-of-doors and leaned against the cottage wall to watch Wren tend to flock and herd. The hens happily scattered when Wren opened their coop, and whilst none would approach him with grain cupped in his palm, they snatched it up once he tossed it down to them. Thus occupied, they ignored his retrieval of their eggs. The goats wouldn't stand to be milked until Shrike beckoned them over and scratched behind their ears, which distracted them long enough for Wren to fill the copper pail. Though not accustomed to such labour, Wren took to it readily. Shrike found more satisfaction than he'd anticipated in seeing Wren shrug off his frock coat and roll up his shirtsleeves to bare his freckled forearms. This, combined with the warmth of said frock coat folded over Shrike's elbow as Wren worked, left Shrike feeling quite content. Though, as the minutes passed, his head seemed to grow heavier, and the throbbing ache returned until he found he could no longer bear the sunlight filtering down through the forest canopy and striking his eyes. But by then Wren had finished the morning's chores and, linking his arm through Shrike's, led him back indoors.

Shrike sat down hard on his bed and gingerly kneaded his brow with his fingertips while Wren fixed him a second cup of lavender laudanum—this time with goat's milk. Then, whilst Shrike sipped at his medicine, Wren threw milk and eggs together in a pan over the hearth. Pain had distracted Shrike from hunger since he'd awoken. Now, with the savoury scent filling the cottage, he found himself ravenous.

Wren scraped the eggs out of the pan with a knife and divided them into two clay bowls, one considerably more full than the other. Then, glancing 'round, he asked, "Do you have any forks?"

Shrike blinked up at him in confusion. Surely Wren had seen for himself that Shrike had no hay-fields and thus no need for a pitchfork. "Nay."

Wren frowned down at the eggs. "I suppose a spoon will do."

Shrike agreed and took the fuller bowl Wren proffered with murmured thanks. He wolfed down the eggs. Wren watched with undisguised amazement.

"I can make more if you're still hungry," said Wren, who was but half-done with his own portion. When Shrike hesitated to answer, he added, "You look like you haven't eaten in weeks."

"Aye," Shrike replied, for he felt much the same. Though loath to admit weakness, he thought there was little use in denying his hunger and little harm in divulging it to Wren in particular. Despite the substantial fare Wren had cooked up, the hollow sensation continued gnawing at him from within. The ache that had begun in his brow now seeped into his very bones, as though he'd jolted them to splinters with a fortnight's riding on a wild steed. It seemed his body would consume itself to nourish his growing antlers unless he offered it something more.

Wren took the empty bowl with a wry half-smile and returned to the hearth. He hadn't yet put his frock coat on—it lay beside Shrike on the bed—and once again Shrike's gaze fell to the rolled-up shirtsleeves and how thin the white fabric seemed over the muscles of his arm and shoulder.

"D'you have anything else to hand?" Wren asked.

Shrike thought a moment and rose from his bed. A grunt of pain escaped his clenched jaw. Wren cast a concerned look over his shoulder, but Shrike waved him off and continued on to the hatch in the floor on the north-west side of the cottage. His joints protested climbing down the ladder into the larder, but it was worth it to sate his hunger. That, and for the astonished look on Wren's face when Shrike re-emerged with a venison flank slung over one shoulder.

"That'll do," said Wren, his dark eyes very round.

Shrike grinned.

The sweet and savoury scent of the maple-cured meat filled the cottage as Shrike sliced off portions of the flank and added it to Wren's pan of eggs. The gnawing hunger within him grew to an all-consuming roar. Though Wren had declared himself full after the first serving, Shrike persuaded him to try a bite or two of the venison. The flavour seemed to surprise him.

"Maple sap," Shrike explained. "Boiled down to sugar."

"Good stuff." Wren took a third bite. "D'you do it all yourself?"

"Not the sugaring," Shrike admitted, passing him another slice. "But the hunting and curing, aye."

Wren appeared far more impressed by this than Shrike thought warranted, but it pleased him nonetheless to know his labours were appreciated. Wren's wonder never failed to amaze Shrike in turn. To share his spoils with him seemed to redouble the joy he found in them.

It satisfied something within him he hadn't realized he wanted. And now that he had it, he wished to gather it close and guard it against all who would dare attempt to steal it away.

Yet as matters stood, even with a second helping of eggs and venison in him, he hardly felt equal to the task. Though the hunger had receded for the moment, the bone-deep ache remained. His shoulders in particular seemed determined to punish him for climbing down into the larder and carrying the flank out of it. He bit back another groan, his hand rising unbidden to rub the ache. His eyes fell shut against the throbbing in his skull.

Then another hand alighted on his shoulder.

Shrike opened his eyes just enough to see Wren had sat down on the bed beside him. He sighed in relief as Wren kneaded the knots out of his muscles. He let his own hand fall from his shoulder and slumped forward to rest with his elbows on his knees and his head bent. When he untied the lacings at the neck of his tunic, Wren took the hint and delved beneath his raiments to reach down Shrike's aching back and better alleviate his suffering. The familiar touch warmed Shrike's heart as well as his skin. To have Wren so near to him, to feel the heat of his body and inhale the scent of his hard-labouring sweat, to know the hands that graced his flesh were as tender as they were strong and held as much affection for him as he felt in turn, brought an immeasurable relief he'd never before imagined.

The relief proved short-lived as Wren withdrew his hand.

Shrike raised his head to find Wren had stood up and walked away entirely. He opened his mouth to question this, but his tongue stilled as he watched Wren approach the hollowed stump and turn its copper handle. Hot spring water gushed from the pipes into the hollow. The rising steam coiled in the air above it and dissipated in the shafts of sunlight streaming in through the windows. Just seeing it released some of the tension in Shrike's shoulders. Despite his pains, a smile came to his lips, a fraction of the thanks he felt Wren deserved for contriving such a notion as this.

"I daresay you'd have thought of it yourself, if you weren't in such a state," said Wren, which confused Shrike for a moment before he realized his silent thanks must have slipped off his tongue after all.

Wren returned to his side and slipped his hands beneath Shrike's tunic once more—this time to lift it over Shrike's head. Shrike raised his arms to allow him to pull it off, though it cost him considerable effort to do so. It took Wren far longer than usual to divest Shrike of his clothes, half due to Shrike's leaden limbs, and half, Shrike suspected, due to Wren's insistence upon handling him as gently as possible. No tearing of laces or ripping of seams, as so many of their other, more urgent encounters had entailed.

By the time Wren had set aside Shrike's tunic and hose on the bed, the copper tap had half-filled the hollow stump. Shrike's body sinking down into it sufficed to bring the water up past his chest. He groaned as he leaned back against the smooth-polished wood, stretching his legs out beneath the water and his arms across the rim above. The warm current stirred up by his slipping into the tub swirled around his aching limbs. He let his eyes fall shut with a sigh.

Then the water rippled anew, disturbed by something beyond him.

Shrike blinked his eyes open to behold Wren divested of his myriad layers and on the brink of stepping into the tub himself.

A lackadaisical grin spread across Shrike's face. Ripples rose to the rim as Wren straddled him, the water rendering him weightless. His arms twined around Shrike's shoulders and his soft fingertips kneaded through knotted muscle. Shrike tilted his face so their lips might meet, and still more interesting things occurred beneath the surface that allowed him, for a few blissful moments, to forget all his aches.

Afterward, Shrike found himself fit only to stand still whilst Wren rubbed him dry with a linen towel, then crawl back into his bed. Wren lay beside him, dressed again, though bereft of his coat and boots.

"Good of you to look after me," Shrike muttered as Wren's warm bulk nestled against his own. "Great deal of trouble."

"Nonsense," Wren replied. "You're much easier to look after than any of my university mates were in their cups—or on the mornings after."

Shrike chuckled.

Wren brought his sketch-book into bed with them, and the rhythmic scrap of pencil across parchment soon soothed Shrike down into something like sleep.

Monday dawned bright with golden sunshine turning green through the newly-unfurled leaves of the forest canopy.

"I'll be all right," Shrike told Wren—not for the first time since they'd woken.

Wren didn't appear convinced. "Don't forget the laudanum. Is there no way you might recall me to Blackthorn if you find you have need of me?"

Shrike couldn't think of anything at the moment—though that might have been due to the dull throbbing pain that had plagued him throughout the past few days and only seemed to grow worse with the bright dawn. Still, "It's only a day. I'll survive a few hours alone."

Yet when Wren at last tore himself away from Shrike's side, Shrike didn't remain alone for long.

At first Shrike turned to his work-bench as a distraction from his discomfort. Sitting at it proved easy enough. But when he attempted to tool another leather oak-leaf, the strike of the mallet shot twin bolts of agony up his arms to stab his budding antlers. His vision flashed white, then spotted black. Both mallet and leather fell from his hands as he clutched the rim of his work-bench to keep from collapsing. When his sight returned some moments later he staggered upright and groped his way back to his bed. His brow continued to throb with the echoes of the blow, and so the sleep he returned to left him fading in and out of consciousness.

Soft footsteps interrupted his uneasy slumber. Too soft for Wren, who, though he had a light tread for a mortal, still thudded his boot-heels into the ground with every stride in a manner that carried throughout the forest. These present footsteps, by contrast, proved almost too soft for even Shrike's keen ears to hear. And yet he heard them. Which meant whoever made them wished him to hear.

"Nell," Shrike muttered without opening his eyes.

He could hear the smile in her voice as she replied, "Aren't you a sight."

Shrike didn't feel the need to dignify that remark with anything more than a groan.

Nell laughed, but lower and more gently than she was wont. "How do you like them?"

"What?" Shrike grumbled, though he knew better.

"The antlers, you dullard."

Shrike thought that a very foolish enquiry. "I'll tell you when they're grown in."

"Fair enough. Where's Lofthouse?"

"Staple Inn. London," Shrike told her through gritted teeth. Why she'd chosen today, of all days, to pepper him with questions, he couldn't fathom. She had a way of needling that he'd oft seen her turn upon others. She hadn't turned it upon him in decades. Not since their first meeting, in the aftermath of a particularly bloody hunt, whereupon he'd aroused her curiosity. She'd heard stories of the Butcher of Blackthorn—everyone had—and had taken it upon herself to learn the truth of the matter from the Butcher himself. Now, it seemed, her curiosity had renewed. "I go to meet him at sunset."

"And d'you think you'll be in a fit state to journey by sunset?"

"I must," said Shrike. "And so I shall be."

"D'you suppose it wise, then, to wander amongst mortals with such a pair of buds upon your brow?"

Shrike had to admit he hadn't considered that. He forced his eyes open.

Nell stood in the centre of the cottage, leaning against the hollowed stump with her arms crossed as she regarded Shrike with a cocked eyebrow. He wondered how long she'd held that expression whilst waiting for him to awaken and witness it.

"If so," Nell continued, when it became apparent that not only did she have his full attention, but he had no answer for her, "then you're half as foolish as my twin. And a quarter as foolish as my half-brother."

Nell didn't oft speak of her family. Shrike knew of them from a misadventure early in his acquaintance with her that had forged their friendship in fire. Few others could claim such knowledge of either of them.

"What would you suggest instead?" asked Shrike.

"Don't go. Or, if you must, contrive a disguise. Or find a clever friend to contrive one for you. You'll forgive me for saying you don't seem fit to contrive much of anything at present."

Shrike could hardly deny it. "I suppose the hidden folk are used to it by now."

"They have the sense not to shed the antlers once they've grown them." She paused, and Shrike almost thought she'd said all she meant to, until she added, "I'd supposed your mortal dalliance was your last hurrah, after a fashion. But he seems determined to see you survive."

"No less determined than myself," said Shrike.

"Is there anything I might do for you?"

Shrike wondered if she meant the antlers or the solstice. Both, he supposed. "Have you heard whom the Queen of the Silver Wheel has named her Holly King?"

"No," said Nell. "Whom?"

Shrike didn't have will enough remaining to hide his frustration. "I know not. That's why I've asked."

Shrike expected her to laugh at him again. She did not.

"Oh," she said instead, sounding almost contrite. Then, "Shall I find out?"

"I'd owe you a debt if you would," said Shrike.

"You'd owe me naught," she shot back—more like her old self. "I'll see to it now, if you like."

"I'll make you a quiver."

"So many men have promised," Nell replied with a smirk. "And yet none have delivered."

"You know what I meant," Shrike grumbled, an answering smile tugging at the corner of his mouth despite his gritted teeth.

Nell laughed. Shrike shut his eyes again. A silence fell, which Shrike presumed meant she'd slipped away, until the creak of the door cut through it.

"Well met," Nell said—to someone other than himself.

Shrike forced open his eyes.

And on the threshold stood Wren.

Shrike surged upright—regretting it as his pulse sobbed against his brow with pounding pain that rang in his ears and robbed him of his sight for several heartbeats. By the time his vision cleared, Wren had flown across the cottage to lay his gentle hand on Shrike's shoulder.

"I'm all right," Shrike assured him. "What brings you so swift from London?"

"You," Wren replied bluntly.

Shrike supposed he ought to have known. "But so soon?"

Wren furrowed his brow. "No earlier than usual."

Shrike blinked at him, then looked past him to Nell, who'd resumed leaning against the hollowed stump. Over her shoulder, the cottage door hung half-open, and through it Shrike glimpsed the golden light of sunset against the briars.

"No wonder you thought me foolish for declaring I'd recover by sundown," Shrike said to her.

A half-smile curled up her cheek.

"Are you feeling worse?" asked Wren.

"No," Shrike replied. "Just the same. No trouble between here and London?"

"None at all. It's just as you said," Wren added with a note of wonder in his voice. "If one knows the way, the path is very short indeed."

"Indeed," Nell echoed with more amusement than Shrike thought warranted. "Now that I know our Butcher is in good hands, I'll take my leave."

"Stay a moment," Wren blurted.

Nell paused in the midst of turning and arched an eyebrow at him. Shrike could hardly blame her as he levelled a similar bewildered look on Wren.

"If you've a moment to spare," Wren added. "I'd like a word or two in confidence."

Nell glanced between him and Shrike, who had no answer for her evident curiosity. She seemed to realize this and resumed her pose at the hollowed stump with a shrug.

She waited there for some while. Wren wouldn't be satisfied with Shrike's assurance of his well-being until he'd lain his hand on his brow to check for fever, brewed a pot of lavender tea with honey and goat's milk—gathered by Wren himself that morning, between leaving Shrike's bedside and going off to London—and dosed Shrike's mug with laudanum.

"Essence of poppies," Wren explained in response to Nell's glance of undisguised suspicion as he pressed the mug into Shrike's hands. "For pain."

Shrike wrapped his fingers around the warm clay with gratitude. The lavender scent wafting up with the steam worked well upon his brow. The first sip of the medicinal brew did still more.

Nell seemed to accept Wren's explanation, though she remained wary even as she accepted the mug Wren offered her. Only after Wren drank from his own cup did she taste hers. Judging by the angle her brows assumed afterward, its flavour surprised but did not displease her.

Soon enough, as Shrike sipped his tea, the pounding in his head faded from a sharp stab to a dull thud, and then ebbed to an occasional twinge. It left him far more comfortable yet no less exhausted than before. Wren gently retrieved the empty mug from his grasp and drew the furs up over his shoulder as he laid down to catch the true sleep that had eluded him all day.

Nell's hardly audible footsteps and Wren's mortal tread alike retreated across the flagstones. The cottage door creaked open and shut. Voices arose from the garden. Wren had brought her out of human hearing, but Shrike's keen ears caught almost all.

"Are you certain this is normal?" Wren demanded.

"Aye," Nell answered. She had much the same ears as Shrike, and therefore must know he could hear them, which gave her no excuse for speaking as loud as Wren. In a tone bespeaking more indignation than concern, she returned, "Does it trouble you if it is?"

Shrike tensed. Nell's heritage gave her a particular sensitivity towards mortal perceptions of the fae. While he could hardly blame her for that, the implied threat in her voice shot past the ache in his bones, through his ribs to his heart, which burned to defend his Wren. All sense of sleep left him, laudanum or no laudanum, and he lay as one waiting to strike.

Wren matched her ferocious undercurrent as he replied, "It troubles me to see him in such pain. If there's anything that may alleviate his suffering, I'll not cease until I see it done."

A silence fell.

"Glad to hear you say so," Nell replied at last in a tone much changed. "You'll forgive me for my suspicion. I seek to protect a dear friend."

"Nothing to forgive," Wren quickly added. "I'd do the same in your place."

At length the murmurs ceased, and shortly afterward the cottage door creaked open. Familiar footsteps padded across the flagstone floor. A warm weight settled onto the bed beside Shrike. A soft hand stroked through his hair and alighted gentle on his brow. Then it withdrew, and the crackling of the hearth-fire rekindled in Shrike's ears. The scents of lavender and honey wafted through the cottage alongside eggs and maple-cured venison. Soon Wren returned to his side and laid his palm on Shrike's shoulder.

"I'm awake," Shrike muttered, drawing himself upright despite the throbbing pain in his temples. The mug of laudanum-dosed tea Wren handed him dulled the pain enough for him to appreciate the offered repast. His gnawing hunger sated for the moment, he returned to his quiet rest with Wren curled up against his side.

Shrike had hunted deer for many, many years. From his careful observation in stalking quarry over the centuries, he knew the antlers of a stag grew in by a quarter of an inch per day, in the course of four full moons.

The morning after Nell's visit, Shrike awoke to find his own antlers had grown another full inch overnight.

Again, Wren proved reluctant to leave Shrike to his fate alone. Only after laudanum tea and toasted goat cheese had revived Shrike somewhat did Wren consent to return to London. His parting kiss to Shrike's brow soothed more pain than he might ever know.

After Wren had gone, Shrike made another attempt at his workbench. Nell had spoken many true things the previous day—not the least of which was that Shrike couldn't show his face in the mortal realm again until he found a way to disguise his budding antlers.

The scraps of leather left over from his Ostara work would suffice for his plan. He didn't try his wooden mallet again, for it felt too much like tempting fate with the dull throbbing ache still behind his eyes, but his half-moon blades and awl he could wield without plunging his skull into agony. Even so he found his vision blurred within the hour. Retreating to his nest to shut his eyes a while restored his sight, and the day became a back-and-forth from bed to bench as he returned again and again to his work.

What he might have finished in a day when he had his health, he now supposed would take perhaps a fortnight. This didn't trouble him overmuch. Its completion would require Wren's particular talents, for which he must wait for Wren's return.

The hours Wren spent in Mr Grigsby's office in Staple Inn did not pass pleasantly.

Not that Mr Grigsby knew it. Mr Grigsby continued on in his merry ignorance, smiling at his newspaper, humming to himself over tea, and making occasional polite enquiries of Wren.

Wren, meanwhile, stewed in private agony. His thoughts continually wandered far from London's clattering fog to the quiet cottage and the better half of his heart he'd left behind. Antlers sprouting oak leaves grew from the margins of the rent-collection ledgers whilst precious few figures made it into the columns between. In the rare moments when Wren could consider his present surroundings, it was with the expectation that someone—Felix or Tolhurst—would contact him either privately or, Heaven forbid, publicly, to reveal their knowledge of his worst manuscripts and threaten to expose him to the full wrath of English society and English law.

When at last Mr Grigsby departed for his dinner, Wren hardly paused long enough to lock up the office before he dashed down Oxford Street. The fog lay thick on the ground in Hyde Park. He depended on it to obscure him from view as he fell through the toadstool ring and landed amidst the ruins in the wood.

While the brisk air of the fae realms never failed to invigorate him, he could not breathe easy until he'd reached Blackthorn and beheld Shrike once more. He felt a brief reprieve as the wall of thorns parted to allow him up the path to the cottage. The door swung in at the barest touch of his fingertips.

And any peace he'd found vanished as he beheld Shrike slumped over his work-bench.

Wren strangled an instinctive cry of alarm as he dashed to Shrike's side. Yet no sooner had he laid his hand on Shrike's shoulder—warmth suffusing his night-chilled fingers even through Shrike's woollen tunic— Shrike stirred beneath his touch. Moving as if his head bore the weight of an anvil, Shrike arose and sat blinking in bleary bewilderment at Wren.

"What happened?" Wren demanded, though he kept his voice low. His hand went to Shrike's face at once, stroking his cheek and cupping his jaw. "Are you all right?"

Shrike nodded and winced. "Fell asleep at my work. As I've oft done this day."

"How's your head? Did you take any laudanum? Wait," Wren added, all too aware that his babbling couldn't be helping Shrike's head-ache and very likely made it worse, yet powerless to halt his tongue. "What do you mean, your work?"

"Fine. Some. And this," Shrike answered him, turning and fumbling at his bench until he brought forth a masterpiece-in-progress and held it out to Wren.

Wren took it from him warily. It didn't look like the handiwork of a sickly man. Indeed, it looked like the beginnings of an improved version of the masks Shrike had crafted for Ostara. Like a Venetian domino in pattern, designed to conceal just the upper half of a face, with its edges pointed and curled like fallen oak leaves. At the peak, where the mask would cover the brow, the oak-leaf pattern mirrored from left to right and formed two particular rounded dales that Wren realized would match perfectly with the budding protrusion of Shrike's new antlers.

"Nell reminded me," Shrike added as Wren gazed at the mask. "I need something to disguise my oddities from mortal eyes."

"They're not oddities," Wren said without even considering the matter, the words spilling forth from his heart rather than his head.

If Shrike minded, it showed neither in his face nor his speech. "I need your help to finish it."

"How?" Wren blurted. He'd felt desperate to alleviate Shrike's agonies since they'd begun and equally hopeless he might ever do so in his own mortal failings.

Shrike reached out his forefinger and tapped the centre of the mask's brow, where a smooth field devoid of veins spanned between the two antler valleys. "It requires a cunning sigil."

Wren's unease increased. Even after all the hours they'd spent in each other's company, hours in which Wren thought it woefully apparent his own mortal skill couldn't hold a candle to Shrike's fae mastery, Shrike thought him some manner of wizard. "What ought it to look like?"

"I know not," said Shrike. "I've no gift for glamour. I'm ill-accustomed to seeming anything other than what I am."

Wren had spent more than three decades disguising his truest self from society's judgment. Shrike could not have chosen a more experienced practitioner in the art of deceit. When it came to enchanting, however... "I'm hardly magical."

Shrike remained undaunted. "You devised the sigil for our Samhain ritual."

"I didn't devise anything," Wren protested. "I copied it out of *Gawain and the Green Knight.*"

"Perhaps. Though Gawain didn't use it as you did. Unless I've very much misunderstood the tale."

A breathless huff of laughter escaped Wren despite his best efforts.

"As you will. But first, I think, more laudanum."

Shrike did not object. Wren tried to take it as a sign of Shrike's trust in him, rather than indicating an increase in Shrike's pain.

For Shrike, time passed with a steady, if not entirely comfortable, rhythm. Each morn he awoke curled 'round his Wren, the dull throb of his brow rousing him from his slumbers. They broke their fast and tended the flocks together before Wren departed for Staple Inn. Shrike spent the daylight hours alternating rest with work on his glamour mask. The sunset heralded Wren's return, whereupon they supped, and Wren coaxed Shrike to an early bed. Thus each day continued on much like the one before it.

And each day, another inch gained on Shrike's antlers.

The third day saw them split into their first prongs. Over the course of the ensuing se'en-night they split again, and again, and again, until they attained six points between them.

At the close of the se'en-night, Nell returned.

"Lofthouse not arrived yet?" she said by way of greeting as she ducked into the cottage.

The sun's rays had just begun to fade to scarlet. Shrike, still at his work-bench, set down his mallet and awl beside his half-finished mask. Despite her continued suspicion towards Wren, Shrike found himself glad to see her again. "Soon."

Nell approached the work-bench in a wandering way that appeared haphazard, though Shrike knew her every step deliberate—for she stalked her prey in much the same manner. She bent over his shoulder to peer at his handiwork. "I half expected to find you gone to meet him."

"I will when this is complete," Shrike said, handing her the mask.

She gave it close examination. "There's no glamour in it."

"Not yet," Shrike admitted. "What word from the Silver Wheel? Who is the Holly King?"

"No one," said Nell.

Shrike stared at her. "None?"

Nell's own curious gaze remained fixed on the half-finished mask as she ran her fingertip along its curving points. "Your queen appointed none on Ostara and has granted the title to none since. Perhaps she waits for your attendance on Beltane."

"Then she waits in vain."

Nell raised her head and brows alike at that. "You mean to defy her."

"To my last."

She appeared no less sceptical as she held out the mask in return. "And your last it will prove indeed, if you refuse all foreknowledge of your opponent."

"Then so be it," said Shrike, taking it from her.

"So be what?"

Both Nell and Shrike whirled to face the threshold where Wren now stood. As glad as Shrike had felt for Nell's company, his heart rejoiced anew to see Wren. Breathless, with a slight rose hue blooming beneath his freckles and one stray lock of chestnut hair falling across his brow—all of which told Shrike he must have dashed, rather than ambled, from Staple Inn to Blackthorn. His jaw set in determination and his eyes afire with curiosity sparked a similar blaze within Shrike. His cravat had just begun to loosen its knot in his journey. His frock coat fluttered open to reveal the merest glimpse of white shirt-sleeve beneath his shoulder and his waistcoat with its long line of buttons down its front, which Shrike's fingertips knew as well as his own tunic ties.

"Beltane," said Shrike.

"Or May Day, as your folk would call it," Nell added. "Whereupon the Oak King crowns the Queen of the Court of the Silver Wheel."

Wren furrowed his brow. "A new queen?"

"No," Shrike interrupted before Nell could confuse Wren further. "It's a farce. The queen demands the pageantry of a coronation for herself each spring, and her reigning king must perform the office."

"And as the Oak King reigns in spring..." Nell continued.

"Unless it's a year without a summer," said Wren. As they spoke, he'd fully entered the cottage and shut its door behind himself, swung his satchel down from his shoulder and hung it on the hook beside Shrike's coat, and seemed about to shrug off his frock coat likewise—

but paused with an uncertain glance at Nell. Shrike had noticed the presence of a lady, or ladies, prevented Wren from doing certain things which would otherwise be commonplace. He supposed it another mortal superstition. He hoped Wren might overcome it in time, as he'd overcome the mortal realm's law against men with men, but for the moment he had patience enough to let him do so on his own.

"Unless that," Nell conceded. "But this year, while she has her Oak King, she'll not have him crown her. Or so I'm told," she added, turning to Shrike.

"Then her Holly King must do so," concluded Wren.

An awkward silence descended upon Blackthorn.

Wren glanced between Shrike and Nell. "Who is it, then?"

"No one," Shrike answered just as Nell spoke the same.

The furrows in Wren's brow deepened. He raised one towards Shrike in query.

"The queen named none at Ostara," Shrike explained.

"Perhaps she shall at Beltane," Nell added.

And thus the talk had run in a complete circle. Shrike's headache, kept at bay by laudanum since dawn, began to gnaw at him anew. He resisted the urge to knead his knuckles against his brow.

"Then perhaps," said Wren, "we ought to attend Beltane. If only to hear her choice as she announces it and lose no time in acquainting ourselves with our opponent. Or," he added, shooting a worried look at Shrike, "perhaps I might conduct reconnaissance alone—"

"No," said Shrike. His head shot up as he spoke, the single word erupting from his heart as much as his mouth, both without any forethought. He withheld a wince at the resulting knell of pain from within his own skull.

This did nothing to dispel Wren's growing concern. "What occurs at the Beltane festivities?"

"An orgy," said Nell.

Wren choked on nothing.

Shrike glared at Nell. She rearranged her smirk into something that hid her delight in shocking Wren.

"It's a fertility rite," Shrike explained. "As the fae folk join together, so does the realm increase in wealth and splendour."

Wren appeared only slightly less alarmed. "All together? At once?"

Nell snorted.

Shrike did not give her the satisfaction of another glare. "Not all together, no. In groups of varying sizes—alone, or in pairs, or more—as is their wont throughout the day. Some make it a game to see how many partners they may satisfy in the celebration. Others pair as swans from beginning to end and acknowledge naught but each other."

This last seemed to allow Wren to relax his tense posture. Still, his gaze flicked to Nell before he answered Shrike. "Then perhaps we ought to attend as a pair. If you're willing, that is."

"An' it so please you," Shrike replied, finding a smile came to his lips as he spoke the words. He could hardly deny his Wren.

The following se'en-night passed much like the first. By the end of it, Shrike's antlers bore twelve points, and spread far beyond the breadth of his shoulders to span over a yard—very nearly an ell.

This made passing through the cottage doorway rather more difficult than otherwise.

The first time he knocked his antlers against the door-frame it rang through his skull to his very teeth. He staggered back to clutch at the rim of the hollowed stump for support whilst he waited for the pain to recede and his vision to return. He only felt thankful Wren hadn't witnessed his stupidity. Still, he repeated his error twice over that very morning before he learnt to turn his head aside and duck and so work his way through.

As for the pots, cobwebs, and bundles of dried herbs hanging from the hooks on the rafters—well, he gave thanks again to fortune that Wren didn't see him tangled up in sprigs of rosemary or knocking a copper cauldron down onto his own head. Shrike spent much of the afternoon taking down the herbs and pots and stowed them elsewhere in the cottage wherever he could fit them.

For some minutes after Wren's arrival, in the evening, Shrike hoped his idiocy might remain unknown. Until, after Wren had kissed him, he pulled away to gaze in confusion at something over Shrike's head. Before Shrike could ask after it, Wren reached up gingerly between his antlers and plucked something out of his hair.

"Is this... parsley?" Wren asked, turning the sprig over betwixt forefinger and thumbs.

"Aye," Shrike admitted, and hurried to turn their talk toward supper.

The end of the se'en-night saw Shrike's mask almost complete. The delicate tooled veins threading throughout the leather oak leaves only awaited a coat of deep green stain—and Wren's promised sigil nestled in the centre of the mask's brow.

Shrike sat back at his bench to admire his own handiwork whilst he awaited Wren's arrival. Soon, no doubt, as the sun's glow had already begun to fade from gold to plum though the branches over Blackthorn.

The growth in his antlers had slowed over the past few days, and the ache in his head had ebbed along with it, leaving him with a mere twinge to grit his teeth through. However, without his work to distract him, he found his antlers itched. He'd avoided touching them as they grew, finding the merest pressure redoubled his agonies. Now he laid his fingertips gingerly on the points that most troubled him. The velvet proved soft as its namesake. The twinge in his brow seemed no worse for the touch. He dared to scratch. The itch abated.

And the velvet came away on his fingertips.

Shrike stared down at the scrap of skin in his hand. He supposed he ought to have expected as much and cast it aside into the fireplace.

No sooner had he satisfied the first itch than another sprang up in its wake. Shrike resigned himself to an evening of shedding. He gave thanks he had hands, at least, and needn't scrape his antlers against tree trunks as a wild stag must.

"How's your head?"

Shrike glanced up to find Wren standing on the cottage threshold. He'd been so occupied with his own head that even his keen ears hadn't caught wind of Wren's footsteps.

Wren stared back at him with an uneasy expression.

"Better," Shrike replied, though the sudden strain in Wren's aspect made him wary. "What troubles you?"

Wren continued staring at him. "There's a lot of blood."

"What?" Shrike bolted upright. He saw no blood upon Wren's person, but Wren wore enough layers of dark wool to disguise a great deal of it. A single stride closed the distance between them. Shrike slipped a hand beneath the lapel of Wren's frock coat, swift yet gentle, and drew it away from his body to better see what damage might lie beneath. No gash in fabric or flesh appeared, nor any dark stain spreading through his waistcoat. Still, the wound might lie deeper yet. "How are you hurt?"

Wren answered him with silence. Shrike glanced up to find him looking no less bewildered than alarmed.

"I'm not hurt," Wren said at last, and Shrike realized his gaze had fixed above his head. "I meant—"

Following Wren's gaze, Shrike reached up to his antlers and found a palm-sized scrap of velvet dangling by a thread of sinew. He tore it away with a wince, the cold blood smearing across his fingers.

"Is that *normal?*" Wren asked as Shrike cast the scrap into the fire.

"Aye," Shrike answered him. When Wren's shocked expression changed not a whit, he added, "Have you never seen a buck shed his velvet afore?"

"No," said Wren.

"Oh." Upon reflection, Shrike supposed it must prove an alarming sight to one unaccustomed. "Forgive me, I didn't mean to affright you."

"Nothing to forgive," Wren replied almost before Shrike had finished. "Just so long as you're not hurt."

"Not hurt," Shrike assured him, and continued on to the hollowed stump. The copper tap swiftly washed the crimson stain from his hands. "The blood will cease when the velvet is gone. Naught but bone remains."

"Comforting," Wren said dryly, but Shrike turned to find him wearing a wry half-smile.

Shrike retrieved his almost-finished mask from his work-bench and held it out to Wren for his approval.

"Marvellous," Wren murmured as he took the mask with greater reverence than Shrike thought it deserved. His fingertip ghosted over the barren field of its brow. "Is this where the sigil will go?"

"Aye."

Wren returned the mask to Shrike's keeping and delved into his satchel for his gyrdel-book. "I have some designs worked out if you'd like to see."

Shrike liked nothing better, and said so.

Wren flipped through the vellum leaves. Many beautiful and arcane sketches fluttered past like so many moth-wings in the moonlight. He halted on a particular page and held it out for Shrike's inspection.

Amidst a multitude of glyphs, one caught Shrike's eye—a crest of antlers bound in spiderweb knots.

Shrike tapped it with his forefinger. He looked up to find Wren wearing a wry smile.

"Have you seen your reflection today?" Wren asked.

Shrike confessed he had not.

Wren laid his gyrdel-book on Shrike's work-bench beside the mask and retrieved his shaving mirror from where it lay atop the medicine chest. He held it up before Shrike.

Above Shrike's head, the silvered glass showed a cobweb of ruined flesh strewn between branches of bone.

"Ah," said Shrike.

Wren set the mirror aside on the rim of the hollowed stump. He sat beside it, shrugged off his frock coat, rolled up his shirtsleeves, and beckoned Shrike to follow him there. As if Shrike did not already feel called to follow wherever Wren chose to lead him.

No sooner had Shrike joined him then Wren raised his hands towards his antlers—then hesitated. "If I may?"

Shrike nodded.

Ever so gently, Wren's fingertips alighted on Shrike's antlers. Shrike felt no pain, even as Wren's hands came away with bloodied scraps of velvet like fallen leaves wet with crimson rain. Wren threw it into the fire as Shrike had done before him.

Shrike would not have begrudged Wren if he'd gazed on the gory mess of it all with revulsion. Yet Wren didn't shy away from getting his hands as dirty as Shrike's own. Again and again Wren peeled away the velvet with all the delicacy of a bard strumming a harp stringed with maiden's hair. A touch brimming with mercy paired with eyes bereft of pity. Meeting his gaze felt like returning home.

The sunset had faded to full twilight when Wren ceased plucking the withered blooms of velvet and turned to the copper tap in the hollowed stump. He rinsed his hands, then, taking linen from the medicine chest, he soaked it through and brought it to Shrike's antlers, polishing them as if they were blades of glass. The linen came away vermilion, then rust, then blush, then, at the final rinse, bearing just the faintest golden tinge. A dry clout daubed what he'd washed, then he brought up the shaving mirror again for Shrike's inspection.

The soft rounded tips of chestnut velvet had fallen away to reveal gleaming points of ebony bone.

CHAPTER
TWENTY-SIX

The first of May fell upon a Thursday.

Which meant Wren would have to ask Mr Grigsby for the day off in advance if he wished to join Shrike in dancing 'round a maypole at the Court of the Silver Wheel.

By Wednesday morning, the final day of April, Wren had not yet invented a plausible excuse. He had, however, concocted an improbable one, and as he retrieved the day's first delivery of the penny post, he slipped a letter from his waistcoat pocket into the bunch before handing the pile off to Mr Grigsby. Then he returned to his own desk to wait.

"Why, Lofthouse!" cried Mr Grigsby not a minute after. He held up a particular letter. "You've missed one for yourself! Here you are, and don't feel you need wait to open it."

Wren smiled and accepted his own letter back from Mr Grigsby. He read over the words he'd penned himself in his garret that very morning and let his face fall into an expression of sober concern.

"Nothing grave, I hope?" said Mr Grigsby, who of course watched him throughout.

"I'm afraid it is grave indeed, sir," Wren replied. "My friend Mr Butcher has fallen ill and is in want of nursing."

Not entirely a lie. Mr Grigsby needn't know the peculiar particulars regarding Shrike's ill health. Nor that Wren had already tended him by night for the past month and more.

"Dear me!" said Mr Grigsby in a tone of such genuine concern as to wrench even Wren's withered conscience. "Has he no relations who might look after him?"

"No, sir," Wren answered honestly.

Mr Grigsby clucked his tongue in sympathy. "Of anyone else I might ask if he had any friends to look after him—but I know he could have no nearer or more stalwart friend than yourself, Lofthouse."

Wren's conscience gave another feeble pang. He ignored it.

Mr Grigsby drew himself up with a look of great resolve. "You needn't ask, Lofthouse. I grant you leave to see your friend. Stay as long as he requires you. And, if I might be so bold as to recommend, you may find the services of Dr Hitchingham most amiable."

"Thank you, sir," said Wren.

Mr Grigsby gave him a hopeful smile and returned to his post.

Wren tucked his forged letter back into his waistcoat pocket. Mr Grigsby hadn't even asked to see it.

Wren almost didn't recognize the tourney field.

The sea of dead grey grass limned with frost had transformed and rejuvenated into a verdant meadow of lush new growth. Fragrant clusters of common yarrow scattered across the deep green field like foam capping waves in the open sea, interspersed with golden buttercups and cowslip, the powder-blue harebell, the pale pink of ladies' smock, and flowing purple heather. A multitude of bowers had sprung up since midwinter with trellises bedecked with honeysuckle and apple blossoms woven through willow lattice. Their sweet perfume wafted over the whole field and, for Wren, mingled with the vanilla wood-smoke musk of Shrike beside him.

Still more blooms adorned the fae who wandered between the bowers. Tiny white bells of lily-of-the-valley tucked behind pointed ears, the fluttering petals of blue aquilegia braided through the hair to match the wings of the wearer, and woven bands of purple foxglove encircled the delicate wrists of one who bore a tufted tail. The folk of the Court of the Silver Wheel, as they gathered in trios and pairs and occasional clusters, reminded Wren more and more of the fashionable *ton* of London strolling through Hyde Park by day, as much to be seen as to see.

The fae, however, did not content themselves with mere flirtation of glances and pouts. Ungloved hands clasped ungloved hands, arms twined 'round bare shoulders, and lips drank as deeply of kisses as they did of wine.

At least, Wren assumed it was wine, for it had the right colour and smelled of elderberries when a passing couple offered their shared goblet up to Wren and Shrike. Shrike glanced to Wren to seek his opinion before he declined with a silent shake of his head.

The revellers simply shrugged and moved on to one of the many bowers. This offered some privacy from prying eyes, though, when Wren considered the multitude of fae engaged in carnal relations in the open field, he concluded the fae did not believe privacy an absolute necessity for those pursuits.

And rising above it all stood the proud maypole.

Of course, Wren didn't suppose the fae called it that. But its ribbons and garlands would not have appeared out of place at a mortal village fête. The folk dancing around it might have turned a few heads, with their pointed ears and fluttering wings and gently curving horns, but the pole itself, even topped by a moon-like hoop strung with myrtle and lily-of-the-valley, seemed familiar nonetheless.

The only aspect that remained of the tourney field Wren had known was the tower of intertwined hemlock trees at the far end of the clearing with the ring of knights standing guard at its base and a balcony of branches growing out of the top where Wren could just barely glimpse the vague outline of a golden-haired figure.

And when he turned to his companion, he found Shrike's gaze likewise fixed on that same figure, with narrowed eyes and his jaw set in a hard line.

"Well!" said Wren, gazing over the field once more. "It seems the rite of Ostara bore fruit."

Shrike shot him a startled glance. Then his low rumbling laugh overtook him and Wren rejoiced to see his slight and handsome smile return.

Wren took full advantage of this to add, "Shall we not reap the fruits of this harvest?"

Shrike quirked his brow in a manner which told Wren he could not mistake his meaning. His smile likewise turned coy.

With fingers yet entwined, Wren led Shrike to a particular bower.

The bower Wren chose had white stars of flowering myrtle woven together with love-in-idleness. It was the love-in-idleness which struck him, much like how Cupid's arrow had struck the blooms and turned them "purple with love's wound," according to the Bard's legend. The Beltane celebrants had already reminded Wren of those affected by the love potion in *A Midsummer Night's Dream*. To see amongst them the myrtle, five-pointed like Gawain's pentangle and white like the mistletoe which had surrounded his and Shrike's Samhain ritual, only reinforced his decision.

Shrike, for his part, shot Wren an approving and mischievous smile as he parted the flowery curtain draped over the bower's entrance and held it aloft so Wren might pass under it. The interior occupied about the same circumference as the nest in Blackthorn. Stray blooms of myrtle and love-in-idleness dotted piles of moss as soft as swan's down.

No sooner had the flowery curtain fallen into place behind them than Shrike took Wren's face in his hands and caught his lips in a kiss. Wren, his blood thrumming with anticipation, wrapped his arms 'round him for support as Shrike broke away to bruise another kiss onto his throat, then nip his way up his jawline to his ear.

"What my lady offered to me," Shrike murmured as he went, his lips brushing Wren's ear, "I should like to offer to my lord."

All Wren's breath left his body. How many uncounted evenings had he abused himself with fantasies of Gawain surrendering the spoils of his hunt to the Green Knight—though whether Wren himself played the role of the Green Knight or Gawain he could never quite say. He knew only that the mere thought of it sufficed to send him spilling out of his hand. Shrike could offer him no more potent temptation than this.

A wry half-smile curled the corner of Shrike's handsome mouth. "Would I not make a worthy vessel?"

"You would indeed," Wren assured him before his mind had quite caught up with his tongue. "But I..."

He trailed off, the words sticking in his throat. Irrational, he told himself, and yet it remained; an instinctive aversion to the risk of the act under English law. The spectre loomed over his mind now as it always had, tainting his fantasies with the poisonous bloom of anxiety. The same fear that had kept him out of Hyde Park at night. The same fear that had kept him from giving voice to his overwhelming emotion at university. The same fear that had kept the deepest, truest parts of himself relegated to villains in his own manuscripts. The knowledge that any penetration of man by man sufficed for the capital offence of sodomy —no matter how willing the participants.

Despite Wren's trailing off into silence, an understanding came into Shrike's eyes. The wicked gleam of desire softened. His grin grew gentler until it became a warm and no less handsome smile. "Something else, then. Perhaps—what did you call it? The Oxford rub."

Such a reply ought to have reassured Wren. And in some respects, it did. To know Shrike would never demand anything of Wren that he did not wish to grant.

And yet.

Wren wished to grant it. He wished it more than anything. Decades of self-denial, of self-reproach, of self-abuse, had given him a surfeit of restraint. He wearied of suppressing his desires. His own cowardice exhausted him. Everything he'd ever wanted lay before him in the form of a handsome and willing partner. He hadn't the chivalry of Gawain. He couldn't satisfy himself with giving and receiving mere kisses. Not now.

Besides, English law held no sway over the Court of the Silver Wheel.

"No," Wren said. Then, as Shrike withdrew, he hastened to add, "I mean—I want whatever you wish to offer me."

This did nothing to dispel the confused furrow on Shrike's noble brow. Still, he did lay his rough hand on Wren's face and stroke his cheek with the pad of his thumb. Wren leaned into the touch with everything he'd withheld for nigh on fifteen years.

"Are you certain?" Shrike murmured.

"I am."

Yet Shrike made no further move towards him. "If you change your mind—"

"I won't," Wren promised.

After a moment's pause, Shrike continued. "Give me any sign you wish to cease, and I shall do so."

Despite his own exasperation, Wren could appreciate what Shrike intended. "And you have my word that I will give you such a sign, if I deem it necessary to do so."

"Very well." Shrike's gaze fell to Wren's lips as he bit his own. "I wish to have you in my mouth."

Wren's breath caught. He swallowed hard. "I should like that as well."

He didn't need to see Shrike's smile or feel the deep rumbling of his breathless laugh to know he'd failed to keep his voice steady in reply. Still, Shrike leaned in, and Wren opened his mouth hungrily beneath his kiss. When Shrike broke it off, Wren found himself following him to reclaim it.

But he opened his eyes to behold Shrike sinking to his knees before him.

Antlers already dotted with fallen sprigs of myrtle bracketed Wren's hips and encircled his waist. His heartbeat stuttered in his chest—and further down, as well.

Shrike met his eye with a gaze which shot true to his very core. Then he lowered his lashes and turned his clever hands to trouser buttons.

Wren's cock, already at half-mast in his trousers just from hearing what Shrike wished to do to him, quickly pulsed to a full stand as Shrike took it in his firm grip.

And as the head of his prick slipped between soft lips, Wren bit his own to keep from spending at once.

Then Shrike swallowed him down.

The sensation proved beyond anything Wren could have anticipated

—hot, slick, soft, enrapturing, all-consuming. Every flick of Shrike's tongue, every swallow of his throat, every alternate stroke of mouth and hand threatened to send Wren spiralling over the precipice from which he might never return. He choked off an oath as he struggled to master himself. In search of an anchor, his hands fell to Shrike's broad shoulders. He clenched his fingers hard enough to bruise.

And still, Shrike devoured him.

Wren found his hips rolling to meet Shrike's ministrations. All the moreso as Shrike's hand grasped his arse and pulled him forward. The drag of his tongue along the vein on the underside of his cock as it slipped out of his mouth, then back inside, sent shivers up Wren's spine.

His grip on Shrike's shoulders proved insufficient. His fingers scrambled for an anchor and tangled in Shrike's raven locks before flowing through them as through rainfall. He followed them up to stroke Shrike's jaw, his cheek, his brow.

And the base of his antlers.

Without thinking, he wrapped his hands 'round them.

Shrike groaned.

Wren snatched his fingers away as if burned. "Sorry, I—"

Shrike glanced up at him. Then, seeing Wren's distress, he withdrew his prick from his mouth—though he kept it in his palm. "That wasn't pain."

"Oh," said Wren. Then, "*Oh.*"

The familiar half-smile wound its way up Shrike's cheek. His fist idly stroked Wren's cock.

Wren bit back an unseemly sound. He reached out his hand again and gingerly traced the root of Shrike's antler.

Shrike shivered as his eyes fluttered shut.

Emboldened, Wren wrapped his fingers around it. He kept his hold loose as he ran his thumb along the grain of bone.

Shrike's breath hitched. He leaned in and took Wren in his mouth again. Took him to the hilt, his throat opening to swallow Wren down.

Wren gasped. His fists clenched upon instinct.

Around Shrike's antlers.

Shrike's responsive moan reverberated through Wren's cock in the soft wet heat of his throat.

Wren choked out an oath.

Shrike's eyes smiled up at him as he withdrew until just the head of Wren's prick lay between his lips. He raised his own hand to cover Wren's fist and close it tighter. Gently, he pushed towards Wren.

Wren hardly needed more prompting to pull Shrike's face down onto his cock by the antlers. He felt Shrike's groan of satisfaction in his prick, in his thighs, in his chest, echoing down to the very core of him. He released him and drew him down again—and again—and again—

Fucking his throat.

"Oh," Wren gasped, sheer sensation driving all thought from him. "Shrike!"

What would have burst from Shrike's lips as an ecstatic cry thrummed through Wren's whole being as if he were a plucked bowstring. With his own wild exultation, Wren spent, his seed pouring down Shrike's throat. Shrike swallowed it all, clenching around Wren's cock as he did so until pleasure peaked and verged upon pain. Wren choked it back.

Shrike let his softening prick fall from lips glistening with drops like pearls. Wren dragged him up by his antlers until he could kiss him as ravenously as he desired, tasting himself on Shrike's tongue, drinking it like ambrosia. All too soon, his need for breath demanded he break off.

"Shall I...?" Wren began, as hoarse as if he'd already done the thing.

Shrike's laugh sounded as breathless as Wren felt. "Not for a while yet."

Intrigue broke through Wren's blissful fog. "Did you really...?"

"Aye," Shrike replied, and kissed him again before he could question it further.

"My lord?"

Wren's heart ceased beating.

Shrike broke off the kiss. Wren opened his eyes to find his features twisted in vexation and his gaze fixed on the bower's veil. The voice had come from beyond it, and the speaker remained without, much to Wren's relief.

Wren tucked himself back into his trousers. Shrike turned to put himself between Wren and the bower entrance. When Wren had restored his decency, Shrike threw back the veil.

There, blinking up at them both, stood a diminutive page in a cobalt blue tabard with a silver wheel embroidered on its front.

"What," barked Shrike.

The page flinched. "My lady requests the presence of her king in her bower."

Shrike glowered down at the page, then across the field toward the hemlock tower, then back to the page again. "You've delivered your charge. Now be off."

The page scampered.

Wren watched the page go all the way to the roots of the hemlock tower. When he returned his attention to Shrike, he found him glaring in the same direction.

"Shall we have done with it?" Wren enquired in a low tone.

"Aye," Shrike muttered, and strode off.

Wren hastened to catch him up. But mere paces passed before Shrike halted and glanced down at Wren in apparent bewilderment.

"I'm coming with you," said Wren.

Shrike didn't look any less unsettled. 'She's unlike your mortal queen."

"Dangerous, you mean."

Shrike nodded.

"All the more reason for you not to face her alone," Wren concluded.

A warm fondness came into Shrike's considering gaze. With another nod, he relented and continued on towards the queen's bower with Wren in tow.

The ring of knights at the tower's roots made way at Shrike's approach, though they cast suspicious glances at Wren as he passed through their ranks. The courtiers he encountered on his way up the spiralling wooden stair within the tower were likewise astonished by the presence of a mortal in their midst, judging by their wide eyes and hissing whispers. Wren's own gaze flitted over them in search of anyone who looked particularly like a Holly King. None resembled the one

Shrike had slain on the Winter Solstice—the only Holly King whom Wren had ever known.

The spiral staircase opened up to a feast hall likewise filled with fae gawking at Wren and Shrike. Shrike paid them no heed. He strode with purpose across the hall toward the balcony with its twin thrones; one empty, the other holding the queen upon whom Shrike fixed his fierce glare.

Wren followed his gaze and his path alike. Long had he harboured a curiosity to meet the one who wielded such influence over his beloved's fate.

The Queen of the Court of the Silver Wheel bore the same strawberry-golden hair and emerald-green eyes as when Wren had glimpsed her from a distance on the Winter Solstice. Since then, however, she had discarded her silver-blue gown in favour of one in honeydew which shimmered towards white-gold at the peaks of its folds and ivy-green in its shadowed valleys. Embroidery in golden thread along its hems depicted the hunt of a unicorn. Her belt of slender bronze chain—a proper medieval gyrdel—draped around her waist to cling to her hips, with the remainder of its length trailing down her lap like a sword-blade dividing a waterfall of silk. It joined together links the size and form of ivy leaves with those delicate enough to resemble the vine, the leaves enamelled glass-green and the vine tarnished to a matching shade.

Shrike halted some paces before her throne and made a small bow. Wren hastened to follow suit. When he straightened up again, he saw the queen's rosebud lips curled in something like faint amusement, and her emerald gaze flitted between Shrike and Wren with equal curiosity.

"Good morrow, my Oak King," she said. Her voice, soft yet sonorous, carried command throughout the bower.

Shrike muttered something in kind.

"When I called upon you to crown me," the queen continued, her eyes trailing across the breadth of his antlers from point to point, "I did not think to see you wearing a crown of your own make."

Courtiers standing behind Wren and Shrike tittered. Shrike did not deign to so much as glance in their direction. Wren resisted the urge to do so.

"It becomes you," the queen added when it became apparent Shrike had nothing to say to her idle observation.

Shrike gave his thanks.

The queen's emerald-green eyes slid towards Wren. Instinct bid him lower his gaze. He found he could not.

"Pray," the queen said to Shrike even as she fixed Wren with her attention like an entomologist might pin a beetle beneath glass. "Do introduce us to your companion."

"Lofthouse," said Shrike. "Of London."

"Lofthouse of London," the queen echoed, like a child toying with a new word in its teeth. "We bid you welcome."

Wren attempted to thank her. His mouth moved in silence. He cleared his throat and managed a rasp in reply.

This seemed to satisfy her. She released him from her gaze and turned her eye toward something behind him.

Wren glanced back to see a pair of handmaidens carrying between them a crown woven from flowering boughs. Jewel-bright hummingbirds struggled feebly against their spiderweb bonds between the sprigs of aquilegia and foxglove.

At the queen's signal, the handmaidens handed the crown over to Shrike, who accepted the charge with stoic indifference. In the span of a few strides he stood behind the queen's throne. He lowered the crown onto her head in solemn silence. Then sank to one knee and bowed his own.

The resulting cheer from the throng assembled beneath the balcony startled Wren, who had forgotten the presence of almost all save Shrike and the queen.

The queen basked in their adoration. Then, to the astonishment of Wren and her courtiers alike, she rose from her throne and turned to Shrike. Their astonishment only increased as she dropt her delicate ivory fingertips to the curve of her hips and unclasped her gyrdel from about her waist. The green chain gently jingled as she wound it between her hands and held it out to Shrike.

A gesture which Wren knew must mean as much in the Court of the Silver Wheel as it had done in Lord Bertilak's castle.

Shrike's face remained cast in stoic stillness as he accepted it from her. He bowed. Her smile beamed down upon him.

Then he arose and turned to Wren.

And held out the gyrdel for him to take.

Wren, surprised and amused alike, repressed the urge to laugh aloud. He satisfied himself with biting back a smile as he accepted the gift from his beloved.

Yet over Shrike's shoulder, Wren saw the queen's own smile turn from sunshine to ice. Her emerald-green eyes ignited with cold flame.

Shrike, still not deigning to glance back at her, laid his hand on Wren's arm and made as if to guide him out of the bower.

"Stay, my lord," the queen called out. "We would have a word with your gallaunt."

Shrike froze. His expression remained unreadable as he faced his queen. His hand clenched to a fist around Wren's arm.

"Come forth, Lofthouse," the queen continued. "And kneel before us."

Wren's heart ceased beating. His eyes darted to meet Shrike's, seeking explanation, advice, a sign.

Shrike's dark gaze locked on his own. For an instant, Wren beheld fury tinged with fear. Then, like a bright-blazing ember flying from a bonfire, no sooner had it arose than it went out. A stoic tide washed over any emotion as Shrike flicked his gaze to the throne.

"Forgive me, my lady," he said in a low burr which begged no such thing. "We must away."

The queen narrowed her eyes. Her lips parted for speech.

"No, it's all right," Wren hastened to interrupt. "We can stay a moment longer."

Better, he thought, to face whatever wrath she held for them both now than to risk the increase of her ire with disobedience.

Shrike fixed him with a penetrating look. For a moment Wren feared he would prove stubborn. Then he nodded and withdrew his hand from Wren's arm.

Wren returned his gaze to the queen, bowed his head, and sank to one knee before her.

The queen withdrew her sword from its sheath with a scrape that sent a shudder down his spine.

"Kneel, Lofthouse," she intoned as she laid her sword on his left shoulder.

Wren, already kneeling, remained motionless. His mind raced. Perhaps the queen would grant him youth and beauty beyond all mortal expectation. Perhaps she would make him a knight in her court. Perhaps she would name him her amanuensis and his art would find its staging in her woodlands, far out of the reach of England's Lord Chamberlain.

"And arise," said the queen, shifting her sword to Wren's right shoulder, "our King of the Holly."

SUMMER

CHAPTER
TWENTY-SEVEN

"No!" Shrike shouted.

A roar of approval rose from the throng in the same instant, swallowing his voice.

Wren's head shot up. He whirled, and his bewildered gaze locked with Shrike's own.

The queen sheathed her sword. She took great pleasure in wreaking her vengeance upon Shrike, judging by the elegant moue of her smile.

Shrike did not waste another moment on her. He leapt to Wren's side, seizing his arm as he arose.

"We're leaving," Shrike told him.

Wren didn't argue.

The cheers had become a wild rejoicing. Courtiers flocked 'round their queen, creating a writhing wall of bodies between Shrike and Wren and the spiralling staircase down from the queen's bower.

Shrike grappled a lady-in-waiting by the shoulder and shoved her aside. Then he snatched up a page by the throat and flung them out of his path.

By then, the rejoicing crowd began to realize Shrike intended to carve through them, and those nearest to him scrambled to make way. Shrike hardly heeded them. He strode forth, the tide of courtiers parting before him, Wren half-dragged along behind. More fae fled from Shrike's wrath as he stormed down the spiral stair, out of the bower, and across the flowering field. He met no gaze as he went, looking ahead to the treeline.

Nor did he cease once he reached the forest, instead marching on in furious silence. The Beltane revels faded to the merest echoes behind him. He heard nothing from Wren at his side all the while. The silence grew as they drew within sight of the briars encircling Blackthorn, as the vines parted before them, and as they entered the cottage garden.

No sooner had the thorns grown over the path behind them than Wren jerked to a halt.

Shrike, still holding him by the arm, halted as well. He turned to look at Wren—the one thing he couldn't bear to do ever since the queen had laid her sword upon his shoulder.

Wren still held her gyrdel in his fists. His palms turned white where the chain's links dug into his flesh. Shrike felt those same links wrapped around his heart and cutting tighter with every beat.

"What just happened?" Wren said, his voice low and urgent.

Shrike forced the impossible words out despite his clenched jaw. "The Queen of the Court of the Silver Wheel has named you her Holly King."

"Has she ever crowned a mortal Holly King before?" Wren demanded.

"All Holly Kings are mortal by definition."

"That's not what I meant," Wren snapped. "And you know it."

"No," Shrike admitted. "She has never done so, to my knowledge."

"Then what the Hell is she playing at?"

"I don't know."

Wren stared up at him, his gaze darting between Shrike's eyes in search of answers he didn't have.

To see Wren look upon him in fear clove Shrike's heart in twain.

"I should never have brought you before her," Shrike blurted. "I ought to have left you safe in the bower. Or better yet, in Blackthorn."

Wren stared at him. "You cannot possibly blame yourself for this."

Shrike could see no one else to blame. "If I'd swallowed my pride and lain with her—"

"If you *what!?*"

Shrike balked at the sudden outburst from his beloved. In an instant, Wren's aspect had shifted from fear to rage. Jealousy, Shrike thought— yet even as it occurred to him, he realized he erred. He'd had jealous lovers before, not keeping them long after he realized their flaw, and what he saw in Wren's face now wasn't that same maelstrom of envy and wrath. Wren's rage was borne of something else.

"To give your gyrdel to another is to declare your intention to lie with them," Shrike explained, though it didn't seem to do much good.

"And by giving it over to me," said Wren, "you declared your intention to lie with me instead?"

"I made my preference clear," Shrike admitted.

"If your preference isn't for her," Wren continued, no less heated than before, "then why is your lying with her even a possibility?"

Shrike thought the answer obvious. Still, he said nothing. This didn't seem to do much good, either.

"What claim has she to your body?" Wren demanded. "None, but what you grant her of your own will. Only a coward would ask you to submit yourself to her whims to preserve his own hide."

"If it would keep you safe—" Shrike protested.

"If it would keep *you* safe," Wren shot back, "would you want me to sacrifice my own body to her bower?"

The very thought sent a flood of wrath through Shrike's veins. "I would slaughter her and her whole court if she tried to take you."

Wren raised an eyebrow at him, as much as to say he thought Shrike ought to realize his impulses were mirrored in Wren's own soul.

"The fault is yet mine," Shrike insisted. "If I'd not given you her gyrdel—drawn her eye to you—it would never have occurred to her to name you her Holly King."

"Balderdash," said Wren.

Shrike stared at him.

"If she didn't intend to name me," Wren explained, seeing Shrike could form no words, "then why leave the post vacant all these long months? She must have known about me since Midwinter at least. Our embrace on the duelling field could hardly have escaped her notice. She's planned it since then, I'd bet my eye-teeth on it—and only held off so long in proclaiming it to toy with you as a cat toys with a wounded mouse. The gyrdel just gave her a convenient excuse to put her plans into motion."

Shrike continued staring at Wren as the threads wove together before his mind's eye until the resulting tangle knotted around his throat. Then he ran a hand over his face to clear his head. It didn't work. When he met Wren's gaze again, Wren looked no less exhausted and lost than Shrike felt.

"What shall we do now?" Wren asked.

"London," said Shrike. "You must return to London. It's choked with iron. No fae may touch you there."

"You kissed me there," said Wren.

How long ago and far away that seemed. Shrike tried again. "No fae will *harm* you there."

"Will you come with me?"

Shrike gazed down at Wren in disbelief. To think, after all that had befallen Wren this day, that Wren would still want him near—Shrike hadn't dared hope half so far.

Wren must have mistaken his confusion for aversion, for he hastened to explain. "I know the iron is a trial for you, but I should like to have you nearby all the same. Perhaps, if you were to follow me as a bird, you might tuck yourself away in Staple Inn. Perched on a windowsill. Or," he added, as it seemed inspiration struck him, "I could open the window to my garret, and you could remain safe indoors."

"Do you truly want me there?" Shrike murmured, scarcely able to believe him even now.

Wren blinked at him. "Of course. More than ever."

"Then you shall have me."

The faintest smile flickered across Wren's bespeckled lips—more of a smile than Shrike had ever hoped to see again.

"Let's go for the day at least," said Wren. "I can hardly abandon Mr Grigsby without explanation, but I should like to return to Blackthorn this evening." In reply to Shrike's bewildered gaze, he added, "I feel far safer here than in London."

Shrike wished he could say the same.

If Wren had found it difficult to return to clerking in Mr Grigsby's office after his previous adventures in the fae realms, it felt nigh-on impossible after he'd been declared the Holly King. Yet go he must. He desperately needed a dose of the familiar, however mundane.

"Lofthouse!" Mr Grigsby cried as Wren entered the office at half-past nine. "Pray, tell me Mr Butcher is not worse?"

"What?" Wren halted on the threshold. Belatedly he recalled the fib that had seen him out of the office just the day before. How long ago that seemed now. "No, not worse."

"I'm much relieved to hear it! You looked so grave, I had feared—but quite glad to know Mr Butcher is better."

Wren attempted to master his face. "I would not say he is better."

"No?" Mr Grigsby made no effort to disguise his confusion.

"Not worse," Wren insisted, his tongue running on whilst his mind whirled elsewhere, spinning out truth whilst his nerves remained too raw to suppress it as he ought. "But not better."

"Oh." Mr Grigsby didn't appear any less confused. But as he did not enquire aloud what had prompted Wren's return to Staple Inn if Shrike's condition remained unchanged, Wren saw no need to volunteer an explanation.

"As such," Wren said instead, "I had intended to go back again this evening. With your permission, sir."

"Of course! You hardly need my permission for that, Lofthouse—your hours are quite your own once we've locked up."

Wren hesitated. "I would not intend to return before morning, sir."

But Mr Grigsby waved him off. "I would hardly expect you to. Only think of it, leaving the poor invalid alone all night."

Wren could never quite tell if Mr Grigsby truly did not comprehend what other men would find suspicious, or if he simply chose to ignore it. He decided it didn't matter. "Thank you, sir."

"You're very welcome, Lofthouse!" Mr Grigsby returned to his newspaper in what appeared to be perfect contentment.

Wren went to his desk, opened his ledger, and sat staring at unending columns of figures with unseeing eyes for uncounted minutes.

He was the Holly King.

Though no crown had yet touched his brow, he nevertheless felt the weight of it keenly. A hollow and heavy weight around his mortal temples in which Death kept his court—or so the Bard had said through the mouth of Richard II. The histories, and the *Henriad* in particular, had always been Wren's favourite plays. He couldn't help thinking of them now. Kit Marlowe came to mind as well. Like Edward II, Wren and Shrike both bore the name of King and wore the crown, yet found themselves controll'd by their unconstant queen. Both Richard II and Edward II had died for love of their favourites. Wren felt he could not escape their fate. The bookshelves surrounding the office seemed to close in upon him with every passing moment.

As if the day had not yet proved trying enough, a merry rapping fell upon the door.

The familiar knock jolted Wren from his ghoulish musings and redoubled the knot of dread in his gut. With leaden limbs he crossed the office to let in the supplicant.

Felix Knoll sauntered over the threshold, bright as ever, and handing off his hat to Wren without looking him in the eye. Wren distracted himself from his irritation by making tea whilst Mr Grigsby fawned over his prodigal ward.

"I had wondered," Felix said, sitting in Wren's chair with a cup of tea after an excruciating quarter-hour of polite conversation, "if I might have your assistance in applying for a special licence?"

After a moment's stunned silence, Mr Grigsby answered him. "I would of course be only too happy to assist you in any way I can. But— if I may be so bold as to ask—why do you require a special licence? You and Miss Fairfield are young, yes, but it would require only the permission of your guardians to marry, and as I am guardian to you both, you need but ask. However, in my opinion, a bit of patience in the matter may go a long way. You will take your degree within the month and attain your majority by midsummer. Then you may begin your career in earnest to set up a proper household for Miss Fairfield and marry her before summer's end. I realize a few months may seem a great deal of time to wait, particularly when your affection for her is so strong, yet surely you have nothing to gain by applying for a special licence, except expense, and little to gain from my permission save a few weeks' haste."

And a hundred awkward rumours, Wren thought but didn't say.

"I should like to be married much sooner than summer's end," said Felix.

Mr Grigsby waited patiently for Felix to explain why.

Felix did not.

Mr Grigsby hesitated a moment further, then ventured in a more delicate tone, "Is there, perhaps, a reason for Miss Fairfield to likewise desire to wed earlier rather than later? Is she—forgive me—in a state of particular expectation? Does she fear a certain consequence if she should fail to marry soon?"

"Oh," Felix replied with an easy shrug. "She's not in trouble, sir."

This euphemism proved still too direct for Mr Grigsby's sensibilities. A startled cough escaped him, and he fumbled for his handkerchief.

"Or if she is in trouble," Felix continued, either enjoying Mr Grigsby's distress or in ignorance of it, "it ain't by my doing."

Wren had long thought that, after all Felix had already done, nothing else would surprise him. Yet it seemed Felix had found the means to burrow beneath Wren's lowest expectations.

A tense pause ensued.

"Forgive me, my dear boy." While Mr Grigsby's voice remained mild as ever, the good humour had fallen away to leave something stark in its wake. "I'm afraid I misheard you."

Felix said nothing.

"I had thought," Mr Grigsby continued in the same low tone when it became apparent Felix had no reply, "that you had insinuated a grave slur on the character of the young lady you intend to marry. Perhaps you meant it as a jest, though I would hate to think one would make such a jest even in the lowest of company."

Felix remained silent, his expression sober for the first time in all Wren's acquaintance with him.

"Or perhaps, Mr Knoll," Mr Grigsby concluded, "you merely misspoke."

Relief broke over Felix's face—too soon, by Wren's reckoning. "I must have, sir."

Mr Grigsby didn't appear in the least bit relieved. "Then, pray tell, for what purpose do you require a special licence?"

"Nothing serious," Felix answered quickly, with a breathless chuckle that Mr Grigsby didn't share. "It's only the matter we spoke of before."

Mr Grigsby raised his brows.

Felix hastened to explain. "That is, I asked you before if I might draw any further upon my trust this quarter—and you've assured me it is impossible. So I must seek out an alternative solution."

Mr Grigsby's brows flew still further toward his receded hairline.

Felix smiled in a wan imitation of his once-effortless charm. "Flora wishes to help me, but her power over her fortune is limited until she attains her majority—or until she and I wed, at which point all that is mine is hers, and all that is hers is mine."

Mr Grigsby stared at him.

"And I'd very much like to have the money as soon as possible," Felix babbled on. "So it's necessary that we marry as soon as possible, rather than waiting until I finish university and attain my majority."

A resounding silence crashed down upon them all in the wake of Felix's proclamation.

"How strange," said Mr Grigsby at last. "I've heard nothing from Miss Fairfield regarding the matter."

Felix frowned. "She came to ask you about it in person."

"Is that what she told you?" asked Mr Grigsby.

"It's what I told—" Felix cut himself off. Whether because he'd finally realized he'd said too much, or due to the pallor that had descended upon Mr Grigsby's visage, Wren couldn't say.

Yet Mr Grigsby's voice remained low and calm as ever. "What is the extent of your financial difficulty?"

Felix, through much circumlocution, admitted to a variety of debts—debts of honour to friends, debts of business to tailors and tavern-keepers and stable-masters, and debts of debts to money-lenders.

Mr Grigsby listened to the whole with far more patience than Wren thought Felix deserved. Even as Wren tallied up the rapidly-accumulating sum in his head and realized the whole would wipe out Miss Flora's fortune entirely, and knew Mr Grigsby must realize the same, still Mr Grigsby said nothing, nor let any hint of the creeping horror show in his sober face.

After many minutes, Felix concluded his evasive accounting.

Mr Grigsby let the ensuing silence stretch on for another moment before he spoke. "Is that all, Mr Knoll?"

Felix swallowed hard. "That's all, sir."

Mr Grigsby levelled a severe look upon the boy, and his voice at last took on the slightest timbre of emotion—rage. "Under the circumstances you've outlined, I will by no means apply for a special licence on your behalf. As Miss Fairfield's legal guardian, I have every intention of withdrawing my consent to the match unless you settle your outstanding accounts and show how you will treat her with the respect that she—or indeed any living creature, but particularly she—deserves."

Wren wondered if he ought to dash out and fetch a physician. Mr Grigsby looked on the verge of becoming apoplectic in the literal as well as the figurative sense.

Despite the quiet and solemn tone, Felix appeared at last to understand how far he'd erred. "Sir, I—"

Mr Grigsby's well of patience had run dry. "If you require assistance in settling these debts, I offer you this advice: cut off whatever friends have led you down this path. Withdraw from university and begin employment without delay. Sell off whatever goods you own—I daresay you can get on without most of it, much more than you realize—and return whatever goods you don't. Quit the rooms you now occupy and apply to your uncle for assistance. His fondness for you is without peer and he will no doubt shelter you."

Nothing in this plan seemed to appeal to Felix. "But Mr Grigsby—"

"Until you follow my advice," Mr Grigsby spoke over him, "I have nothing further to offer you. Good day, Mr Knoll."

Felix stood staring at Mr Grigsby. Then, unaccountably, he turned to Wren.

Wren maintained his stone-faced silence.

Felix looked to Mr Grigsby again. Seeing no change in the old gentleman's aspect, he scoffed, snatched up his hat, turned on his heel, and strode out of the office.

Wren shut the door behind him.

Mr Grigsby sat looking at the closed door for a long while. Then he slumped over his desk with his face in his hands for many minutes more. He remained there long enough for Wren to brew a pot of tea. Only when Wren poured a cup and set it by his elbow did Mr Grigsby rise again. While no one would have ever mistaken Mr Grigsby for a youthful man, he'd never looked quite so old to Wren as he did in that moment.

For years, Wren had awaited the day when Mr Grigsby would see Felix for what he truly was—as Wren had seen him all along. But now that the hour had arrived, Wren wished he could drape the veil over Mr Grigsby's eyes again, if only to spare the poor gentleman the immense turmoil he now suffered.

Mr Grigsby spent another half-minute or so in silent regard of the teacup before he picked it up. After a small sip, he set it down again and resumed his far-off look. Without meeting Wren's eye, he spoke.

"When his parents passed on and left the boy to my guardianship," Mr Grigsby said in a dull tone unrecognizable as his ebullient self, "I resolved to do my best by him. He was so very young, and quite alone in the world, save for his uncle. As his uncle has become something like a father to him, I suppose that I have, after a fashion, become the mother. And in doing so I fear I've indulged him far too much." Mr Grigsby paused. His fingertips trembled upon the teacup handle. "I've failed him."

"Mr Knoll is almost a man grown, sir," Wren said softly in the ringing silence that followed. "You cannot blame yourself."

"I'm afraid I must," replied Mr Grigsby. "Otherwise it will fall square upon Mr Tolhurst's shoulders—and I believe we can both agree he is not responsible for what Mr Knoll has become."

Wren did not agree, in fact, but held his tongue. And as Mr Grigsby sipped his tea and stared off into nothing, Wren found himself wondering if Mr Grigsby would grieve him half so hard as he grieved Felix if he knew the depraved depths to which Wren had sunk. Whether Mr Grigsby would be more distraught to realize he'd raised up a spendthrift or a sodomite, Wren couldn't say. His pessimistic nature inclined toward the latter possibility.

Yet despite all this, one curious spark ignited in Wren's mind. Felix, desperate for money, would stoop to any depth to obtain it. A man willing to beg his guardian for a special licence—and ruin his innocent betrothed in the bargain—would hardly do less to those for whom he cared not a whit. And while Wren didn't have a particularly high opinion of Felix's intelligence, he thought him clever enough to make more than one attempt at the acquisition if he believed he had the upper hand.

Such as, perhaps, by convincing his guardian's clerk to apply for a special licence in secret, under the threat of blackmail. Or demanding the clerk withdraw further from his trust. Or simply command the clerk to fork over his own wages and savings outright in exchange for keeping his terrible secret.

Felix had done none of this. He'd made no mention of Wren, had hardly glanced toward him throughout his visit. Nor had he contacted Wren to confront him with the hideous evidence.

From this, Wren could draw but one conclusion.

Felix did not have his manuscripts.

"Tolhurst, then," said Shrike.

Wren had divulged the day's events the moment they stepped through the toadstool ring into the fae realm, and Shrike had reached his conclusion almost as quickly.

Having thought the matter over for hours beforehand, Wren felt forced to agree. Still, "I hardly know what he would want with it. He certainly hasn't blackmailed me yet, and I can't imagine what would drive him to do so—while he's not so well settled as his nephew, he has a comfortable enough living in Rochester. Certainly more comfortable than myself. One would think his moral fibre would demand my arrest. Or perhaps," Wren added, though he didn't really believe it, "he did what I could not, and threw the whole into the fire, lest it corrupt any more idle readers."

"I should hope not," said Shrike.

Wren gave him a sharp glance. "Why not?"

"Your work is wonderful. To burn it would be a terrible waste."

"I'm very much afraid no one in the mortal realm shares your opinion. But—thank you," Wren added, for his words had warmed his heart nonetheless.

This earned him a smile, though wan and fleeting.

The remainder of the winding walk to Blackthorn passed in silence. Wren felt no need to break it as the briars receded from their approach of the cottage. Nor as Shrike opened the door and reached inside.

But when Shrike brought out an arming sword and held it out, scabbard and all, towards Wren, Wren thought it prudent to speak.

"What's this for?" he asked as he took it from Shrike. The leather scabbard, tooled in a pattern of ivy leaves, reminded Wren of a leather-bound book. The sword weighed more than a book, though it felt better balanced in his hand. It didn't look like the one Shrike had used in the solstice duel or the dance at Ostara.

Shrike had already gone into the cottage again and retrieved that very sword. Then he unsheathed it. The blade sang out as it came free, the ringing metal echoing all throughout the briar.

Dread seized Wren's heart. "What are you doing."

Shrike swung the blade back and forth as if testing it. He adjusted his grip on the hilt and motioned to the scabbard in Wren's hand with the wickedly pointed tip. "Draw your sword."

Wren swallowed. His mouth remained dry. "Why don't we go inside?"

"I would recommend against sparring indoors," Shrike replied.

Sparring. Wren, who'd not excelled in fencing at university, replied, "I don't want to hurt you."

"You won't," said Shrike.

Wren very much doubted that—inexperience begat accidents that no amount of practice could set right—but relented nonetheless. It took two tries to pull his own sword from its scabbard, producing dull and disjointed clatter rather than the magnificent ring of Shrike's blade. And when he held it before him, it wavered in his grip, his arm not accustomed to holding the weight of a blade steady. Sixty hours a week hunched over a desk had not done much to increase what meagre strength he possessed.

Shrike, meanwhile, dropped into a half-crouched fighting stance as naturally as most men dropped off to sleep. "Come at me."

Against his better judgment, Wren did his able best to imitate Shrike's pose, then slashed out at Shrike's sword with his own. It glanced off with a clang.

Shrike frowned. "Strike at me. Not at my blade."

Wren hesitated.

Shrike thumped his own chest with his free fist. "Aim here."

"Why the deuce should I aim at something I've no wish to hit?" Wren shot back.

Shrike remained unmoved. "Because it's the only way you'll survive."

Wren stared at him.

"You are the Holly King," Shrike continued. "You must duel upon the solstice. And you must win."

"What?" Wren barked out a bitter laugh. "Do you intend to kill me?"

"No."

"Then why—"

"I'm not training you to defend yourself against me," said Shrike. "I'm training you to defeat the Oak King she crowns in my stead, and every Oak King that comes after."

Wren dropped his arm. His sword's point struck the dirt. "What?"

"It will be worth it to know you will survive after I'm gone."

"Not to me, it won't!" Wren snapped.

Shrike balked. "What?"

"I'm supposed to *murder* you?" Wren continued, his voice dripping with indignant sarcasm. "And then what? Just keep on cleaving Oak Kings in half until Judgment Day? What sort of plan is that? Even if I wanted to kill you—which, and I cannot emphasize this enough, I do not, though my patience is sorely tested—what happens to the rest of the world if an Oak King never reigns again? Another year without a summer? Another decade? Another *century?*"

Shrike had no answer for him.

Wren tossed his sword aside entirely, his eyes fixed on Shrike as the pommel thudded against the ground unseen. "I'm not doing it. I don't care what you think or what you want or what you say. I'm not killing you, and I'm not condemning everyone else to suffer along with us."

"Very well," said Shrike, his voice dull and distant. "When our duel begins, I will yield and fall on my own sword."

Cold dread seeped through Wren's veins. He pushed it back with a hiss. "You will do no such thing!"

"Then," said Shrike with a face that seemed carved from stone, "if you hope to prevent my doing so, you had better practice your swordplay."

"If you so much as drop to one knee, I will slit my own throat."

Shrike's eyes flew wide with a horror that matched Wren's own.

"I'm human," Wren said before Shrike could protest. "Mortal. I'll bleed out within a minute. And there's no coming back from that. No force of will, no determination, no promise will prevent me from dying on the field. You *will* outlive me—if only by a few moments."

Shrike continued his silent regard of Wren for some time after Wren ceased speaking. Then, in a stricken voice, he asked, "What do you propose instead?"

"Neither of us dies upon Midsummer," declared Wren.

Shrike waited. When it became apparent Wren had said all he meant to, Shrike asked, "And how shall we accomplish this?"

Wren didn't know. Yet. "You trusted me to find a way to see you safely through the Winter Solstice. Trust me again to find a way to see us both through Midsummer."

Shrike fixed him with a steady gaze that seemed to burn through his stoic visage and strike Wren to his very core. Then he threw down his sword—his arm moving faster than Wren could perceive, only realizing what had happened when he heard the blade thud against the ground. Two strides brought him to Wren. His strong arms swept him into a fraught embrace, his rough palm cradling Wren's jaw as tenderly as one might hold a wounded bird, and the kiss he pressed to Wren's lips held an oath, a promise, a vow of eternal faith.

Wren knotted his fingers in Shrike's silver-shot tresses and returned the kiss with bruising determination.

CHAPTER
TWENTY-EIGHT

Wren's kiss, as ever, proved a balm for Shrike's wounded heart. Shrike slung his arm around his waist and guided him into the cottage to settle down for the evening as best they could, considering their trials.

While they shed their garments and nestled into bed together, Shrike's mind kept whirling away at the problem. Wren had bid Shrike trust him to think of something. And so Shrike would. Still, that needn't prevent Shrike from devising alternatives.

But his allies and resources, once he'd numbered them, proved few indeed. Even with Wren warm and safe in his arms, he felt a cold dread seep into his veins.

"Shrike," Wren murmured.

The sound of his true name, however faint, sent a shiver through Shrike's core—all the moreso when it fell from those beloved bespeckled lips. "Aye."

"Have you heard the tale of Saint George and the Black Knight?"

Shrike had not, and said so.

"Perhaps you know him as the Redcrosse Knight," Wren added, though Shrike did not. "He slew a dragon once, but that's not the tale I'm thinking of. It's just a mummer's play. The same mock pageant every year. The Black Knight challenges the good Saint George, and they fight to the death, until the Black Knight is slain by Saint George."

It had a certain ring of familiarity to it, Shrike had to admit.

"But," Wren continued, "when Saint George realizes he's killed the Black Knight, he's overcome with remorse and grief, and begs the doctor to return the Black Knight to life. The doctor does so, and Saint George and the Black Knight embrace as comrades." He paused. "I don't suppose there are any such doctors in the fae realms."

"There are rumours," Shrike admitted. "It would take a quest to find them."

"If they exist at all." Wren sighed. "Still, it's a thought."

They lapsed into silence again. Shrike's hand wandered to Wren's hair and began braiding knots into it absent-mindedly.

"Your turn," Wren murmured.

"Mine?" Shrike replied.

Wren nodded against Shrike's collar. "Tell a story."

One couldn't live centuries in the fae realms without hearing at least a scrap of story or song. But Shrike had never tried his hand as a bard. His quiet nature made him ill-suited to recounting epics or reciting poetry.

Still, there remained one tale he knew by heart. One oft whispered at the margins of his presence in hunts, though none knew it so well as him. One he'd not told but the once, many years ago, and yet burned in his mind now. He forced himself to begin. "I would have you know the truth of how I came to be called the Butcher of Blackthorn."

Wren's body took on the aspect of a taut bowstring as Shrike felt rather than saw his gaze fix on his face with intense interest.

"I've already told you how Larkin raised me through my first century, until he perished." Shrike hesitated. "He did not die a natural death."

While Shrike couldn't see Wren's face in the darkness—could not search his dark eyes for what he thought of his tale—he felt Wren's body tense against his own in his embrace. He waited to see if Wren might speak. But Wren did not. And so Shrike spoke on in his stead.

"On a September eve, Larkin bid me bring our wares to the Moon Market to barter. The day's work had wearied him, and he remained home to rest. I left him abed and went out. The moon was full. The market was bright. Amongst the throng I stumbled across a fae peddling pomegranates—a particular favourite of Larkin's. I brought some back with me alongside the rest of the night's spoils. I walked home. When I came within a half-mile of our hovel, I beheld a curious light that rivalled the moon. A golden glow flickering through the trees.

"Belatedly, I recognized it as a towering flame.

"I dropt all I held and ran.

"By the time I arrived at the remnants of our home, most of the fire had burnt out. The ruin of our hovel still smouldered. Larkin…" Shrike forced his words out past the catch in his throat as the memory flickered once again into his mind. The dark stains spreading o'er the homespun tunic stitched by Shrike's own hand. The strong arms which had carried Shrike through his childhood and taught him to wield axe, scythe, hammer, and bow, now fallen at fixed angles never to rise again, the iron dagger yet clutched in his rigid fist. The crow's-feet wrinkles around eyes that had smiled warmly on Shrike all his days, now fixed unseeing on the night sky beyond. "His body lay beyond it."

Shrike's voice failed him. His own ragged breath resounded in his ears. He knew not how to continue his tale.

Then Wren caressed his cheek, a touch familiar and warm, and with more comfort in a single gesture than Shrike's heart could well bear.

Shrike cleared his throat and spoke on. "He'd been cut down by three blades. I buried him. Then I slipped his iron dagger into my belt and took up his iron scythe in his stead to seek my vengeance.

"Tracing the path his murderers had taken proved little challenge. I had spent the prior century tracking game through the woods. And the hooves of their war-chargers had torn up the forest floor like plough-shares.

"Their trail led to a tavern between realms. Outside stood the three war-chargers I'd tracked, their bridles—one of silver cord, one of copper chain, and one of leather riveted with pewter—all tied to low-hanging branches as they awaited their masters. Inside, fae from all courts gathered to exchange tales and share drink. On this particular eve I threw its door wide to find three knights amongst the throng—one in silver scale, another in copper chain, and a third in a pewter-studded gambeson. They'd discarded their suits of armour—silver, copper, pewter—in piles around the bench on which they caroused. They'd removed their helmets and wore instead leather masks wrought by Larkin's own hands, looted from our home." Shrike found his fingers trembled with rage just as they'd done on the very night he spoke of. "I strode to their bench and told them I intended to avenge Larkin's murder. The silver knight smiled to hear it.

"I carved a second smile into his throat."

A stifled gasp escaped Wren's lips. Yet he did not speak. Nor did he move to withdraw from Shrike's embrace. Shrike waited to hear him draw breath again before he continued his tale.

"The silver knight fell. The copper knight and pewter knight leapt to take up arms. Surprise had taken me as near to victory as it could. From thereon out I depended on skill and luck. More of the latter. In a fair fight with either I should have fallen. Yet in the tavern on that night I had some advantage. For one, all the knights had shed their armour to carouse. For another, they'd already caroused for some hours before I found them, and now they fought from deep within their cups. And thirdly, I wielded weapons of iron—and few tournaments are fought with scythes.

"None else in the tavern came to the knights' aid, nor mine. The copper knight fell beneath Larkin's scythe soon enough. The pewter knight stood longer. Long enough for their longsword to force the scythe from my hands. Yet as they lunged to strike me, Larkin's dagger found its way into their heart."

Shrike paused to hear what Wren thought of this. Wren said nothing. But nor did he withdraw from Shrike, so Shrike went on.

"Having defeated the three knights, I claimed their steeds, armour, and weaponry as my rightful spoils. None moved to prevent me, just as none had moved to interfere in the fight. I brought my spoils home to what remained of our hovel, though I could ill bear the sight of them. I slept in the burnt ruin. I awoke to find briars had grown all around me. Rings within rings of tangled thorns encircled me in a labyrinth of my own grief. And the well-spring beneath, from which we drew our water, had transformed into a scalding geyser of my howling rage. Thus this patch of forest became Blackthorn Briar. This very cottage stands over the ruin of Larkin's hut.

"At the next Moon Market I bartered my ill-gotten gains away. If tales carried from the tavern that fateful night hadn't already sealed my reputation amongst the folk, bringing bloodied arms and armour to the Moon Market did. For the first time folk took notice of me—not for my or Larkin's craft, but for what havoc I could wreak. The blood has never ceased flowing. I threw myself into the Wild Hunt, seeking a channel to draw off my rage. There I met Nell, and others, who understood somewhat. All have their own reasons for joining the Hunt. Through this all heard of my talent for bloodshed. Despite my craft, my garden, and my flocks, it seems the fates have formed me for death and death alone. Perhaps my fellow fledglings sensed this in me and hence shoved me out of the nest. Ever since the night of Larkin's murder, I'm called Butcher by all who care to know me. Save you."

Silence fell. Shrike waited for Wren to withdraw. He wouldn't blame him for it. Not after he knew what blood soaked Shrike's hands.

But when Wren moved at last, it was only to turn his head to press a kiss to the inside of Shrike's wrist and entrust his cheek to the care of Shrike's palm. His arm twined 'round Shrike's collar in a hold as strong as the stout branch of an oak and as gentle as a summer breeze overturning a leaf. Far better than Shrike deserved.

He had failed to protect Larkin.

He refused to falter in his quest to protect Wren.

"Butcher!"

Wren bolted upright from Shrike's nest-bed. Morning had broken. Dust motes danced in the sunbeams streaming into the cottage. Shrike lay beside him and seemed altogether far less alarmed at the rude awakening than Wren felt.

"Nell," Shrike muttered in reply to Wren's confused glance. He rolled over and arose to don his tunic, hose, and boots in a remarkably lackadaisical fashion.

Knocks fell like hammer blows on the cottage door. Wren hastened to follow Shrike's example. Waistcoat, trousers, and boots he donned easily enough, but he couldn't reach his frock coat before Shrike went for the door, leaving him standing in bare shirtsleeves when Shrike let Nell in.

Despite being the first female to see Wren in such a state since his father had dismissed his childhood nursemaid, Nell didn't appear appalled or astonished in the least as she looked him up and down. One hand she kept on the hilt of the arming-sword at her waist. The other gripped the strap of her quiver with her unstrung bow slung over her shoulder alongside it. "Good morrow, Lofthouse. Butcher."

"What brings you here?" Shrike asked with more calm than Wren possessed.

"Beltane." She shot another significant glance at Wren.

"You've heard, then," said Shrike.

"Aye," she replied. "I come to offer my bow and quiver to the Oak and Holly King. I think you may at last have encountered a predicament which a well-placed arrow might solve."

"A tempting offer," said Shrike, echoing Wren's own thoughts. "But there may yet be some course for us to pursue before we come to that."

Nell's mouth twisted up one side in a doubtful expression. Yet all she replied was, "Very well. What would you have of me instead?"

"Find a duelling master," said Shrike. "One willing to instruct in the art of the blade—"

"I'm not going to fight you," Wren snapped.

Nell raised her brows and shot an enquiring glance at Shrike.

But Shrike's solemn gaze remained fixed on Wren. "I know. But for us both to survive the coming solstice, it may prove necessary for you to defend yourself. If you cannot bear to raise your hand against me then I must find another worthy opponent to teach you."

"Fine," Wren conceded.

Nell acquiesced with a bow that would've done any young buck at Almack's proud. "Allow me to make enquiries."

"Discreet enquiries," Shrike added.

"I am capable of subterfuge," replied Nell. "Though I may not oft choose to employ it."

And with that, she turned on her heel and strode out of Blackthorn, the briars parting before her as she went and twining together again in her wake.

"Will you return to London?" Shrike asked, jerking Wren's attention back to him.

The temptation to remain within Blackthorn—with Shrike—proved even stronger now than it ever had before. And yet, "I must."

Returning to the mortal realm felt no less surreal than it had yesterday. Mr Grigsby appeared to notice nothing amiss when he came down to find Wren mechanically slicing open the morning offerings of the penny post. Wren managed to echo his employer's greeting. Further conversation proved beyond him—not that Mr Grigsby seemed to mind.

"Oh, Lofthouse!" Mr Grigsby piped up mere minutes after Wren handed over the mail. "You may find this an amusing diversion."

Wren glanced over from his ledger to Mr Grigsby's desk. Mr Grigsby held one letter in particular before him.

"It seems," Mr Grigsby continued the moment he had Wren's attention, "Miss Fairfield is doing charitable works for the Society of Friends of Needful Seamen, and requires our aid. She asks if we have any gentlemen's clothing—something out of fashion or in need of mending—which we might like to pass along to sailors who find themselves down on their luck. Not that I suggest anything you own is out of fashion or in need of mending, of course! But I myself have some raiments of which I've outstripped the seams and the canvas of which would better outfit a young seaman's rigging than a swollen hulk like myself. Would you be so kind as to fetch them down and bundle them off to Miss Fairfield? They ought to be in my cedar chest, if I recall correctly."

Far be it from Wren to decline a distraction. He accepted his employer's charge and retreated upstairs.

Mr Grigsby had allowed Wren into his chambers on scattered occasions throughout their years together in Staple Inn—most notably, during a fortnight some five years back when Mr Grigsby had come down with a devilish cold and required Wren to nurse him through it. Thus the sight of the bed, desk, chest of drawers, and cedar trunk proved more familiar than otherwise to Wren's eyes.

Yet never before had every nook and cranny of the warm and cheerful chamber appeared a perfect hiding place for his missing manuscripts.

Finding the articles of clothing Mr Grigsby had hinted at took mere moments. Just as he'd said, the cedar chest at the foot of his bed contained trousers which had begun in the fashionably slender cut of some quarter-century past and had their seams let out again and again throughout the intervening years until no fabric remained to contain Mr Grigsby's growing girth, at which point he'd tucked them away. Three pairs altogether—one brown, one blue, and one black. Good enough yet for a gentleman who'd fit them, and certainly good enough for a sailor, Wren thought as he set them aside, along with several shirts whose buttons could never again hope to close around Mr Grigsby's considerable middle.

His assigned task complete, Wren set about turning over the rest of the room. Not quite so swift and silent as Shrike, yet quicker and quieter than Mr Grigsby might ever notice, Wren emptied out the entire cedar trunk, as well as the chest of drawers; then stripped the bedclothes, shook out the pillows, and flipped the mattress; then crawled beneath the bed-frame itself and all over the floorboards besides in search of any particular plank that might resound as hollow as the one under his own garret.

He found nothing but a sense of shame—both for invading Mr Grigsby's privacy and for ever suspecting him of the theft in the first place.

The shame drove Wren up to his own garret. He had no intention to return to England after Midsummer and thus thought some of his wardrobe might be put to better use in clothing Miss Flora's indigent sailors. At length he found two waistcoats—one black wool duplicate of the one he wore, the other flannel—which he couldn't imagine missing over-much.

Yet despite returning downstairs to the office with garments laid over both arms, he felt empty-handed. His stolen manuscripts remained missing.

And his hollow head remained empty of plans to survive the Summer Solstice.

CHAPTER
TWENTY-NINE

The remainder of the week passed without word from Nell. Wren had high hopes for Friday evening, which he had the liberty to spend in Blackthorn, but while he and Shrike wandered through the briar retrieving conies from snares, they neither saw nor heard any sign of her.

By Saturday morning, Wren felt ready to give the matter up. He had precious little to do in Staple Inn and thus not nearly enough to distract himself from his growing despair as the hours dragged on. Some small relief found him when the mantle-clock struck noon, and after polite refusal of Mr Grigsby's invitation to tea, he could escape from the dreary grey noise of London to the quiet greenery of the fae realms.

Wren breathed easier as he wandered the woodland and came to the familiar sight of the wall of briars marking the boundary of Blackthorn.

Yet as the brambles withdrew, a few vines remained tangled together in the midst of the path.

And something hung suspended within them.

Wren slowed his step. The thing in the vines appeared about the size of the cats he'd sometimes glimpsed scrambling through the alleys of Staple Inn. But not the same shape. Thinner, and with its lanky body as much twisted around the vines as the vines twisted around it, as if it had writhed itself into a knot. Its already-dark fur matted darker still with a crusting stain that had dripped into a pool beneath it. Wren halted altogether a yard or so away to bend and squint at the thing which looked more and more disturbing the longer he stared. Its maw had frozen in a fanged snarl, and its beady eyes had clouded over in death.

"Weasel."

Wren bolted upright and staggered back at the voice, though he knew it well.

Shrike likewise gazed down at the wretched thing, though with less disgust and more nonchalance. He nudged the knot of briars with the toe of his boot. The vines withdrew, scraping against the packed dirt of the path as they went, leaving the weasel's corpse behind with its serpentine form still twisted mid-convulsion. Shrike picked it up by the scruff of the neck embedded with broken thorns and cast an appraising look over it.

"Does this happen often?" Wren asked, rather than the question which had occurred to him whilst he stared at the strangled corpse and tried not to imagine what the briars might do to a larger foe.

"Now and again. They seek the hens. Sometimes they think they're clever and burrow under the vines. Then the roots ensnare them."

"Oh," said Wren.

Shrike glanced from the weasel to Wren. "Does it trouble you?"

Wren wished he knew how to appear less transparent than a window-pane. "No," he lied.

Shrike looked to the weasel again with a more considering gaze. "It's a good omen. The flesh will feed the soil, and the hens will reap the harvest from the garden. Those who attack us will only make us stronger."

And gazing into the soft dark eyes beneath the stern and heavy brow, Wren almost believed it.

If nothing else, it emboldened Wren enough to twine his arm through Shrike's and follow him back into the cottage—even as the weasel's corpse yet dangled from Shrike's other hand.

The sun had just begun to sink below the canopy when a call rang through the wood from beyond the cottage door.

"Hail and well met, Butcher!"

Wren, seated upon the bed with his sketch-book across his knees, shared a glance with Shrike at his work-bench.

"Nell?" Wren guessed.

"Aye," said Shrike, and went for the door.

Wren shut the cover on his drawing of Shrike at work just as Nell strode into the cottage.

"Thought I'd give you fair warning," she announced with a grin. "Didn't want to meet you at sword's-point again."

As she spoke, another figure entered the cottage in her wake—one small enough to remain hidden 'til now in the shadow of her slender frame. Smaller even than Wren. And yet not unfamiliar to his eye.

"You remember the ambassador," Nell continued, gesturing towards her guest with a careless wave.

"Good morrow, my lords," chirped the spiderweb fae from behind his mask.

Shrike balked—a small gesture on his part, the slightest backward jerk of the head that might have gone unnoticed on any other man, and which lasted for the merest instant, but a balk nonetheless, and one which Wren's keen interest readily perceived. He recovered quickly and nodded in reply. "Well met."

The ambassador smiled. "Nell tells me you require the services of a duelling master?"

Shrike nodded again.

The ambassador swept down into his extravagant wrist-twirling bow. "Allow me to offer my expertise for your consideration."

"And what do you ask of me in return?" said Shrike.

"I would beg a boon, my lord," the ambassador continued. "Of your companion."

Wren looked to Shrike, who appeared no less astonished than Wren felt. Still, if it would gain them the knowledge they sought, Wren saw no objection. "What would you ask of me, then?"

"You are a clerk by trade?" asked the ambassador.

"I am." Wren wondered where the ambassador had learnt that—Nell, he supposed—and if he ought to explain how the profession had changed since the fourteenth century.

The ambassador did not give him the opportunity. "You have the gift of letters?"

"I do," said Wren.

The ambassador beamed. "I would like the gift of letters."

This, of all things, Wren hadn't expected. The ambassador bore all the marks of refinement and culture of one accustomed to holding rank in court. And yet, evidently illiterate. Given this, a few lessons in literacy seemed a small enough price to pay for potentially life-saving tutelage. Wren opened his mouth to say so.

Shrike flung out an arm across Wren's path as though to shield him from the ambassador. His other hand went to the hilt of his sword at his belt.

Wren jerked back and shot Shrike a look of total confusion.

Shrike did not return his gaze. His dark eyes remained narrowed at the ambassador. In a cold voice unlike anything Wren had heard from him before, Shrike asked, "You would take the gift of letters from him?"

The ambassador had not moved a fraction of an inch despite the looming threat of Shrike before him. "Forgive me, my lord. I will speak more plainly. I would like the Holly King to teach me to read, whilst he retains his own literacy."

Horror washed over Wren as it dawned upon him what he had almost surrendered—without a thought.

Shrike slowly lowered his arm but kept his hand on his sword hilt. He glanced back at Wren with a look both enquiry and offer; enquiring what Wren thought of the bargain and offering to refuse it with violence if Wren deemed such action necessary.

Wren gave a slight shake of his head to stay Shrike's sword-hand and turned to the ambassador. "I accept your terms."

"Splendid!" The ambassador clapped his hands. "Which weapon do you prefer?"

"The quill," said Wren.

The ambassador blinked. "Ah. I'm afraid I've no skill whatsoever in that particular arena. Have you any experience with a blade?"

"Some practice with a fencing foil," Wren admitted. His education, while prematurely cut off, had seen to that. "Nothing with an edge, aside from pen-knives."

To Wren's astonishment, the ambassador smiled. "All the better, then, for you'll have fewer bad habits to break. Which weapon would you most like to learn?"

"Whichever one you think I've any chance of mastering before the Summer Solstice," Wren replied flatly.

The ambassador didn't seem in any way put off by Wren's sarcasm. He merely cocked his head to one side as his bizarre cat-slit eyes flicked up and down Wren's length in a piercing glance. "I myself am partial to the rapier. As you seem to hold yourself in a similar frame—if I may be so bold as to say so, my lord—and you have practiced with fencing foils already…"

"The rapier, then," said Wren, as the ambassador seemed to wait for his answer, no matter how many times he deferred.

The ambassador beamed again. "Then shall we begin on the morrow?"

Their plans made, Shrike led Nell and the ambassador out of Blackthorn. Not a strictly necessary gesture—the thorns would withdraw for them to depart just as they had withdrawn to allow their entrance—but it was courtesy to do so nonetheless, and he certainly owed both of them a debt for their aid in his present difficulty.

Shrike did not know much of his fellow riders in the Wild Hunt. He knew their feats and follies in the course of the Hunt itself, and he knew the bodies of those few he had lain with—knew them intimately, indeed—but little else of substance had passed between them. And they understood as little of him as he did of them. That was part of why he liked riding in the Hunt. No one questioned anyone's presence or purpose in it. They simply rode and ran and hunted together. No call for conversation or demand for declaration.

Aside from Nell.

Not because he'd approached her—quite the reverse. On the occasion of his first Hunt she had strode up to him and demanded to know his purpose.

"I know an outcast when I see one," had been her only explanation.

Shrike didn't take offence at the plain-spoken truth. And as Nell herself soon explained, divulging her own history as she learnt his in turn, she considered herself an outcast as well—a half-fae child born into mortal society, neither her nor her twin brother ever truly accepted by their father and his lawful wife. Only when she sought out the fae realms did she find the simple joy of freedom. Her brother had remained in the mortal realm and found something akin to happiness there, to her bewilderment, as an outcast.

Nor were her brother and Shrike the sole outcasts of her acquaintance, for she seemed to have struck up a familiarity with the ambassador of the Court of Spindles, as well.

Shrike knew as little of the ambassador as he knew of any other rider in the Hunt. He'd observed his evident skill, the poise with which he carried himself and the finesse with which he struck a killing blow, but he couldn't say with any honesty that he'd given him much thought over the decades.

Only when the ambassador approached Wren at Ostara did he come to the forefront of Shrike's mind. Then, in a flash of cold dread, Shrike had recalled all the rumours flying through the Hunt—of a forgotten son trained in the subtle art of murder and his deft and bloody escape from the most ruthless court in all the realms. From what Shrike had seen in the ambassador's conduct with Wren, nothing with even the barest hint of a threat had passed between them. Still, Shrike hadn't survived centuries in the fae realms unaligned with any court without nurturing a sense of wariness which proved difficult to dispel. As he watched the ambassador now stroll out of Blackthorn with a light and graceful step not unlike Nell's own slinking pace, he noted too the perpetual smile on the lips beneath the cobweb mask and the dancing glint in the cat-slit eyes.

"I've oft heard tell of Blackthorn Briar," the ambassador chirped, startling Shrike out of his study. "I must say it well outstrips its legend—quite beautiful, indeed. Rather of the sort of beauty many courts strive for and fail to capture."

"Thanks," Shrike muttered, ignoring Nell's laughing glance.

They'd reached the distant boundary of Blackthorn by then. The ambassador took his leave with another low bow and much wrist-twirling before striding off into the forest and vanishing into the mist.

Nell, however, lingered.

"Well?" she asked when the ambassador had thoroughly gone.

Shrike waited for her to say more.

"You mislike this plan," she added when the silence between them had stretched beyond its breaking point.

Shrike thought it useless to deny the truth. "It's my own plan. I've no one to blame but myself."

"Even if the ambassador becomes your Lofthouse's tutor?"

"Even so." Shrike hesitated. "Do you trust him?"

"With my twin's life."

Shrike stared at her. She'd spoken without hesitation. Others might have said such a thing in jest. Her blunt tone, which Shrike knew well, suggested she spoke from experience.

Nell cocked her head to the side to meet his stare. "Take heart—if Lofthouse learns something from the ambassador's tutelage, then he is certainly better off than before. And if he learns nothing, you may still truthfully say he's been instructed in the deadly arts by the Ambassador of Spindles." A wry half-smile plucked at the corner of her mouth. "Which would give even the most ambitious assassin pause."

Shrike had to admit she made a compelling argument. It was certainly more of a plan than he'd proved capable of concocting since Beltane.

Nell clapped him on the back and strode off.

"Is there anything to hand I might use for writing?" Wren asked as Shrike entered the cottage. "Larger than my sketch-book, I mean."

No sooner had Shrike left to show Nell and the ambassador out than Wren had set to work on the question of teaching literacy. His own education had begun at home with his mother reading to him from her copy of Audubon's *Ornithological Biography* whilst he stared at its accompanying engravings. The combination of his mother's scientific enthusiasm and the vivid watercolours had set fire to his youthful imagination, inspiring him to both art and literature. His father sold off book and prints alike within a fortnight of her death.

Aside from his mother, however, Wren had learnt from seeing the alphabet laid out before him, hearing what sounds corresponded to which letters, and copying it out again and again until he knew it all by rote—enough to sound out words which struck him unfamiliar and to seek them out in Johnson's *Dictionary*.

Wren had not yet seen anything like Johnson's *Dictionary* in the fae realms. An alphabet, however, he thought he could manage.

At present, Shrike fixed him with a puzzled look, his antlered head cocked to one side like his songbird namesake.

"About yea wide by yea high," Wren added, holding his palms roughly two feet apart in either direction.

Shrike nodded and went to his work-bench. From a cedar chest beside it—rather like a bride's trousseau, stocked with leather instead of linen—he retrieved a remarkable delicate sheet of pale ivory vellum.

"Not fit for your gyrdel-book," Shrike explained as he gestured to a thin dark blotch running across the page.

Wren thought it more than fine enough for what he intended and said so, which provoked a smile from Shrike.

Wren smoothed out the vellum over Shrike's work-bench, retrieved his pen and ink from his satchel, and, with Shrike peering over his shoulder in fascinated silence, began to draw. Small letter followed large letter, and beneath each a simple illustration of a single word, with the word itself written out below. Apple, bee, cat, duck... Wren hoped the ambassador wouldn't think it too childish, but each letter had to be something he might have already encountered in order to make a useful point of reference, and nature, from what Wren had seen, seemed the connective tissue between the fae and mortal realms. This left him struggling towards the end of the alphabet. Few enough words began with X or Z. Fewer still which one could illustrate in a simple drawing. He settled upon "axe," with two lines under the X, as he'd seen one in Shrike's own woodpile. And as for Z...

"Do the fae have astrology?" Wren asked.

"Aye," Shrike replied, though he looked no less puzzled by the question.

Wren supposed that would suffice and wrote out "zodiac," drawing the twelve signs beneath. If worse came to worse, the ambassador could interrogate him on the point when he returned for the second lesson.

"Would you teach me as well?"

The sudden speech after so many moments spent in reverent silence startled Wren almost as much as the question itself. He knew Shrike didn't have his letters, as he'd said, but had assumed he felt content with his considerable skill in myriad other pursuits. Had he realized Shrike desired to learn, he'd have offered to tutor him long before now.

Wren glanced up from the parchment page in time to catch a curious expression on Shrike's face—a hesitant uncertainty tinged with wistful longing. The sight of it tugged at Wren's heart-strings. He could do no less than reply, "If you'd like."

A shy and handsome smile graced Shrike's lips.

CHAPTER
THIRTY

"Hail and well met, my lords!"

Wren jerked his head up from the sketch-book page he'd scrawled on for the past hour or so. Sunday had dawned early over Blackthorn Briar with all the splendid refulgence of spring on the cusp of summer. Wren could have hardly resisted the temptation to spend the morning amidst the green. And so he followed Shrike out of doors, first to tend the hens and goats, and then to sit on the flat rock by the stream and draw whilst Shrike moved on to weeding the garden. Wren had intended to sketch Shrike, or the goats, or the surrounding forest, but he found his pencil drifting aimless across the page to form small and simple images from his own mind—swords and skeletons and moths like those which had filled the margins of his Latin grammar at Eton.

The cry which broke him from his inane stupor echoed across the garden from the far side of the cottage. Its bright and ebullient tone left little doubt as to who had spoken.

Still, Wren turned to Shrike and asked, "The ambassador?"

"Aye," said Shrike, rising and dusting the soil from his palms on his hose.

At the same moment, a spiderweb mask peeked out from around the corner of the cottage, the angle suggesting the ambassador had folded almost in half to achieve the view. Cat-slit eyes darted from Wren to Shrike and back again. A smile curled beneath the mask. The ambassador drew himself up as nimble as a bent green branch springing back into shape, and as the rest of him emerged into the back garden, Wren beheld a rapier cradled in the crook of his arm like a bouquet of roses.

"Hail," Shrike offered in reply to the ambassador's extravagant bow.

Wren took the opportunity to rise and set his sketch-book aside to approach the ambassador. As the ambassador held out the rapier to him, Wren held out a leather scroll-case to the ambassador in turn.

The rapier Wren received was no mere fencing foil. A delicate spiderweb of gossamer silver strands formed the guard of the hilt, complete with glistening beads of once-molten metal scattered across the threads like dew-drops. Wren glanced at the rapier hanging from the ambassador's belt, assuming they made a pair, but found the ambassador's of far plainer make. Despite its beauty, one could never mistake the spiderweb rapier for a purely decorative piece. Its slender blade's doubled edge came to a wicked point. And even a novice like Wren could feel its perfect balance in his palms.

The ambassador, meanwhile, received Wren's offering with evident interest. He uncapped the scroll-case and unfurled the alphabet. His cat-slit pupils changed from merest slivers to enormous round ink-blots as his eyes traced the letters and illustrations. As his gaze fell to the zodiac Wren had drawn for Z, he gave an approving nod. "The beasts that stand by the naked man in the book of moons, defend ye."

Wren, having no idea how to reply to this assertion, instead explained, "This chart is the key to letters—a map, if you will. Begin by studying it and copying out its symbols. When next you return, I'll have slate and chalk for you to practice on."

It felt odd to give instruction to one certainly far older and more powerful than himself. Yet the ambassador appeared in no way offended —on the contrary, his smile bespoke gratification. He rolled the alphabet up once more and tucked it back into the scroll-case with more reverence than most schoolboys regarded their textbooks.

Wren glanced around the garden and came to the belated realization that, between the abundant flora and fauna, it might prove too crowded to practise swordplay. He certainly wouldn't like to strike the bee baskets by accident. "Er..."

The ambassador likewise glanced 'round, though with a far more approving air. "Perchance, my lords, is there a staircase at all convenient to your holdings?"

Wren looked to the cottage—the single-storey cottage, which had remained so since the ambassador's arrival and could not have escaped his notice. He didn't dare look at the ambassador again, lest his expression reveal something that might give offence, and so instead he turned to Shrike.

Shrike didn't appear anywhere near so puzzled as Wren felt. He stepped forward. "Follow me."

Much astonished, Wren did so, and the ambassador likewise seemed to have no objection.

Shrike led the queer coterie past the hen-house and bee baskets, across the babbling brook and then, to Wren's surprise, into the briar, the thorns parting before him.

It had never occurred to Wren that the briars enclosed anything more than the cottage and its humble garden. Now, however, as Shrike forged their path through ever-unfurling thorns, he recalled how the entry to Blackthorn had always formed a tunnel of briars supported by pillars of living trees rather than a mere archway. And how the road to Blackthorn itself could prove miles and miles long to those who did not know it.

Then, just when his wonder had grown fit to burst from his throat in enquiry, the wall of thorns parted like a curtain to reveal a meadow of clover and heather limned in briars and verdant forest. In the midst of the meadow stood a squat tower of dark stone. Arrow-slits dotted its rounded walls in a pattern that spiralled all the way up to the crenelated parapet some three storeys above.

"The old warren watch-tower," Shrike explained in response to Wren's incredulous look.

The ambassador clapped his hands. "Splendid! And the staircases all intact?"

"You may see for yourself," Shrike said as he led the way to the open Gothic arch of the entrance.

The warm spring air in the meadow didn't quite penetrate the cool dark interior of the tower. As Shrike had promised, a stone staircase spiralled upward against its curved wall. Shafts of sunlight shone through the arrow-slits to cross the tower like luminescent strands of spider-silk. More extraordinary still, the staircase had a living banister. A lilac bush grew in the centre of the tower, sprouting from where the flagstone floor had sunken into dirt, and its branches curved upward alongside the stone steps, weaving themselves together into a braided rail at a height a little above Wren's waist. Heart-shaped leaves of vibrant green and fragrant blooms in royal purple appeared all the brighter against the cold dark stone of the tower interior. Whatever trellis had guised the branches had long since rotted away; or perhaps, Wren thought as he studied it, some arcane rite had coaxed them into proper shape.

"Perfection!" the ambassador declared. He skipped three steps up the stair before turning to face Wren again. "We shall begin by acquiring speed. The rapier is not required for this, strictly speaking, though you may wish to wear it to grow accustomed to its weight, however slender it may seem."

Wren, who'd wondered for some minutes now what staircases had to do with fencing, thought he'd found the solution. "You want me to run up the stairs?"

"Precisely. I cannot make you as quick as myself," the ambassador explained with what sounded like sincere regret. "But I can make you far quicker than most will expect of a mortal. Which will grant you the element of surprise. And within the span of surprise, one may often find room enough to slide a blade beneath the skin."

Wren didn't know what else to say to that but, "Indeed."

The ambassador's sharp teeth flashed in a swift smile. "You may wish to remove your wool."

Wren relinquished his frock coat to Shrike's proffered arm. It felt odd to bare his shirtsleeves out-of-doors; even moreso in front of a near-stranger. The ambassador, for his part, appeared in no way offended. From what Wren had seen of the fae realms, it didn't seem like they had overmuch regard for modesty.

Thus disrobed, Wren began to climb, with the ambassador darting up ahead of him and Shrike bringing up the rear.

Wren had never proved a particularly athletic youth. In his years with Mr Grigsby, living above the office, he rarely walked more than a few streets in a day. And while he'd spent the past few months in daily hikes from Staple Inn to Blackthorn Briar and back again, that would hardly erase almost a decade of sloth.

All of which meant that by the time he reached the top of the watch-tower—several minutes after the ambassador, who stood waiting for him with his head cocked to one side like a curious hound—Wren felt certain he would die.

His heart pounded in his ears. His legs and lungs alike burned. His throat and stomach conspired rebellion. He leant forward and braced his hands on his knees to keep from collapsing altogether as he drew great gulping breaths. His awareness of his surroundings on the watch-tower roof dwindled to the sheer relief of the breeze rusting the leaves of the canopy in the surrounding woods—and, more importantly, wicking the rivulets of sweat streaming down the nape of his neck.

When he could raise his head again—he knew not how long after—he beheld Shrike and the ambassador standing before him; Shrike gazing down at him with brows knit in concern, while the ambassador watched him with bemused intrigue. Neither seemed in any way affected by the strenuous climb.

The instant his eyes met Shrike's, Shrike wordlessly handed him his water-skin. Wren drained half of it in a single draw which left him gasping for breath anew when he finally let it fall from his lips.

"Shall we go down?" the ambassador enquired.

Wren had to admit the notion appealed to him. Yet it felt like a trap. "To go upstairs again?"

"Naturally," the ambassador chirped.

Every bone in Wren's body screamed for him to refuse.

Something of this must have shown in his face, for Shrike stepped forward. "Another day, perhaps."

As much as Wren wished to agree with him, he waved him off. "I'll do it thrice before the day is out."

He regretted saying so as soon as the words left his lips, but he didn't take them back—no matter how high Shrike's brows rose. Half-measures would not serve to ready him for the solstice. As the ambassador had said, he must acquire speed to attain surprise. After all, no one knew what to expect of Shrike before he became the Butcher of Blackthorn, and to hear Shrike himself tell it, the element of surprise had accounted for much of his success in that particular endeavour. Wren would grit his teeth and do what he must to equal him.

He did, however, dispense with his waistcoat before he began the descent.

The downstairs journey had two points in its favour. For one, it was all downhill. For another, it went at a far more sedate pace. Shrike had volunteered to lead the way; whether to enforce the slow and steady rate of descent or to catch Wren if he should collapse on the stair, Wren knew not. His gratitude knew no bounds in either case.

At the bottom of the tower they paused whilst Shrike let Wren have another draw off his water-skin and went to refill it from the brook that babbled throughout Blackthorn. Then the ambassador leapt up the steps with all the grace of a cat, leaving Wren to drag his burning legs after him.

The second climb went slower than the first, but Wren made it to the top again nonetheless. He took his welcome descent with one hand on the lilac railing and the other braced against the stone wall.

On the third climb, Wren turned his mind away from the pain dragging his body down and toward imagining a slavering wolf chasing after him. The thought of fangs sinking into his flesh and tearing him apart did wonders for motivating each successive footfall.

Until, mere steps away from the lilac ladder leading up the trap-door to the roof, the sole of his boot slid off the corner of the time-worn stone and left him plunging backward into the void.

For an instant the horrifying sensation of wind whirling in his ears and the stone slipping away beneath his boot-heels consumed his world as he fell.

Then strong hand seized him by the shoulders from behind.

Wren's heart fluttered for reasons beyond mere exertion as he let his eyes fall shut and leant into Shrike's embrace. Yet, having found his footing again, he allowed himself but a moment's respite before he resumed his climb. Only when he took another step did Shrike release him.

His momentum broken, Wren had to drag himself up the final few steps hand-over-hand on the lilac banister. Yet up he went, and soon enough stood with shaking legs against a parapet on the roof of the watch-tower.

The ambassador heaped praises upon him. Wren hardly heard a word. He locked eyes with Shrike, and the smile he saw there bespoke pride enough to make all the agonies worthwhile.

"Is Mr Knoll in?"

Wren blinked at the stranger with the red-and-yellow checked sack-coat and silver-tipped cane standing on the threshold of Mr Grigsby's office. It was the first of June, and the first Wren had heard of Felix since his departure in disgrace on the second of May. "I beg your pardon?"

"Mr Felix Knoll," the stranger continued. "I'm given to understand his guardian resides at this address."

"May I ask what business you have with Mr Knoll or his guardian?"

The stranger drew out his pocket-watch, huffed on its crystal face, and polished it with a silk handkerchief monogrammed in garish purple. Without looking up from his watch, he replied, "Mr Knoll has an account with my employer."

Wren knew full well where this conversation must lead—and indeed had expected to encounter its like for some time now—but waited in silence for the stranger to make his point more plain. After all, the attention to the watch suggested the stranger had other such appointments to attend today, whereas Wren need not move from where he stood until eight o' clock that night.

The stranger coughed into the monogrammed handkerchief before tucking it back into his waistcoat pocket, where at least half of it hung out in an audacious display. "I come today to remind Mr Knoll of the account."

"I regret to inform you Mr Knoll is not at this address." Wren felt safe enough admitting that much. "Perhaps you had better try his uncle—"

"Mr Tolhurst?" the stranger drawled. "Already been. Not there, so he says. And before you suggest, he's not up at Oxford, neither. Must be somewhere. My employer would very much like to know where. We fear Mr Knoll has forgotten us."

Wren put on his most placid face and said nothing.

The stranger tapped his cane against the threshold. "You tell him I've been by when you see him next, eh? Say Mr Woodbridge sends his regards."

"Happily," Wren replied.

The stranger gave him a grin as broad as it was insincere and turned to go out at last.

"Your pardon, sir!"

The stranger turned back with brows raised.

Wren withheld a sigh and stepped aside so Mr Grigsby need not shout over him again.

"You say, sir," Mr Grigsby went on now that he had the man's full attention, "that Mr Knoll is not in Oxford nor Rochester?"

"I do say so, sir," the stranger replied. "Leastwise I've not found him there."

"And you've spoken with his uncle?" Mr Grigsby pressed. "And his uncle has no notion where he may have gone?"

"No notion he's tellin' me," the stranger replied, evidently annoyed at having to repeat himself.

Mr Grigsby had not finished. "And your name, sir?"

The stranger balked. Wren suppressed a smirk. Names did not have power over fae alone, it seemed.

"Your name," Mr Grigsby insisted. "*Sir.*"

The stranger pursed his lips and chewed the inside of his cheek for a long moment before he spat out at last, "Smith."

"Then, Mr Smith," Mr Grigsby continued, nothing daunted, "when you do find Mr Knoll, tell him Mr Grigsby would very much like to speak with him."

Smith blinked. "I'll do that."

And with a touch of two fingers to the brim of his hat, he turned his back on the pair of them and descended the stair.

Wren shut the door.

"Well!" said Mr Grigsby.

Wren waited.

Mr Grigsby pressed his lips into a thin white line and gave a solemn shake of his head. His brows knit together in a mixture of worry and shame. He ran both hands over his face, then wrung them. At last, he turned to Wren.

"Lofthouse," Mr Grigsby began.

"Yes, sir," said Wren.

"It would seem Mr Knoll has vanished once again," said Mr Grigsby.

"Yes, sir," Wren repeated.

"I must say you proved quite instrumental to his return after Christmas."

"Thank you, sir."

"Would it perhaps be possible," Mr Grigsby asked, "for you to make similar enquiries today, so we might find him once more?"

Wren took his genuine relief at Mr Grigsby's finally arriving at his point and used it to put on a sincere smile. "Of course, sir."

A faint echo of that same smile flickered across Mr Grigsby's aged features. "Then I leave the matter in your capable hands."

And so saying, he returned to his desk and his newspaper.

Wren retrieved his hat, coat, and satchel and set out from the office for Hyde Park.

Shrike, in the midst of tending the garden, appeared astonished but by no means displeased to see Wren come running up the path to Blackthorn.

"Felix is missing," Wren gasped, bracing one hand against the cottage wall as he caught his breath.

"Again?" said Shrike.

"Yes." Wren described his encounter with the money-lender's agent.

Still, he didn't think Felix had vanished through mortal means. "Have the huldra reclaimed him, d'you think?"

Shrike arose from where he knelt amidst the sprouting beetroot and brushed the soil off his palms. "They're not fool enough to touch him before Midsummer."

Wren didn't share his certainty, but supposed Shrike had more experience with the ways of the Court of Hidden Folk. "Then I confess I know not where he might have flown. Can you find him as you found me? An acorn, wasn't it? Or how you found the Restive Quills, with knuckle-bones?"

Ever-obliging, Shrike reached into the pouch at his belt and withdrew four stark white bones. He cast them onto the dirt, between the neat rows of carrots, then knelt to examine the pattern in which they fell. Something changed in his face; a slight knit across the brow, and a hardening of the eyes.

"Well?" Wren asked after Shrike had remained silent for a very long moment. "Where is he?"

Shrike looked up and replied in a voice as flat as his expression. "He's dead."

CHAPTER
THIRTY-ONE

Wren stared at him. "What?"

"Felix Knoll is dead," Shrike reiterated.

"How do you know?"

Shrike indicated the knuckle-bones with a sweep of his hand.

Wren fought against the rising panic in his chest. It couldn't be so. The bones were wrong. Or Shrike had misinterpreted them. "Cast them again."

Shrike raised an eyebrow that suggested he could hear Wren's doubts as clear as if he'd spoken them aloud—but he took up the bones and threw them down again regardless.

Wren blinked. If he didn't know better, he'd say they had fallen not only on the exact same sides as before, but in the exact same pattern and position as well. No doubt a combination of coincidence and Wren's imprecise memory. "Again."

To his credit, Shrike gave no hint of exasperation as he cast the bones a third time.

Now there was no mistaking the exact repetition of their fall. Their magic had never before seemed so unnatural to Wren.

"And this means he's dead?" Wren forced himself to ask.

"Yes," said Shrike. Not a trace of impatience entered his tone, though Wren thought he well deserved it.

Wren, meanwhile, tried to contend with the mortality of Felix Knoll. "How did he die?"

Shrike shrugged.

Wren withheld a sigh. "Where is his body?"

Another toss of the bones—falling this time in an entirely different configuration, much to Wren's relief.

Less soothing was Shrike's interpretation of their pattern. "It no longer exists."

"What the Devil does that—?"

"It has returned to nature," Shrike explained as Wren bit off his frustrated exclamation. "It has been devoured by wolves, or picked apart by ravens, or decayed into soil beneath tree-roots, or in some other way transformed from death to life."

Wren didn't think wolves particularly likely in England. Ravens, perhaps. But that would require a body lay undiscovered for some time. And Wren, who'd seen Felix depart Mr Grigsby's office not quite a month past, didn't think that sufficient time for Felix's corpse to disintegrate naturally. Not even if Felix had dropped dead the moment he stepped out the door into Staple Inn.

Shrike scooped up the bones and dropped them back into their pouch. "Shall we tell your master?"

"Is there no way to know what killed him?" Wren asked, parrying Shrike's question with his own. "Or where? Or when?"

Shrike pulled an uncertain face.

Wren began to pace as he wracked his brain for a solution. "A natural death, considering his age and means and general good health, is not, I think, particularly likely in his case. Even if he'd fallen ill, someone at the university would have contacted either his uncle or his guardian. No one has contacted either, so he must have left university before he perished. Likely withdrew on Mr Grigsby's advice—which would be the first sensible thing he'd done in all his days—and so no one thought anything of his absence. Perhaps he encountered some accident whilst traveling. An over-turned carriage or drowning at a water crossing. But I don't think his body would vanish before it could be discovered, and once discovered, enquiries would be made which ought to have led, again, either to Tolhurst or Mr Grigsby."

Shrike nodded.

Wren continued. "If his cause of death is unnatural, then it must be super-natural—or criminal, I suppose. As he dresses better than he could ever afford, an enterprising mugger might take it upon himself to relieve him of his supposed fortune. Though I daresay Felix was prime enough to fend off an attack, and a mugger would give up when he realized his prey would not prove easy. I can't imagine who would want Felix dead. Enough to act upon it, I mean," Wren added, knowing all too well how such a motive applied to himself. "His creditors wouldn't murder him—he can't very well pay them back if he's dead. A suicide?"

Shrike looked no more comfortable with the idea than Wren felt. "You knew him better than I did."

The notion incensed Wren more than he'd expected. For Felix, with all his privileges and promise, to take the coward's way out of a perfectly surmountable difficulty, when Wren had not yet conceived of a plan that would allow both himself and his lover to survive past the Summer Solstice—but no. "Felix loved himself too well for that."

"Not suicide, then," Shrike concluded.

"I think not. Perhaps the super-natural. Are you absolutely certain the huldra wouldn't seek him out?"

"They are not foolish enough to break their vow before Midsummer," Shrike repeated.

"Then if Felix's death be not natural, super-natural, or criminal, I know not where to turn except to those who knew him best."

Shrike raised an eyebrow. "Mr Grigsby?"

Wren shook his head. "Knows nothing of Felix's disappearance, much less his death. Tolhurst and Miss Flora, however, might yet tell some hint of what became of him, if given an appropriate prompt. Smith no doubt asked the very same questions of the very same people, but they likely lied to protect Felix. As Mr Grigsby has Felix's best interests at heart, and as I am Mr Grigsby's creature, they need not tell such lies to me."

"And what shall you tell Mr Grigsby?"

"I cannot tell him the truth without revealing how I learnt it. And so I must find some proof of it beyond the bones. All the more reason for me to go to Tolhurst and Miss Flora and demand answers."

"Then," said Shrike, "we are off to Rochester."

The journey to Rochester through the stable-yard well proved far easier for Shrike than the first. He took on his bird form before they left the fae realms. Wren glimpsed him flitting about ahead and behind and alongside him as he strode down the quiet streets to Mrs Bailiwick's Academy.

The girl-of-all-work appeared slightly less surprised to see Wren a second time.

"Mr Lofthouse to see Miss Fairfield," Wren recited. "On behalf of Mr Grigsby."

Rather than let him into the parlour, she bid him wait on the doorstep while she ducked inside. Some minutes later, the door opened again to reveal Mrs Bailiwick herself, but no sign of Miss Flora.

"A thousand apologies, Mr Lofthouse," Mrs Bailiwick trilled before Wren could state his purpose. "I'm afraid you've come a very long way all for naught. Miss Fairfield is not at-home to visitors today."

Wren, caught off-guard, recovered himself just enough to reply, "Not ill, I hope?"

Mrs Bailiwick assured him Miss Flora was not in the least bit ill—but nevertheless, not at liberty to entertain her guardian's clerk.

This did nothing to allay the suspicions teeming in Wren's mind. Quite the reverse. If Miss Flora were somehow involved in Felix's disappearance, then it proved very convenient for her not to be available to speak with Wren or with anyone else involved in Felix's fortunes.

However, as Wren could hardly explain any of this to Mrs Bailiwick, he instead forced a stiff smile, bowed, and departed.

Once the front door had closed upon his back, he continued on down the garden path to rejoin the thoroughfare, strolling purposefully on down the street with his shoulders straight and head erect. He walked until he reached a crossroads, turned left, went on until he encountered another cross-street, turned left again, and repeated the exercise a third time to bring himself around to the academy again.

Approaching the edifice from the rear brought him to the high hedges bordering its back garden. An iron gate barred the gap in the hedge along the path leading from the street to the kitchen door. While the mistress of the establishment had rebuffed Wren's attempt, he thought perhaps the staff might prove more accommodating. One maid in particular he knew for Miss Flora's favourite. If only he could remember the girl's name…

But as Wren laid his hand on the gate to open it, a curious murmur reached his ear. Not from the street behind him. From the garden ahead.

A garden which proved far less empty than he'd anticipated.

The gate was unlocked. No reason to lock it, Wren supposed, during daylight hours in a town as quiet as Rochester. Still, given its weather-beaten state, he took especial care to ease its latch open, muffling the clinks and squeaks with his fingertips. He lifted it as he pushed it inward, lest the weight dragging against its hinges made them screech. No sound arose save chirping finches in the hedge and human murmurs beyond.

Wren stepped through the gate, though he hung back short of passing the hedge. Peering around its leafy corner, he espied two figures in the garden beside a purely ornamental sundial.

Miss Flora in conversation with Tolhurst.

Or rather, Wren realized as he stared in stunned silence, Miss Flora with her hands folded in front of her in a demure posture, whilst Tolhurst loomed over her, hat in hand. Hardly a hair's breadth stood between them. From this angle Wren could just make out Tolhurst's profile as he leaned so near to her that his murmuring lips almost touched her ear. The back of his head obscured Wren's view of her face.

It was not so unusual for a young lady to stand in an academy garden in the company of her music master. It was unusual, however, for Tolhurst to bend his head so low towards Miss Flora's. Rather nearer than a sensible *chaperon* would permit, Wren thought. But of course there was no *chaperon* in sight. Why should there be, when Tolhurst was Miss Flora's tutor and a perfect gentleman besides.

Still, something twisted in Wren's stomach to see how near Tolhurst stood to her.

This feeling did not improve when Tolhurst reached out to grasp Miss Flora's ungloved hand in his own naked palm. Nor when he took the further liberty of raising her hand to his mouth so he might press his lips to her bare knuckles.

As Tolhurst bent to kiss her hand, his head no longer blocked her from Wren's sight. Not a single feature so much as trembled in her face, as cold and still as carved marble. Her eyes, however, burned with a hatred the likes of which Wren had never beheld before.

Then her gaze met his.

Wren had no chance to hide. And, as she had already espied him, he knew it would do him no good to duck behind the hedge now.

So instead he rolled his shoulders back and strode into the garden, calling out as he approached the pair, "Good morning, Miss Fairfield. Mr Tolhurst."

Tolhurst bolted upright and whirled toward him at the first syllable. For an instant, Wren saw his brow knotted, his jaw clenched, and his mouth twisted in an impatient scowl. Then, in the space of the blink, it melted away so completely that Wren almost doubted it had ever existed, replaced by a look as blank as it was benign. "Ah, Mr Lofthouse. A pleasant surprise. What brings you to Rochester this day? Glad tidings, I hope?"

Nothing in his casual and even-toned speech could possibly raise the hackles of even the most discerning society matron. Yet Wren felt as if he'd interrupted a wolf feasting on a lamb and found its ravenous stare fixed on him.

Miss Flora, meanwhile, said nothing. Nor could Wren read her expression with any confidence. Though as her attention shifted from Tolhurst to Wren, it seemed the hatred in her eyes had faded to mere indifference.

"Tedious tidings, I'm afraid," Wren said, forcing the words to assume a disinterested shape. "And such as must be imparted to Miss Fairfield in confidence. On her guardian's behalf, you understand."

"As her guardian is likewise the guardian of my nephew," Tolhurst replied in affable tones, "one might consider myself an uncle to her, as well. Surely you may speak to her and feel assured of my silence on whatever matters you bring to her attention."

Wren didn't think what he'd witnessed of their meeting had in any way resembled the behaviour of an uncle, much less a trustworthy one. Aloud, he kept his voice flat as he reiterated, "My master will not permit me to speak my charge to any ears save Miss Fairfield's. I beg your pardon for the inconvenience, sir."

No hint of irritation showed in Tolhurst's face. Yet Wren noted how his fingers twitched at his side.

"No inconvenience whatsoever," said Tolhurst. "Good morning, Mr Lofthouse. And I shall rejoin you for your piano-forte lesson this afternoon, Miss Fairfield," he added, his smile returning as he bowed to the young lady.

Wren watched him march off, not toward the academy as Wren had expected, but out the garden gate into the street.

And a little grey bird with a queer black mask flitted after him.

Prior to Shrike's transformation, he and Wren had agreed to meet at Rochester Cathedral, on the assumption that Wren would enter the academy where no bird could follow. While things had not quite gone according to that plan, it would serve just as well to allow Shrike to follow Tolhurst whilst Wren investigated Miss Flora.

"What is it you have to tell me, Mr Lofthouse." Miss Flora's sharp words jerked Wren out of his avian musings. Her impatient tone did not allow for the slightest hint of a question.

Wren thought it prudent to come straight to his point. "It's not so much what I have to tell you as it is what I hope you will tell me. Do forgive my impertinence in asking, but when did you last hear from your fiancé?"

Miss Flora's glower suggested she had endured more than enough impertinence already that afternoon. Yet her voice remained cold and indifferent as she replied, "I had a letter from him in the first week of May."

Some weeks prior. "Again, I hesitate to enquire, but I assure you I must. What, pray tell, did this letter impart?"

Miss Flora raised her brows.

Wren supposed he must offer up information of his own if he expected to receive anything from her in return. While he couldn't tell her of Felix's death, he could give her something truthful for her trouble. "It is only, I fear Mr Knoll may have begun to reap what he has sown."

Comprehension dawned upon Miss Flora's face. Surprise did not arrive alongside it.

Wren continued. "A gentleman has visited Mr Grigsby to enquire after Mr Knoll's debts. It seems this gentleman has not succeeded in contacting Mr Knoll for some months now. Mr Grigsby himself has neither seen nor heard from Mr Knoll since the second of May."

Still, Miss Flora didn't appear in any way astonished.

"Did his letter mention any intention on his part to travel?" Wren asked. "Abroad, perhaps?"

"Nothing of the kind," Miss Flora replied. "He said only that unfortunate circumstances necessitated his withdrawal from university, and he did not anticipate our wedding could occur before he returned to take a degree."

"Any hint as to his intentions between withdrawing from university and returning to it?" Wren pressed.

"He claimed certain matters of business required his attention. I presume," she added dryly, "from your presence her, that he alluded to his debts."

"You presume correctly." Wren could admit that much, at least.

Miss Flora looked neither shocked nor satisfied to hear it. "Have you found the missing papers yet?"

"What?" blurted Wren, startled.

Miss Flora remained the very picture of perfect calm. "The certain papers which vanished from Mr Grigsby's office on the same day Felix came to Rochester to convalesce."

Ah. Those papers. Wren tried his best to appear indifferent to their fate. "No, I haven't."

"Has Mr Grigsby noted their absence?"

Wren had never expected her to remember his asking after them in the first place. He found himself ill-equipped to answer her with anything other than honesty. "No, he hasn't. They were not so important to him as they are to me."

"I see." She glanced away from him to consider the middle distance. "May I task you with something, Mr Lofthouse?"

Wren's surprise wasn't enough to overpower the instinctive reply of, "I am at your service, Miss Fairfield."

A pained and bitter smile twitched at the corner of her mouth. "Would you be so kind as to discourage Mr Grigsby from meeting with Mr Tolhurst?"

This did nothing to lessen Wren's astonishment.

"Ideally," she continued when it became apparent his bewilderment overcame his speech, "with subtlety and discretion. Only, I do not wish Mr Tolhurst to be alone with Mr Grigsby at present. I am concerned he may make certain enquiries or ask certain favours which would make matters awkward for... well, for everyone, really."

Wren could barely follow her reasoning. Still, it seemed easy enough. As a clerk he would as a matter of course remain in the background of Mr Grigsby's office and bear witness to all that occurred within it. If his mere presence would prove enough to prevent Tolhurst from saying whatever it was Miss Flora did not wish him to say, then Wren saw no reason not to do as she asked. "You have my word, Miss Fairfield. And my discretion."

Before he could question her further on the point, she had curtsied, turned on her heel, and vanished back into Mrs Bailiwick's Academy.

She had not seemed overly concerned with her betrothed's disappearance, Wren reflected as he wandered out of the garden. Then again, considering she was betrothed to Felix, he could hardly blame her for her disinterest. All the better for her if he should mysteriously perish. And while it certainly made matters convenient for her, convenience need not make her a murderer.

Wren reached the cathedral without drawing a definitive conclusion as to Miss Flora's involvement in Felix's death. He intended to say so to Shrike, but as he entered the vaulted sanctuary, he found Shrike already in conversation.

With Tolhurst.

Shocking enough to see Shrike in the form of a man when he'd left him in the form of a bird. More shocking, still, to see his broad ebony antlers reaching toward the vaulted ceiling. He wore the leather domino mask of oak leaves with its notches for his antlers and the antlers-bound-in-spiderwebs sigil that Wren had devised. Shrike had donned it before they left Blackthorn. Even then, Wren hadn't seen it make any difference in the appearance of Shrike's antlers. Yet Shrike had seemed pleased with it.

And now, while Wren found it difficult to tear his gaze away from those very antlers, Tolhurst seemed not to notice them at all.

Tolhurst and Shrike stood together by the ruin of Gundulf's tower and beneath the green man carving in the groined roof. Wren felt quite certain of that last point, as Shrike had his arm upraised to indicate said carving and his gaze fixed upon it, with Tolhurst following his direction. That is, until Wren dared to venture further into the sanctuary, at which point his boot-falls echoing from the floors to the rafters alerted all to his presence.

"Ah, Mr Lofthouse!" said Tolhurst in a tone which suggested all his geniality had returned since Wren had seen him last. "Your friend Mr Butcher was just telling me the legend of the Green Man. What a queer pagan fixture in this house of God."

"Very medieval," Wren agreed, forcing his words to remain conversational even as his pulse raced. "If I might have a moment of your time, sir, in private?"

Perhaps, Wren hoped, Tolhurst might speak more freely than Miss Flora had on the subject of his nephew. But he could hardly expect Tolhurst to speak candidly on the subject of Felix's fate if Shrike were looming over his shoulder.

Tolhurst glanced at Shrike with raised brows. Shrike's expression remained blank stone as he bowed and retreated to the cathedral entrance. He went beyond the range of human hearing—but not beyond that of fae. Wren gave silent thanks for Shrike's evident trust in him, while feeling relieved that Shrike hadn't wandered too far off to respond if Wren should require his intervention.

"Perhaps you've heard, sir," Wren ventured in a low tone, "that Mr Knoll has withdrawn from university?"

"I have heard so, yes," Tolhurst replied. "From his creditors."

Wren, surprised at Tolhurst's apparent ease, took a moment to respond. "You've not spoken with Mr Knoll yourself?"

"I haven't," Tolhurst said with a faint smile. "Nor have I seen him. As such, you see, it becomes much more difficult for me to reveal his present location to said creditors."

"Your loyalty to your kin is commendable," said Wren, his mind whirling all the while. "However, should you come to discover where Mr Knoll has hidden away, perhaps you would be so kind as to mention it to Mr Grigsby? He has his ward's best interests at heart, I can assure you of that. And he would by no means betray—"

Tolhurst waved off the remainder of Wren's speech. "Your employer's concerns are admirable, but unnecessary."

Wren bit his tongue and grit his teeth, yet could not quite prevent himself from replying, "If I may be so bold as to mention it, sir... you do not seem particularly worried regarding your nephew's welfare."

Tolhurst raised his brows, though his tone remained mild. "I beg your pardon, Mr Lofthouse. But as Felix has already vanished and returned within the last year, and as one might argue vanishing is the best thing he could now do to escape his present predicament, I see no cause for concern."

Wren had to concede that reasoning seemed sound. At least when one didn't have the benefit of fae sooth-saying to tell one otherwise.

Tolhurst's smile widened. "Particularly when he has such good friends as yourself looking after him."

Wren forced a smile to match it.

CHAPTER
THIRTY-TWO

Wren could not say in truth he mourned Felix's death.

However, whatever Wren's own thoughts on the matter, when he returned to Staple Inn and stepped over the office threshold, he couldn't fail to notice how Mr Grigsby bolted upright at his entrance, or the spark of hope that lit up Mr Grigsby's eye as he peered over Wren's shoulder, expecting Felix behind him.

Something in Wren's withered conscience likewise twisted as he informed Mr Grigsby of his failure to find his ward. The glint in Mr Grigsby's gaze guttered out like a spent candle stub drowning in its own wax as Wren described, in broad terms, his meetings with Miss Flora and Tolhurst alike. He made no mention of Shrike; it wouldn't have helped matters, and indeed might have confused them much. He took care to prevent his gaze from wandering toward the black-masked songbird perched outside on the windowsill just over Mr Grigsby's shoulder.

Yet, wan though it had grown over the course of Wren's recital, still Mr Grigsby's smile remained as he expressed his belief that, in time, Wren would discover his ward. Perhaps sooner rather than later, he added with a sage nod.

"I do hope," Mr Grigsby continued, "that we may find him before any danger befalls him."

Wren fixed an answering smile onto his own features. He needn't tell Mr Grigsby that Felix now lay beyond all hope and beyond all danger.

The sparrows nesting in the nooks and crannies of Staple Inn took more than a passing notice of Shrike as he perched in their territory. Their song turned from a warning chirrup to an angry trill. Shrike puffed up his own feathers and fixed his keen eye on the figures within the window-glass.

The death of Felix Knoll did not affect Shrike quite so much as it perhaps ought. Mortals died every day; most of them undeserving of their fate. Felix, from what little Shrike had known of him and what fragments he'd heard from Wren, might have deserved his fate more than most. It wasn't for Shrike to say. His own concerns lay entirely in how the death of Felix would affect his Wren.

The mystery, likewise, lay beyond Shrike's power to judge.

The happenstance of following Tolhurst to the temple hadn't given Shrike as much insight into the man as he thought Wren might have gleaned in his stead. Fortunately for Shrike, Tolhurst had seemed happy enough to carry both halves of a conversation. Shrike had only to point to the Green Man in the roof to explain his purpose in the temple to Tolhurst's satisfaction. And the leather oak-leaf mask, with Wren's ingenious sigil, glamoured away any hint of Shrike's antlers to Tolhurst's eyes.

But despite Tolhurst's friendly regard, Shrike remained wary. In the fae realms a smile all-too-oft served to bare fangs.

Shrike had merely the barest glimpse of Miss Flora. Which struck his curiosity all the more. If Wren needed to solve the mystery of Felix's death, then Shrike could do no less than seek her out and discover what role she had to play.

A shrill cry was all the warning Shrike received before a particularly bold sparrow swooped down. Shrike whirled to shriek his riposte. The sparrow veered off back up to the rafters to continue its angry chirrups.

Shrike paid it no heed. He posed no threat to sparrow fledglings. Nor did the sparrows themselves pose any real danger to him.

The remainder of the afternoon passed into evening without further incident. Mr Grigsby left the office without taking any notice of Shrike yet perched on the window-sill. Soon after, Wren emerged. From the moment his boot-heel touched the cobblestones, he turned his head in all directions in search of Shrike.

Shrike flitted down to land on his shoulder.

Wren jumped in astonishment, which threw Shrike from his perch, but he regained it soon enough.

"Forgive me," Wren murmured, and ventured to stroke Shrike's feathered head with gentle fingers.

Shrike didn't think Wren had done anything to forgive, and he hoped he knew it from how he chirruped and flew up to follow Wren down the lane to Hyde Park.

They passed through the toadstool ring to the Grove of Gates. No sooner had Shrike regained his true form than Wren cleaved to him, taking Shrine's arm in both his own and leaning his head against his shoulder. The tedium with an undercurrent of dread that prevailed in Staple Inn drained him. His only consolation throughout had been the thought of an evening in Blackthorn in Shrike's company.

Yet as they drew near to the wall of thorns, Wren halted at the sight of dark spots on the path ahead. He glanced up at Shrike to find his attention likewise fixed on the crimson drops crusting to black.

"Is someone hurt?" Wren asked.

Shrike said nothing, though as he continued, the length and speed of his stride increased, forcing Wren to trot to keep up.

Wren's worry came to a head when he turned a corner in the tunnel of briars to find a hulking figure looming before the cottage. As broad-shouldered as Shrike was tall, with a waist slender as a whip, and bones jutting out one side. He couldn't see a face or even a head—they had their back to the path.

Then the figure turned toward them. In the same instant, the sun sunk beneath the canopy. The figure was no longer silhouetted, and as Wren's eyes adjusted to the change of light, he recognized the face.

It was Nell.

With a dead stag larger than her own body slung across her shoulders.

"Oh good, you're home!" she said. "I've been knocking for an age. I didn't want to kick the door in because, well..." She levied a knowing look at Wren.

Wren cleared his throat. "Your discretion is appreciated."

Nell laughed. "Since your royal duties detain you from the hunt so often, I thought I'd bring the spoils to you."

Wren, who still felt rather stupid about mistaking Nell for a troll, couldn't keep from thinking of a cat. A cat who, seeing its human companions as very poor hunters indeed, might lay a fresh-slain dormouse on the threshold to sustain them. He had to admit venison made a more palatable offering.

Shrike accepted the stag from Nell, bending to allow her to shrug it from her shoulders to his. For a moment, Wren feared the stag's antlers would lock with Shrike's own, but Shrike righted himself without further trouble.

"I'd stay to butcher it," Nell continued. "But I've a friend expecting me in the Court of Hidden Folk."

Shrike, seemingly unbothered by the blood smeared across his shoulders from the hollowed cavity where the stag's entrails had once lain, wished her well.

But as she began to depart, sudden impulse seized Wren. "Wait!"

Nell paused mid-stride with her boot still upraised. She glanced between Shrike and Wren. "Aye?"

"Before you go," said Wren, ignoring Shrike's puzzled look. He didn't know much of women, but he knew better than to ask a lady her age. Instead, he enquired, "I'd wondered if you might tell us anything of past Oak and Holly Kings?"

This question did nothing to dispel Shrike's evident confusion.

Nell, however, looked more intrigued than otherwise. "Rather little, I'm afraid. I don't concern myself overmuch with the affairs of the Court of the Silver Wheel."

Wren supposed that'd been rather too much to hope for. The dearth of knowledge regarding the solstice duels had driven him to desperation.

"Go to Lady Aethelthryth." Shrike's voice, low and soft though it might be, still startled Wren with his sudden speech—though, as Wren jerked his head up to face him, he saw Shrike had fixed his dark gaze on Nell. "Tell her I would have my boon from her afore Midsummer. If there is anyone in her acquaintance who may answer the Holly King's questions, I bid her send them to Blackthorn."

Nell met his gaze with a grim nod.

Wren knew nothing of Lady Aethelthryth. Nor did he have much to offer any fae. Yet he felt Nell's quest could not go unrewarded. "Would you like the gift of letters, as well?"

Nell's dark brows rose. "I have my letters. Though I don't oft find use for them."

"Oh." Wren wondered what formed the difference between her and Shrike, or her and the ambassador, which might account for how she attained literacy whilst they did not. He didn't think she'd take well to being asked. "Well, is there something else we might do for you in return?"

Her gaze drifted toward Shrike even as she answered Wren. "You've done enough."

"I've done nothing," Wren couldn't keep from saying.

Nell's dark eyes darted back to meet his. "Butcher has done enough."

It wasn't that Wren didn't believe Shrike capable of doing something magnificent and marvellous enough to earn Nell's loyalty in addition to her interest. Rather, he had an insatiable curiosity to know the details of his beloved's heroic exploits.

And though he didn't voice this enquiry aloud, he supposed something of it must have shown in his face, because Nell took it upon herself to respond to the unspoken question.

"He rendered aid," she explained, with another glance at Shrike, "when our acquaintance was yet too fresh for one to expect anything of the kind from him."

"It was nothing," Shrike said almost before she'd finished speaking.

Nell raised an indignant eyebrow. "If you consider my brother's life and liberty 'nothing,' then our friendship is sorely tried indeed."

Shrike's lips parted, but no sound emerged. Evidently he couldn't think of a way to demur her praise of his actions without disparaging her brother.

Yet even as he failed, he succeeded, because judging by her smirk, the sight of Shrike flustered by her words proved ample balm for her wrath. In an instant her ill-temper had vanished. With a wink and a bow, she took her leave. The briars of Blackthorn grew together behind her as she wandered off into the wood.

"I suppose," Wren said, eyeing the stag slung across Shrike's shoulders, "tonight is the night I learn how to butcher a fresh-slain hart."

Shrike smiled, and together they went to begin their work.

Wren returned to Staple Inn the next morning.

Shrike would have liked to go with him. However, Wren had before insisted he would be safe without Shrike's protection in Mr Grigsby's office—and, given the iron-choked air of London, Shrike had to admit it unlikely any fae threat could find him there.

Still, Shrike felt determined to do something toward defending Wren against the slings and arrows that seemed ever to beset him in the mortal realm.

And so, after Wren had gone, and after Shrike had tended his fields and flocks, he left Blackthorn behind and journeyed on through the Grove of Gates to the stable-yard well in Rochester.

He emerged from the well in his feathered form. Neither steed nor stable-boy took note as he flitted past them and on down the quiet cobblestone lanes of Rochester. None of the travellers he passed on foot glanced up to see him swoop under the arch of Cemetery Gate and wheel up around to peer in its second-storey windows. He didn't see

Tolhurst in his bed nor at his desk. Nor did he find any sign of Wren's manuscripts from without. Or any trace of Felix Knoll.

Mrs Bailiwick's Academy, however, lay not far distant from Cemetery Gate. And Tolhurst, as its music master, might well be observed there.

Shrike arrived at the academy to find its garden occupied. A flock of some dozen-odd mortal youths in gowns fluttered about within the enclosure of hedges and gates. They bore no weapons, unless one counted the pencils and sketch-books clutched in their hands. Shrike, curious, settled onto a particular twig atop the hedge.

He'd barely glimpsed Miss Flora when last he visited Rochester. Yet this glimpse, combined with his study of the portrait he'd found in Tolhurst's rooms, might allow him to recognize her again. Most of the young mortals he could disregard at once, their hair not holding a sunshine hue. One had strawberry-blonde tresses framing her heart-shaped face, but straight rather than curled, and eyes of warm tawny brown instead of blue.

Then, just when Shrike supposed Miss Flora hadn't joined the garden flock after all, he espied slender fingers tucking a lock of kingcup-gold back beneath the brim of a bonnet trimmed in blue ribbon. When the face turned toward him, the blue eyes widened. Whilst the colours proved true, the portrait in Tolhurst's rooms was not an otherwise faithful representation—the artist's skill had not lived up to the true face, which looked far more handsome than otherwise.

And yet.

The figure Wren called Miss Flora didn't carry themselves quite like the other young ladies. In some aspects they reminded him of Nell—or so he thought at first glance, though the longer he watched them the more he realized his error. While they had the same keen gaze and held their chin just as high, the figure some called Miss Flora lacked Nell's slinking swagger. Their expression, too, had none of Nell's impish delight. The flat severity of their mouth and the furrow of their brow seemed greatly at odds with the fanciful giggling of their companions; nothing like the smirk perpetually playing about Nell's lips when she found herself surrounded by nymphs and huldra. And the figure's alert posture, as Shrike observed them, appeared less like Nell's huntress stance and more like the wary anxiety of the hunted—a cornered beast whose fear had reached the brink of wrath.

In other aspects the figure who wore Miss Flora's face reminded him of something hiding in another shape. A bell-wether amidst a flock of ewes. Or a gelding in a herd of mares.

Or, perhaps, a murderer amongst innocents.

The pupils had scattered across the lawn and put their sketch-books and pencils to work, each choosing a subject to draw from their surroundings. Most picked flowers. One took great interest in the ivy creeping up the corner of the academy itself. Another set her sights on the ruin of Rochester Castle rising on the hill above the town to the south-west.

The figure who wore Miss Flora's face, however, turned and fixed their keen blue eyes on Shrike.

Shrike remained perched on his twig, still and silent.

The figure who wore Miss Flora's face continued staring as they raised their sketch-book and hunched their shoulders over their drawing. Their gaze flicked furtively between Shrike and the page as they dashed rapid pencil-strokes across it in hasty, jagged lines which dug deep into the paper.

As if, Shrike realized, they expected him to fly off at any moment, and wished to capture his image before he vanished. Most birds would.

Shrike, however, would not.

Shrike assumed the same stillness he took on whenever Wren drew him in his other form. For, as long as the figure who wore Miss Flora's face watched him, he might watch them, in turn.

Gradually, as moments passed into minutes and Shrike remained still and silent, the figure who wore Miss Flora's face relaxed their hunched posture and their grip on pencil and sketch-book alike. At length they dared—ever so slowly—to turn the page and begin their drawing anew. The second sketch began with lighter strokes, drawing forth delicate shapes which gradually resolved into a form Shrike recognized as his own, as if he had emerged from the thick fog hanging over London to appear in the garden of Rochester. The drawing did not look quite so well as Wren's handiwork, to Shrike's eye at least, though he supposed he had a certain partiality in that regard. It looked better by far than the portrait of Miss Flora in Tolhurst's rooms.

Then the figure who wore Miss Flora's face turned the page again. But before they brought pencil-point to paper, they walked with slow measured steps—rather like how Nell stalked her prey in the hunt—toward a bench nestled in the hedge. They sat upon it and withdrew from a pocket in their skirts a folded handkerchief. This they laid out on the bench beside them. Unfolded, the handkerchief held the crumbled remains of some sort of tea-cake, its pinkish hue suggestive of rose-water or strawberry.

Or, perhaps, blood.

Having done with the handkerchief, the figure who wore Miss Flora's face returned their attention to their sketch-book. But though they held their pencil poised over the page, it did not move. Nor did their eye fix on anything to draw. Though Shrike did catch their deep blue gaze flicking towards him once or twice.

Shrike cocked his head to examine the trap laid out before him. From what he'd observed, he didn't think the figure who wore Miss Flora's face could snatch him out of the air bare-handed. Still, he remained wary as he hopped down from the twig in the hedge and settled on the handkerchief.

The blue eyes flew wide. As if their bearer couldn't quite believe the trap had worked.

Shrike waited for the figure who wore Miss Flora's face to strike.

No blow fell. Instead the blue eyes flicked from Shrike to the page and back again as the pencil began its delicate work anew, sketching yet another portrait of a black-masked bird.

Many minutes passed. Shrike pecked at the crumbs more out of curiosity than interest. They tasted of strawberry. More cloyingly sweet than Shrike would've preferred. He gave up crumb-pecking in favour of preening, then settled into a pose he could comfortably hold whilst the figure who wore Miss Flora's face practiced their art.

"Ladies!"

The shrill cry startled Shrike into flight. Abandoning the bench, he took to the hedge again. From a hidden perch within its tangled branches he peered out to see what beast had raised such a tumult.

The figure who wore Miss Flora's face remained seated on the bench, though they looked no less annoyed than Shrike felt at the interruption. Their gaze and that of all the other pupils besides had snapped toward the woman in the centre of the garden who yet clapped and called for their attention.

"Come along, ladies!" she trilled like an angry sparrow. "Inside for your dancing lesson! Your music master awaits!"

At this, the figure who wore Miss Flora's face glanced up. Shrike followed their gaze to a third-storey window of the academy. Through clouded glass he could just make out the looming form of Tolhurst.

Shrike wondered how long Tolhurst had watched over the garden. He felt he ought to have noticed him earlier. Still, with the figure who wore Miss Flora's face before him, it had never occurred to him to look skyward.

The young pupils gathered their drawing tools and trickled toward the academy door. The figure who wore Miss Flora's face trailed behind despite the woman's continued trilling. They glanced all around before shoving their handkerchief back into their pocket. Shrike realized, belatedly, they might well be looking for him.

Shrike kept hidden until all the pupils, including the figure who wore Miss Flora's face, had vanished within the academy. Only then did he fly up to that third-storey window where he'd glimpsed Tolhurst.

But he arrived in time to see the tail of Tolhurst's coat vanish through a doorway within the house. The door close after him, leaving the room he'd occupied empty. Indeed, it looked quite empty even of purpose. Lumps covered in dusty sheets seemed the only furniture within it. The room offered no advantage save that of gazing down upon the garden and those who wandered within it.

Shrike waited some minutes for Tolhurst to reappear. Yet he did not do so. And so Shrike went 'round the whole academy to peer in every window in turn. Musical notes resounded loudest at one particular window, but its lace curtains lay closed, obscuring any view Shrike might have of the occupants at their dancing lesson.

By then the afternoon had passed toward evening. Soon Wren would leave Staple Inn. If Shrike intended to meet him in Hyde Park, he would have to begin his flight there now. His efforts had gathered few hints towards solving the mystery of Wren's missing papers.

And if the figure who wore Miss Flora's face had indeed murdered Felix Knoll, Shrike knew it not.

CHAPTER
THIRTY-THREE

"Any news of our Mr Knoll?" asked Mr Grigsby.

Wren's head shot up from the penny post he'd been in the midst of sorting. In truth, he'd hardly thought of Felix since Shrike had informed him of Felix's death, and he and Shrike had gone all the way to Rochester to learn nothing. "Not yet, sir."

"Oh." Mr Grigsby didn't give voice to his disappointment, but Wren could read it on his weathered features as plain as he could read the letters piled on his desk. "Is there nowhere we might search for any hint of him?"

Felix being dead, and his body being returned to nature, and no one who knew him willing to give any information on what might have become of him, Wren had rather put the matter of Felix out of his head altogether in favour of obsessing about the Summer Solstice. He certainly hadn't bothered with the trouble of searching for a corpse he'd never find. Not that he could say so to Mr Grigsby. "I thought it vital to remain here to be of service to you during office hours, sir."

Mr Grigsby nodded in an amiable way which nevertheless told Wren he didn't agree in the slightest. "You are, of course, indispensable, Lofthouse. However," he added, tapping the open ledger before him without glancing at its columns, "I could survive without a clerk in office for an afternoon or two—or more—if it meant our Mr Knoll might be found sooner."

Wren hesitated. He knew full well searching for Felix would turn up nothing. However, the prospect of an excuse to leave the office sounded very tempting indeed. His time would certainly be better spent training his body for the Solstice than moving figures from one column to the next in Staple Inn. He swallowed his conscience and said, "If you'd prefer it, sir, I could go out to make enquiries regarding Mr Knoll."

Mr Grigsby's smile of unmistakable relief did nothing to assuage Wren's ever-increasing guilt.

The guilt continued gnawing at him as he donned his frock coat and hat to leave the office. It remained as he walked to Holywell Street. Not the worst idea for someone seeking Felix—if he were alive, the booksellers there would certainly cater to his vices—but as Wren knew Felix to be dead, he asked after second-hand dictionaries, slates, and chalk, rather than young blond gentlemen of means.

Nor did Wren ask any questions of anyone he passed on his way back through Hyde Park to the faerie ring within.

He did make some effort to justify his actions, if only to himself, as he journeyed from the Grove of Gates to Blackthorn Briar. By spending his present hours training for the solstice, he would stand a better chance of discovering what had become of Felix in the future. After all, Wren couldn't very well find Felix if he were also dead. At present, the best he could do for both Mr Grigsby's and his own sake was to commit himself to the ambassador's training and wait for word from the Court of Bells and Candles.

Thus far nothing had come of Shrike sending Nell to demand his boon of Lady Aethelthryth. Wren didn't expect to hear anything soon. He spent his days in Blackthorn racing up and down the warren watchtower and tutoring Shrike and the ambassador in literacy.

On a particular Friday afternoon, rain fell in the fae forest—a rarer phenomenon there than in London, but not unheard of. Wren weathered it on his way to and from the Grove of Gates to spend his morning in Staple Inn. It had not abated upon his return just after noon, which kept both him and Shrike indoors. Shrike studied the dictionary at his work-bench, murmuring words to himself as he worked them out and copied them down into the memorandum-book Wren had provided. Wren, meanwhile, sat himself on the nest-bed and studied Shrike through the medium of pencil lightly sketching on vellum. He didn't get far, however, for not an hour after he'd returned from his token duties in Staple Inn, a knock fell upon the cottage door.

Wren raised his head, puzzled. The knock had sounded nothing like Nell's battering-ram demand. "Bit damp for the ambassador, isn't it?"

Shrike, likewise interrupted in the midst of his academic toil, looked as though he agreed. He shut the dictionary with more care than it warranted and arose from his work-bench to approach the door. Wren leapt up from their nest-bed and hastened to follow him. He did his able best to calm his frayed nerves with the recollection that no one who wished Shrike harm could pass through the wall of thorns.

Still, he noted how Shrike held his arm behind him as if ready to shield Wren from whatever lay beyond their threshold.

The door swung open to reveal a figure smaller than Wren's own stature—smaller than the ambassador, even—standing in the steady rainfall with as much disinterested dignity as if they stood in sunshine. A fae figure garbed in a mottled grey woollen cloak, one side dark as storm-clouds and the other a silvery shade of moonlight, topped by a thick grey fur ruff that swallowed up everything between chin and breastbone—the same fae that had wielded the crystal dagger in the Wild Hunt before Samhain. They appeared no less bizarre by the full light of day. Long grey tresses belied their smooth and youthful face, every feature small and sharp save for the enormous eyes. Wren could discern neither whites nor irises in their gaze, only glittering darkness of pure pupil; the round black eyes of a goldfinch or harvest mouse. Their uncanny gaze was well matched by their brows, likewise long and grey, with a feathered texture that lifted them off of the face altogether to curl in the air as a gentleman might wax his moustache. Though, as Wren stared, he thought he saw the tip of one eyebrow furl and unfurl like the tail of a house-cat on the hunt.

"Well met," said Shrike, as if such visitors were matter-of-course in any given afternoon.

"Well met, my lords," the fae echoed in a voice like a whispering wind.

Shrike stepped back to allow the fae entrance into the cottage. Likewise he dropped his arm from its shielding posture, which Wren took as a good sign. As Shrike shut the door behind them, the visitor tilted and turned their head with slow and steady poise in all directions to take in the whole of the cottage from rafters to flag-stones. All the while Shrike said nothing, and Wren, in his eagerness to follow his lead, hardly dared to breathe.

"You may call me Tatterdemalion," they said. "My Lady Aethelthryth sends her regards and bids you grant me hospitality in your briar."

Shrike gave Tatterdemalion a nod which bordered on a bow. "Welcome."

Tatterdemalion served him a similar nod in turn. "My Lady Aethelthryth tells me you seek information regarding the ways of the Court of the Silver Wheel."

"We do," said Shrike.

"I've lived amongst the courts for many ages," said Tatterdemalion, "and am acquainted with those who have lived among them for many ages more. I will answer with truth any question you care to ask."

"And what would you ask in trade?"

Tatterdemalion levelled a considering look at Shrike. Then their beetle-black gaze slid over to Wren. He couldn't follow which exact points their eyes focused on, but as their infinite pools of pure ink glistened in their sockets, he gathered the impression that they looked him up and down and fixed him where he stood like an entomologist's pin fixed a butterfly.

"Perhaps," said Tatterdemalion, "your teeth."

"What?" Wren blurted.

Beside him, Shrike went absolutely still.

"I ask for your teeth," Tatterdemalion said in a very sensible tone. "Not so rare as hen's teeth, but precious nonetheless."

Wren quite agreed. Still, as the prospect sunk into his mind, the wheels in his head began to whirl, and he thought he knew a way to give

Tatterdemalion what they wanted without losing too much of himself in the bargain. His lips parted to make his counter-offer.

Shrike's hand fell upon Wren's shoulder in a bruising grip. Wren followed that hand up to meet his eye, but found Shrike's gaze fixed on Tatterdemalion.

"A moment, if you will," said Shrike in what Wren recognized as forced calm.

Tatterdemalion blinked up at him, then nodded.

To Wren's astonishment—as if the past few minutes hadn't already proved astonishing enough—Shrike used his vise-grip upon Wren's shoulder to steer him out the door into the rain. The door fell shut behind them as they left Tatterdemalion alone in the cottage. Shrike never looked back. Wren started to ask what the deuce had come over him, but Shrike silenced him with a look and strode on into the back garden. Only when they reached the point where the stream flowed in a waterfall through the brambles did Shrike halt and turn to Wren.

"May I speak now?" Wren asked with ill-concealed impatience.

"Aye," Shrike said warily.

"If all they want is my teeth," said Wren, "I may grant their wish."

Shrike stared at him. "No."

"You misunderstand me," Wren hastened to explain. "I don't mean the teeth I have in my jaw now. My milk-teeth fell out years ago. My mother kept them in her jewellery chest along with a lock of my hair. It's all still there, in my father's house, and between the two of us I think we can manage a little house-breaking—"

"No," Shrike said again with still more emphasis.

Wren choked on the remainder of his intended speech. He furred his brow as he studied Shrike's face in vain. "Is it the house-breaking that troubles you? You didn't object to it when we searched Tolhurst's rooms."

"Break any house you like," said Shrike after another moment of bewildered regard. His voice took on a low and urgent emphasis as he continued. "But do not give anyone your teeth. Particularly not those teeth."

Wren withheld an impatient sigh. "I appreciate your sensitivity for their sentimental value, but—"

"Sentiment," Shrike cut him off, "is the highest value any artifact may attain. It would grant powerful magic to its wielder. Your milk-teeth, imbued with a child's innocence and a mother's love, would prove potent indeed."

Comprehension dawned for Wren at last. "Oh."

"Aye." The ghost of a wistful smile flickered across Shrike's lips. "Though I admire your daring."

Wren thought that a charitable term for idiocy. "With what else do we have to bargain? In this particular contract negotiation we're at all disadvantage. Our survival may depend upon what knowledge Tatterdemalion chooses to give us—and as far as I can tell they only offer it for their own amusement."

"Then perhaps," Shrike replied, "we should find something more amusing than your teeth."

"Doesn't sound like a terribly tall hurdle to clear when you put it like that," Wren felt forced to admit. "Though I confess I've not the slightest notion how we might manage it. Unless," he added as an idea struck him.

They returned to the cottage to find Tatterdemalion perched on the rim of the hollowed stump with their head tilted back to examine the rafters. At Shrike and Wren's entrance, Tatterdemalion fluttered down to stand before them with one curious unfurling eyebrow raised.

Wren cleared his throat. "I have some talent which might please you."

Under Tatterdemalion's piercing gaze, Wren went to the nest-bed and retrieved his gyrdel-book from where he'd set it aside not a quarter-hour past—yet how long ago that already seemed. Against his better judgment he held it out to Tatterdemalion, who received it with indifferent curiosity. Wren watched and waited as Tatterdemalion turned the pages. Gently, though whether out of respect for the contents or the construction Wren couldn't say.

"It's both our handiwork," Wren explained. "His without, mine within."

Tatterdemalion appeared neither pleased nor displeased. The beetle-black eyes didn't seem to condemn the drawings of Shrike in various aspects. Wren supposed he ought to feel thankful for that at least. At length, they came to the vellum not yet scored by Wren' pen. Tatterdemalion flipped through a few more blank pages.

"Some talent, aye," Tatterdemalion declared. "It might blossom forth into something truly beautiful, given time enough." They glanced up from the gyrdel-book and caught Wren's eye. "More time than would pass between now and next Midwinter."

Wren held his breath.

Tatterdemalion cocked their head in consideration. "A century, perhaps. A century and a day."

Wren swallowed. "And then?"

The smile which stole over Tatterdemalion's face spread wider than their minuscule pout would have suggested possible. Indeed, it spread wider than any Wren had seen on a mortal face, a thin spiderweb crack of a line in their porcelain cheeks. All at once it vanished, and only the faintest flicker of amusement lingered in their delicate moue of a mouth. "Then, in a century and a day, I shall return to commission a masterwork."

"I look forward to the challenge," Wren uttered with more courage than he felt.

Tatterdemalion's soft laughter reminded Wren of nothing so much as the whistling wind over-turning leaves before a thunderstorm.

Wren held out his hand to seal their bargain. Tatterdemalion took it not with the strident clasp of a gentleman but by laying their fingers across Wren's palm with all the delicacy of a lady acquiescing to an invitation to dance.

In that same instant, Wren felt as if a draft gelding had kicked him in the gut. His veins seemed to twist 'round the pain in a gnarling knot. It held all the power of the Samhain rite with none of its pleasure.

As quick as it arrived, the sensation vanished. Wren felt harrowed in its wake. Only when he heard himself gasp did he realize how the bargain had driven the breath from him.

Tatterdemalion withdrew their hand with a smile.

Wren thought he ought to say something, but his weakened state precluded his recalling what polite reply the situation demanded. The cottage seemed to slide sideways. Strong hands gripped his shoulders and hauled him upright again.

"Steady," Shrike's voice echoed above him.

"I'm all right," Wren heard himself say half out of habit. But soon enough his vision cleared, and he stood strong upon his own two legs. Tatterdemalion held out the gyrdel-book. Wren took it warily.

Tatterdemalion's soft smile remained. "Ask your questions."

Wren had his enquiries well ready, for they'd filled his mind since before Samhain. "Who was Holly King in the summer of 1816?"

Tatterdemalion blinked.

Wren tried again. "The Year Without a Summer."

"Ah," said Tatterdemalion. "A knight-errant of no small renown. She came to the Court of the Silver Wheel in Imbolc. She lost her heart to the queen at first sight and slew many a rival suitor to win her place at her side. Her love spurred her to victory in winter and summer alike. And when she realized the queen did not love her in return, she strode out to the duelling field on the winter solstice, unsheathed her blade, and threw herself upon it."

So much for that. Wren tried another. "What of the duel itself? How did such a custom come to pass?"

"Your queen came to power through the rites of Beltane," said Tatterdemalion. "Wherein the fae host would crown the two most beautiful as lord and lady. Their ritual coupling invoked the verdant blooming of the land in spring, and they abdicated on the Summer Solstice. Except, of course," Tatterdemalion added, a wicked smile pinching the corners of their mouth, "your queen chose not to follow that particular tradition."

Neither Shrike nor Wren shared in their mirth.

"Instead," Tatterdemalion continued, "upon the Summer Solstice, she slit the throat of her lord. Broken hearted by her betrayal, he died where he fell. Holly bloomed from his spilled blood. She named another lover her king, crowned him with a wreath woven of that same holly, and coupled with him on that same scarlet ground to bring on autumn.

By Midwinter she tired of him. Another of her consorts leapt at the chance to become her new champion. She declared him her king of oak, in opposition to her king of holly. The Oak King slew the Holly King in her name and enjoyed many months of apparent bliss at her side until the queen found another Holly King to slay him and assume his position in her bower. Thus the bloody cycle began and continues to this very day. As the seasons ran on into centuries she withdrew from the spectacle, no longer coupling on the blood-stained duelling field itself but rather whisking her kings away to her bower to join with her in more secluded rites. Some say this enhances the mystery and makes others still more eager for the chance to take part—even when it means their certain death."

"Is death so certain?" asked Wren. "I've heard the fae can survive even the most grievous wounds."

"And yet death comes to all her kings," Tatterdemalion replied. "Some say she supplies her usurping favourites with iron weapons to strike wounds that can never heal. Others say she doses her reigning kings with a tincture of iron to ensure their wounds prove mortal. Still others claim she entices her kings whilst in the throes of passion, holding them upon the brink of exquisite release until they give up their true names, and then uses their names to command them to die at their opponent's hands upon the solstice. Or perhaps, like the knight-errant in the Year Without a Summer, those that truly love her lose the will to live when they understand their affections can never be returned."

"And her subjects approve of this?" Wren asked, unable to keep his incredulity out of his tone.

"Their approval concerns her not," said Tatterdemalion. "The gentry delight in the spectacle regardless. Do not underestimate the novelty of true death amongst the fae. The Queen of the Court of the Silver Wheel has turned this ultimate sacrifice into magnificent pageantry, buoyed by staggering romance—a queen so beautiful that hundreds of kings will die to spend but half a year at her side."

"I am not at her side," Shrike interjected.

"You are not," Tatterdemalion admitted with another small yet wicked smile. "Which makes this year's spectacle far more interesting.

Whatever will become of the kings who scorn their queen's bower? What marvellous punishment will she concoct for them?"

"Methinks being her king is punishment enough," said Shrike, his voice devoid of emotion. "But evidently she did not agree."

Tatterdemalion's smile remained unchanged. "Raising a mortal to the rank of Holly King is certainly unprecedented. Perhaps she thought your chosen companion, being worthy of a king, must be worthy of the title himself. Every court is tittering with theories. I daresay this coming Summer Solstice shall double, if not triple, the host of spectators."

"Is that what she intended when she chose me?" Shrike asked.

Tatterdemalion shot him a curious glance. "I doubt so. But she will turn it to her benefit all the same."

"Then why?" Shrike demanded. "Why choose me at all, if I do not act according to her design?"

Wren gazed upon Shrike's high cheekbones, strong jawline, noble profile, and the silver-shot ink-spill waterfall of his hair flowing down between his broad shoulders to halt just above his lithe waist, but kept his own suspicions to himself.

"The tide of her taste has ebbed and flowed throughout the centuries," Tatterdemalion continued undaunted. "For the season, at least, it would appear to have settled upon you. Perhaps she wearies of her courtiers' refinement and yearns to taste more feral fruits. Or perhaps it is due to your overwhelming victory in her mêlée. She does adore a violent spectacle above all else. That much has remained true throughout her reign."

"Or it could be because he's dashed handsome," Wren deadpanned, unable to stop himself.

Shrike shot him a startled glance. Wren offered up only a sheepish look in explanation. Colour came to Shrike's high cheekbones as he faced Tatterdemalion again.

"Aye," Tatterdemalion conceded. "Perhaps your lordship's countenance played its part."

The colour in Shrike's cheeks deepened.

Tatterdemalion turned to Wren. "Is this all your lordship wished to know?"

"For the moment," said Wren.

Tatterdemalion's beetle-black eyes sparkled. "Then you shall hear from me in a century and a day—unless you call for me before."

And with a bow, they took their leave.

Shrike continued staring at the closed cottage door after they'd gone. Then he turned a bewildered look upon Wren.

"You *are* handsome," Wren offered.

A huff of laughter escaped Shrike. He ran a hand over his face and smiled in its wake, as much as to say, *If you insist.*

"It would seem," Wren said, working the problem out as he went, "that we require a ritual that will rival the pageantry of the Eglington tournament."

Shrike raised an eyebrow at him.

"A recent mortal affair," Wren explained. "Very shiny. Very expensive."

Shrike twisted his mouth to one side, unconvinced. Wren had to admit the difficulty of imagining Shrike in pompous pageantry. Even his limited participation in the ceremonies at the Court of the Silver Wheel had cut through their finery and filigree to their sanguinary core.

"Or," Wren continued as he realized this, "perhaps we require something raw and primal. Something to strip away all the queen's artifice and drag the rite of Oak and Holly down to its bare and bloody roots."

"Aye," said Shrike, gazing down at him with a quiet mixture of surprise and admiration, the mischievous gleam Wren loved so well returning to his dark eyes. "That we might."

CHAPTER
THIRTY-FOUR

"What do you know," Wren asked the ambassador as they met in the dappled afternoon sunlight of Blackthorn's garden, "of fighting with a scythe?"

The ambassador hesitated. "It's more often a weapon of desperation than of design."

"I should hesitate to describe myself as anything short of desperate."

The ambassador appeared more intrigued than otherwise. "Very well. I shall endeavour to acquire a scythe before we meet on the morrow."

"No need."

Under the ambassador's curious and increasingly amazed eye, Wren went to the wall of thorns growing behind the chicken coop, just like Shrike had shown him the evening after they struck their bargain with Tatterdemalion. The briars withdrew from his hands as he outstretched them to reveal Larkin's scythe—centuries old and still as sharp as the eve it had cut down three fae knights. Its curving wooden handle, polished smooth with many years of use, weighed heavily in Wren's palms.

"Ah," said the ambassador. His cat-slit eyes ran up and down the length of the wicked instrument with undisguised interest. "If I may be so bold as to enquire—have you ever wielded a scythe before, m'lord?"

Wren admitted he had not.

The ambassador nodded in a way which said quite without words that one could tell as much from how Wren carried it. "It may then be prudent to first give you greater familiarity with its intended purpose."

Wren led the way through the ever-shifting wall of thorns toward the makeshift training grounds. As they arrived at the warren meadow and the briars grew together behind them, the ambassador turned and twirled his wrist in a beckoning motion towards the thorns. Wren watched and waited in silence to see what he meant by it. A moment passed. Nothing happened.

The ambassador gave a thoughtful hum. "Interesting."

"What is it?" Wren asked.

"I had thought, mayhaps, since the briars have been so kind as to withdraw at my approach, I might persuade them to advance as well." The ambassador turned to Wren and glanced down at the scythe he carried. "We'll need something for you to mow down, after all."

"Oh." Wren thought it a reasonable notion. A shame it hadn't worked in their favour. "Perhaps Butcher could do it?"

"Perhaps," the ambassador echoed, stretching out the word in an uncertain timbre. "Or, m'lord, if I may be so bold as to suggest, you might make the attempt yourself?"

Wren didn't think he'd ever grow used to that title. Nor did he think he, a mere mortal, could ever hope to exert his will over the magic of Blackthorn when a fae like the ambassador had failed.

Still, the ambassador watched him with such a hopeful air that it seemed only polite to make an attempt.

And so Wren handed the scythe off to the ambassador and approached the wall of thorns.

Like the ambassador had done, Wren held out his hand to the briars —palm upraised, fingers at rest, a gesture not unlike he might use to reach for Shrike. He felt more than a little ridiculous as he did so. He expected no result whatsoever.

And yet, to his astonishment, the briars which had heretofore retreated from his every approach now sent tentative tendrils of thorns spiralling up to meet his fingertips.

Wren jerked back. The briars ceased to grow towards him. He whirled to face the ambassador.

The ambassador appeared pleased but by no means surprised.

Wren remained unnerved. He supposed that this newfound power must be the result of his role as the Holly King. Though upon further consideration, as he returned to the briars and raised a tentative hand toward them again, he couldn't ever recall making an attempt to draw forth the briars before today. Perhaps if he had...

At present, under the ambassador's approving eye, Wren trailed his fingertips through the air and watched amazed as briars followed. Fresh green tendrils unfurled across the meadow and quickly matured into thick thorny black vines. Wren withdrew and beckoned the thorns to follow him. Soon they blanketed the meadow.

The ambassador, smiling, returned the scythe to Wren's charge. Wren wrapped his hands around its smooth-worn wooden handle. The ambassador gently adjusted his grip on the two knobs.

"These are the nibs," the ambassador explained as he went. "And the snath," he added, lightly touching the curved length. "The blade is called a blade—convenient, no?—and it attaches to the snath at the tang. The great advantage of a scythe, other than mowing, is in its reach. Pray forgive me for mentioning it, my lord, but the Oak King is rather longer in the arm than yourself."

Wren saw no reason to deny the truth of it.

"A scythe should do well to make up the difference," the ambassador continued. "But first, we must get you acquainted with its true purpose. Approach the thorns, if you will."

Wren did so.

"Excellent!" the ambassador trilled. "Now bend your knees until the back of the blade rests on the ground."

Against all logic, Wren followed the instruction.

"And now," the ambassador declared, "simply turn your waist from right to left and let your arms fly out as they will."

Feeling rather like a foolish windmill, Wren spun. Laying against the ground as it did, the scythe seemed to weigh almost nothing in his hands. He expected the blade would snag against the fresh-grown briars with a jagged thud. To his astonishment, however, it sliced a half-moon arc clean through the thorns with a faint whispering sound. The stems lingered for but a moment before withering and withdrawing into the ground.

The ambassador clapped his hands. "Splendid! Just so!"

Wren had, of course, seen cottagers wielding scythes in his father's fields, but had never before taken one up himself. If his father could see him now... The thought brought a smile to his lips, as he considered the apoplectic fit that would ensue.

Back and forth, back and forth, sliver by crescent-moon sliver, Wren carved through the thorns. By the halfway point his shoulders had begun to twinge; by the end of the work some hours later, a low burn had settled into his arms and back.

"We'll continue on the morrow," the ambassador decreed as Wren ceased scything.

Wren straightened up with a grimace. While the ambassador's regimen of running up the warren-tower stairs had done miracles for his stamina, it had not yet undone a decade of hunching over a desk.

He wondered, too, as the ambassador led the way back through the tunnel of briars to Blackthorn cottage, how a fae with so deadly a reputation had acquired the knowledge of practical scything. At length this wondering grew so great he found it impossible not to give it voice.

"Were you a farmer?" Wren enquired, wary of giving offence.

"Oh no, I haven't the talent," the ambassador demurred. "However, a dear friend of mine lives in a little village, which I've visited in harvest time oft enough. She taught me how to swing scythe and flail."

"And the rapier?" Wren couldn't keep from asking.

The ambassador laughed. "Learnt long before I met her."

The ornate rapier yet hung from Wren's hip—had done so throughout the scything lesson. He gestured to it now with his free hand. "If I'm to fight the solstice duel with a scythe, then..."

The ambassador gave a sympathetic nod. "I'm afraid we must wait until after the solstice to continue your lessons in swordplay. Still! Something to look forward to."

Wren, who'd intended to suggest returning the rapier to the ambassador, hesitated.

The ambassador smiled. "You've given me the gift of letters. It's the very least I may do to repay you."

A wiser man might have kept his own counsel. Wren, however, couldn't prevent himself from replying, "It costs me far less than you value it."

Still the ambassador smiled. "All the better for you, m'lord."

"If I may ask," Wren said, emboldened by the ambassador's ability to take every foolish thing that fell out of his mouth in stride, "why did you want the gift of letters? It aids me in my vocation, certainly," he added, "but you seem to get on very well without it.

The ambassador hesitated long enough for Wren to fear he'd given offence at last. Yet when the ambassador did reply, his words carried an apologetic tone. "It's not considered worthwhile to teach the skill to superfluous heirs."

Primogeniture, Wren supposed. It hadn't affected him personally, as the solitary offspring of a gentleman, but he'd heard tell of the misery it inflicted on the second sons he'd attended school with, and seen how it fell out in the estate affairs he and Mr Grigsby had untangled in their career in Staple Inn. Though it'd never yet prevented a mortal man from learning to read, so far as he knew. "You have many elder brothers?"

"Sisters," said the ambassador. "All of whom bring glory to our mother. Whereas I, as a son, am shaped only for shame."

Not primogeniture, then. Wren had much to learn yet regarding fae inheritance law. "I see."

"I never thought I'd find the opportunity to acquire my letters," the ambassador went on. "Until! A mortal clerk is crowned the Holly King, and better for me, an acquaintance informs me said Holly King wishes to learn the art of combat. Trading art for art seems fair enough, and so I offer my services. And here we are!"

For indeed, they'd just arrived at the humble cottage in the heart of Blackthorn.

"While not designed for combat," said the ambassador when next Wren met him in the training meadow, "there are certain benefits to the scythe. It has considerable reach. Its sweep will encourage your opponent to keep their distance. And the curvature of the blade does nicely for disarming."

Wren, with the scythe in his hands, saw no reason to disagree. Though he wondered how the slender silver rapier the ambassador held would stand up against the more substantial oak and iron.

"As it cuts down wheat, so may it cut down your opponent." The ambassador fell into a fencing stance with the ease of a clerk falling into an office chair. "Begin!"

A moment passed in bewildered silence.

Wren blinked. "What, just have at you?"

"Indeed!" the ambassador chirped.

The ambassador, while rather shorter than Wren, stood taller than briars or wheat. Given this, Wren raised the scythe to the height of his waist. He felt the difference in its weight at once. Still, he swung it.

The ambassador scampered backward out of reach. "Again!"

Stuck now with his waist twisted to one side, Wren saw nothing for it but to try and thump him with the flat of the blade on the back-swing.

The ambassador leapt nimbly away. "And again!"

Not fast enough. Never fast enough, despite all the hours he'd spent running up and down the warren watch-tower. He needed more strength behind the scythe, he thought, and this time put his shoulders as well as his waist into the swing as he advanced.

It flew high. It flew wide. It flew so far out of his expectations that he struggled to halt its spin before the blade drove into the ground.

The ambassador ducked beneath the swinging iron—but only just.

Wren stared at him, then at the traitor blade, then back to the ambassador.

"I could've killed you," Wren blurted.

"You could have," the ambassador conceded with a half-shrug. "But you didn't!"

Wren stared at him. The ambassador seemed not to notice.

"Boiled leather ought to withstand iron's first blow," the ambassador reasoned. He stroked his pointed chin as he considered the weapon in Wren's hands. "But I wouldn't depend upon it to withstand a second or third."

The ambassador didn't wear any armour that Wren could see. Certainly not boiled leather.

Shrike, on the other hand…

Wren swallowed hard. "So I shall have but one chance to err."

"If that," chirped the ambassador.

Wren could not dismiss the notion so lightly. Shrike stood taller than the ambassador. Far taller. Wren's wild swing might well have clipped him beneath his chin.

Or slit his throat.

Either ignorant of Wren's dawning horror, or indifferent to it, the ambassador continued. "There is a method to cure wounds of iron. One must carve out the wound itself with a silver knife and stitch the remaining flesh together with threads of silver—or spider-silk—and a silver needle. It is not a pleasant prospect, and must be performed with haste."

"How much haste?" Wren asked almost before the ambassador had finished the word.

"Within minutes."

Minutes Wren doubted he and Shrike would have in the wake of the solstice duel.

The ambassador fought with a different figure—a different stride—a different weapon. Wren might learn to strike with the scythe, true enough. But the ambassador couldn't teach him how to duel Shrike. Or how to keep from killing him.

Shrike alone could do that.

And as Wren lifted his gaze from his iron weapon to the ambassador's masked face, he saw those cat-slit eyes patiently waiting for him to draw that very conclusion.

They returned to the garden of Blackthorn cottage some hours before Shrike expected them, judging from his confused expression as their entrance drew him away from picking strawberries in the little thorn-fenced garden.

"Will you join us in the warren meadow?" Wren asked.

Shrike arched an eyebrow at the scythe but nonetheless replied, "Aye."

"And bring your sword and armour," Wren added.

Both Shrike's brows arose, and an unmistakable gleam of intrigue lit his dark eyes.

"I'm not going to fight you," Wren insisted. "But if we are to dance a deadly waltz to rival Ostara, it would do well for both of us to know the steps."

Shrike answered him with a smile.

Staple Inn, London
June 6, 1845

Wet ink glistened on the letter Wren had just penned. Four prior drafts lay scattered across his desk, crumpled and smeared. This final attempt, however, he thought might serve.

Though his heart still sank to read over his own words.

Before his courage could fail him, he forced himself to grasp a pinch of dust and sprinkle it over the letter to absorb what ink remained wet, then blew on it for good measure before he folded it up. He rose from his desk and took three strides across the office to stand by Mr Grigsby.

Mr Grigsby looked up from his newspaper with a quizzical expression.

Without a word, Wren handed over the letter.

"What's this?" asked Mr Grigsby, bemused.

Wren gazed down on his wrinkled features, their delight and curiosity in no way dulled by age, and forced himself to say the words that would banish joy. "My fortnight's notice."

If Wren slew Shrike, Wren would be compelled to remain in the Court of the Silver Wheel to reign as the Holly King and duel the new-crowned Oak King upon the Winter Solstice. If Shrike slew Wren—well,

Wren would be dead. And if all went according to plan, and both he and Shrike survived... Either way, he could not return to clerking in Staple Inn.

Mr Grigsby's smile withered. He unfolded the letter and read.

Wren clasped his hands behind his back and waited. Another minute passed in silence save for the ticking of the clock on the mantle.

"'Overseas'?" Mr Grigsby read aloud, glancing up at Wren. "You've not yet decided where to seek your fortune?"

"Not yet," Wren lied. "I'll go wherever the wind takes me."

Some of Mr Grigsby's good humour returned. "How whimsical! Dear me, what adventures you shall have. You'll be missed, of course, but far be it from me to stand in the way of destiny. Only, you will write, won't you? I should like to hear from you now and again and know how you get on."

"Of course, sir," Wren said, the well-practiced reply falling from his lips before he had time to think it through.

Mr Grigsby smile and refolded the letter to tuck it into his waistcoat pocket. Then he returned to his newspaper as if Wren had never interrupted him.

Wren envied his serenity. Though he maintained his impassive mask as he returned to his desk and resumed mechanically paging through his ledger, the wheels of his mind spun at a frantic pace. His off-handed promise to write to Mr Grigsby could not be kept. Not unless he survived the coming solstice and found a way to send penny post through the fae realms, besides.

In the midst of this bitter maelstrom, the office door burst open.

Wren leapt to his feet before he fully recognized who had entered. In his defence, the wild-eyed and hatless man with the morning's stubble still on his cheeks bore very little resemblance to Tolhurst's customary calm and collected demeanour. Indeed, Wren hadn't seen him so distressed since Felix failed to appear for Christmas.

"Mr Grigsby," Tolhurst gasped as the startled old gentleman spun in his chair to regard him. "I'm afraid I bring you most dreadful news."

Wren's heart sank. Only one thing could distress Tolhurst more than his nephew's initial disappearance. Somehow, Tolhurst had discovered that Felix had perished.

"What is it?" asked Mr Grigsby.

Tolhurst ran a distracted hand through hair which did not look as though it had touched a comb since last night. With a hollow voice and a haunted gaze, he replied, "Miss Fairfield has vanished from Mrs Bailiwick's Academy."

CHAPTER
THIRTY-FIVE

A queer mixture of disappointment and alarm overcame Wren. Alarm at Miss Flora's disappearance, naturally enough, but also disappointment that the knowledge of Felix's death remained his burden to bear alone.

"Vanished?" cried Mr Grigsby, oblivious to Wren's conflicted thoughts. "But how? And to where?"

"I'd hoped she might have only gone to London, perhaps to beg your assistance in whatever misadventure has befallen her—but you've not seen her?" Tolhurst concluded, his desperate gaze flicking between Wren and Mr Grigsby.

Mr Grigsby shook his head in mute horror and turned to Wren.

"We have not, sir," Wren replied.

"Have you any notion where she may have gone?" Mr Grigsby asked Tolhurst.

"Yes," Tolhurst said softly. "I'm very much afraid I have." In a stronger voice, he continued. "Neighbours of Mrs Bailiwick's Academy report seeing a young lady departing before dawn... in the company of a young gentleman."

Mr Grigsby bolted upright in his chair. "Mr Knoll! Can it be?"

Wren thought it particularly cruel of happenstance to taunt Mr Grigsby with this impossible hope. Yet, without any material proof of

Felix's demise, he could say nothing against the supposition Mr Grigsby had formed.

Tolhurst likewise seemed more defeated than roused by this prospect. "I dare not hope so, sir. If the young gentleman is indeed my nephew, he is making a grave mistake and dragging Miss Fairfield down with him."

"If it is Mr Knoll," Mr Grigsby continued regardless, "I cannot imagine how he might have procured a special licence without my knowledge or assistance, much less yours. We must therefore conclude —however dreadful it must be to suppose—that he has taken Miss Fairfield over the border, where there are no such obstacles to their marriage."

"Assuming it is my nephew," Tolhurst reminded him in a gentle yet firm tone.

"Miss Fairfield has said nothing of their engagement being broken," Mr Grigsby countered. "Nor is she the sort of young lady to entertain suitors when her heart is promised to another. You may know your nephew, sir, but I know my ward, and to run away with a stranger is quite unlike her."

Tolhurst regarded Mr Grigsby in stunned silence, then turned to Wren with an expression that implored him to reason with his master. Unfortunately for Tolhurst's sake, Mr Grigsby followed his gaze and alighted upon Wren as well.

"Lofthouse!" cried Mr Grigsby. "You found our dear Mr Knoll once before!"

Wren did not fail to notice how Mr Grigsby's tact prevented any mention of how Felix could not be found a second time.

"Pray," Mr Grigsby continued, "employ those same methods in searching for Miss Fairfield. I've every faith you shall find her!"

Tolhurst didn't look anywhere near so convinced of Wren's capabilities.

"Did the neighbours happen to mention," Wren asked him, "what gown the young lady wore? What colour or pattern?"

Tolhurst's gaze shifted away from Wren's face toward some mark in the middle distance over Wren's shoulder. "They claim to have seen her in a blue gown. I suspect it is Miss Fairfield's morning dress—a ribbon-trimmed poplin, no less handsome for its modesty, and of a cornflower-blue hue which brings out her eyes to great advantage."

Wren stared at him. Some might excuse the minute description by supposing that, as a music master for Mrs Bailiwick's Academy, one must expect Tolhurst to have some familiarity with the garb of the students he taught every day for years on end. However, Wren doubted Tolhurst could describe the dress of any student other than Miss Flora if Wren were to ask him here and now. But Wren refrained from performing the experiment at present and restrained himself to reply merely, "I shall keep a weather eye out for such a garment."

Tolhurst cleared his throat. "I regret I cannot stay further, gentlemen. If Miss Fairfield is not here, then I must find her elsewhere. I ask only that you keep your door open to her should she by chance return."

"But of course!" said Mr Grigsby, looking more shocked that Tolhurst could think he'd do anything less for his ward.

Tolhurst excused himself with a nod and fled the office.

Wren snatched up his hat and coat and hastened to follow his example.

By the time Wren had rambled down the stairs to the courtyard, Tolhurst had vanished from it. Which was just as well, as Wren didn't want Tolhurst to see him head not towards the train station or any other conveyance northward, but down Oxford Street to Cumberland Gate and into Hyde Park.

Few passers-by bothered casting a first glance, much less a second, at an unassuming clerk walking alone. Fewer still saw him wander into the woods. And none, he thought, saw him step through the toadstool ring and vanish out of London altogether.

"What's wrong?" Shrike asked the moment Wren came into view.

Wren supposed his distress showed in his face. Or perhaps Shrike simply remembered the last time Wren had arrived in Blackthorn without warning in the middle of his work day. Just now Wren had run into the back garden to find him cross-legged on the flat rock by the bend in the stream, plying his whetstone to the sword laid out across his knees, sunlight glinting off blade and water alike.

"Miss Flora is missing," Wren blurted.

Shrike set his sword aside and stood. The request had not yet left Wren's tongue before Shrike's hand dropped to the pouch hanging from his belt and withdrew the knuckle-bones to scatter across the flat stone.

Wren held his breath.

Shrike furrowed his brow at the knuckle-bones.

"What is it?" Wren demanded. "Has she been taken by the fae as well?"

Shrike shook his head. "Miss Flora does not exist."

Wren's heart plunged as cold panic flooded his veins. "She's dead?"

"No." Shrike raised his head, his expression of mild confusion turning to concern as he caught sight of the stricken look on Wren's face. "She's not dead. She doesn't exist."

"Well," said Wren. "I don't know how it works in the fae realms, but in England that means she's dead."

"If she were dead, the bones would say so," Shrike replied with more patience than Wren probably deserved. "They do not say Miss Flora is dead. They say there is no such creature as Miss Flora."

"Balderdash," said Wren.

Shrike raised an eyebrow.

"I've met her!" Wren insisted. "I've spent the last decade managing her fortune! You've seen her yourself—she's as real as you or I!"

"We met a mortal," Shrike explained. "A mortal whom you called Miss Flora. Whether that is said mortal's true identity... the bones don't seem to agree."

"Then the girl we know is an impostor?" Wren asked, unable to keep the sardonic tinge from his tone. "From her infancy?"

"Did the mortal you know as Miss Flora name themselves?"

Wren blinked. "Of course not. What infant names itself at birth?"

"Most of them," Shrike replied.

Wren stared at him. "Did you?"

"How else would I recognize the sound of my true name?"

Wren had no answer for that. Yet, "That may hold true for the fae, but for mortals, I assure you, it is another matter entirely."

Shrike did not look as though he believed him. "Be that as it may, the mortal you call Miss Flora does not call themselves Miss Flora. If you wish to find them, we must find a way to call them which their essence would recognize."

Wren didn't think they had time to go down a list of every name he could think of in the hopes that Miss Flora had given herself the same nickname. "If that's true, then how did we find Felix?"

"Evidently Felix Knoll had no quarrel with what society chose to call him."

Wren didn't doubt Felix lacked the imagination required to name himself something other than what name he'd been given. "And how did you find me before you knew my name was Wren?"

"I did not ask for you by name. I asked the fates to bring me to the one who would secure my victory."

"Oh," said Wren. He considered the matter a moment, then added, "Could we ask the bones where to find the young lady whom Felix Knoll would have married, had he lived?"

Shrike cast the bones again, examined them, then shook his head.

Wren supposed that the match may very well have dissolved even if Felix had survived. Another thought occurred to him. "The young lady formerly known as Miss Flora Fairfield, who has now taken her husband's name."

The bones continued to deny the existence of such a person.

Wren had thought that solution rather clever—but not clever enough, apparently. He turned his mind to simpler definitions. "The only child of the late Mr and Mrs Fairfield."

God willing, neither had sired nor borne a bastard prior to their premature demise.

Shrike cast the bones. Wren held his breath. He couldn't be certain, but it seemed to him the bones had fallen on different sides and in a different pattern than before.

"The only child of the late Mr and Mrs Fairfield," said Shrike, "is headed west of London."

Wren frowned. "Not north?"

"Further west than north."

"You're certain?"

Shrike cast an exasperated look up at him.

Wren supposed he deserved that. "How far west?"

"To the sea. And across it. They've not reached the sea yet," Shrike added as Wren stifled an oath. "But it is their intention to continue through it to lands beyond."

Wren studied the bones, though their pattern did not speak to him as it did to Shrike. "I don't suppose you could persuade the bones to be more specific as to the present location of the one we seek?"

"No," Shrike admitted. "But we might seek them as I sought you."

As Wren watched in fascination, Shrike dropped the knuckle-bones back into the leather pouch. In their place he withdrew a delicate sun-bleached songbird skull. Then he reached up to the top of his head and plucked a single silver strand from amidst the dark raven locks. This done, he threaded the hair through the eye-sockets of the skull and tied it off in an intricate knot.

"Acorns are out of season," Shrike said apologetically as he held for the result for Wren's inspection.

Wren had no complaint. "And this will find the individual I knew as Miss Flora?"

Shrike laid a strong yet gentle grip on Wren's wrist. Wren took the hint and opened his hand. The bird skull seemed to weigh little more than a feather when Shrike dropt it into Wren's grasp. Then, as Shrike's clever fingers drew arcane signs in a sort of benediction over it, the skull became heavy as a stone—and pulsed with faint warmth. Instinct bid Wren close his hand over it, and no sooner had he done so than he felt the skull press softly against the inside of his fist, as if it wished to fly beyond the bounds of Blackthorn Briar. Shrike looped the strung hair over Wren's neck, and Wren tucked the bird skull under his shirt-collar to lay against his heart. It fluttered still, too faintly to be seen from without, but keenly felt by Wren.

"Would you," Wren asked, "be willing to remain in Staple Inn whilst I go where the charm leads?"

Shrike cocked his head to one side.

Wren tried again. "If Tolhurst should realize his mistake and return before I do... I've been warned not to let him alone with Mr Grigsby."

Shrike's jaw tightened. He gave a grim nod.

They separated the moment they stepped through the toadstool ring into Hyde Park; Wren to find his employer's ward and Shrike to Staple Inn on the pretence of looking for Wren. Shrike wore his oak-leaf domino mask with Wren's cobweb sigil to disguise his antlers from all mortal eyes save Wren's. Mr Grigsby, being all politeness, would of course invite Shrike to stay, which would in turn allow Shrike to keep watch over Mr Grigsby in case of Tolhurst's early return. Wren, meanwhile, hailed a passing omnibus and hopped aboard for a ride to the train station and thereon northwest as Shrike had said. The bird skull pulsed encouragingly beneath his shirt.

To ask after particular unremarkable individuals amidst the general crush of London would prove useless. However, Wren had a somewhat profitable conversation with a particular ticket clerk regarding a young gentleman of means accompanied by a young lady in a blue frock. Enough to induce him to procure train passage to Liverpool—further west than north, a stepping-stone to lands across the sea, just as Shrike had said—and the thrum of the bird skull as he made the transaction gave him confidence to step aboard.

Hours passed away rattling over the rails. All the while Wren had the bird skull strung on Shrike's hair 'round his throat, tucked beneath his shirt to lie warm against his heart and to beat its own pulse faintly and tug him ever onward, telling him he trod the true path. Then the train halted, at last, in Liverpool, and he disembarked. The bird skull fluttered stronger than ever before as his boot-heel struck the cobblestones.

Wren's eagerness turned to uneasiness when the bird skull tugged him toward the harbour. If Miss Flora had already taken to the sea, Wren could hardly hope to catch her now.

Yet as he wandered down the docks in a meandering pattern that must have irritated every sailor who crossed his path, the bird skull did not seek the waters nor the ships, but rather the edifices lining the street; ship-builders, chandlers, warehouses, and taverns.

The bird skull gave a pulse that forced Wren to a halt beneath a black-lacquered sign carved in the shape of a spouting leviathan. The door it hung over opened into a particularly greasy public house. The very rafters seemed soaked in whale oil. To say nothing of the seafaring folk gathered within. Wren ignored the salty stares and strode to the bar.

"Pardon me," Wren asked, after clearing his throat several times to catch the barkeep's attention and succeeding at last. "Have you seen a young lady with golden hair and a blue gown? Travelling in the company of a young gentleman? Or possibly unattended?"

Nothing moved in the barkeep's face as he gestured with his rag towards a low doorway in the back.

Wren thanked him and put a shilling on the counter for his trouble as he went.

The private dining room of the Black Whale looked only slightly less greasy than the public room. The armchairs clustered around the soot-streaked hearth bore heavy stains on their antimacassars. Yet on the edge of one seat perched a young lady in cornflower-blue poplin with a veiled bonnet covering her face.

Wren withheld a triumphant smile. The situation required delicacy. As such, he approached at a sedate pace.

Though he couldn't see her face, Wren could tell she'd spied him by the sudden stiffening of her posture. Yet she made no move to prevent his standing before her.

Wren bowed. "Miss Fairfield, I presume?"

The girl hesitated, which Wren had never seen Miss Flora do before. Then she raised her hands from where she'd held them folded in her lap and slowly withdrew her veil to reveal dark eyes framed by deep mahogany locks. Despite the lack of black-and-white uniform, Wren recognized the girl-of-all-work from Mrs Bailiwick's Academy.

"Forgive me, Miss Sukie," Wren managed when he'd recovered from the shock. Privately he congratulated himself on remembering her name at last. "But perhaps you may assist me in this matter. Do you perhaps know where I might find Miss Fairfield?"

Sukie continued to regard him in wide-eyed silence.

Wren tried again. "Mr Grigsby is quite anxious for her sake. If she is in distress, I'm at her disposal to relieve it."

Sukie said nothing. But her eyes flicked away from Wren's face toward something over his shoulder.

Wren turned to find Felix Knoll standing in the dining room doorway.

CHAPTER
THIRTY-SIX

All breath left Wren as if he, too, had gone to the grave.

The ghost of Felix Knoll looked almost as astonished as Wren felt. Those familiar blue eyes widened, those rosebud lips parted, and the whole expression fixed upon Wren in shock.

Yet as the moment dragged on, and Wren and the ghost stood staring at each other in stunned silence, he realized his error. The face, whilst remarkable in its similarities, did not belong to the deceased. Though Wren recognized them all the same. He'd seen those blue eyes, those severe brows, and that sharp chin held high on several occasions within the last year—and in a particular miniature portrait on several occasions prior. Many other things, however, had changed since then. The flouncing gown of ribbons and lace had changed places for a sober grey frock coat and trousers which looked very much like the taken-in versions of garments Wren and Mr Grigsby had donated. The bonnet had become a top hat to match. The faint peach-down of fine pale hairs had vanished from cheeks and chin; in its wake they appeared all the sharper and stronger. The most striking change had come atop the head. Where once had stood a pile of golden tresses that must have tumbled down past the knees when brushed out, now there remained only close-cropped flaxen curls. Even so, Wren still knew the youth.

A youth who was not—and had never been—Miss Flora Fairfield.

"I warn you, Mr Lofthouse," the youth said. The voice sounded both lower and more natural than what Wren had heard from those lips before—and still more determined. "If you attempt to remove us from this establishment, I shall resist you by force."

"I would not make such an attempt on any account, sir," Wren replied.

At the word "sir," the youth's aspect changed at once from suspicion to intrigue. Indeed, in the brief flicker of astonishment passing over the familiar-yet-unfamiliar features, Wren thought he beheld something like delight.

"Indeed," Wren continued, "I find this an excellent opportunity to renew our acquaintance. A pleasure, Mr...?"

"Durst," the youth said without hesitation. Either he'd rehearsed it, in which case he could prove a most excellent thespian if he ever decided to live upon the boards, or his answer, on some level, rang true. "Mr Daniel Durst."

"Mr Durst," Wren echoed with an attempt at a reassuring smile. Upon reflection, Daniel seemed rather fitting for the young gentleman who stood before him. He had certainly come through the lion's den.

"Allow me to introduce my cousin," Daniel continued, with careful emphasis upon the last word. "Miss Euphoria Durst."

The former maid ducked her head in a very pretty curtsey.

Wren bowed. Of course Mrs Bailiwick hadn't bothered to mention a missing maid. What did she care for a mere servant when an heiress had vanished?

"If you've not come to drag us away," Daniel asked, drawing Wren from his musings, "then why are you here?"

"Mr Grigsby is much distressed by the disappearance of his ward," Wren explained. "He has sent me to investigate the matter. For myself, I am satisfied with the answer I find here and see no need to enquire further, save on one point; where do you intend to go?"

Daniel hesitated. "You will not tell anyone of the particulars of our plan."

Wren did not hesitate to reply, "I will take it to my grave."

Daniel studied him before he continued. "We've booked passage to Canada. I've saved enough to make our way easy. And my cousin has relations already settled there."

For a moment, Wren glimpsed the story in which he might have taken part, if only he'd cared to see the mortal realm beyond his own thwarted ambitions.

"Will you promise me one thing before you depart?" Wren asked.

Daniel shot him a wary look. "That depends upon what you ask."

Wren could hardly blame him for his suspicion. "Will you write to Mr Grigsby after your arrival and tell him you're safe and sound?"

Daniel's suspicious look became something like consideration.

Wren hastened to press his advantage. "He'll not seek you out. Nor will he make any attempt to bring you back. And," Wren added, with his own terrible conjectures as to what pursuit drove Daniel to this desperate flight, "he will not reveal your location to anyone else. If you tell him to destroy your missive upon reception, you may depend on him to do so. Only—he does care for you, and he will worry his life away for want of a resolution. All he desires is to know you are safe and happy. Even if he may never guess what shape that happiness takes."

A lengthy pause ensued, during which Wren feared he'd failed to impress upon his audience the gravity of his concerns.

Then Daniel nodded. "I shall write to him."

"Furthermore," Wren continued, unable to repress an apologetic wince, "if I may be so gauche as to mention it, he can send you the remainder of your fortune once you come of age."

A huff of wry laugher escaped Daniel.

Wren indulged in a reciprocal smile. "Have you enough to tide you over until then?"

Daniel nodded again and gestured toward his fresh-shorn locks with a swift and decisive hand. Wren realised Daniel had proved clever as well as daring, for in selling his hair, he'd not only acquired funds for his adventure but also rid himself of the most recognizable evidence of his past. Wren only wished he could have seen the expression on the wig-maker's face as Daniel handed over gold for gold.

And yet, Wren still couldn't keep from wondering why Daniel hadn't exhausted all possible source of funds. While it seemed Daniel never expected Wren to condone this most unusual scheme, much less offer assistance in it, Wren's objections might be easily overcome by the use of the missing manuscripts against him. Yet Daniel had made no mention of the papers nor Wren's unnatural predilections.

Which led Wren to a singular conclusion.

"I hesitate to ask," said Wren, "but have you by some chance discovered anything of the papers that went missing from Mr Grigsby's office some months hence?"

Daniel blinked at him with undisguised bewilderment. "No. In truth, Mr Lofthouse, I'd assumed you'd found them ages ago."

Wren withheld a sigh. "I have not."

"Then I regret I cannot repay your kindness by solving this mystery for you," Daniel replied. "Still, if Mr Grigsby hasn't noticed the papers' absence by now, then he likely never will. You needn't fret over them any more than he does."

Wren wished it were so simple. Despite his own predicament, he found himself smiling for Daniel's sake. "Then all that remains is for me to wish you *bon voyage*."

Daniel accepted his well-wishes with a gracious nod; Miss Euphoria with another curtsey. Wren tipped his hat to both and showed himself out.

But when he reached the threshold of the Black Whale and stepped out into the streets of Liverpool, he had no intention of turning his boots toward Staple Inn.

If neither Felix nor Daniel had stolen Wren's manuscripts, then it fell to Tolhurst. And Tolhurst had gone north, across the border, to seek a schoolgirl who didn't exist.

Wren had no time to waste in stopping in Staple Inn to explain his purpose. Particularly not in front of Mr Grigsby. Nor did he want Shrike to leave Mr Grigsby's side just yet—not when Tolhurst might return from his ill-conceived expedition at any moment. He must go straight on to Rochester without delay.

If ever there were an opportunity for an uninterrupted search of Tolhurst's rooms, it must be tonight.

It was fortunate, Shrike thought, that Mr Grigsby favoured a copper kettle lined with tin.

Mr Grigsby had at first appeared astonished to find Shrike on his doorstep. But the very moment Shrike explained he wished to see Wren, Mr Grigsby invited him into the office to await Wren's return. Though Shrike dipped and ducked to get his antlers in through the door-frame, Mr Grigsby noticed them not, thanks to Wren's clever sigil on his own half-mask.

And now, as Shrike sat in Wren's desk chair while Mr Grigsby puttered about with kettle and tea leaves, he reaped the harvest of a sense of hospitality which would have put even the most scrupulous fae to shame.

"I've sent Lofthouse away on a matter of business," Mr Grigsby explained as he stoked the fire. "But I hope he may return by evening—and if not, you're more than welcome to visit again on the morrow. I'm very glad for the company."

Shrike nodded, and this was enough for Mr Grigsby to continue chattering on about some articles he'd found interesting in that morning's paper and what rumours he'd heard in town of late.

"Very fanciful ones!" Mr Grigsby added as he took the whistling kettle off the flame. "Out of Hyde Park in particular."

"Oh?" said Shrike, the first word he'd spoken in several minutes.

"Indeed!" Mr Grigsby poured tea from kettle to pot and set out a cup and saucer before Shrike. "Beggars tell of will-o'-th'-wisps bobbing about in the dark beneath the trees, and the ghost of a medieval outlaw stalks the barracks!"

Shrike said nothing, lest Mr Grigsby draw any connexion between the rumours and Shrike's own garb. He had no fears for his own sake. Yet he thought of Wren and what fate might befall him if the mortal realm realised what they had wrought together.

Perhaps sensing Shrike's growing unease, Mr Grigsby added, "Of course it's likely nonsense. But amusing nonsense nonetheless. Cream? Sugar?"

Shrike, relieved at the change in the conversation's course, thanked Mr Grigsby but declined both offers. Mr Grigsby took this with good cheer and settled into his own chair at his desk across from where Shrike sat.

"I suppose," said Mr Grigsby, "Lofthouse has told you of his intention to leave my employ."

"He has."

Mr Grigsby stirred his tea. "He said he wished to go and seek his fortune. Would I be correct if I were to suppose that he intends to do so with you?"

It seemed safe enough to admit that much. "Aye."

A faint smile twitched at the corner of Mr Grigsby's mouth. "I'm glad of it."

This, Shrike had not expected.

"I know not what Lofthouse has told you of himself," Mr Grigsby continued as Shrike stared in astonished silence. "But I may tell you what I've observed. To wit, when he first entered my employ, he went out a great deal. Visiting friends in the City, attending trials to hear the testimony and take notes on the witnesses and evidence in preparation for sitting at the bar, and ever working diligently on his artistic aspirations—though he has never yet permitted me even a glimpse of the fruits of those last labours." Mr Grigsby smiled, apparently not offended by Wren's reticence in that regard. His expression grew wistful as he continued. "Gradually, however, he stopped attending trials. Then he ceased visiting with friends. And I began to fear he'd even given up his art. Not that he ever faltered in his duty toward me, you understand. Quite the reverse. But still I could tell he was quite unhappy, and it grieved me to see it."

Again, Shrike said nothing.

"Then you arrived," said Mr Grigsby.

Shrike blinked.

Mr Grigsby had returned his attention to stirring his tea and did not lift his gaze from it no matter how Shrike stared. "It was as if you'd returned him to life. I know not what you've done to revive him, as it were, but whatever it was has done him a great deal of good, and I am glad of it."

Shrike found his voice. "I confess I know not, either. But if it has made him happy, then I, too, am glad."

Mr Grigsby glanced up at last and met Shrike's gaze with serenity. "You seem a very sensible fellow, Mr Butcher. And Lofthouse seems most happy in your company, and yourself likewise in his. I'm glad he'll have someone looking after him. Particularly when he's done so well looking after me all these years. Not that I am helpless without him!" Mr Grigsby interrupted himself with a chuckle. "Though I'm sure he'd tell you otherwise. I will miss him very much, of course, but I can look after myself. I did so for forty years before he came along, and I may do so for however many weeks pass until I can find a suitable replacement for him. Not that I consider Lofthouse at all replaceable! Rather the inverse, in fact. Irreplaceable," he added with a sage nod, evidently pleased to have found the exact word he wanted. "But needs must, and as he need no longer clerk for me, so I must find another clerk. Likewise must I entrust Lofthouse to your care and keeping, Mr Butcher."

It became apparent in the ensuing silence that Mr Grigsby had finished expressing his thoughts on the subject and would require more than a nod from Shrike in reply.

"I cannot promise much," Shrike said, his words coming low and slow. "But I shall cleave to him against all onslaught."

Mr Grigsby's startled blink bespoke confusion. Shrike wondered if he'd said more than he ought.

But then the serene smile broke through as Mr Grigsby replied, "And I shall go forth with an easier heart knowing he has you by his side."

CHAPTER
THIRTY-SEVEN

Wren stood beneath the arch of Cemetery Gate in Rochester, against the wall and out of the road, hidden from view amidst the evening's shadows. Rochester did not have the same silence as the forests of the fae realms, yet it proved far quieter than London after nightfall. He'd arrived in London by train at half-past eight and dashed straight to Hyde Park to the toadstool ring, and from thence to the stable-yard in Rochester, alone. The journey didn't seem to tire him in the same way it tried Shrike's strength. He reached Cemetery Gate on foot some quarter of an hour afterward. He'd passed no one along the way. The good citizens of Rochester went down with the sun, so it seemed.

Despite the quietude of the sleepy little town, Wren found the door to Cemetery Gate locked. Perhaps due to his and Shrike's prior burglary efforts. Or perhaps because Tolhurst had known the sun would set before he returned from seeking the individual he called Miss Flora.

Either way, Wren still had his button-hook and Shrike's silver awl tucked into his coat pocket from their last adventure and used them now to the same success.

The narrow stair held deeper shadows than the night-time streets of Rochester. Wren crept upward more by touch than by sight, the steps beneath bowed by centuries of tread. No noise reached his ear save the creak of the floorboards under his boots and the pounding of his heart in his throat. With each step it seemed as if he dragged his legs up from fathomless depths. Their strength almost failed him when he alighted on the upper landing.

Against his better judgment, Wren approached the second door.

Cupping his ear to it gave him no hint as to what might lie beyond. He steeled his nerve and rapped his knuckles against the wood panel with a none-too-steady hand.

No one answered.

The silence did nothing to calm Wren's nerves. Yet he forced his fumbling fingers to grasp the knob and turn.

This door, too, was locked. It took the work of a moment for Wren to pick it. The clicking sounds of his progress against the lock seemed to resound like whip-cracks in his ears in the overwhelming silence of the gloomy stair.

The tumblers fell into place. Wren gathered what small courage he possessed and pushed the door open.

The door swung inward to reveal the self-same chamber he and Shrike had failed to burgle some months past. A slender shaft of silver moonlight shone through the window before the desk, slicing the room in twain with just enough brilliance to distinguish the silhouette of a candle-stick on the corner of the desk.

Wren crept across the room and picked up the candle. The moonlight wouldn't be enough to search by; however ill-advised, he knew he must risk a candle-flame. No one else in Rochester was awake at so advanced an hour. And with any luck, a passing insomniac would mistake his shadow in the window for Tolhurst. He only hoped, as he struck a match from his pocket and brought it to the withered wick, that Tolhurst wouldn't notice its having burnt down another inch or two when he returned. Wren would be long gone by then.

Reflections of the pale golden flame glimmered against the glass-fronted barrister bookshelves lining the walls. Wren, candle in hand, went to them and began methodically pulling down books to flip through them one-by-one in case his own manuscripts were tucked between their pages. Shelf by shelf, emptying and refilling, he found they were not.

Still, he held out hope as he moved on to the bedroom. Perhaps Shrike, in his unfamiliarity with mortal customs and manners, had missed something Wren might yet discover. When he'd overturned the mattress, emptied the chest of drawers, and sounded all the floorboards without finding even a scrap of his own work, he felt forced to conclude that Shrike's search had proved thorough. He ought never have doubted him, though it boded ill for his present efforts.

Wren had saved the desk for last in a half-superstitious effort to fulfil the prophecy of lost items always being found in the last place one looked. In his heart he knew simple logic would show this phrase existed because one would not continue looking for a lost object after one found it, and therefore the last place one looked must be the one wherein the lost object was found, but nevertheless he set upon the desk drawers with button-hook and awl and something akin to hope.

Some time later, the candle-flame had dwindled to a guttering stub. Wren knew its withered state could hardly escape Tolhurst's notice. He lowered his hopes to merely being many miles off by the time Tolhurst returned. Of greater concern to him at present was the mountain range of piled papers surrounding him as he sat on the floor amidst all the drawers he'd pulled out. Not a single sheet belonged to his missing manuscripts.

The rattle of the key in the lock seemed to fill the whole chamber. The scrape of the door against its frame rang in Wren's ears. He had time enough to leap to his feet—no more.

"Good evening, Mr Lofthouse. You had a pleasant journey from London, I hope?"

The words held the shape of a warm welcome, yet the sound of them filled Wren with cold dread. He turned to find Tolhurst standing in the doorway, looking not quite as astonished as one might expect to find a common clerk digging through his desk drawers.

Wren opened his mouth intending to reply in kind. "If it's all the same to you, Mr Tolhurst, I would prefer to arrive straight at the point."

So much for intentions.

Tolhurst's brows elevated a fraction of an inch. "Very well."

His hand delved into his coat towards a slight bulge in the wool that had previously gone unnoticed against the general bulk of his brawny frame. Wren held his breath as Tolhurst withdrew a familiar sheaf of papers tied together with black ribbon. A pang struck his heart, half relief and half anxiety at seeing his work again.

Tolhurst untied the black ribbon with the delicacy of a lover unlacing a bodice. He began to turn the pages over with slow deliberation, as a curator might display prints for auction.

"They are complete," he said. "Kept precisely as they were found. I'd thought I might have use of them today in London if you proved less tractable than I required in our efforts to discover Miss Fairfield, though I suppose they may serve the same purpose here."

Wren could feel Tolhurst's unrelenting gaze upon his face as he spoke. He did not meet it. He couldn't tear his eyes away from the manuscripts. Just glimpsing his work in Tolhurst's hands brought forth a wellspring of memories, even after so many months' separation. Every pen-stroke held a story. The illustrations of Sir Gawain and the Green Knight sent his pulse pounding with the same indignant rage that had flooded his veins as he stormed out of the Restive Quills. Snatches of birdsong and the babbling brook filled his ears as Tolhurst turned over watercolour sketches of the garden enclosed within Blackthorn Briar. In a drawing of Shrike working at his bench, Wren could smell his vanilla woodsmoke musk, hear the tap of his mallet on leather, and feeling the warmth of the cottage all around him. More intimate portraits recalled still more stirring moments.

"You are satisfied as to their condition?"

Wren, jolted out of his spiralling thoughts, blinked and forced himself to meet Tolhurst's gaze. He swallowed hard. "I am."

Tolhurst smiled and withdrew his fingers from the manuscripts, leaving them set aside on the desk. The instinct to snatch the pages and bolt threatened to overwhelm Wren's better sense. With his hands already in fists at his sides, he dug his nails into his palms to hold himself in check.

"Did Mr Knoll show you where I'd hidden them?" Wren asked in a tone of forced disinterest.

"No," Tolhurst replied. "I don't suppose he ever knew your body of work existed."

Wren hid his astonishment beneath his indifferent mask. "Really."

"Mr Grigsby's mention of your particular friends and your frequent meetings at night in Hyde Park piqued my curiosity." Tolhurst chuckled. "I confess at first I suspected you'd thrown your lot in with the Chartists. Particularly after I espied *Wat Tyler* amongst your books. But I didn't begin my investigations in earnest until I returned with Miss Fairfield and found you half under the bed whilst my nephew slumbered above. Then I knew you had something to hide. I waited until Miss Fairfield returned to Rochester, and Mr Grigsby and Dr Hitchingham had left me to nurse Felix alone. As he seemed in no danger, and as your secret seemed very dangerous indeed, I slipped under the bed myself. Imagine my astonishment at what I discovered. Not a manifesto of revolution, as I'd feared, but something I could never have imagined. Something I daresay most gentlemen could never imagine."

Wren knew Tolhurst did not intend the remark as a compliment.

"In hindsight, of course, it was obvious," Tolhurst continued. "I should have noticed before had I not been so preoccupied with my nephew's well-being. I was educated at Harrow. I know full well what some boys get up to there. And what habits some men fail to break when they go on to university."

Wren said nothing.

Tolhurst smiled. "Tell me, Mr Lofthouse—in all your years of service, have you ever met a boy as feckless as my nephew?"

"No," Wren admitted.

Tolhurst chortled. "That's what I like about you, Mr Lofthouse. Brief and to the point. I'm certain you must share some of my feelings on the matter. You, who have managed the trust since the day Felix inherited all. The sheer wealth he came into. And how he has squandered it. On drink, on dissolute friends, gambling, the company of unfortunate women—there is no vice left unexplored. Well," he added with a wry smile, "save yours."

Wren clenched his jaw to keep his silence.

"But unlike Felix," Tolhurst continued, "you need not let your vice destroy you."

Wren did not see fit to tell him it already had.

"If you are here," said Tolhurst, "rather than out in pursuit of Miss Fairfield, I must conclude you are either extraordinarily negligent in your service to Mr Grigsby, or that you have enjoyed more success than myself in your search for her."

Wren, startled by the shift in subject from Felix to Miss Flora—or rather, Daniel—caught his prepared speech on his tongue. Which was something of a feat, given that his prepared speech explained not only how much of Felix's fortune remained and how Mr Grigsby would manage it in his absence, but also how the trust, upon Felix attaining his majority, would doubtless be claimed by his remaining creditors, unless Felix himself called upon Mr Grigsby to attempt have the debts declared void on account of his youth. This, and how, for the purpose of inheritance, the courts would presume Felix alive and able to reclaim his trust at any moment—until seven years had passed, at which point Tolhurst might petition the courts to declare Felix dead and, as his nearest living relative, inherit all. Not that there would be much left to inherit after the money-lenders claimed their due.

"When I ponder the many terrible fates that may befall a young lady alone in the world separated from her guardians..." Tolhurst shook his head. "Where did you find her? Or perhaps I should ask, where have you put her for safe-keeping?"

To this, Wren could give but one answer. "I'm afraid I've given my word that I will not reveal her whereabouts. It must be enough for you to know that she is beyond harm."

Tolhurst's smile faded. "No, Mr Lofthouse, I'm afraid it is not enough. I must ask a great deal more of you."

Wren spared a glance for his manuscripts on the desk before meeting Tolhurst's gaze again. In a dry tone, he replied, "I admit you've assumed a position of significant advantage in our negotiations. What would you have of me?"

"You're a practical man, Mr Lofthouse, despite your artistic endeavours. You must understand my concerns in this regard. Though you've sworn yourself to secrecy, and it speaks well of your character that you wish to keep your word, surely you feel no such compunction towards a mere slip of a girl who has no idea of her own best interest? You see how it would be better to entrust the knowledge of her present location to a steady and forthright man of the world."

"Such as yourself, I presume you mean," said Wren.

Tolhurst smiled. "If I may flatter myself so far, yes."

"As a steady and forthright man of the world, would you then tear Miss Fairfield away from what happiness and security she has found for herself?"

Tolhurst's smile faded. "Her greatest hope of happiness and security lies with me."

Wren sincerely doubted it.

Tolhurst didn't require Wren's commentary to continue his speech. "You have managed Miss Fairfield's fortune ever since you came into Mr Grigsby's service, but you never met her before last year. You cannot hope to know her as I do. From the very moment she first entered Mrs Bailiwick's Academy, at the tender age of eleven, an orphan all alone in the world and bereft of protection. To watch her sweet innocence bud into the fragrant blooms of womanhood. If you had known her as I have known her—guiding her growth as the trellis guides the rose—even a man of your own predilections could not fail to love her."

Wren had assisted Mr Grigsby in choosing which finishing school would bring up his ward. They'd settled on Mrs Bailiwick's Academy not only for its sterling reputation of respectability in churning out fine young ladies but also because Tolhurst had taken the position of music and dancing master. Mr Grigsby had assumed Tolhurst would prove as much an uncle to his nephew's betrothed as to his nephew himself. Wren's guts twisted to think how Tolhurst had betrayed what ought to have been his familial love for his future in-law. Small wonder Daniel had felt loath to trust Wren. Wren had thrown him into the very den of lions he sought to escape.

"And when Mr Knoll returns?" Wren asked—though he knew no such thing could occur, and it seemed Tolhurst knew it, too. Still, if

Felix's engagement had kept Tolhurst at bay for all these years, then perhaps the reminder of it would recall him to reason now. Or at least convince him to abandon his pursuit long enough for Daniel to evade his grasp. "What then?"

As if to confirm Wren's suspicions, Tolhurst replied, "I do not anticipate my nephew intruding on Miss Fairfield's happiness after she has become Mrs John Tolhurst."

"While Mr Knoll has flown his creditors," Wren said, forcing himself to speak as if he believed it, "he must intend to return when he has gained the means to deal with them. And when he does, surely he will wish to return to his betrothed, as well. I cannot imagine him well pleased if he returns to find she is wed to his uncle. Such an occurrence must make life very difficult for her, no matter her husband."

Tolhurst appeared in no way moved by this argument. "I assure you, my nephew has quite given up Miss Fairfield."

Wren weighed his words with careful consideration. "If I may be so bold as to ask, sir, how is it you can feel so certain of your absent nephew's intentions?"

Tolhurst regarded him for a moment. Then, to Wren's astonishment, he raised his hands to his cravat, untying it and unbuttoning his shirt to dip his hand under his own collar. From beneath his shirt-front Tolhurst withdrew a chain, from which dangled a minuscule object.

"He relinquished this," Tolhurst said as he drew the chain over his head and held the item out for Wren's inspection with as much reverence as a bishop would show the relic of a saint. "Prior to his departure. You cannot believe he would do so if he ever meant to return for her."

Wren stared at the painted miniature of a blonde, blue-eyed, sweetly smiling young lady. It bore every resemblance to Miss Flora, and none to Daniel, which rendered it unnerving to Wren's eye. Yet he recalled it as the one which Felix had carried with him ever since its commission in his first year at university. The warmth of Tolhurst's flesh suffused it still.

"He gave it into my care," Tolhurst continued as Wren regarded the miniature in disbelieving silence.

"And the lady as well?" Wren managed despite the sudden dryness in his mouth.

Tolhurst gave him a speaking look, though Wren couldn't fathom what it meant to impart.

"When he did so," Wren went on, "did he make any mention of where he intended to go after departing your company?"

Tolhurst said nothing.

"It speaks well of your loyalty to your kin for you to go so far to hide your nephew from his creditors," said Wren. "Yet I hope you'd see fit to take Mr Grigsby, if not myself, into your confidence, so we might render what assistance we may. I assure you, while Mr Grigsby is disappointed in Mr Knoll, he wishes to see him well nonetheless."

Still, Tolhurst said nothing.

Wren waited a moment further before coming to his point. "Where is your nephew, Mr Tolhurst?"

Tolhurst gave him a long and solemn look. "Where no one will find him and from whence he shall never return."

Wren pressed on. "But how can you be certain—"

"Where is Flora?" Tolhurst demanded.

Wren drew up short. He'd never heard that tone from Tolhurst before. Nor had he thought Tolhurst bold enough—despite his evident passion—to refer to an individual he believed to be a young lady by her Christian name alone in conversation with a near-stranger.

And yet, though his words flared with impatience, the stare Tolhurst levelled at Wren felt as cold as frost creeping over a grave.

Wren endeavoured to match it with an expression of perfect indifference as he echoed back, "Where no one will find her and from whence she shall never return."

Tolhurst's face drained of blood. He fell back a full stride and choked out, "What—dead!?"

Wren waited in silence, watching the façade ripple and shift—the change from white to ashen grey as the cheeks regained their colour, the eyes that had flown wide in shock narrowing to suspicious slits before returning to half-lidded sangfroid, the parted lips pressing together in a thin line—as Tolhurst realised all he'd revealed in those two fateful words.

"It seems," Tolhurst said when his equilibrium had returned, "we are evenly matched, Mr Lofthouse. I have in my possession matter enough to send you to the prison hulks, if not the gallows. And now that you know my nephew's fate, you may say the same of me."

"I know nothing I didn't already suspect," Wren admitted, not bothering to disguise his dry tone. "Though I'd like to learn the full truth of the matter, if you're willing to tell it. We need have no secrets between us now."

Tolhurst didn't reply in words. Instead, with a heavy sigh, he dropped into his desk chair.

Wren tried again, his voice low and soft. "Where is the body, Mr Tolhurst?"

Tolhurst ran a hand down his face, not meeting Wren's eye. His gaze fell upon some unfixed point between the fireplace and the window.

"When did it happen?" Wren pressed. "Can you tell me that, at least?"

A long minute passed before Tolhurst spoke. "On the second of May."

The very day Felix had left Staple Inn in disgrace. How often, upon Felix's habitual departures from Mr Grigsby's office, Wren had wished he'd seen the last of him. Little did he realize upon that day that his wish had been granted. Rather than relief, a gnawing void bloomed within his chest, a hollow sickness that threatened to consume him.

"He came to me in the evening," Tolhurst continued without Wren's prompting. "Mr Grigsby had advised him to do so—or so he claimed. I suppose you might verify?"

Wren forced himself to nod.

"It seems Mr Grigsby likewise advised him to sell off all he could bear to part with," Tolhurst went on. "To that end, he drew out this miniature—this portrait of his betrothed, which I had commissioned for him to mark the occasion of his eighteenth birthday—and endeavoured to induce me to purchase it from him, as if it were so much dross."

Wren suppressed a flinch. Tolhurst had spat those final words with a violence Wren had never expected to hear from him. Much as Felix, Wren supposed, had never expected violence of any sort from his uncle.

Venom infused Tolhurst's voice as he continued. "He told me he'd known for some time how I watched after Flora. Admiring her from afar. Never doing anything more, out of respect for my nephew's claim. Respect I've since realised was in no way his due. Regardless, he said I ought to buy it off him, to have something to remember her by when he took her to wife. And when I hesitated… he said he might be persuaded to break it off with her entirely, if I agreed to take on his debts alongside his bounty." Tolhurst met Wren's eye at last with the same cold gaze as before. "He offered me her honour as if it were shillings and pence."

Wren winced. For Daniel's sake and not Tolhurst's, though Tolhurst needn't know it.

"I ask you, Mr Lofthouse," Tolhurst continued. "What gentleman could hear such an insult and not feel moved to answer it?"

Wren waited for further details. When none came, he made another attempt. "The body, Mr Tolhurst. Where did you hide the body?"

Tolhurst did not turn his head, but his eyes slid sideways to the indigo night beyond the window. "I agreed to his terms with my tongue. My heart spoke differently. Felix suspected nothing. We shook hands upon it. With the matter settled in his mind, it was easy to persuade him to take an evening stroll to cool our heads. It was only natural such a stroll would take us down to the river-bank, so convenient to Cemetery Gate. Even more natural that, as we stood side-by-side admiring the clear night, I should lay an uncle's comforting hand upon my nephew's shoulder. It felt still more natural for my other hand to come to rest upon his throat."

Wren's own throat went dry.

"I had assumed the body would be found before now," Tolhurst continued, either not noticing how his words unnerved Wren, or not caring. "I suppose it sank beyond retrieval. Or floated away to meet the Thames. Picked over by mudlarks and sunk into the sediment."

Returned to nature, Shrike had said. Wren could only imagine what manner of eels had gnawed upon the corpse until nothing remained.

"You needn't fear I share my nephew's spendthrift habits," said

Tolhurst, drawing Wren's mind away from sepulchral thoughts. "Miss Fairfield's fortune shall not go to waste under my care. As you can see by the rooms you stand in, I am a practical man and well accustomed to living within my means."

Wren stared at him. Household economy could not have been further from his mind in that moment. If Tolhurst thought his financial standing, rather than his confessed murder, would prove the greatest impediment to Wren believing him a fit suitor for Daniel, then his conscience had twisted further than Wren could ever imagine.

Tolhurst raised his own brows at Wren's disbelief. "You cannot deny Felix proved himself unworthy of Flora's hand in marriage. He never deserved her."

Wren could not deny it. He cleared his throat and assumed a tone of cool indifference. "And what does Miss Fairfield deserve?"

"A delicate flower such as she deserves the commanding presence of an older, wiser gentleman to guide her through the correct path in life."

Wren's gorge rose.

"Keep your silence regarding his fate," Tolhurst continued, "and I'll keep my silence regarding your sins—so long as you tell me where I will find Flora."

His voice fell to a growl upon those last few words. He rose from his chair and advanced a step. Wren fell back in kind. Tolhurst had just confessed to one murder. Wren couldn't assume he'd feel any reluctance to commit a second.

Yet, while Tolhurst had proved monstrous, Wren couldn't help feeling his malice was nothing compared to the inhuman wrath of a faerie queen. And despite Tolhurst's menace, blackmail could have little effect upon one who planned to either die or leave England forever on the twenty-first of June.

"I will find her," Tolhurst went on. "Whether you tell me or no, I shall hunt her down. There is no covert she may run to that I will not sniff out. I'll not rest until I have her. So you may as well tell me."

Wren didn't trust himself to lie without revealing more than he ought.

And so rather than speak, he darted for the desk.

The ambassador's training regimen had done wonders in just a few short weeks. It had made Wren quick enough to snatch up his manuscripts before Tolhurst could do more than rock back on his heels in alarm.

But not quick enough to decide between dashing for the window or the door before Tolhurst set on him.

Hands like talons seized his shoulder. Wren whipped one arm out of his coat sleeve, ready to sacrifice it in his escape, but his compulsive hold on his manuscripts, while he swapped them from one hand to the other, lost him the vital moment required to fully elude Tolhurst's grasp. The frock coat fell to the floor well after Tolhurst's fists clenched Wren's shirt-front.

Thrust back against the barrister shelves with enough force to crack the glass behind him, Wren dropped his manuscripts. They fluttered down around him like so many dying moths.

"Where is she?" Tolhurst snarled in his face.

Wren couldn't summon any words, much less the ones Tolhurst wanted.

Tolhurst lifted him until his boots no longer touched the floor and slammed him against the bookshelves again. "Where!?"

Wren shook his head.

"Tell me!"

Wren, his vocal cords tight with fear, just managed to murmur, "Never."

Tolhurst stared at him in frank disbelief. He removed one hand from Wren's shirt-front.

And wrapped it around Wren's throat.

Instinct drove Wren to grab at the wrist of the hand now crushing his windpipe. This changed nothing. Tolhurst, larger, stronger, and more practised in murder, had every advantage. Still, his lungs burning, Wren wrenched Tolhurst's wrist again and again. He kicked out, his boot-heels breaking the glass behind him and proving just as futile against Tolhurst's shins as his hand proved against Tolhurst's arm. Dark spots clouded his vision like swarms of flies. He grit his teeth, and through them he whispered with the last of his breath.

"Shrike."

Tolhurst didn't seem to hear him any more than he noticed his kicks and blows. His snarling rage had turned to cold indifference. Eyes frozen in their hatred fixed on Wren's face. He hoped it wouldn't be the last thing he saw.

Even as his vision went black.

He could still hear Tolhurst's ragged panting over him, though with every agonizing second that passed, it sounded further and further off, as if he'd slipped beneath the waters of the River Medway alongside Felix and drifted down, down, down...

The crashing chimes of shattered glass broke through the haze. The crushing force vanished from his throat—though the pain remained—and he drew choking gasps of woodsmoke scent as he fell into darkness.

Then he hit the floor in a heap.

Over his own wheezing breaths he heard Tolhurst bite off an oath. More thuds and crashes followed. Fading in with the rhythm of the blood pounding in his ears, his vision returned. The coffered ceiling of Tolhurst's rooms swam above his eyes. He rolled his head toward the muffled cacophony.

And beheld Tolhurst laid out flat with a familiar figure kneeling on his chest like a vengeful incubus.

"Shrike." Wren's mouth formed the word without any breath behind it.

Nevertheless, Shrike's head shot up. His warm dark eyes fixed on Wren's own. The slender point of his misericord remained against Tolhurst's throat. Silver moonlight streamed through the shattered window behind him, and this, combined with the guttering gold of the candle-stub beneath the desk, illuminated the shards of broken glass scattered across the fallen papers like glittering ice over a field of snow.

Tolhurst's hand closed over a particular shard.

A ragged cry sprang from Wren's broken windpipe.

But even as Tolhurst raised his jagged weapon, Shrike's misericord slid into his throat.

The terrible wet sputtering noise lasted the merest instant. Then silence fell.

And in a heartbeat, Shrike knelt at Wren's side.

"Easy," Shrike murmured, cradling Wren's face in his gentle hands. "It's all right. Are you hurt?"

Wren shook his head and rasped, "Only my throat."

He tried to rise. Shrike laid a palm on his chest. It weighed almost nothing, yet it kept Wren pinned.

"We must go," Wren croaked. "Now. The neighbours will have heard something—"

"We will," Shrike assured him. "Catch your breath first."

Wren felt as if he never would. Still, as he drew in shuddering gasps of woodsmoke and vanilla, the overwhelming thud of his own pulse in his skull dimmed, and the room no longer tilted when he raised his head. At length, he clung to Shrike's arm, and with his assistance got his legs under him.

Tolhurst's body lay as if sleeping on a bed of papers and broken glass. The dark crimson stain trickling from the hole in his throat looked almost like a ribbon tied 'round his neck. Wren forced his gaze away from the sight. His eye fell on his manuscript pages heaped against the cracked barrister bookshelves.

"Wait," he said, though Shrike hadn't yet taken a step. His head swam as he bent to pick up the manuscripts.

Wood scraped against wood.

"Here," Shrike murmured overhead, and Wren realised he'd pulled out the desk chair for him to rest on.

Against his better judgment, Wren settled himself into the dead man's seat whilst Shrike gathered the pages much as he gathered herbs from Blackthorn garden. Quickly, too, for Wren hardly had time to think on the oddity of it before Shrike arose and handed his own life's work back to him. Unaccountable relief washed over his heart to feel those familiar pages beneath his fingertips again. And yet...

"There is a slender chain," Wren said, even as he avoided looking at the object. "Around his collar."

Shrike asked nothing further. He left Wren's sight as he went to Tolhurst's body but returned soon enough and opened his palm to reveal the miniature of Daniel. He didn't question why Wren wanted it so. There would be time enough to explain later, if they managed to escape.

No sooner had Wren taken it from him than voices began echoing up from the street below.

Shrike crouched before him. Wren, whose knees yet trembled, clambered onto his back with welcome relief and wrapped his arms tight around Shrike's shoulders, just as he'd done when they rode the stag in the Wild Hunt. His manuscripts vanished into Shrike's cloak pocket. The miniature of Daniel remained clenched in his fist hard enough to bruise his palm.

It seemed Wren weighed nothing to Shrike as he slipped out the broken window to perch on the sill beyond. Wren expected him to scale the wall down to the cobblestones—if not outright leap. Both particularly dangerous propositions when lanterns bobbed and voices rang out in the street beneath them.

Yet as Shrike began his climb, he went not below, but above.

The rooftops on High Street stood close together. Shrike ran along them as swift and silent as a hunted hart darting through dense forest. Those few awoken by the incident in Cemetery Gate were too intent on discovering what had happened within to look without, and it never occurred to any of them to look up. Their lantern lights faded away like so many will-o'-th'-wisps as Shrike carried Wren across Rochester to the stable-yard. The horses slept on as he descended to the well, and Wren held tight as he plunged into the depths, eager to leave England behind forever.

CHAPTER
THIRTY-EIGHT

The Court of the Silver Wheel
The Fae Realms
Midsummer

An eerie silence descended over the gathered crowd as Wren and Shrike entered the Court of the Silver Wheel. It parted before them as they strode with purpose toward the hemlock bower standing tall on the opposing side.

In the corner of his eye Wren glimpsed some familiar figures beyond the denizens of the Court. Lady Aethelthryth, seated atop her grey steed, could hardly be missed. Nor could he fail to spot Tatterdemalion flitting about overhead in their dual-toned fur coat and trailing silver tresses. Several milk-maid huldra wandered through the throng, which Wren had come to expect, but he also recognized their queen, whose antlers outstripped Shrike's, accompanied by the blue roan incubus who'd played the queer fiddle in the mead hall. He almost missed the silver glint of a spiderweb mask amongst strangers—for even the ambassador's fearsome reputation couldn't keep such a throng as this from crowding in at each other's elbows. Fae had gathered from courts far and wide to stare at the Kings of Oak and Holly.

Well might they all stare at Shrike and Wren. Shrike, wearing the queen's gyrdel fastened around his waist over his boiled leather armour, and Wren with Larkin's scythe slung over his left shoulder. Whether the wide berth the crowd gave them was due to Shrike's bloody reputation or the iron blade, Wren couldn't say.

The knights encircling the hemlock bower's base stepped aside to allow them entry. The sun shone bright above the tourney field and cast a green hue over everything beneath the needle-leaf roof. The courtiers' low murmur of conversation died into a stunned hush at Shrike and Wren's approach.

The queen sat alone on her throne at her balcony. Her delicate fingers held a crown. Not, as Wren had expected, braided holly leaves jewelled with crimson berries, but instead woven from evergreen thorns. He wondered if the fae understood the mortal symbolism of such a crown. He doubted it.

"Kneel, my Holly King," she purred.

Wren bent on one knee as he'd seen Shrike do so many months ago.

The queen laid the crown on his brow with a gentle hand. It did not weigh upon him as heavily as he'd expected. Nonetheless, he felt it difficult to raise his head to meet her gaze again. He found her smiling. He didn't return it.

Without a word, he and Shrike turned as one and descended to the duelling field.

Wren gave one last glance across the gathered crowd in search of friendly faces. Someone waved a scrap of white linen with a dark stain over their head. Belatedly Wren recognized his own bloodied cravat and the young man who wielded it, flanked by the statuesque woman and the crone. Further off, he espied a hint of blue amidst the green and found Nell perched in the fork of a tree at the edge of the field. With bow in hand and quiver slung over her shoulder she stood watching and waiting for the duel's result.

Shrike and Wren took their places marked on either side of the three-ells-wide ring burned into the grass of the tourney field.

The queen's herald held out a handkerchief embroidered with the symbol of the silver wheel. At a sign from her, they dropt it and leapt back from the combatants.

So began the duel.

The melodrama Wren had scripted commenced with he and Shrike circling each other around the marked edge of the duelling ring. Shrike had his sword unsheathed in an instant. Wren, with the scythe already in hand, had only to raise it in front of him as shield and weapon both.

Shrike attacked first, darting forward almost faster than Wren could perceive. He brought the scythe up just in time to ward off the sword.

Blade clanged against blade. Wren thrust the flat edge of the scythe at Shrike's chest to force him back. Then, with a wild spin, he swept the scythe at his face.

Shrike ducked beneath the blade.

But not swift enough to prevent it striking an antler.

The iron blade did not slice clean through the bone but hacked halfway before ceasing, caught. This, Wren had not written. Nor had they rehearsed such a thing.

Shrike, however, improvised by seizing a prong in his own hand and breaking off the antler with a sickening crack.

Blood oozed from the jagged edge. Wren stared in horror. Antlers were supposed to fall off, he told himself, and when the rest of this one took its natural course, it would take the ever-bleeding wound with it. Shrike need not bear it over-long.

Still, the sight of the crimson gore beading along the craggy break did nothing to ease Wren's conscience.

Shrike swung his sword just as Wren swung the scythe. The notch between iron blade and wooden handle caught the sword below the hilt. A twist of the scythe wrenched the sword from Shrike's grip and flung it aside.

Nevermind that the hilt only dropt from Shrike's fist because he chose to open his hand. The duel need not appear beyond convincing to the most discerning eye. After all, everyone watching the sword dance at Ostara knew it for mere play and rejoiced in it nonetheless. It need merely be a splendid spectacle.

Wren spun a full circle to bring the scythe 'round again. It caught Shrike at the waist. The gyrdel links chimed against the blade. The boiled leather held out against the iron.

For now.

With a mighty yank, Wren drew Shrike to him. Near enough to feel his breath on his face and fill his lungs with his woodsmoke-vanilla scent. Near enough to press his woollen waistcoat to his leather armour.

Near enough to seize his silver-shot midnight locks in his fist and drag him down for a kiss.

Rough and ravenous.

No sooner had Shrike's hands rose to embrace Wren in turn than Wren drew back—Shrike's teeth tearing through his lip—and got the scythe between them to shove Shrike away.

Far enough to swing the blade again.

Iron struck leather. Straps already scored once now gave way. The armour slid from Shrike's body and fell to the field.

In a flash, Shrike had his misericord in hand from some hidden sheath. He held it back-handed as if he hoped to defend himself from the iron scythe with a bit of silver as slender as a needle. Then he struck.

But not at Wren.

The silver blade sliced through the remaining straps. Every scrap of leather fell like golden leaves in autumn. The gyrdel was not spared; Shrike stuck the point of his misericord through the links of the chain and with a vindictive twist broke it from his body.

Wren gave the scythe a few wayward spins to either side, rolling the length of the handle along each arm, then sent it in a decisive upward arc at Shrike. He redoubled his efforts to draw it up short, his muscles straining against the wood.

Shrike jerked his head back. The point of the blade halted just beneath his chin.

A hair's breadth from drawing blood.

Wren threw the scythe aside and leapt at him.

Cries of alarm ensued as the scythe thudded into the field some yards off. Wren could only imagine how the crowd must have dived out of the path of the iron weapon, as his whole world had reduced to

Shrike. He recaptured his mouth in a kiss. His own blood smeared across Shrike's lips.

Scattered gasps arose, announcing the next action of their little play, wherein Shrike raised his misericord behind Wren's back.

Wren made no move to halt him.

A single scream rang out as the blade descended. Shrike's tongue tasted sweeter than honey against his own.

The ripping of wool resounded across the field as Shrike cut Wren's waistcoat from his body.

Gasps of fear turned to murmurs of confusion, and unless Wren was much mistaken, excitement. Shrike brought the misericord down again and again, tearing through the ties of his own garb, until tunic and hose alike lay discarded on the duelling field.

The final act of their spectacle had been written—planned—but never rehearsed.

An act which would see him hanged if witnessed in England, now performed before a fae audience of hundreds.

Wren had rather thought Shrike might sit astride him, as he had sat astride Shrike at Samhain. But when Shrike bore them both to the ground, it was Shrike who lay with his back against the grass and who pulled Wren in between his thigh, and threw his own knees up over Wren's shoulders in an acrobatic feat that only one of the fae could hope to accomplish, bending himself double beneath Wren's weight as he dragged Wren down to kiss him. It couldn't possibly have felt comfortable for Shrike, yet, as Wren slid his hand up the inside of Shrike's bare thigh, he found a cock as rigid as his own. He fumbled the spermaceti oil out of his trouser pocket and uncorked it to spill over his prick and Shrike's fundament alike. The empty bottle fell to the grass and rolled away with a hollow ringing sound. Wren took his slick cock in hand and aligned its head with Shrike's hole, leaning his weight against it, testing the boundary not yet breached.

"Do you yield?" Wren whispered.

The wicked spark in Shrike's eyes had flared up into a roaring flame of determination and desire. His fangs gleamed as he grinned and growled, "I yield."

Wren gathered his courage and drove his sword in.

It could never have found a more perfect sheath. A single thrust sank him in halfway to the hilt, the tight rings of muscle opening to embrace the very core of him. Wren gasped, the sensation driving the breath from him like a hammer-strike. The sheer heat that blazed within Shrike and how it clenched 'round him—he bit his lip to keep from spending at once and reopened the wound, fresh blood trickling forth.

Shrike arched his back beneath him with a hiss of satisfaction.

Yet Wren couldn't allow himself to feel satisfied. For the ritual to work, Shrike must spend first—must surrender and die a little death, under the power of the Holly King.

"How—?" Wren began, and found he hadn't the self-command required to both restrain himself and finish his question; to ask what he must do to increase Shrike's pleasure over his own.

Shrike understood regardless. His lips brushed Wren's as he whispered, "Roll into me."

Wren rolled his hips, his prick sliding in a fraction of an inch, then out again, his cock-head grazing a certain hard point within Shrike that made him shudder in Wren's arms. Even these minute movements proved almost too much for Wren to bear—particularly when combined with Shrike's trembling in his embrace and around his cock in the hot, tight, slick velvet sheath consuming Wren's blade. What little presence of mind remained in Wren allowed him to take Shrike's cock in his fist and stroke it swift and sharp in rhythm with his own thrusts.

"Now," Shrike hissed. "Fuck me, fuck me, fuck me—"

Any further command cut off as Wren withdrew until only the tip of his lance remained within Shrike—then in a swift powerful thrust, plunged it in again, this time to the hilt.

Shrike shuddered so, Wren feared he'd hurt him, until Shrike's clenched teeth split into a breathless laugh, and in a broken gasp, he demanded, "Harder."

Wren obeyed.

Shrike clawed Wren from his shoulder-blades down to his buttocks, gripped the back of his thighs hard enough to bruise, and slammed Wren into him again and again.

Wren held on—barely—and stroked Shrike's prick, matching the rhythm Shrike set. It pulsed against his palm in time with the hammering of his own heart. Pearls of seed leaked from its tip with every pull. He could almost feel the power between them growing, rising, like a sunrise about to break over the horizon, like wildflowers on the brink of bursting into bloom. Wren couldn't hold himself back much longer.

Never ceasing, Wren bent to bring his lips to the pointed tip of Shrike's ear. "Are you—?"

The restraint required to rein in his own spend forced him to bite off the end of his enquiry.

In a voice broken with overwhelming sensation, Shrike replied, "Command me, my king. I am at your mercy."

To hear those words nearly sent Wren over the edge. He gasped, bit his bloodied lip, and choked out at last in a rasping whisper, "Shrike—come."

Shrike obeyed. His cock pulsed in Wren's palm. Seed spilled through Wren's fingers and onto Shrike's belly, drops falling like mistletoe amidst the scars. His back arched, his whole body trembling taut like a bow-string, his inner heat clenching rhythmically around Wren. Then, with a final gasp of the breath he'd held throughout his spend, Shrike collapse beneath him, his eyes fluttering shut.

The sympathetic magic of surrender.

An instant after—yet an instant proved enough—Wren's stones drew up. He poured his essence deep within Shrike, his sword driving in blow after blow, long and sharp, fit to impale, spilling what felt like torrents of ecstasy. Shrike groaned, biting his lip with a grin of deep satisfaction. With the last of his strength, Wren bent forward to capture his mouth in a kiss, one which Shrike hungrily returned. The ritual's power thrummed through both their bodies in a final paroxysm of pleasure. Spent, exhausted, wrecked, Wren fell into Shrike's embrace, the strong arms around him the only thing anchoring him to consciousness on the tides of bliss.

A wild roar filled his ears.

Wren opened his eyes, too stunned to do more than stare back at the raucous crowd leaping and flailing in their wild celebration.

Shrike arose, slipping from beneath Wren as if he weighed no more than a feather quilt. Wren hastened to tuck himself back into his trousers, though Shrike seemed to feel no such shame. He bent to draw Wren up beside him. Hand clasped forearm to do so, then lingered afterward, trailing down the inside of Wren's wrist to thread their fingers together in an unbreakable knot.

Though all the whooping throng watched them, Wren found he had eyes for Shrike alone. Shrike gazed down at him in turn, with warm dark eyes yet gleaming with desire and his small, handsome smile of satisfaction. Something more had changed in his face; belatedly, Wren realized the antlers, broken and unbroken alike, had fallen away, leaving his bronzed noble brow as smooth as if they'd never grown in.

"My lords?"

The herald had returned to the rim of the duelling circle, though as of yet they dared not do more than perch on its perimeter. Their gaze flicked between Shrike and Wren, returning again and again to a spot just above Wren's brow.

Wren raised a hand to the crown of thorns and found it softer than he remembered. He plucked off a piece and brought it down for inspection. A golden flower bloomed in his fingertips. Not just a crown of thorns, he realised, but a crown of furze.

Shrike, meanwhile, had bent to regather their discarded garments and implements. He'd already tied his hose with shortened knots and shrugged his tunic back over his head. The broken gyrdel jingled as he slung it over his shoulder.

The herald cleared their throat.

Shrike didn't look up.

"Your queen," the herald continued, "bids you attend her in her bower."

"We have no queen," said Shrike.

The herald balked. Wren stifled a half-hysterical laugh.

Shrike glanced up at last with an arched brow. "You may go and tell her so, an' it so please you."

The herald looked as though they would very much rather not do so. Still, as Shrike returned his attention to the scythe, the herald retreated.

A muffled thud came from behind them. Wren whirled to find a familiar rabbit-fur cloak thrown on to the duelling field and looked up just in time to catch a spiderweb mask fading back into the crowd. He hastened to snatch up the cloak and, with an effort, threw it over Shrike's shoulders. His own shoulders, back, and arms burned from the exertion of the fight. Even so, for the first time in all his days, he felt suffused with inner strength. Perhaps it was the lingering effects of the ritual. Or perhaps it was the awed smile shining down at him from Shrike.

"When Wren delved and Shrike span," Shrike murmured, so low Wren could hardly hear him above the throng, "who then was the gentleman?"

A bark of laughter escaped Wren. He pulled Shrike down for another kiss to renewed cheers from the gathered fae.

Then a hush descended on the crowd. At first, Wren supposed this was due to Shrike handing him the iron scythe again; no doubt the fae felt wary of such a weapon. But then he beheld the crowd parting like the sea before the prow of a ship.

And the figurehead sailing toward them was none other than the Queen of the Court of the Silver Wheel.

Wren could do naught but stare at her. Her presence held all the light of summer sunshine with none of its warmth. As she came to a halt at the edge of the duelling ring, Shrike stepped forward with sword in one hand and the other held out to shield Wren.

The queen spared an amused glance at the sword, then raised her emerald-green gaze to Shrike's face. "Well met, my Oak King."

Shrike said nothing.

The queen waited another moment before turning to Wren. "And well met, my Holly King."

Wren set his jaw.

She beheld them for a moment longer, then to Wren's astonishment, smiled and lifted her arms toward Shrike and Wren in turn, palms upraised as if to receive some tribute. "I bid you both join me in my bower to take your rightful places at my side."

A king for each hand. Wren almost admired her audacity. Yet he found a spark of courage within himself as well and replied, "Our rightful place is in our own realm."

The queen stared at him with an expression suggesting she'd never expected he could speak. She shot a demanding glance at Shrike.

Shrike's wry smile curled across his cheek.

Wren could almost feel the cold fury rolling off her in waves. She lowered her outstretched arms. By this time her retinue of knights had caught up to flank behind her.

Yet even as Wren brought his scythe out in front to defend himself, a low growl sounded from behind him.

Hardly daring to take his eyes off the queen, Wren turned his head prepared to see some fell beast at her beck and call ready to tear out his throat.

Instead, he saw the young man yet holding Wren's own bloodstained cravat, teeth bared and a glint of feral mania in his eye as he stared daggers at the queen.

Nor was that young man alone. His wolfish companions stood at his side, naturally. But likewise Wren saw Lady Aethelthryth had drawn her grey steed up to the edge of the duelling ring and held a slender silver longsword in her delicate white hand. The ambassador in his spiderweb mask had emerged from the crowd as well with his rapier at the ready. More astonishing, the Court of Hidden Folk had gathered, their Mistress of Revels surrounded by huldra, and her blue roan fiddler held his instrument as if he could wield it with all the deadly art of a blade. Beyond the crowd, Wren just glimpsed the distant figure of Nell perched in the fork of the tree with an arrow notched to her bow. And above them all flitted Tatterdemalion with their crystal dagger.

Wren returned his gaze to Queen of the Court of the Silver Wheel to find her likewise taking stock of his unexpected allies. Her eye seemed particularly caught on Tatterdemalion. It occurred to Wren he didn't precisely know who or what he'd allied himself with in them. They were old indeed—old enough to have beheld the true origin of the solstice duels. And the queen seemed very nearly unnerved to face them now.

"We take our leave of you," said Shrike.

Her emerald eyes flashed fury as they snapped back to him. "If you leave now, you return at your own peril."

Shrike merely smiled. The hand he'd held out to shield Wren settled onto the small of Wren's back.

Side-by-side, flanked by their friends, Wren and Shrike turned their backs on the Court of the Silver Wheel and set out for Blackthorn Briar.

THE END

ABOUT THE AUTHOR

Sebastian Nothwell writes queer romance. When he is not writing, he is counting down the minutes until he is permitted to return to writing. He is absolutely not a ghost and definitely did not die in 1895.

If you enjoyed this book, you may also enjoy the following by the same author:
Mr Warren's Profession (Aubrey & Lindsey, book one)
Throw His Heart Over (Aubrey & Lindsey, book two)
The Haunting of Heatherhurst Hall
Hold Fast

CPSIA information can be obtained
at www.ICGtesting.com
Printed in the USA
LVHW030054220222
711617LV00011B/320

Shrike, the Butcher of Blackthorn, is a legendary warrior of the fae realms. When he wins a tournament in the Court of the Silver Wheel, its queen crowns him as her Oak King - a figurehead destined to die in a ritual duel to invoke the change of seasons. Shrike is determined to survive. Even if it means he must put his heart as well as his life into a mere mortal's hands.

Wren Lofthouse, a London clerk, has long ago resigned himself to a life of tedium and given up his fanciful dreams. When a medieval-looking brute arrives at his office to murmur of destiny, he's inclined to think his old enemies are playing an elaborate prank. Still, he can't help but feel intrigued by the bizarre-yet-handsome stranger and his fantastical ramblings, whose presence stirs up emotions Wren has tried to lock away in the withered husk of his heart.

As Shrike whisks Wren away to a world of Wild Hunts and arcane rites, Wren is freed from the repression of Victorian society. But both the fae and mortal realms prove treacherous to their growing bond. Wren and Shrike must fight side-by-side to see who will claim victory—Oak King or Holly King.